The
Suspicion at Sanditon

The
Suspicion at Sanditon

OR, THE DISAPPEARANCE OF LADY DENHAM

A Mr. & Mrs. Darcy Mystery

Carrie Bebris

A TOM DOHERTY ASSOCIATES BOOK

NEW YORK

THE SUSPICION AT SANDITON

Copyright © 2015 by Carrie Bebris

A Tor Book
Published by Tom Doherty Associates, LLC
175 Fifth Avenue
New York, NY 10010

www.tor-forge.com

Tor® is a registered trademark of Tom Doherty Associates, LLC.

The Library of Congress Cataloging-in-Publication Data is available upon request.

ISBN 978-0-7653-2799-4 (hardcover)
ISBN 978-1-4299-4307-9 (e-book)

Tor books may be purchased for educational, business, or promotional use. For information on bulk purchases, please contact the Macmillan Corporate and Premium Sales Department at 1-800-221-7945, extension 5442, or write to specialmarkets@macmillan.com.

First Edition: July 2015

Printed in the United States of America

0 9 8 7 6 5 4 3 2 1

*For Uncle Mike,
one of my favorite storytellers*

Acknowledgments

So many individuals have lent their support—directly and indirectly—to the creation of this book that now, given the opportunity to formally thank them, I fear accidentally leaving someone out. However, I shall attempt to mention here as many as I can.

The best family anyone could wish for. Special mention goes to my daughter, who not only served as a sounding board when I plotted myself into corners but who also baked scones when Mom was on deadline.

My editor, Kristin Sevick, who kept the faith through this novel's numerous incarnations, helped me shape it into the story it was meant to be, and gave me the time necessary to do it. And her assistant, Bess Cozby, for her attention to and deft handling of so many details.

My agent, Irene Goodman, a source of calm in a storm, humor when it is most needed, and wisdom at all times.

Artist Teresa Fasolino, whose paintings so perfectly represent each Mr. & Mrs. Darcy Mystery that I am happy to let readers judge my books by their covers.

Tom Tumbusch and Leah Withers, for helping me reach readers next door and on the other side of the world.

Acknowledgments

Fellow authors Maddy Hunter, Pamela Johnson, Victoria Hinshaw, Kim Wilson, Sharon Short, Ed Greenwood, James Lowder, Anne Klemm, and Joan Strasbaugh, who at various stages in the book's development served as sounding boards, brainstorming partners, first readers, informational resources, and mentors. Also, my Wisconsin writers group, for renewing retreats and many years of community and camaraderie.

Historical interpreter Kristopher Shultz, my on-call expert on eighteenth-century life, and reference librarian Chris May, who helped me track down chamber horse images and other obscure information.

The staff of Our Lady of the Pines, where I wrote portions of this book while staying in an actual hermitage. Fortunately, it was not quite as rustic as Ebenezer Woodcock's.

The Jane Austen Society of North America, which for more than two decades has not only enhanced my appreciation of Austen and brought me into contact with experts on her work and the Regency era but also enriched my life with lasting friendships formed with members near and far.

Friends Janine Borneman, Constance Crafton, Jean Long, Meredith Stoehr, and others who help keep the rest of my life in balance.

Jane Austen, whose writing continues to entertain, inspire, and move me. Even after years of perpetual rereading, I cannot open one of her works without discovering something new.

And you, my readers, for your interest in and enthusiasm for the series; for the praise, criticism, comments, and questions that have contributed to its development; and for the notes and e-mails that seem to serendipitously arrive on my toughest writing days, sharing with me how one of my books has touched your life. You have all touched mine.

"Those who tell their own Story you know must be listened to with Caution."

> —Mr. Thomas Parker,
> *Jane Austen's original
> unfinished manuscript of* Sanditon

The
Suspicion at Sanditon

Prologue

"My early hours are not to put my Neighbours to inconvenience."
—*Lady Denham*, Sanditon

A Gentleman and Lady, being induced by business to travel towards that part of the Sussex Coast which lies between Hastings and Eastbourne, entered the village of Sanditon little anticipating that the small but developing watering-place would become a scene of intrigue shortly upon their arrival.

They should have known better.

The Gentleman and Lady were, you see, Mr. Fitzwilliam Darcy and his wife, the former Miss Elizabeth Bennet. Four years of marriage had brought them much happiness, including two dear children and an ever-increasing circle of friends. Yet it seemed that wheresoever Mr. and Mrs. Darcy went, some unexpected event was bound to occur. On a good journey, it was something vexing but tolerable. To this category, Darcy consigned ordinary travel inconveniences, less than ideal weather, and anything involving his mother-in-law. There had, however, occasionally arisen disturbances of a more serious nature, and Darcy fervently hoped that the present confusion would not number among them.

A haughty sigh from the young lady near his side commanded his attention. For the third time in as many minutes, Miss Esther

Denham's gaze drifted to the sitting room doors. "Whatever can be keeping her?"

The "her" in question was the dowager Lady Denham, mistress of Sanditon House, wherein was assembled a party of thirteen neighbors and visitors to the village—fourteen, if one included her ladyship, which unfortunately one could not, as their hostess had thus far remained absent from her own gathering.

At first, the neglected dinner guests had been content to wait patiently in the main sitting room, with its view of the park in full summer and large portrait of the late Sir Harry Denham observing them all from above the fireplace. They were clustered in several small groups. Darcy stood near the hearth with Miss Denham, her brother, and Mr. Thomas Parker, the person in the house (other than Elizabeth) with whom Darcy was best—if not particularly well—acquainted.

Across the room, Elizabeth and her friend Charlotte Heywood were immersed in a lively discussion with two of the other guests. Their conversation seemed of far greater interest to Miss Denham than the one in which she herself was engaged. Darcy suspected the fact that the participants included the party's two most eligible single gentlemen had something to do with her diverted attention.

Mr. Parker's youngest brother and two sisters sat with another young lady on a sofa in the middle of the room, where they carried on a discussion of their own. The thirteenth guest, a gentleman of advancing years, sat apart from the others, occupying a chair nearest Darcy's party.

Many of the guests had known each other all their lives, so conversation flowed easily, although attempts to engage the lone gentleman met with indifference. Nobody seemed to know him, and other than being introduced as one Mr. Josiah Hollis, he appeared inclined to keep it that way. As Lady Denham's first husband had been a Hollis, all assumed Josiah was a relation, although he did not bear much resemblance to the dignified miniature depiction of the late Mr. Archibald Hollis displayed in a corner of the room. Perhaps in his late fifties, Josiah was a thin man whose small eyes, long teeth, and grey hair lent him the appearance of a rat. Darcy might have pitied him this unfortunate rodential resemblance were it not for his equally unpleasant demeanor. He spoke little, studying the room and its occupants with the eye of a scavenger and an air of resentment.

Although Miss Denham's impatient query had been expressed in a voice loud enough to be heard by half the company, it was her brother, standing on her other side, who answered.

"We all know that Lady Denham conducts herself on her own schedule," Sir Edward Denham said. "'Assoiled from all encumbrance of our time.'" The current baronet, Sir Edward had inherited his title upon the death of his uncle, Sir Harry, several years earlier. He had also inherited the family estate, Denham Park, where he resided with his sister.

"Then she ought to have consulted her schedule and considered *our* time before designating four o'clock as the hour at which we were all to arrive," declared Mr. Hollis.

"While it is true that Lady Denham keeps her own hours, they are country hours," Mr. Parker said. "She prefers her dinner and tea early, and planned this party accordingly. She must be insensible of the time." He lowered his voice. "She seldom hosts events this large," he reminded Darcy, whose invitation to the affair had derived primarily from the Darcys' connection with Mr. Parker, as they had met Lady Denham only two days previous. "And she is seventy, after all. Perhaps she withdrew to her chamber to rest before the demands of the evening, and slept longer than she intended."

In the limited time Darcy had spent in Lady Denham's company, she had not impressed him as a woman who, seventy or not, slowed down long enough for afternoon naps. Darcy, however, would not question Thomas Parker's excuse. Josiah Hollis was less generous.

"Insensible? Inconsiderate, more like it. How long have we been waiting?"

Sir Edward's hand moved to his fob pocket, only to find it smooth and flat. "I seem to have forgotten my watch."

Mr. Hollis released a sound of exasperation and looked pointedly at the chain hanging from Darcy's waistcoat.

Darcy withdrew his watch and opened its lid. "Most of us have been here nearly an hour." Mr. Hollis, for all his complaints, had been one of the last to arrive, but comported himself so disagreeably that Darcy felt as if the gentleman had been there longest of all.

Mr. Hollis scowled. "This delay is deliberate, no doubt. An attempt to remind us that she still has control of this house, after all these years. Well, I have no patience for such manipulation." He turned to the young lady on the sofa—Miss Clara Brereton, the only other resident of Sanditon House. "Are you not supposed to be her ladyship's companion? Why is she not with you, or you with her?"

So startled was the young woman by his accusatory tone, that she could not immediately reply. A flush spread across her cheeks.

"Here, now, sir!" said Sir Edward. "That is no way to address a lady. Will you apologize, or must you and I—"

"Thank you, Sir Edward," Miss Brereton gently interjected, then turned to Mr. Hollis. "Lady Denham said she had no need of me this afternoon. I was simply to make sure I appeared here in the portrait room by four o'clock."

"Like the rest of us. Hmph!" He looked about until he spotted the footman, who, like any well-trained servant, had been doing his best to ignore the developing quarrel and fade into the wallpaper. "You— inform Lady Denham that Josiah Hollis has done with her waiting game."

Miss Brereton rose from the sofa. "I shall look in on Lady Denham myself." The mildness of her voice and manner admonished his rudeness more effectively than any barbed retort could. "I did not realize so much time had passed."

She quit the room, leaving behind an awkward silence that Thomas Parker intrepidly attempted to fill. "I am sure all is well," he assured Darcy, "and I am equally certain that her ladyship's delay in personally receiving us is not motivated by an attempt to manipulate anybody."

Darcy nodded politely, but his gaze traveled beyond Thomas Parker until it came to rest on Elizabeth. Her returning gaze reflected his own misgivings.

He pushed them from his thoughts and attended Mr. Parker's discourse once more. Were there trouble, they would know soon enough, and in the meantime he would not dwell upon it. For the next quarter hour, Mr. Parker and Sir Edward enumerated the attractions Not To Be Missed during the Darcys' two-week stay in the village, while Miss Denham huffed, Mr. Hollis glowered, and the other guests resumed their own conversations.

———

On the other side of the room, Miss Brereton's departure created a momentary pause in the otherwise diverting banter of Elizabeth's party. Upon their arrival, she and Charlotte Heywood had fallen into conversation with Thomas Parker's brother Sidney, and Sidney's friend Mr. Granville. The two gentlemen were handsome in both countenance and manners, and Elizabeth could not help but notice the pleasure Charlotte took in their unexpected attention.

"Miss Heywood, I leave to you our next subject of conversation," Sidney Parker said. "What shall we speak of while we all pretend we are not wondering whether our delayed dinner will be served stone cold or overcooked?"

"I believe the weather is always a safe topic of discourse," Charlotte offered.

"Oh, it is, indeed! One can never say too much about the weather; it is society's greatest equalizer. Everybody from a ploughman to a prince may hold an opinion, and confidently state it with little risk of giving offense. There is usually general agreement as to whether conditions are fair or foul, too hot, too wet, too sunny, too grey; and where opinions differ, nobody has much need to prove himself right, for the weather will do what it will, and tomorrow the same conversation can be had all over again. In fact, I daresay we are negligent in not having already dispatched our social obligation to discuss it. How fortunate that we are standing so near a window." He glanced outside. "The sky has grown overcast since we arrived. Mrs. Darcy, do you think it will rain?"

"My husband and I are on a seaside holiday," Elizabeth said. "Of course it will rain."

He laughed. "I can say the same for myself—Sanditon is never so wet as when I return for a visit. But will it rain *today*? What do you think, Miss Heywood? Mr. Granville and I have more than a passing interest in the matter, as we walked here from the hotel."

A low rumble spared anyone the necessity of a prediction. It was not a welcome noise, as Elizabeth and Darcy also had walked to Sanditon House. "It sounds distant," Charlotte said. "Perhaps the rain will hold off until we are all safely returned to our respective lodgings."

"Are you always an optimist, Miss Heywood?"

"Only after considering all the possibilities, and talking myself out of the worst ones."

As Charlotte spoke, Elizabeth saw Miss Brereton reenter the portrait room. From the anxious expression of the younger woman's countenance, she did not think the news they were about to hear would prove at all optimistic.

Miss Brereton scanned the room as if in deliberation, then headed toward Darcy's group. She had just reached Thomas Parker's side when Josiah Hollis caught sight of her.

"Well, does Lady Denham intend to join us at all this evening?" Mr. Hollis's volume drew the attention of all the guests, and conversation ceased.

Miss Brereton flinched at his querulous demand. "I do not know."

Mr. Parker was more sympathetic. "As you have returned without her, I can only suppose something significant prevents her from joining us. Is Lady Denham indisposed?"

Her composure suddenly breaking to reveal her distress, her gaze swept all the guests before returning to Mr. Parker.

"Lady Denham is missing."

Volume the First

IN WHICH IT IS RELATED HOW THE DARCYS CAME TO BE
AT SANDITON HOUSE ON THE NIGHT IN QUESTION

"I am not easily taken-in my Dear. . . . I always take care to know what I am about and who I have to deal with, before I stir a finger."
—Lady Denham, *Sanditon*

One

"Yes, I have heard of Sanditon," replied Mr. Heywood. "Every five years, one hears of some new place or other starting up by the Sea and growing the fashion."

—Sanditon

*O*ur tale properly commences a fortnight ago, in another part of Sussex, where a small but congenial company gathered at Brierwood House, the home of Colonel and Mrs. James Fitzwilliam. The Fitzwilliams were relative newcomers to Brierwood, for though the family of Mrs. Fitzwilliam—née Anne de Bourgh—had owned the property for generations, it was only upon the transfer of Brierwood to Anne three years earlier as part of her marriage settlement that the seldom-used minor holding of Lady Catherine and the late Sir Lewis de Bourgh became the primary residence of their daughter and her new husband.

While the estate lay in a fair-sized parish, the house was remotely situated, standing so close to the border that its nearest neighbors were in fact part of the adjacent parish of Willingden. A collection of modest cottages hard-pressed to merit the title "village," Willingden could boast little in the way of commerce or conveniences—not a shoemaker nor surgeon to be found. But Brierwood House soon became the Fitzwilliams' home in all the best senses of the word: the place where they welcomed old friends and new neighbors into its rooms, and their firstborn child into the world.

The colonel and Anne presently enjoyed a visit from their cousin Mr. Darcy and his wife, Elizabeth. The Darcys were regular guests at Brierwood, as the Fitzwilliams were at Pemberley, the Darcys' home in Derbyshire. The two couples shared the most ideal of connections—not merely the accident of kinship, but also genuine friendship—and from the (predominantly) happy sounds that emanated from the nursery, where the Darcys' three-year-old Lily-Anne and one-year-old Bennet played with the Fitzwilliams' little Lewis, it appeared that relations among the next generation of cousins would prove equally amiable.

The children were presently nestled all snug in their beds, napping in the care of their nurses while the adults anticipated the imminent arrival of some of the Fitzwilliams' neighbors for tea.

"Will Miss Heywood be among the party?" Elizabeth asked.

The Heywoods were a genteel family with whom the Fitzwilliams had developed a close acquaintance since coming to Sussex, and whom the Darcys had met on previous visits. A warmhearted couple as attentive to their neighbors as the responsibilities and distractions of raising fourteen children allowed them to be, Mr. and Mrs. Heywood had done much to make the colonel and Anne feel welcome upon the Fitzwilliams' first taking up residence at Brierwood. Miss Charlotte Heywood was the eldest of their daughters still at home.

"Indeed, she will."

"It will be good to see her again." At two-and-twenty, Miss Heywood was only three years younger than Elizabeth, who found her a pleasant, sensible young lady, and very much enjoyed her conversation whenever they were in company together. "How are all the family?"

"They have unexpected houseguests at present whom we have also invited to tea," Colonel Fitzwilliam said. "A Mr. and Mrs. Thomas Parker, of Sanditon. The Parkers were traveling through Willingden when their carriage overturned near the Heywoods' house, leaving Mr. Parker with a badly sprained ankle. The Heywoods offered their hospitality while the carriage was repaired and he recovered. His ankle is enough improved that he and his wife plan to return home tomorrow, and to reciprocate the Heywoods' hospitality, they have invited Miss Heywood to accompany them."

"Have they a long journey home?" Elizabeth asked. "I am not familiar with Sanditon."

Colonel Fitzwilliam and Anne exchanged a smile. "You will be, once you meet Mr. Parker," the colonel said, "for he is quite an enthusiast on the subject. Sanditon lies on the coast, near Eastbourne, and it is gaining some renown as a new bathing-place. Mr. Parker is one of its chief landowners, and is working hard to develop the village into a thriving resort."

"The coast is already so full of such places that I cannot imagine the need for another," Darcy said.

"Mr. Heywood is of the same opinion," Colonel Fitzwilliam replied, "but Mr. Parker claims the village is particularly well suited for such a purpose. Indeed, he speaks of Sanditon in such glowing terms that I am considering investing in it myself."

Darcy regarded his cousin shrewdly. "Has Mr. Parker solicited you to do so?"

"No—it is entirely my idea, and I intend to keep silent until I have had an opportunity to evaluate Sanditon with my own eyes. I do not even know if he and his speculation partner would be open to an outsider buying or building in the village. He told me of several projects he would like to initiate, including the building of a Crescent, so they might welcome new capital that would help advance those plans."

"Speculation is a risky business, and I have never known you to be much of a gambler," Darcy said. "What is it about this particular enterprise that attracts you?"

"Mr. Parker and his partner, Lady Denham, seek to make Sanditon a respectable resort that draws families of good character, without the crowds and glamour and problems of the large, highly fashionable places—a quiet, private village; much more a Lyme than a Brighton. It is an attainable goal, and this would be a minor investment—you know that I never wager more than I can afford to lose, whether at cards or anything else. Nevertheless, I would appreciate your more objective counsel in determining whether this is indeed a sound decision. Anne and I want to visit soon—will the two of you come with us?"

"How long a visit do you have in mind?" Elizabeth asked.

"A week, perhaps two," Colonel Fitzwilliam said. "Long enough to obtain a general sense of the place."

"We can leave our children here with their nurses," Anne added. "We think to go in a fortnight or so. By then, Ben and Lily-Anne will feel so at home at Brierwood that they will scarcely notice your absence."

Elizabeth turned to Darcy. "I like the prospect of returning to the sea."

"Very well, then," Darcy said. "Let us all go to Sanditon."

Two

Sanditon was a second wife and four Children to [Mr. Parker]—
hardly less Dear—and certainly more engrossing.—He could talk
of it for ever.—It had indeed the highest claims;—not only those of
Birthplace, Property, and Home,—it was his Mine, his Lottery,
his speculation and his Hobby Horse; his Occupation, his Hope and his
Futurity.—He was extremely desirous of drawing his good friends
at Willingden thither.

—Sanditon

*C*harlotte Heywood entered the drawing room of Brierwood
full of happy anticipation. Tomorrow she would embark on the
greatest adventure of her young life.

She supposed that for many young ladies, a journey to a quiet
coastal village a few hours from home would not constitute an "adventure" at all, let alone a significant one. But Charlotte had not often
traveled from Willingden. Her parents never left home themselves, the
expense of raising such a large family requiring a certain degree of
economy and restraint. And while they did encourage their children
to take advantage of opportunities to broaden their experiences and
connections, so far Charlotte's opportunities had primarily been
limited to visiting her older married siblings and other relatives.

But now, happenstance had brought adventure to her door, in the
form of Mr. and Mrs. Parker, and when the amiable, openhearted
couple had invited her to accompany them to Sanditon—a rising seaside resort—her parents had deemed it a good opportunity for her to

step out into the larger world. Tea with their friends the Fitzwilliams and Darcys, and last-minute preparations for the morning departure, were all that remained before her journey began.

Mrs. Darcy smiled upon sighting her, and advanced toward Charlotte immediately. Charlotte returned the smile. She liked Elizabeth Darcy very much. Like Charlotte, she was the daughter of a gentleman of comfortable but not impressive means, and though she had married very well, sensed that the elevation of her social status had not changed her nature. She was a warm, genuine, sensible woman, and Charlotte felt fortunate in her friendship, even if occasions to enjoy it were limited to the Darcys' visits to Brierwood.

"It is very good to see you again, Miss Heywood."

"Likewise, Mrs. Darcy. I am glad Mrs. Fitzwilliam invited us to tea before I left Willingden, or you and I would have missed each other. Have you heard that I am traveling to Sanditon with Mr. and Mrs. Parker?"

"I have indeed. How long do you expect to be gone?"

"At least a month, depending upon when an opportunity arises to return me home. The Parkers would like me to stay for six weeks. Mr. Parker is of the opinion that everybody should visit the sea for at least six weeks each year, in order to truly benefit from the bathing and breezes."

"You are not in need of the sea's medicinal properties, I hope?"

"Oh, not at all! My health is excellent. If the sea fortifies what is already strong, so much the better, but this is primarily a pleasure trip—an opportunity to get out into the world—or at least, a small corner of it—to see a new place and form new acquaintances."

Their tête-à-tête was temporarily suspended by introductions between the Darcys and the Parkers. A gentleman of good family and comfortable means, Mr. Thomas Parker was about five-and-thirty; his wife, Mary, several years younger. They were a pleasant couple, and conversation with them flowed easily.

"We heard of the injury that has kept you in Willingden," Mr. Darcy said. "You must be anxious to return home."

"We are," Mr. Parker replied, "though we have spent a most enjoyable fortnight with Mr. and Mrs. Heywood. A sprained ankle seems a small nuisance to endure for having gained such good friends in consequence."

"However did you come to be in Willingden when your carriage overturned?" Mrs. Darcy asked. "It is hardly a place one passes through on the way to anywhere."

Mr. Parker laughed. "A fool's errand, as it turns out. I would like to bring a physician or surgeon to Sanditon, and as I was leaving London, I saw a pair of newspaper advertisements announcing the dissolution of a medical partnership in Willingden. The former partner wishes to start an independent practice. The circumstances sounded ideal, and when my enquiries determined that Willingden was no more than a mile or so out of our way, I decided to come here, meet the man, and—I hoped—settle the matter. Unfortunately, I did not realize until talking with Mr. Heywood after the accident, that there are two Willingdens in Sussex, and the one with the surgeon is seven miles from here."

"Will you travel there to meet the surgeon now that your ankle is improved?"

"I wrote to him, but he has already committed to another opportunity. I shall, however, continue my search. Having a medical man in residence would not only enhance Sanditon's reputation and bring in more visitors, but also serve a personal end: I would like to bring my own two sisters to Sanditon this summer, but being invalids, they could never contemplate an extended stay in a place where medical advice is not immediately available."

"Your sisters no longer live in Sanditon?" Elizabeth asked. "Did marriages take them elsewhere?"

"No, they are both single, as are my two younger brothers. My sisters live in Hampshire with our youngest brother, Arthur. All three of them are independent, as is my brother Sidney. In fact, Sidney, through a collateral inheritance, is as well-off as I. He has a country house of his own, although he spends most of his time in London, or traveling about."

Tea was brought in, and as they sat down to take refreshment, talk turned to Sanditon itself. Mr. Parker, full of pride in and plans for his native village, told the Darcys more about his home. Eventually, though, the general conversation broke into several smaller ones, and Charlotte and Mrs. Darcy were able to resume their earlier discussion.

"Your visit with the Parkers sounds idyllic," Mrs. Darcy said. "When you and I next meet, you shall have to tell me whether Sanditon satisfies your expectations."

"By then, my visit will be so far in the past as to benefit from the softening effects of memory, whatever the actuality might have been."

"We might meet sooner than you think. Mr. Parker praises the village so effusively, that I am now all curiosity to see it for myself before we leave Sussex."

This announcement elicited not one but two expressions of surprise—the first, a smile which crossed Charlotte's countenance; the second, a glance from Mrs. Heywood, who was seated nearby.

"It would be wonderful if you visited while I was there," Charlotte said. "I have no doubt of being well taken care of by the Parkers, but never before having traveled from home except to visit relations, I confess a bit of trepidation at going to Sanditon by myself. The prospect of your being there sometime in the course of my stay removes even that small anxiety, leaving me nothing to anticipate but pleasure."

"Then consider it a certainty. Mr. Darcy and I had been considering a brief holiday, and I now find myself quite persuaded that Sanditon is the very place for it." Mrs. Darcy glanced at Mrs. Fitzwilliam. "I think the colonel and his wife might even join us."

Such delightful news could not help but reach Mr. Parker's hearing with the rapidity of a pistol shot, his attention so finely attuned to anything regarding Sanditon that a whispered mention in the next county might have drawn his notice.

Within minutes, all was settled. The Parkers offered the hospitality of their own home, but the Darcys and Fitzwilliams gently declined, citing a reluctance to inconvenience their family. Mr. Parker would have to content himself with merely engaging lodgings for them ("Something on the Terrace—I have the very house in mind, if it has not been taken in my absence") and with serving as their personal guide during their stay.

As the Parkers and Heywoods departed, Charlotte's mother

expressed to Mrs. Darcy and Mrs. Fitzwilliam the additional comfort it brought her to know that her daughter would have old friends with her in unfamiliar surroundings. "If it is not too great an imposition, would you mind keeping an extra watch over her for me?"

"Looking after a friend is never an imposition," Mrs. Darcy assured her.

To Charlotte, Mrs. Darcy smiled and said, "I will start by advising you to get a good night's rest before your journey."

Charlotte wished she could comply. But so high were her spirits, she doubted she would be able to sleep at all.

Three

"Miss Heywood, I astonish you.—You hardly know what to make of me.—I see by your Looks, that you are not used to such quick measures." The words "Unaccountable Officiousness!—Activity run mad!"—had just passed through Charlotte's mind.
—Miss Diana Parker and Charlotte Heywood, Sanditon

*T*he best-laid schemes of mice and men often go awry, and such was the case for Colonel and Anne Fitzwilliam. Just as the two couples were about to depart for Sanditon—trunks already loaded on the Darcys' carriage, good-byes with the children already exchanged—a missive arrived from Anne's mother, Lady Catherine de Bourgh, announcing her imminent arrival. Traveling to visit a friend, Lady Catherine had taken it into her head to stop at Brierwood en route for a stay of at least a se'nnight, perhaps two, and would arrive in mere hours.

Both Anne and the colonel were needed at home to prevent her ladyship from harrying the servants and directing "improvements" throughout the house. (Experience had taught them that managing Lady Catherine was at minimum a two-person undertaking, especially at Brierwood, which her ladyship tended to forget was no longer hers.) They were determined, however, that this news should not alter Elizabeth and Darcy's holiday, nor delay the evaluation of Sanditon as a potential investment. They urged the Darcys to make the journey as planned; the Fitzwilliams would join them as soon as Lady Catherine departed.

And so it was that Elizabeth and Darcy were the sole occupants of the carriage that approached the village of Sanditon one sunny July day. Though the scent of salt air and cries of seabirds reminded Elizabeth of Lyme Regis, Sanditon appeared to possess a character all its own. Where many of Lyme's oldest buildings lined the steep streets closest to shore, the most established portion of Sanditon lay in a wooded valley on the opposite side of the down from the sea, while its modern dwellings and businesses stood on the great sunny hill overlooking the water.

As they climbed, the lodge and gates of a large estate caught their attention. Beyond, the top of a great house was visible above the grove.

"I believe that is Sanditon House," Darcy said, "Lady Denham's home. Mr. Parker told me it was the last residence we would pass before reaching the newly built portion of Sanditon."

As the carriage emerged from the woods and onto the open down, several neat rows of new houses and buildings in various states of construction lined the hill. The broadest street boasted Sanditon's hotel, livery, billiard room, and library, punctuated by smart, modern houses and shops, all standing at attention along a wooden walk that descended toward the sands and sea. Elizabeth surmised that this petite mall was the "Terrace" of which Mr. Parker had spoken, and in which stood the lodgings he had taken for them.

Just beyond the Terrace, a large, airy, elegant house occupied the highest settled point on the hill. Surrounded by a small lawn and young park of saplings and seedlings, it overlooked a steep but unpretentious cliff. It was at this dwelling that their carriage drew to a stop.

They had not yet alighted when Mr. Parker emerged from the residence, all delight at their safe arrival. "Welcome! Welcome to Trafalgar House!" He heartily shook hands with Darcy and helped hand down Elizabeth. "Where are Colonel and Mrs. Fitzwilliam?"

"Unfortunately, they are detained at home by a family matter," Darcy said. "They hope to join us here next week."

"Oh, dear! I hope it is nothing too dreadful?"

Elizabeth exchanged a glance with Darcy. If only Mr. Parker knew.

"No, just something that required their personal attention," Elizabeth said.

"Well, sometimes the unforeseen occurs—such as spending a fortnight in Willingden recovering from an injured ankle."

"How *is* your ankle?" Elizabeth enquired. Mr. Parker had not appeared to favor it when he hastened forth to greet them.

"Good as new, I assure you, though my sister Diana will not believe me. She has come to Sanditon, along with Susan and Arthur— an unexpected surprise. Now I shall have the pleasure of introducing you to nearly the whole Parker family, save my brother Sidney." As he spoke, Charlotte and Mrs. Parker came round the side of the house, apparently in the midst of a stroll about the grounds. "Aha! And here are two people already familiar to you."

Charlotte's countenance broke into a smile upon sighting Elizabeth, and she closed the gap between them with quick steps. "I thought I heard a carriage. How good to have you here at last!" Charlotte's eyes seemed a bit brighter, her color a little fuller, than when they had last been together.

"Sanditon appears to agree with you," Elizabeth replied. "How has your visit been thus far?"

"Wonderful—I could not ask for better hosts, nor more pleasant surroundings."

Mr. Parker beamed at Charlotte's praise. "Nor Mary and I, a more delightful guest. Is that not so, Mary?"

"It is, my dear," Mrs. Parker said. "Little Mary is quite taken with her—I don't know what she will do when you leave us, Miss Heywood."

Mr. Parker turned back to Elizabeth and Darcy. "I expect you are wanting to see the cottage I took for you, but can I first persuade you to come inside and refresh yourselves?" He gestured toward the house.

Though indeed eager to settle into their lodgings, Elizabeth and Darcy gratefully accepted Mr. Parker's offer. Several hours in their carriage had made attending to creature comforts a more immediate priority than commencing their exploration of Sanditon.

Mr. Parker happily ushered them toward the door. "As of your arrival, the Terrace is fully occupied," he informed them. "In fact, my siblings have taken the cottage next to yours."

"You and your speculation partner must be pleased," Darcy said.

"We are, we are," Mr. Parker replied. "I told Lady Denham that it is a sure sign of growth—Sanditon's reputation is ascending, and more visitors will certainly follow. If we are this populated now, imagine the end of summer, and next season! We are building several more small houses on the hill, and Sir Edward—Lady Denham's nephew, the baronet—has built a cottage ornée on his property. I enquired about it—it would have been the very place for you to stay—but he said it is not quite finished. Even when complete, however, Sir Edward's cottage and the other few will not be enough. We need to move forward on building the Crescent—which I plan to name for Waterloo, by the way. If only I could convince Lady Denham of the need for it! I cannot act without her."

"Are you prohibited by the terms of your partnership?" Darcy asked.

"No—our arrangement would not restrict me from independently financing the Crescent—or any other venture—but with my other investments I have not the capital."

While their trunks were delivered to the cottage, Darcy and Elizabeth entered Trafalgar House with their hosts and Miss Heywood. It was a fine house—at first impression all new, all modern, fitted out with the latest furnishings and fabrics. Yet upon closer observation, Elizabeth noted here and there older pieces—a random table, or armchair, or fire screen—and it was these objects that lent the house the warmth of a family home.

As dinner was still some hours off, Mrs. Parker ordered a light repast to be served. While they all dined on fruit, cold pork, warm rolls, and cake, Mr. Parker's conversation was full of Sanditon news and praise. He seemed to want to show the Darcys everything—the sands, the sea, the shops—at once, and to introduce them to everybody—Lady Denham, Sir Edward, his siblings—without delay.

Elizabeth wished to ask Miss Heywood more about her visit, but so boundless was Mr. Parker's enthusiasm, that she had time to exchange only a brief greeting with her friend, and promises to speak at greater length during dinner, before Mr. Parker escorted the Darcys to their cottage.

The quaint dwelling sat on the village's high street, across from the hotel. Its sitting room ran the length of the house, so that it offered a view of the Terrace at one end and the sea at the other; its remaining main rooms and half the bedchambers were also situated so that as many of them as possible offered at least a glimpse of the sea. Mr. Parker showed them through its rooms, then led them back outside for another view from the front.

"I hope it meets with your approval?" he asked.

"It is altogether charming," Elizabeth assured him.

"I am glad it passes inspection. Now, shall I show you more of Sanditon, or leave you to yourselves for a few hours? Either way, you must promise to return to Trafalgar House for dinner."

Before such a pledge could be given, their joint attention was drawn to a woman charging down the street toward them at full speed.

"Ah, here you are, Tom! I have been to Trafalgar House and back in search of you. Thankfully, it was not out of my way—I have been running errands since before breakfast; in fact, I have not eaten a thing all day—but then, I eat so little, you know, that I did not even realize I had forgotten until talking to you just now."

Mr. Parker's countenance clouded. "Is all well with you, Susan, and Arthur?"

"Well? Oh, yes—that is, as well as we ever are. I think Susan needs leeches. Have you found a surgeon yet to take up practice in Sanditon? If not, I have administered leeches before, provided we can obtain some."

"I will summon the surgeon in the next village," Mr. Parker said.

"Thank you. Tomorrow is soon enough for him to attend Susan. I declare, we cannot fit another thing into this day! Now, are you going to introduce me to your friends, or leave me to assume they are one of the couples you told me you were expecting today?"

"Yes, of course! Mr. and Mrs. Darcy, I present my sister Miss Diana Parker. We are lucky to have the Darcys here," Mr. Parker said to Diana. "The Fitzwilliams, the other couple of whom I spoke, had to remain at home on unanticipated family business."

"How unfortunate! Well, at least they did not have to subject themselves to the rigors of travel," Diana said. "Susan, Arthur, and I travel only when we must. We have been here four days and have scarcely recovered our equilibrium."

To Elizabeth's eye, Diana Parker held full possession of her equilibrium, along with a mode of address so vigorous that it could knock down an opposing force on its own. This was not the besieged invalid Elizabeth had been anticipating from Mr. Parker's description of his siblings—in fact, Diana was quite the opposite, and Elizabeth wondered whether more serious health complaints on the part of the two siblings with whom she lived had required Diana to habitually exert herself despite her own afflictions.

"Diana, I have just invited the Darcys to join us for dinner. You, Susan, and Arthur do still intend to come?"

"Of course. Though I cannot speak for our appetites, we shall definitely indulge in the pleasure of your company if not your table." She turned to the Darcys. "I look forward to becoming better acquainted then. For now, you must forgive me—I am afraid I must hurry off on another errand: engaging a bathing machine for Miss Heywood tomorrow. I intend to personally examine each one, to ensure hers is the best Sanditon has to offer."

"The Wilsons keep them all in good repair," Mr. Parker said, looking a bit wounded at the implication that anything in Sanditon might be less than perfect.

"I am sure they do, Tom. But Miss Heywood has never been seabathing before, so I am determined that her first experience will be a pleasant one. I have already told her that once she becomes accustomed to the practice, she should return in November—or better still, February—when the water is colder."

Elizabeth suppressed a shiver. "I have enjoyed seabathing in Lyme, but in August," Elizabeth said, "and the water was quite cold enough then."

"The colder, the better. It improves circulation."

"My dear sister," Mr. Parker said kindly, "bear in mind that not everybody has your strength of will." He turned to the Darcys. "We generally dine at six o'clock, but you are no doubt fatigued from your journey and wish to make it an early evening. Shall Mrs. Parker and I anticipate you at half past four?"

"We look forward to it," Darcy replied.

Diana, citing a list of self-assigned commissions as long as her forearm to be completed before that hour, took leave of them and strode down the path to the sands, where she could commence her inspection of the bathing machines. Mr. Parker headed home, leaving the Darcys, at last, to themselves.

"Twopence for your thoughts," Elizabeth said as she and Darcy reentered the cottage. She removed her bonnet and set it on a side table in the small entry hall. A looking glass hung above, and she smoothed a few strands of hair that had been pulled loose.

"Not a mere penny?"

"I am feeling generous." In the mirror, she caught his gaze and offered a smile.

He returned it briefly as he removed his own hat, but then shifted to survey their surroundings with a more critical eye than he had used in Mr. Parker's company.

"Are you dissatisfied with our lodgings?" she asked.

"No, the house is perfectly suitable," he replied. "I am merely vexed with my aunt for managing to undermine the primary purpose of this trip, and am now questioning the value of our coming here without my cousins. An investment in Sanditon is ultimately their decision to make."

"Colonel Fitzwilliam did ask your counsel."

"Yes, but now if he does invest and the enterprise goes poorly, I shall feel all the more responsible."

"We still have much to observe and report before we need contemplate that eventuality."

"All the same, we came to Sussex to visit him and Anne."

She turned to face him. "And now find ourselves alone in a village that we had never heard of a month ago?"

"Precisely." He reached past her to set his own hat on the table, his arm brushing hers.

"A blossoming seaside resort?"

"Yes . . ."

"Without your cousins and without our children?"

He paused, then met her gaze. His dark eyes took on a roguish expression as he released the hat and drew her closer.

"I did not say I objected entirely."

Four

It was impossible for Charlotte not to suspect a good deal of fancy in such an extraordinary state of health . . . The Parkers, were no doubt a family of Imagination and quick feelings—and while the eldest Brother found vent for his superfluity of sensation as a Projector, the Sisters were perhaps driven to dissipate theirs in the invention of odd complaints. The whole of their mental vivacity was evidently not so employed; Part was laid out in a Zeal for being useful.—It should seem that they must either be very busy for the Good of others, or else extremely ill themselves.

—Sanditon

*A*t the appointed hour, Elizabeth and Darcy returned to Trafalgar House. Diana, Susan, and Arthur Parker had arrived only minutes earlier, and the family, along with Charlotte Heywood, were gathered in the drawing room. The ladies occupied the sofa and a small grouping of chairs in the middle of the room, while the brothers stood near the fireplace. Despite the day's seasonable temperatures, a small fire burned.

"I am delighted to meet you at last," Miss Susan Parker said upon introduction. The elder of the two sisters, Susan appeared a thinner, wearier image of Diana, but by no means incapacitated by whatever ailments troubled her. She sat beside Diana on the sofa, clutching in her hand a phial which Elizabeth assumed contained salts. "Drops for pain," Susan explained as a spasm fleetingly contorted her countenance. "Diana prepared them for me. I had three teeth removed just before we departed for Sanditon."

"Good heavens! Three at once?" Elizabeth's own jaw ached at the mere thought.

"She bore it quite well," Diana said. "Better than last time."

Arthur Parker, too, defied all of Elizabeth's preconceived images of his appearance. No delicate invalid in danger of wasting away, he was a stout, broad-shouldered gentleman who stood as tall as his brother. His amiable (if somewhat round) face was pink, with small dots of perspiration beading his brow and upper lip—an effect, no doubt, of standing so close to the unnecessary fire.

"Come, Mrs. Darcy," Mrs. Parker said, leading Elizabeth toward a chair. "Have a seat here among the ladies."

Elizabeth gratefully accompanied her. Because it was not an extraordinarily large room, she found the temperature only marginally cooler away from the fireplace, but as she took a chair next to Miss Heywood, she was grateful for even this slight difference.

Upon the Darcys' entrance, Diana had been narrating a minute account of her bathing-machine inspection. She now returned to it with renewed animation. "I tested every single machine myself," she said. "The process cost me my entire afternoon, but of course I do not mind in the least."

"You took a dip into the sea from each one of them?" Mrs. Parker asked. "Goodness, I think that is more seabathing than I have done in my life."

"No, no—I did not actually submerse myself in the water. You know that seabathing never does a thing for me. Nor for Susan and Arthur."

"How anybody can go seabathing daily astonishes me," said Susan. "I require at least four-and-twenty hours merely to brace myself for the water's chill, and then another eight-and-forty to recover from it afterward. In fact, I grow cold just thinking about it—Arthur, do bank up the fire, if you will."

Arthur dutifully set about selecting a log to add to the one already burning in the hearth. Elizabeth longed to open a window.

"Today, I merely rode inside the machines while the dipper led the horses to the proper depth, then brought the machine back to shore," Diana continued. "I had to ensure that whichever machine Miss

Heywood uses, provides the smoothest possible ride." She looked at Miss Heywood. "I would not have you jostled about."

"I cannot imagine any bathing machine offering a smooth ride," Elizabeth said, "traveling as they do over sand and rocks."

"Well, no machine is perfect," Diana declared, "but I was determined to identify the best Sanditon has to offer. Miss Heywood, I have reserved one of Mrs. Wilson's machines for three o'clock tomorrow. I shall collect you at half-past two."

Elizabeth studied Charlotte. She appeared agreeable to the arrangement, yet apprehensive. "Are you looking forward to seabathing?"

"Oh, yes!" she replied, but then cast a sideways glance at Diana. "At least, I think so. I want to try everything while I am here."

Elizabeth wondered how pleasant Charlotte's bathing experience would prove under Diana Parker's supervision. Reluctant to assert herself with a new acquaintance, Charlotte might be overrun by Diana's zeal.

"I was hoping to do some seabathing myself while in Sanditon." Actually, she was not, but Elizabeth thought Charlotte could use an ally in this particular adventure. "Would you mind if I joined you?"

Charlotte's whole countenance relaxed. "I would enjoy that very much."

"In fact"—Elizabeth turned to Diana—"since you have already devoted so much time to the bathing-machine arrangements but do not intend to bathe yourself, I would be happy to take Miss Heywood while you attend to the many other tasks demanding your attention."

"Oh, it is no trouble for me to take her—none at all, despite everything else I must do tomorrow. However . . . Susan's leeches *will* be at least a three hours' business, and she might need me afterward—"

"Consider it settled, then."

Charlotte silently thanked her with a conspiratorial smile. Elizabeth responded in kind, then said, "I would enjoy hearing how you have occupied yourself since arriving."

"Mostly in quiet amusements," Charlotte replied. "The Terrace offers a lovely view and the weather has been fair, so we have enjoyed a promenade along it each day. I have been to the circulating library several times. Too, Mr. and Mrs. Parker have been so kind as to introduce me to the Denhams, so we have seen Lady Denham, or the baronet and his sister, nearly every day, either here at Trafalgar House or chancing to meet them somewhere in town."

"Mr. Parker has spoken of Lady Denham to us," Elizabeth said, "but we have not yet had the pleasure of making her acquaintance."

"That will soon be rectified, I am certain," Diana said. "Lady Denham has always been one to keep herself apprised of the goings-on in Sanditon. She will want to inspect you for herself, and will create an opportunity to do so if one does not naturally arise. Tom, did you happen to mention to her the charitable campaign I started for displaced goat herds? We have hardly raised a shilling, but if Lady Denham were to make a substantial contribution, I am sure others would follow."

"I have not mentioned it, nor the six other subscriptions to which you hope she will contribute. Lady Denham's generosity—indeed, that of any benefactor—has its limits, and as you yourself just noted, Sanditon and her own concerns receive the greatest share of her attention."

"Well, what is the good of having money if one never spends any of it? Of course, I understand not depleting one's entire fortune—one must retain enough to maintain one's manner of living, and provide for one's heirs. But as Lady Denham has no children, she can afford to be more charitable. If fact, she ought to leave her entire fortune to charity, rather than to Sir Edward or that cousin of hers she has taken in as a companion. They are not nearly as afflicted as are many of the charity cases I have brought to her attention."

Before Diana could enumerate, a servant entered the room with the welcome announcement that dinner was served.

Dinner with the Parker family was an odd affair, with nearly every member dining on something different, or individual variations of the common dishes. Susan ate the pea soup—or, rather, tasted it, consuming so little that Elizabeth thought she did not care for it until Susan declared it perfectly prepared.

"Just the right thickness," she said in compliment to Mrs. Parker, though of course Mrs. Parker had had little to do with it, save conferring with her cook about the menu. "I fear I am quite in danger of making a glutton of myself." Of the meat, she took none, confining herself to small portions of fish that she minced so finely that they reminded Elizabeth of the food Bennet's nurse fed him.

Diana's meal consisted primarily of vegetable marrow on toast, though she did eat a few spoonfuls of soup and allowed Mr. Parker to persuade her to taste the roast mutton. She declined the port, instead requesting egg wine, into which she stirred powdered ginger "to aid digestion."

Elizabeth was begun to think the Parkers must keep an apothecary on personal retainer, when Susan leaned forward and said proudly, "Diana prepares many of our remedies herself."

"You must be very knowledgeable," Elizabeth said to Diana.

"It requires practice," Diana replied, "and a little experimentation. But my decoctions and salves are much more effective than those the average apothecary sells. Indeed, we have had such disappointing luck with the whole medical tribe that we treat ourselves as often as not."

Arthur, in contrast to his sisters, dined heartily on mutton and pheasant, and when offered dessert, enjoyed both a raspberry tart and baked custard pudding with almost childlike pleasure—all to the admonishment of Diana.

"Arthur, you must take care not to overindulge," Diana said. "Do you want to bring on the gout?"

"Of course not," he said, surreptitiously using his forefinger to lift the last few crumbs of tart crust to his lips the moment Diana turned her head. "I have never been troubled by gout," he told Elizabeth in a low voice. "Seems to me that if one is going to eat dinner, one might as well enjoy it."

They had not long returned to the drawing room when a servant brought the news that Lady Denham and Miss Brereton had come to call. The two ladies entered so swiftly upon his announcement, that they might as well have announced themselves.

The elder, whom Elizabeth presumed to be Lady Denham, was of average height, with an upright, sturdy carriage and strong though not unpleasant features somewhat softened by years. Wrinkles gathered round her eyes, two age spots marred her otherwise well-preserved complexion, and what hair showed beneath her bonnet looked to have turned white long ago, but her bearing had not diminished. Though three and a half score in years, she yet moved with agility, and comported herself with the air of one accustomed to being attended.

Lady Denham appeared surprised by the presence of Elizabeth and Darcy. "Forgive our intrusion," she said to Mrs. Parker. "We did not realize you had guests."

"No, no—this is actually most fortunate!" Mr. Parker said. "These are the new friends of whom I told you, the ones who have taken Number Three on the Terrace."

"Number Three?" the lady said, assessing first Elizabeth, then Darcy. "I thought you said two couples were to lodge in that cottage."

"The Fitzwilliams were unable to come because of an unexpected family matter. However, allow me to present Mr. Darcy and his wife, who will remain in Sanditon for a full fortnight. Mr. and Mrs. Darcy, this is Lady Denham of Sanditon House, and her cousin, Miss Brereton."

"You will be quite comfortable in Number Three," Lady Denham declared. "When did you arrive?"

"Early this afternoon," Darcy said.

"Very good. Is the Terrace full, then, Mr. Parker?"

"It is, I am delighted to say!"

"Miss Clara and I are just come from the post office. She had a letter to post to our cousins in London, and it is such a fine evening that we decided to walk it to the postbox ourselves. I never mind a walk, you know, in decent weather. Why, I fancy I could have walked the letter all the way to Gracechurch Street, had I the time."

"Gracechurch Street!" Elizabeth said. "Is that where your cousins live?"

Lady Denham bristled. "Yes . . . they live in Cheapside." She said this as if she had revealed they lived at Newgate Prison. "But they are good people. Miss Clara lived with them, after her parents died, until I invited her to visit me."

Contrary to the image its name suggested, Cheapside was a thriving market district of fashionable shops and tradesmen's homes. Though far from the Darcys' Mayfair town house in more than mere geography, it was a respectable address for those whose income derived from trade.

"I fear you have mistaken the cause of my exclamation," Elizabeth said. "I was simply surprised by the coincidence—my uncle and aunt live in Gracechurch Street. Mr. and Mrs. Edward Gardiner."

"The Gardiners live but a few doors from our cousins' house," Miss Brereton said. "They are a fine family—lovely children. I believe, Lady Denham, you might have met Mrs. Gardiner when you were last in town. She called upon us one afternoon about a church event she was organizing."

"Oh, yes—I recall her now. I had just returned from my solicitor's office when she arrived. She is your aunt, you say? Well, she seemed a nice enough woman, and we cannot help where our relations live— at least, most of our relations. I did help Miss Clara by inviting her to come stay with me for a time."

As this was now her ladyship's second mention of that fact in as many minutes, Elizabeth wondered whether poor Miss Brereton were constantly reminded of the gratitude she owed Lady Denham for her change in circumstances. She also wondered how permanent or precarious her improved condition was.

"Will you stay for tea?" Mrs. Parker asked.

"Not today, I am afraid," Lady Denham replied. "We have already taken ours—you know I prefer it early. But we will not keep you from yours. Besides, I did not sleep especially well last night, so I want to retire earlier this evening."

Diana, who had been remarkably quiet during the Gracechurch Street discussion, pounced upon this mention of poor rest. "What troubled your slumber, Lady Denham? Are you feeling quite well?"

"I am feeling just fine."

"Your color looks a bit jaundiced—"

"It does not!"

"Do you have the headache? Nausea? How is your appet—"

"I am perfectly well!"

"I do not like your complexion—it appears sallow. Why, I believe you are bilious!"

"Bilious? I most certainly am not!"

"Not to worry—I shall prepare you a decoction that will relieve your symptoms."

"What symptoms? I do not have any—oh, never mind!"

Diane rose to her feet. "Wait here—it will not take me long to prepare it."

"No! Only twice in my life have I ever taken physic, or decoctions, or whatever you want to call them—and I do not plan to start a habit of it now."

"Then perhaps a sedative? To help you get a better night's sleep—"

"Diana," Thomas Parker kindly interjected, "Lady Denham was on her way out. I think once she gets home, she will sleep perfectly well."

"I will indeed." Lady Denham moved toward the door with speed impressive for any septuagenarian.

Diana sighed. "Well, if you change your mind—"

"I will not, but thank you all the same. Come, Miss Clara. It was a pleasure meeting you, Mrs. Darcy. You may call upon us tomorrow if you like and talk more with Miss Clara of Gracechurch Street. You are welcome, too, Miss Heywood. You have not yet called at Sanditon House, and Miss Clara should have more young folks about her."

Five

"Sidney says any thing you know. He has always said what he chose of and to us, all. Most Families have such a member among them I believe Miss Heywood. There is someone in most families privileged by superior abilities or spirits to say anything.—In ours, it is Sidney, who is a very clever young Man, and with great powers of pleasing.—He lives too much in the World to be settled; that is his only fault. He is here and there and every where."
—Thomas Parker, Sanditon

Having received a near-summons from Lady Denham, Charlotte set off with Mrs. Parker and little Mary the following morning for a visit to Sanditon House. They had made several attempts earlier in the week to call on Lady Denham at home, but had been thwarted every time by encountering the very active dowager elsewhere beforehand. Today, however, they embarked at an earlier hour, so as to improve their chances of success.

They went by way of the Terrace, where they would collect Mrs. Darcy and proceed to call on Lady Denham together. Mary, delighted to be included (at the venerable age of six) among the "ladies" while her three rambunctious younger brothers stayed home with their nurse, skipped happily between her mother and Charlotte as they walked. She had been allowed to accompany her mother on two previous visits to Sanditon House, and now chattered excitedly about what Charlotte could expect to see.

Charlotte was nearly as excited as little Mary about their destination.

Her quiet life in Willingden afforded few opportunities to visit mansions on the scale of Sanditon House, and she was curious to see where and how the great lady lived.

"The house has a giant park all around it," Mary said.

"A *giant* park?" Charlotte repeated in an exaggerated tone. "How many giants live there?"

The little girl laughed. "Not *that* kind of giant, Miss Heywood!"

Charlotte took pleasure in little Mary's company. The child reminded her of her own youngest sister, whom she missed. While she was enjoying her Sanditon adventure, and the Parkers were thoughtful, attentive hosts, she was also feeling the absence of her own family and the familiarity of home.

Sea mist surrounded them as they neared the Terrace. In the ten days since her arrival in Sanditon, Charlotte had become accustomed to the mistiness of mornings in the coastal village. Today, however, the fog was so dense that as they crested the hill, they could not see the bottom on the other side.

Mary's skipping soon caused her to outpace her mother, but Charlotte, used to helping mind her siblings, easily kept up with the girl. Mary continued her catalogue of delights to be observed at Sanditon House.

". . . and there is a horse that lives in Mr. Hollis's chamber."

Charlotte, whose thoughts had wandered a bit, realized she must have misheard the little girl. However, before she could ask Mary to repeat herself, the child suddenly stopped skipping and pointed into the mist. "Look, Miss Heywood—is that a carriage?"

Charlotte could barely discern a vehicle ascending the hill. "I believe so—a gig, perhaps."

"No—there is more than one horse. It must be a phaeton!"

Mrs. Parker caught up to them and tendered her opinion as the mist continued to roll and obscure their object of interest. "It appears to me to be a tandem."

Little Mary peered hard into the mist. "I can see the coachman." She gasped, then clapped her hands in delight. "'Tis Uncle Sidney, Mama! It is indeed!"

Within a few minutes the carriage was before them, driven by a gentleman accompanied by his servant.

"Uncle Sidney!" At Mary's joyful greeting, the gentleman stopped the vehicle.

"Is that a sprite calling my name in the mist?" He alighted, and the child rushed to him. He lifted her high in the air, to her utter glee, then held her so that her face was level with his. "Why, no—it is Mistress Mary! How does my lady this morning? Not contrary, I hope?"

Mrs. Parker watched them fondly. "Sidney is a favorite with the children," she said to Charlotte.

Charlotte suspected he was also a favorite with the ladies. About seven- or eight-and-twenty, Sidney Parker bore himself with an assured air, and seemed completely at ease in the fashionable clothes cut to show his tall, slender frame to advantage. Short but perfectly tamed curls of light brown hair framed a lively countenance dominated by blue eyes that twinkled as he played with his niece.

"Lift me again, Uncle Sidney!"

He laughed and obliged her once more, then set her down. With a fleeting glance at Charlotte, he turned to his sister-in-law. "And how are you, Mary?"

"Very well, thank you—all the more for this happy surprise," Mrs. Parker said. "Tom will be delighted you are come. Did you know that Susan, Diana, and Arthur are in Sanditon, as well? They have taken lodgings of their own, however, so we have plenty of room for you at Trafalgar House."

"I had no idea the others were here. I am just come from Eastbourne, and thought to spend two or three days at Sanditon before the village changes so much that I no longer recognize it. But the hotel must be my quarters this visit—I expect to be joined there by a friend."

"Your friends are always welcome at Trafalgar House, you know."

"You are most kind, but I am afraid your house will remain empty of guests this time. Next visit, however, I promise to plant myself completely in your way."

"You are never in the way. And our house is not empty." She gestured toward Charlotte. "Miss Heywood is our guest at present."

"Aha! This lady does have a name! You have been so long about introducing her, that I had begun to think her a figment of my imagination, produced by the mist." He offered Charlotte a well-bred bow. "I am happy to make your acquaintance, Miss Heywood."

Charlotte received his address with shy pleasure. She was not often the object of a gentleman's attention, let alone that of a gentleman as sophisticated as Sidney Parker. "And I yours, Mr. Parker."

"How long is your stay in Sanditon? I am guessing my brother Tom has prescribed at least six weeks for your general health—more, if my sister Diana was part of the conversation."

"I think it shall be four."

"Only four? At a seaside resort? You must be a very efficient idler." He smiled and turned back to Mrs. Parker. "Well, Mary, I must be staking my claim on a pair of hotel rooms, before Mr. Woodcock lets them all out."

"Will we see you for dinner?"

"Is Cook by chance making her roast duck?"

"No, but if I mention you are coming, she will prepare it special for you."

"Then give the old woman my love, and tell her I can taste it already." He turned to Charlotte. "The way to a man's heart, Miss Heywood, is truly through his stomach—never let anyone convince you otherwise."

After raising little Mary into the air a final time, he made a charmingly formal bow to his niece—which was answered with an attempt at an equally dignified curtsy—and took his leave.

A brief stop at No. 3 Sanditon Terrace added Mrs. Darcy to their party, and the ladies proceeded down the road to Sanditon House. The broad, landscaped approach took them between misty fields for about a quarter mile before they arrived at a set of gates marking the formal entrance into the grounds of Sanditon Park. Little Mary, having wearied of skipping (at least for the present), walked beside her mother as Mrs. Parker passed through the gates and continued toward Sanditon House.

Charlotte and Mrs. Darcy followed at a slight distance, their pace leisurely as they engaged in light conversation about the beauty of the grounds. A paling that defined the park's boundary ran close to the road, with mature elms and other trees following the fence line. Some of the trees were ancient, towering so high that their tops disappeared into the mist, while their thick, solid trunks boasted the weathering of sea storms that had felled less stalwart companions. Hedges interspersed between the trees created a nearly uninterrupted wall of foliage.

There were, however, gaps here and there in the shrubbery, and through one of them, a glimpse of something white on the other side of the pales caught Charlotte's eye.

She paused, then stepped closer to the fence for a better view. A bank, skirted by a narrow path, sloped down from the paling, and at its foot the seated figure of a woman could be seen clearly despite the mist. A light breeze fluttered the white ribbons of her gown, and it was this movement that had first drawn Charlotte's notice.

It was the woman's identity, however, that now commanded Charlotte's attention: Miss Brereton—with Sir Edward Denham by her side.

The baronet sat very near her, and the couple were engaged in close conversation. Obviously, a desire for privacy had led them to the remote bank, where the morning mist would further shroud their tête-à-tête from observation.

With a start, Charlotte immediately stepped back, uncomfortable in her sudden, unintentional, unwanted role of voyeur.

She looked up the road. Mrs. Parker and Mary continued their approach to Sanditon House, their pace apparently unbroken. Charlotte was glad that Mrs. Parker had not noticed her pause or its cause. A glance at Mrs. Darcy, however, revealed in her answering gaze that she, too, had spied the secret lovers.

"If I am not mistaken, that is Miss Brereton," Mrs. Darcy said as they resumed their walk. She spoke in a volume low enough that there was no danger of Mrs. Parker hearing them converse, let alone being able to discern their topic. "Do you know the gentleman?"

"He is Sir Edward Denham." Charlotte trusted Mrs. Darcy not to spread gossip about what they had just witnessed. "I am—" She could not define precisely how she felt about the discovery. Shocked? Disappointed? The sight of the clandestine meeting had caused both parties to fall in Charlotte's esteem, but she pitied Miss Brereton's situation and did not want to judge her too harshly. "I am quite surprised to see them together in this manner."

"They are not betrothed?"

"No, and Lady Denham is determined that Sir Edward must marry an heiress to rebuild the fortune of the baronetcy."

"I see."

They walked a few paces in silence, Charlotte's thoughts jumbled as questions of duty rose to needle her.

"Do you think—" Charlotte hesitated, then plunged forward. She could use Mrs. Darcy's guidance just now. "Miss Brereton is under Lady Denham's protection. Do we have an obligation to tell Lady Denham what we saw?" She hoped not. Lady Denham would not receive the news with pleasure. Charlotte did not want to be the cause of misfortune or grief to anybody, especially Miss Brereton, whose lot in life was difficult enough as it was.

"I think we ought not form hasty assumptions about the nature of their tête-à-tête," Mrs. Darcy said. "We are but visitors here. However accurate our initial assumptions might prove, we do not know the full story."

Charlotte accepted her friend's counsel with relief, and resolved to put the incident from her mind.

Six

Every Neighbourhood should have a Great Lady.
—Sanditon

A short distance farther brought Sanditon House within sight. It was stately and handsome, rising from the mist like a castle of old, with Gothic window arches and a tower still standing sentinel against the French enemy across the Channel. No one had told it that Napoleon had been vanquished two years earlier, nor would it have cared. Though not as ancient nor grand in scale as the strongholds it was meant to recall, it had stood long enough on this spot of land not ten miles from Hastings to know that two years' peace with France was but an instant on the strip of Anglo-Saxon coastline that had witnessed the Norman invasion. Mr. Parker's proposed Waterloo Crescent might memorialize the French emperor's defeat, but Sanditon House knew that in time, another would-be conqueror would inevitably rise on the Continent to threaten England once more.

Two servants admitted them to the house. Charlotte could not help but feel, upon entering, that the house lacked the warmth of her family home, and that of the Parkers. Everything was propriety and order, and she wondered whether Lady Denham enjoyed the importance of her style of living, more than the style itself.

They were shown into a large, formal sitting room, with old but fine, well-maintained furnishings and appointments.

"Now remember, Mary," Mrs. Parker said, "that whenever we visit Sanditon House, you are to sit quietly on the sofa and Not Touch Anything."

"Yes, Mama." Mary dutifully went to the sofa, sat down upon it, and folded her hands in her lap. Charlotte had enough experience with her own younger siblings to doubt that the child's posture would last more than six minutes, and to know that every one of them would feel to little Mary like a year of her life.

As they waited for Lady Denham to join them, Charlotte and Mrs. Darcy had an opportunity to look about. Their eyes were immediately drawn to the full-length portrait of a dignified gentleman, which hung above the mantelpiece.

"I assume that is some former master of this house?" Elizabeth asked.

"Actually, no," said Mrs. Parker. "That is Sir Harry Denham, Lady Denham's second husband. Sanditon House is the ancestral home of the Hollis family, and traditionally, a portrait of the current master of Sanditon House has indeed hung in that spot—in fact, among the household, this room is called the portrait room for that very reason— and a large portrait of Lady Denham's first husband used to hang there. But when she moved back into Sanditon House after Sir Harry's death, she relocated Archibald Hollis's portrait to the long gallery and installed Sir Harry above the fireplace. Only a miniature portrait of Mr. Hollis remains in this room—in that case over there."

Charlotte could not help pitying the late Mr. Hollis. To be usurped in one's own home and relegated to a corner case while one's successor enjoys a place of prominence! Too, she wondered how Sir Harry might feel about having been removed from his ancestral home to preside over the house of a mere Mister. He did not appear to mind, bearing himself with all the dignity he might have shown in his own drawing room at Denham Park, as his gaze surveyed every corner of the surroundings into which he had been transplanted.

She and Mrs. Darcy wandered over to the glass-fronted cabinet in which the miniatures were displayed. Therein lay a dozen tiny portraits, representing, from the similarity of their subjects' appearances, either several close branches of a family tree, or an uninspired artist. They were not an entirely unattractive group, but neither were they handsome. A prominent nose and long face were apparent characteristics of the family, as was hair in degrees of blond ranging from very pale to dark. All of the sitters had been captured in their youth or middle age, rendering both Charlotte and Mrs. Darcy unable to guess which of the likenesses depicted Lady Denham's late husband. She asked Mrs. Parker to identify him.

"That is he." Mrs. Parker pointed to an image in the middle row, the most amiable-looking gentleman in the display. "I never knew him, of course. He died long before I married Mr. Parker and moved to Sanditon—before I was even born. Mr. Parker is also too young to have known Mr. Hollis, but recalls tales told by his parents and others who remembered the gentleman."

"What sort of man was he?"

"A worthy sort of man."

Charlotte jumped. Though she recognized the voice behind her as Lady Denham's, its proximity startled her. Mrs. Parker and Mrs. Darcy were equally discomposed by the sudden appearance of the dowager, who had entered the room so quietly that none of the women had perceived her approach.

"Your ladyship," Charlotte stammered as her mind raced to recall whether anything she and Mrs. Parker had said in the past minute might reflect poorly on her if Lady Denham had overheard. Though she pronounced her conscience clear, she nevertheless offered a deeper curtsy than was necessary. "I did not realize you had joined us."

"You were examining the miniatures, I see," Lady Denham replied. "They are all Hollises. The middle row is my late husband's generation of the family—Mr. Hollis, three sisters, and a brother. A respectable-looking family, are they not? Well, do not let their appearances fool you. *My* Mr. Hollis—Archibald Hollis—was the best of the lot. The rest of them may live like ladies and gentlemen, but their behavior to me was so uncivil that I washed my hands of them decades ago."

Lady Denham paused, leaving Charlotte with the impression that she was expected to say something in praise of Lady Denham's conduct, or that would, without appearing impertinent, encourage her to divulge the particulars of the Hollises' transgressions. "Doubtless, you had good cause," she offered.

"Mr. Hollis was many years my senior, and was a bachelor the first two-and-sixty years of his life. After decades spent believing themselves secure of inheriting his fortune—even installing a nephew here as his heir for a while—his relations accused me of manipulating him into marriage so that I could 'steal' what they already considered theirs. The presumption! Who are they, to assume Mr. Hollis's fortune would become their own? They, who never paid him five minutes' uncalculated attention?"

Again, Charlotte sensed that some sort of response was expected of her, but Lady Denham went on.

"I did not need his fortune, nor did he need mine. The sum my father settled upon me was enough to grant me independence; I could have remained Miss Brereton forever if I so chose. On his side, Mr. Hollis possessed property and funds passed to him through generations, and he had been a careful owner of his estate during the whole of his long life. When control of the estate was given to me at his passing, his kin were affronted by his decision, believing themselves more entitled to it than I, because they were Hollises by birth, and I only through a marriage he made late in life. That I was the comfort of his old age—his nurse—his wife—his friend—meant nothing to them. And now that my own years number three and a half score, who do you think have come looking for a reconciliation? Those Hollises! Having been overlooked by Mr. Hollis, they now hope to be remembered by me. Depend upon it, though five-and-thirty years have passed, I *do* remember them—and not warmly."

To the contrary, Charlotte observed that Lady Denham had grown quite warm during her recitation of the Hollises' offenses. "Are they the same Hollises—the same individuals?" She expected that in five-and-thirty years, at least some of them had joined Archibald Hollis in the hereafter.

"It makes no difference—they are Hollises."

Their conversation was interrupted by the entrance of Miss Brereton, who arrived with quick steps and a distracted expression. She halted abruptly when she realized Lady Denham and four visitors occupied the room.

"Well, now, Miss Clara," Lady Denham said, "where have you been hiding this half hour at least?"

A faint flush crept into Clara's cheeks. "I have not been hiding, only walking—as you know I like to do of a morning."

"By yourself? In this mist? You stayed within the park, I hope."

"The mist did not trouble me."

Charlotte herself nearly blushed to hear Clara's prevarication, and she could not help but glance at Mrs. Darcy. Neither of them betrayed their greater knowledge of Clara's earlier whereabouts, or that Sir Edward had been her companion.

"Too, the mist is beginning to lift," Clara added.

Lady Denham regarded her a long moment. "Yes, it is." She paused a moment more, her expression unreadable, before turning back to Charlotte and Mrs. Darcy. "There is a larger painting of Mr. Hollis in the long gallery upstairs. Would you care to see it? The gallery also enjoys a fine prospect of the grounds."

The two of them had little choice but to accept. To their surprise, Lady Denham asked Miss Brereton to show the three ladies and little Mary the gallery while she herself remained in the portrait room. The child asked whether she might visit Mr. Hollis's chamber horse while they were upstairs.

"What?" Mary's question seemed to wrench Lady Denham's attention, and Charlotte got the impression that whatever her ladyship's own etiquette weaknesses might be, the dowager was a strict adherent of the "children should be seen and not heard" philosophy of social intercourse.

"I have heard you say there is a horse in Mr. Hollis's chamber. Might I see it?"

"Oh, dear, Mary!" Mrs. Parker exclaimed. "When visiting other people's homes, one does not ask to see rooms into which one has not been invited. Apologize to Lady Denham."

"But when she comes to our house—"

"That is different."

Though her expression held confusion, little Mary offered their hostess a formal "I beg your pardon."

Her ladyship regarded the child for a long moment. "I suppose you may ride upon the chamber horse," she finally said, "but for only five minutes. And take care that you do so gently! I want it to remain in good condition, in the event an opportunity should arise to hire it out to a visiting family."

They left Lady Denham in the portrait room for the time being and headed for the gallery. As they climbed the staircase, little Mary was full of curiosity and speculation about the chamber horse. "What is its name?" she asked Miss Brereton.

"I do not believe Mr. Hollis ever gave it a name," Miss Brereton said with a smile. "But perhaps Lady Denham will allow you to name it."

"If it is a boy horse, I shall name him Star."

"And if it is a mare?"

This required a moment's thought. "Tilly."

Charlotte had never seen a chamber horse either, nor heard of one before meeting Lady Denham. She pictured it as some sort of child's rocking horse, but could not imagine the Mr. Hollis of the miniature, let alone that gentleman in his late sixties, riding such an object. Her interest in seeing the apparatus almost matched little Mary's, exceeded only by her lingering astonishment concerning Miss Brereton's rendezvous with Sir Edward. At least her curiosity on one of the subjects would soon be satisfied.

Given the child's eagerness to meet the horse, nobody harbored any illusions about the likelihood of a peaceful visit to the gallery before she had done, so they went first to the late Mr. Hollis's apartment, where the chamber horse yet stabled in the antechamber. Little Mary was disappointed to discover that it was neither some sort of live pygmy pony nor a wooden rocking horse, but simply an item of furniture: a rectangular leather-covered springed seat about eighteen inches tall, affixed to a tablelike wooden base with a shallow drawer and four legs that raised it another foot off the floor. A footboard protruded in front to assist mounting. On either side of the seat, slits were cut through the leather at each layer of springs, and wooden spindles rose up from the base to form handles for the rider to grip while bouncing on the stationary steed. The only thing genuinely equine about it in form or fact was the hair stuffed under the top to cushion the seat.

"It is a device for taking exercise," Miss Brereton explained as she helped the girl step up on the footrest and from there climb atop. "Lady Denham says that Mr. Hollis used it during inclement weather."

"Does Lady Denham use the chamber horse?" little Mary asked.

Charlotte suppressed a laugh. For all the dowager's vigor, Charlotte was no more able to envision Lady Denham bouncing on the seat than she was able to picture Mr. Hollis. The image was simply too undignified for a woman as conscious of her own importance as was the dowager.

"She does not," Miss Brereton replied. "However, Lady Denham is a mighty walker. On days she cannot stroll in the Park or walk to town, she prefers to take her exercise in the long gallery."

"She must appreciate you as a companion, since you, too, enjoy regular walks in the park," Charlotte said. At Miss Brereton's startled expression, she added quickly, "Or so I understood you to say downstairs."

Clara's countenance smoothed. "Yes. And we do often walk together, although this morning we did not. Lady Denham prefers to walk after the mist clears, and today it hung about later than is usual."

Little Mary gripped the handles and commenced bouncing. Her weight, however, was too slight to compress the springs very far, her legs too short to reach the footboard and push off with her feet. The resulting motion, therefore, was more a gentle bob than an energetic simulation of horseback riding.

Mrs. Parker noticed a framed pencil sketch hanging on the other side of the room and called Charlotte's attention to it. The two of them moved away from the chamber horse for a closer inspection of the sketch.

"Miss Brereton, have you any idea who drew this?" Mrs. Parker asked.

"Mr. Hollis himself, I believe. From what I understand, he became interested in drawing during his later years and could often be seen going out for a walk with a sketchbook in hand."

Mrs. Parker could not identify the drawing's subject, and asked Miss Brereton to come have a look. Miss Brereton's gaze darted to little Mary. At her present pace, a sudden uncontrolled dismount was unlikely, but there was always an unpredictable factor in any activity involving children. And horses, for that matter.

"Go ahead," Elizabeth said. "I will stay with her."

Miss Brereton came to Charlotte and Mrs. Parker, leaving Elizabeth alone with the budding equestrian.

"Are you enjoying your ride?" Elizabeth asked.

"Yes," little Mary said. "But I thought the horse would go faster."

The rough springs seemed to groan in pain. "It sounds as though it has not been ridden in decades. Perhaps it is an old, tired horse."

"I think she is just sleepy."

"Ah—you have determined that the horse is a mare, then?"

"She is not exciting enough to be a stallion. But Tilly is a good horse. She just needs someone to ride her more often. How many more minutes may I ride?"

Elizabeth was fairly certain that Lady Denham's prescribed limit had passed, but she was reluctant to end the little girl's delight. "I believe you have two minutes remaining," she said.

Determined to make the most of them, Mary tried to bounce harder, but with little success.

"Shall I help you bring the horse to a trot?" Elizabeth offered. As Mary's lightweight motions did not compress the seat's springs anywhere near the extent to which an adult's would, Elizabeth doubted the contraption was in any danger of becoming less valuable as a horse-for-hire in Lady Denham's scheme. Besides, was not exercise good for a horse?

"Oh, yes, please!" Mary answered.

"Hold tight to the handles."

Elizabeth placed her hands on either side of Mary and pushed down on the leather top. From her angle, she still could not apply as much force as a seated adult would produce, but it was enough to release air through the side slits in the leather. And to produce giggles from the child.

Mary cantered over the downs of her imagination until Elizabeth grew tired and told her it was time to bring the mount to a halt. With Elizabeth's assistance, Mary climbed down, but lingered beside the chamber horse, running her fingers across the leather. "There, now, Tilly, that's a good horse," she said. "Would you like an apple?"

She produced an imaginary apple from the folds of her dress, but seemed at a loss for how to feed it to a mare that had no head. She walked round the apparatus, starting with the side closest to Elizabeth, then moving to the back of the seat, and finally the far side.

"Oh! What is this?"

Elizabeth moved to Mary's side just as Mary withdrew a folded piece of paper from one of the leather's slits. Black marks and creases suggested that it had been caught in the seat's coils. She opened the paper, revealing the words "woodcock," "tailor," "ivy," and "rose"—the latter two repeatedly—scrawled in childish handwriting, interspersed with simple drawings of leafy vines, flowers, and birds.

"What does it mean?" Mary asked.

"It does not mean anything," Elizabeth said, refolding the paper. "It is only a torn page from a child's drawing book. But it does not belong to us, so let us put it back."

Returning the page to the seat's mechanical interior, where it might suffer further damage, seemed a poor idea, so Elizabeth instead opened the drawer at the horse's front.

"Aha!" Mary said. "Here is Tilly's mouth."

Mary pretended to feed the horse an apple. When she had done, Elizabeth slipped the sketchbook page into the drawer and slid it shut. The sound drew Miss Brereton's attention back to them.

"Have you finished your ride, Mary?" she asked. "Then let us show Miss Heywood and Mrs. Darcy the gallery. Do you think you can remember which portrait is Mr. Hollis?"

Their party removed to the gallery, entering it through an anteroom on one end. The gallery ran the full length of one side of the house and indeed offered a commanding view from its many windows. The mist had almost entirely cleared, revealing a great portion of Sanditon Park and the fence that surrounded it. A hedge maze and fountain were now visible, along with several structures dotting the landscape. A summerhouse that the mist had obscured from notice during the ladies' approach to the Great House, now offered shade from the climbing sun. In another part of the park, a gazebo nestled in the center of a rose garden, while a thatched roof peeked out from the trees in a remote, shady corner of the property.

"This is a lovely view," Elizabeth said. "What is that building with the thatched roof?"

"A hermitage," Miss Brereton replied.

"Indeed? Her ladyship keeps a hermit?"

Although maintaining a hermit was a fashionable folly among some wealthy landowners, Elizabeth had never quite understood the appeal of supporting a recluse—the more eccentric, the better—on one's property for the primary purpose of entertaining one's guests with sightings of him during garden parties. In her opinion, the practice was beneath the dignity of both hermit and landlord. While Longbourn, her childhood home, had a hermitage on its property, it had never known an occupant. She supposed, however, that such arrangements did provide living quarters for the hermit on relatively easy terms, particularly for those who lacked the mental faculties or physical ability to support themselves through other work. Pride could not fill one's belly or warm one's bones on a frigid winter night.

"No, the hermitage has not been used for decades—since the time of Mr. Hollis's father. Archibald Hollis never replaced the last hermit who lived there, and Lady Denham considers hermits a frivolous expense."

From the gallery window, Charlotte could clearly see the sloped bank upon which she had observed Miss Brereton and Sir Edward earlier.

A glance at Clara Brereton showed that her attention, too, was drawn to the bank. She was not, however, regarding it with a soft look of fond memory. Rather, her face held a troubled expression, and Charlotte wondered whether the bank was a regular trysting-place for her and Sir Edward. Was Miss Brereton a persecuted heroine after all, prevented by her dependence on Lady Denham from being openly courted by Sir Edward? Charlotte would like to think Clara possessed better judgment than to swoon at the inflated discourse that Charlotte had observed made up a considerable portion of the baronet's conversation, but hereditary titles had a way of adding imagined sense to even the silliest speeches and speakers.

A window at the far end of the rectangular room overlooked property that lay opposite the entrance gates through which Charlotte and the other ladies had arrived. Through this window, Charlotte had a closer view of the summerhouse nestled beside the shrubbery that formed the park's eastern boundary. On the other side of the shrubbery, not too far distant, another Great House rose from the trees. Charlotte enquired who lived there.

"That is Denham Park," Miss Brereton replied.

"Denham Park? I did not realize it lies so close to Sanditon House." Lady Denham had told Charlotte that Miss Denham and Sir Edward had stayed with her for a full se'nnight the previous summer, and that Miss Denham had lately been angling none-too-subtly for a repeat invitation on the pretext of desiring closer proximity to the shore and seabathing. "Why, one could easily walk between them."

The words left her lips before she considered their potential effect on one who might be burdened with consciousness of someone in particular walking it more often than he properly ought.

"Yes, one can, though Miss Denham generally prefers to take the gig when she and Sir Edward visit."

"Here he is!" Little Mary called the ladies' attention away from the landscape. Her mind still on Sir Edward, Charlotte at first thought Mary's announcement to mean that the baronet had entered the room. But then Charlotte saw that the child pointed to one of many portraits lining the walls. The girl turned to Charlotte. "Here is Mr. Hollis."

Charlotte had greater interest in hearing more about the Denhams than in viewing another likeness of Mr. Hollis, but her conversation with Miss Brereton had been broken. She left the window and walked down the gallery to see the portrait. This full-length oil painting depicted the gentleman at a more advanced age than did the miniature. Despite white hair and a ruddier complexion, he yet appeared a hale man. Perhaps there was something to be said for the chamber horse after all.

"This is the painting that used to hang above the mantelpiece in the portrait room," Mrs. Parker said.

"And that one"—Miss Brereton pointed to a smaller head-and-shoulders watercolor to its left—"also depicts Archibald Hollis, the year he reached his majority." To Charlotte's eye, the older Mr. Hollis appeared more carefree than the younger.

To the right of Mr. Hollis's oil painting hung another full-length portrait, that of a finely dressed woman. "Do you know who this is, Mary?" Miss Brereton asked the little girl.

"Lady Denham!"

"Very good," Miss Brereton said, then addressed Elizabeth and Miss Heywood. "Actually, her name was still Miss Philadelphia Brereton at the time the portrait was painted. It was commissioned upon her engagement to Mr. Hollis, and given to him as a wedding gift."

All things considered, Charlotte thought Lady Denham had aged fairly well. She had not added the weight that many older women did, and her face, though wrinkled, still very much retained the shape and determination of her youth.

There was something in the younger Philadelphia's eyes, however, that seemed to be lost in the dowager's—a vulnerability that age and time had either worn away or buried.

Seven

*Why he should talk so much Nonsense, unless he could do no bet-
ter, was unintelligible. He seemed very sentimental, very full of
some Feelings or other, and very much addicted to all the newest-
fashioned hard words—had not a very clear Brain she presumed,
and talked a good deal by rote.—The Future might explain him
further—but . . . [Charlotte] felt that she had had quite enough of
Sir Edward for one morning.*

—Sanditon

*E*veryone's interest in portraiture sated for the present, including
Elizabeth's, they quit the gallery with the intention of rejoining
Lady Denham. Their progress was slowed, however, as they passed
through an anteroom that held several objects of wondrous distraction at a child's eye level. One of them, a delicate vase containing
three pink rosebuds, rested on a small wooden table. When little Mary
leaned on the tabletop to smell the flowers, the table wobbled—
nearly toppling the vase. Were it not for Elizabeth's fortunate proximity and quick reflexes, the vase would have fallen.

"Mary!" her mother admonished. "What did I tell you about
touching things?"

"I did not touch the vase, Mama! Only the table."

"You should not have pushed against it so hard."

"To be fair," Miss Brereton said, "that table is unsteady—I think
one of its legs is slightly shorter than the others. I nearly toppled the
vase myself last week, but forgot to mention it to the housekeeper."

Carrie Bebris

"All the same, Mary, you cannot run about breaking Lady Denham's things," said Mrs. Parker, "especially if you want to see Tilly again."

That warning proved effective, and they continued toward the portrait room without further incident. As they reached the base of the staircase, they encountered Sir Edward Denham also approaching the portrait room. A momentary expression of—astonishment? alarm? guilt?—flashed across Miss Brereton's countenance, and she hung behind the others as he addressed them.

"Miss Heywood!" Sir Edward doffed his hat with a cavalier flourish. "What an unanticipated delight to meet with you here—'on this gay, dewy morning.' I had no notion of your intent to call upon Lady Denham today."

"Nor I yours," Charlotte said. "Did not Miss Denham accompany you?"

"My sister is otherwise engaged, else she would have come, for she always takes every opportunity to visit Sanditon House. However, it is just as well she could not join me—I appear to be well outnumbered by ladies as it is and will be hard-pressed to divide my attention equally among so many—you, Miss Brereton, your friend . . ." He looked toward Elizabeth expectantly.

"I was just about to introduce you," Charlotte said. "May I present Mrs. Darcy. She and her husband are newly arrived in Sanditon by way of Willingden."

"Yes, of course—Mrs. Darcy! When last I saw Mr. Parker, he heralded your imminent visit. We are a humble village now, but on the rise. And you, Miss Brereton—'fair imperial flow'r.' How are you this morn?"

When Miss Brereton looked up from a spot on the floor that had become the object of her attention, she betrayed no hint of their already having been in each other's company not one hour earlier. "I am well, thank you."

He greeted Mrs. Parker and Mary with equal warmth, minus random poetic quotations, then with a sweep of his arm invited all the ladies to precede him into the portrait room.

"Sir Edward," Lady Denham greeted him. "I thought I heard your voice. Why did not one of the servants announce you?"

66

"I told them I would announce myself. You and I are nephew and aunt, after all, not merely baronet and lady. We need not always stand upon formality."

"In this house we yet retain some protocol. They ought to at least have relieved you of your hat. I will not have my staff becoming lazy."

"Pray, do not reprimand them on my account. It was I who robbed them of the opportunity to perform their duties."

"Hmph. Well, I shall take it up with them later." Lady Denham turned to Charlotte and Elizabeth. "Did you enjoy the view from the gallery?"

"I did," Charlotte replied. "The mist has dissipated, and I could see clear to Denham Park. I had no idea that you and Sir Edward were such close neighbors."

"Yes, when Sir Harry courted me—after a respectable period of mourning, mind you—he had not far to come. And before that, Mr. Hollis was always on good terms with the Denhams."

"Centuries ago, both properties were a single tract of land upon which once stood a medieval castle," Sir Edward said. "The land was granted to my ancestors at the time the Denham baronetcy was created. Alas, by then the castle had long since fallen to ruin; little remained but the foundations."

As Sir Edward spoke, Elizabeth became aware that he assumed the same stance as did Sir Harry in the portrait hanging behind him. In fact, she soon suspected that the similitude was intentional, that he deliberately invited the visual comparison. His formal posture—one leg positioned slightly before the other, hat tucked under his left arm, chin tilted at a slight upward angle—all mimicked that of his two-dimensional predecessor. The only thing missing was the gold watch in Sir Harry's right hand, its chain extending to his fob pocket. Instead, Sir Edward's right hand formed a fist that rested on his hip—a common posture in noble portraits. However, while the two gentlemen shared similar builds, Sir Harry's aristocratic deportment appeared natural; Sir Edward's, affected. Sir Harry's eyes also seemed to reflect more sense in oil than his nephew possessed in life.

"The first baronet built his manor house, Denham Park, within sight of the ruin," Sir Edward continued. "Is that not incredibly picturesque? Imagine looking out one's window on a morning such as this, to see the mist drifting over forlorn, crumbling stones." He sighed, and paused the history to grant his listeners sufficient time to experience the proper degree of sentiment this image evoked.

"Sounds like a death trap to me," Lady Denham declared. "Every time I hear this story, all I can imagine is unsuspecting people and horses tripping on stones and falling into forgotten cellars."

"Nobody fell in cellars," Sir Edward said.

"How would you know? Were you there?" Lady Denham directed her attention to Charlotte and Elizabeth. "The land was put to much better use after it entered the Hollis family's possession. The fourth baronet sold a portion of the land to the Hollises, who built this house on the foundations of the old castle."

"Alas! The ancient stronghold can no longer be seen," Sir Edward said with a heavy sigh, "but the architecture of Sanditon House recalls its glory."

"Well, I am glad you admire it," Lady Denham said. "Mr. Hollis took great pride in Sanditon House, which is why I keep it up the way I do. I would not go to such expense merely for myself, you know. I maintain this style of living to honor his memory."

Without the chamber horse to occupy her, little Mary soon grew restless. Although she made a valiant effort to sit quite still, and not fidget, nor run her hands along the edge of the side table, nor swing her right foot in a steady rhythm, nor commit any other small acts of suppressed energy resisting restraint, Lady Denham—a woman who had never mothered a child and who, even if she had ever possessed the necessary patience, had now been too long accustomed to having all about her precisely to her order and liking—regarded the girl's behavior with escalating displeasure.

Even Mrs. Parker recognized that it was time to end their visit. "I am afraid we must be going."

"Yes," Lady Denham pronounced, "I expect we all have other business to attend to before the day is out. What time is it, Sir Edward?"

The baronet patted his fob pocket, then smiled sheepishly. "I am afraid I have forgotten my watch this morning."

"Indeed? You should take better care of it. You know how dear it was to Sir Harry."

"Of course. I assure you, it is one of my most prized possessions."

Mary tugged on her mother's hand. "Are we going to see Uncle Sidney now, Mama?"

"Not yet, Mary. Later today."

The child's question captured Sir Edward's interest. "Has Mr. Sidney Parker come to Sanditon?"

"He is just arrived," Mrs. Parker said. "We met his carriage on our way to Sanditon House this morning."

"Indeed? Why, I cannot recall the last time I saw him—it would not surprise me to learn it has been nearly a twelvemonth. My sister and I shall have to call upon him. When would be a convenient time for us to visit Trafalgar House?"

"He does not stay with us, but at the hotel," Mrs. Parker replied.

"The hotel!" Lady Denham exclaimed. "Whatever for?"

"He expects to be joined by a friend."

"Well, I suppose the other young gentleman wants to preserve his independence, rather than subject himself to another family's ways and hours," Lady Denham said. "But for Sidney Parker to incur the expense of a hotel seems a foolish extravagance."

"He is in Sanditon only a few days."

"That is all the more reason to save his money and stay with his brother, and I shall not hesitate to tell him so when I see him."

Sir Edward took his leave with as many courtly gestures and lofty quotations as he had indulged in when he entered. Lady Denham summoned a servant "to show him out properly—with the attention due a baronet—in respect for the memories of both Mr. Hollis and Sir Harry."

When he had quit the room and the rest of the visitors were preparing to depart, Lady Denham drew Elizabeth aside.

"I hope, Mrs. Darcy, you do not think I allow visitors to just show themselves in," she said. "That is not the sort of house I maintain. I know the value of money, and I keep a watchful eye on mine, but I also know what is expected of people at our level of society. Ever since Sir Edward and his sister stayed with me for a week last summer, there have been occasions when he seems to feel himself at liberty to enter Sanditon House as he pleases, popping in whenever he likes, and I fear I have been too lax about insisting he adhere to stricter protocol. But that will be changing. For one thing, I do not intend to have him and his sister, Miss Denham, back as overnight guests for some time, especially now that Miss Clara is here."

Elizabeth was surprised by Lady Denham's candor to a near stranger regarding the baronet. "This is your home, and he is your nephew. It is not for me or anybody else to judge the degree of familiarity he enjoys in your household."

"Yes, well—I *am* fond of him and his sister, and of Miss Clara, too. But that sentiment is not something my young folks ought to take for granted. This *is* my home, and while eventually the house will be transferred to someone else, until that day arrives, it is presumptuous for anybody to behave as if it were already theirs."

Eight

"I wish we may get [Sidney] to Sanditon. I should like to have you acquainted with him."

—*Thomas Parker,* Sanditon

While Elizabeth visited Sanditon House, Darcy spent the morning exploring the village of Sanditon on his own. Though Mr. Parker had offered to serve as a guide, Darcy first wanted to see the village as would a newcomer who had not the benefit of established connections to influence his perceptions. And so, several hours before he and Elizabeth were to meet with Mr. Parker, he commenced a solitary stroll through its streets and shops.

He started with the hotel. It seemed a reputable establishment, its lobby hospitably though not luxuriously appointed with Sheraton-style furniture, handsome draperies, and a desk attendant who offered him a genial greeting upon entrance. The few guests loitering in the lobby were well dressed and well mannered. Its dining room appeared to have recently finished serving breakfast; a maid was clearing the buffet of food that looked appealing enough that Darcy ordered dinner for later that day.

From there, he visited the shops and other establishments on the Terrace and in the newer part of the village. He found them typical of an English village this size. The goods seemed well made, the merchants friendly and welcoming to visitors. He spoke at length with a few shopkeepers, and observed others transact business with their customers.

Overall, he came away with a favorable impression. He returned to his cottage with a few minutes to spare before his appointment with Mr. Parker, and looked forward to spending them hearing Elizabeth's impressions of Sanditon House. Upon entering, however, he discovered Elizabeth was not alone; she had invited Miss Heywood, Mrs. Parker, and little Mary to take refreshment before continuing home.

The ladies were just finishing their tea, but decided to stay until Mr. Parker arrived. Apparently, little Mary had news of great moment that she wished to impart to her father before he learned it elsewhere. Indeed, barely had Mr. Parker entered the cottage than she rushed forward to greet him.

"Papa! Three guesses who we saw this morning!"

Mr. Parker knelt to return his daughter's embrace. "Father Christmas?"

"No! It is summertime!"

"Oh! Of course. Robin Goodfellow?"

She shook her head with a broad smile. "'Twas no trickster, Papa! You have one more guess."

"All right, then. Lady Denham?"

"You already know we went to visit Lady Denham. Of course we saw her at her own house. She let me ride Mr. Hollis's chamber horse! I named her Tilly."

"But Lady Denham already has a name." Mr. Parker's eyes twinkled, and from his daughter's poorly suppressed smile, one sensed that they often engaged in teasing banter.

"Not Lady Denham, Papa. The horse!"

"Oh, the horse! So you met a chamber horse named Tilly this morning—that is exciting, indeed, and I never would have guessed."

"No, Papa—I was not talking about the horse. We saw someone else, too."

"Well, I am out of guesses, so I suppose you must tell me."

"Uncle Sidney!"

"Uncle Sidney?" Mr. Parker stood and looked to his wife for confirmation, which she gave with a nod.

"He is just arrived," Mrs. Parker said. "We met him on our way to collect Mrs. Darcy for our walk to Sanditon House."

"Where is he, then? He has not been to Trafalgar House."

"He expects to be joined by a friend, so he is staying at the hotel and stopped to secure rooms. He said he will come later today for dinner."

"Splendid!" Mr. Parker turned to the Darcys. "I am so pleased that you will have an opportunity to meet the last of my siblings while in Sanditon."

Their party now split in two. As Miss Heywood had already been in the village more than a week and had been treated to a personal tour upon her arrival, she accompanied Mrs. Parker and Mary back to Trafalgar House while Mr. Parker commenced the Darcys' tour of Sanditon.

"Let us give Sidney a chance to get settled while I show you the village, then stop at the hotel last," he said. "We are quite proud of it—newly built, as is the livery beside it. It is much bigger and grander than the inn down in the old village was. Three stories of guest rooms, many of the upper ones with fine views of the sea—all quite comfortable. But let us begin with a walk down to the shore. . . ."

After a Grand Tour of Sanditon that rivaled any Continental journey, Elizabeth and Darcy entered the hotel with Mr. Parker. Their guide headed toward the front desk to learn in which room his brother could be found, but stopped upon spying a young gentleman engaged in conversation on the far side of the lobby.

"Oh! That is Sidney over there."

Sidney and an associate sat in a corner pair of chairs, removed from the flow of guests passing through the lobby. A large potted plant partly obscured his companion from view, but as Elizabeth and the others crossed the room, she identified her as Lady Denham.

Sensing the approach of their party, Sidney glanced toward them and rose.

"Why, Tom!" He greeted Mr. Parker with an earnest handshake, his pleasure in the reunion evident. "I did not expect to see you until later today."

"When I heard you were in Sanditon, I could not forgo the opportunity to greet you sooner," Mr. Parker replied. "Especially as I was so nearby, with friends who are lodging in one of the cottages across the way."

He introduced them to Sidney. The usual pleasantries were exchanged, after which Elizabeth expressed happiness in seeing Lady Denham again so soon. "I am, however, sorry to have interrupted your tête-à-tête," Elizabeth said.

"You have not interrupted anything," her ladyship replied. "Sidney Parker was merely keeping me company while I wait for Miss Clara. She is at the library in search of Evelina, or Pamela, or some other unfortunate heroine—I cannot keep them straight—I do not read much myself. But Miss Clara enjoys a novel now and then, and they seem harmless. Sir Edward reads a great many. Young folks must be allowed their amusements."

"Sidney," Mr. Parker said, "Mary told me that you anticipate the arrival of a friend. Do you expect him in time for dinner?"

"No, Granville said he would not arrive until late this evening."

"It will be a family dinner, then." He turned to the Darcys and Lady Denham. "Unless I can persuade you to join us?"

"Mrs. Darcy and I appreciate the invitation, but I have already ordered our dinner here for this evening," Darcy said.

This came as news to Elizabeth, and she half wondered whether he had done so to avoid dining with the valetudinarian portion of the Parker clan a second night in a row.

"Dinner here is bound to be a good one," Sidney said, "the best you will find in the village outside of a private house. Not that Sanditon offers much in the way of competition—only a few cook-shops and pubs—unless, Tom, you have transformed the old inn into a café since my last visit?"

"What," Lady Denham asked, "is a caff-ay?"

"A type of dining establishment one sees in Paris," Sidney replied.

"Paris!" From the expression on Lady Denham's face, he might as well have said "Purgatory." "Why on earth would we want one of those in Sanditon?"

"To entice visitors from across the Channel. Now, Tom, *that* would give Sanditon a leg up on Brinshore! Why, add a pâtisserie, refer to all the shops as boutiques, rename the library 'La Bibliothèque,' and the Terrace could become the next Avenue des Champs-Élysées. Imagine how welcome French travelers would feel! Sanditon would be the destination of choice for every family in France."

"French families!" Lady Denham regarded the brothers in horror. "You cannot be contemplating such a thing? We don't need their like in Sanditon."

"Sidney is not serious," Mr. Parker replied. "He says this only to tease me."

"Well, I certainly hope so. Sidney Parker, sometimes I cannot tell whether you are jesting or not. French visitors! Why not invite the rats off the ships, while we are at it? I would rather the houses sit vacant. We want only good, English folk—Irish, if we absolutely must. None of those mounseers or their cafés here."

"Fear not, Lady Denham," Sidney said. "I was indeed only sporting with my brother." He addressed the Darcys. "I hope I have not made a poor impression upon you. Tom is used to my ways—he will tell you that I would hardly seem myself did I not rail with him when given an opportunity. But it is all in good nature." He turned back to Lady Denham. "If you come to dinner tonight, I promise not to utter a single word *en français*."

"Yes, do come," Mr. Parker said. "The invitation also extends to Miss Brereton, of course."

"As you are so good as to frequently invite Miss Clara and me to dine at Trafalgar House, we will not insert ourselves into your family party the first night all of you Parkers are together," Lady Denham said. "Besides, I was just telling your brother that he must come to dinner at Sanditon House while he is here. Let us make it a large company—you and Mrs. Parker, your sisters and Arthur—Miss Heywood, of course. Sidney, bring your friend—what was his name? Mr. Greenville?"

"Granville. It is most generous of you to extend your invitation to him. I accept on our mutual behalf."

"I shall also invite Sir Edward and Miss Denham, and perhaps one or two others." Almost as an afterthought, she added, "Mr. and Mrs. Darcy, I insist that you come, too."

Mr. Parker appeared surprised by Lady Denham's proposal. "That is indeed a large party."

"It has been a long time since the dining room at Sanditon House held more than half a dozen. My servants are growing lazy and need to earn their keep."

"Very well," Mr. Parker said. "We can celebrate the start of what is shaping up to be a successful season for Sanditon. When will this dinner take place?"

"As Sidney is here but a few days, let us make it tomorrow. Four o'clock. That should keep my staff busy between now and then! I must tell them at once to begin preparations. Ah, where is Miss Clara? She is certainly taking her time at the library. Sidney, will you come with me to retrieve her? I don't believe you have seen Miss Clara since she came to stay with me."

Though Lady Denham's manner was not quite as imperious as Lady Catherine's, Elizabeth could see that this lady was as accustomed to having her way as was Darcy's aunt. Sidney, however, seemed practiced at dealing with her. Having grown up in Sanditon, he had probably done so most of his life.

"I shall do better, Lady Denham. If you like, I will retrieve her for you. Give me but a few minutes."

Lady Denham smiled. "You have grown into a fine young man, Sidney Parker, despite your best efforts."

Sidney laughed, then offered her ladyship an exaggerated bow before heading off on his errand. Thomas Parker, still eager for his brother's company, walked him to the entrance, momentarily leaving Lady Denham with the Darcys.

"Thomas Parker is the best neighbor one could wish for," Lady Denham said, "though when it comes to Sanditon, I wish he were not as eager to spend my money as freely as his own. I did not get where I am in life by rushing headlong into every enterprise that offered." She leaned closer. "But of all the Parkers, I think Sidney is my favorite. I like him for his impertinence, a trait I would not tolerate in anybody else. In him, however, it is a refreshing difference from his siblings. The sisters and Arthur are agreeable enough in their way, but their health complaints! I have no patience for invalids. If they would just go on like everybody else, half their troubles would disappear. And they would save a fortune in doctor fees. Why, the physician who attended my poor dear Sir Harry billed me for ten visits in his final days. Ten! And not a one did him any good. In fact, I believe Sir Harry might be alive today if it weren't for all that doctoring. Mr. Hollis seldom saw a doctor, and he lived to seven-and-sixty. I have never consulted one for myself, nor taken physic more than twice in my life—and then, only at Miss Diana's insistence. She is a good woman, and tries very hard to be helpful, but sometimes a person does not want help. I am glad we will have such a large party tomorrow so that she can spread out her goodwill." She rose from her seat. "Well, I suppose I may as well go meet Miss Clara and Sidney on their way back here. Good day to you."

Before Elizabeth or Darcy could reply, she departed.

Elizabeth's gaze followed the widow out the door. "Did we ever actually accept her invitation?"

"I do not believe we had a choice."

Nine

"Indulge your imagination in every possible flight which the subject will afford."

—Elizabeth Bennet, Pride and Prejudice

*M*r. Parker, by this time, was standing at the hotel's front desk in conversation with the attendant, and Elizabeth had begun to think it his mission in life to spread congeniality wherever he went. She and Darcy approached slowly, not wanting to intrude upon the discussion, but he motioned them forward.

"The hotel is more full than I thought," he announced happily. "Additional guests are expected tonight, including Mr. Granville. Lady Denham will be pleased to hear this news."

"Perhaps it will make up for the French fright she experienced earlier," Darcy said.

"Ha! Yes, Sidney gave her quite a scare, did he not? Though he is right about the need to do something with the former inn. Not a café, of course—the old village is not the place for such an establishment, and Lady Denham would never approve one now. I find it is generally best to submit to her preferences on small matters, so as to reserve my own persuasive efforts for larger concerns such as the Crescent. But perhaps the former inn should be reopened, so that Sanditon can accommodate more visitors. What do you think, Mr. Woodcock?"

"If there are enough visitors to fill it, and I can find enough help to run it," said the man at the desk, apparently the hotel owner. "It hasn't sold, and I've been trying to decide what to do with the place. No sense in leaving it vacant, if it could be earning money for me."

"There's the spirit!" Mr. Parker said. "Since the inn is older and sits in a less sought-after part of the village, you could charge tariffs that would appeal to respectable travelers of more modest means than your hotel patrons. That way the inn and hotel would not compete for the same pool of guests."

"My daughter just got betrothed—after the wedding, I could turn the place over to her and her new husband to manage. . . ."

Though Elizabeth heard the discussion between Mr. Parker and Mr. Woodcock continue, she did not absorb it. The hotelier's name had caught her attention—which was then arrested by a painted wooden sign hanging on the wall behind him.

IVY WOODCOCK
Born 25 July 1717
Disappeared 25 July 1733
Age 16

Her mind returned to the sketchbook page little Mary had found inside the chamber horse at Sanditon House. When at last a break came in the men's conversation, Elizabeth gestured toward the sign. "Who was Ivy Woodcock?"

"Is. Who *is* Ivy Woodcock?" The hotelkeeper smiled enigmatically. "She is Sanditon's resident ghost."

"All the best resorts have at least one," Mr. Parker said. "Ghosts add interest to a place. Visitors love a good ghost story, so long as they do not actually encounter a ghost themselves. Sanditon cannot boast as many as Bath or Brighton, but we are proud of our Ivy—all the more for her being the daughter of Mad Woodcock, another local legend."

"Mad Woodcock?"

"Ebenezer Woodcock. A hermit who lived on the grounds of Sanditon House."

"The hermit had a daughter?" Darcy said. "Hermits are supposed to be solitary."

"He wasn't a very good hermit, what with having a family and all," Mr. Parker admitted. "At least not at first. He always had to keep Ivy out of sight when the Hollises were entertaining—their guests wanted to see a genuine hermit, not a hermit with a little girl in tow. And he was, well, a little too normal—though he managed to affect some tics and other odd behaviors when called upon. But I should allow Mr. Woodcock to share the tale, as Ebenezer was his—what, great-uncle?"

"Great-great," Mr. Woodcock corrected. "Yes, he was not the average hermit. In fact, Mr. Hollis took him on probation—"

"Not Lady Denham's Mr. Hollis," Mr. Parker clarified. "Her late husband was Archibald Hollis. Mr. Woodcock speaks of Victor Hollis, Archibald's father."

"Yes, old Mr. Hollis," Mr. Woodcock said. "Ebenezer had been the village innkeeper till his wife died, leaving him with Ivy. After her death, he no longer had the heart to be social with strangers all the time, so he turned the business over to his brother and moved with Ivy into the hermitage. After a while, a lot of folks pretty much forgot about them, since the hermitage sits in a remote corner of the park, and they kept to themselves so much. Occasionally, someone would catch a glimpse of Ivy wandering the grounds at dawn or dusk, or hear the sound of a girl singing. People say she had a voice more enchanting than a sea siren's."

"A sea siren!" Mr. Parker interjected. "If only Sanditon had its own sea siren! Now, *that* would be an attraction even Brighton and Weymouth could not top—far better than a café."

"But once lured here, visitors could never leave," Darcy pointed out.

"Better still!"

"Until they ran out of money," Mr. Woodcock said. "Then what would we do with them all?"

Mr. Parker thought about this a moment, then conceded that sea sirens were impractical as a tourism strategy. Before the speculator could devise a scheme involving mermaids, Mr. Woodcock continued Ivy's story.

"As Ivy grew up, the village once more took an interest in her, for it was rumored that she had matured into a beautiful young woman," he said. "Young men would hike down to the shore and raise their eyes to the cliff near where the hermitage sat, hoping to see her looking out upon the water. I expect more than one imagined himself the hero who would rescue Ivy from her lonely existence and take her to wife."

Elizabeth smiled to herself. From his lyrical phrasing, this clearly was not the first time Mr. Woodcock had told this tale.

"Then on the night of her sixteenth birthday, Ivy simply disappeared—went to bed as usual, but in the morning she was gone. Her father assumed she had risen before dawn and was walking the grounds, as was her habit, but as the day grew longer, she never returned to the hermitage. The whole village searched for her. Mr. Hollis himself took charge of the hunt—"

"Again, old Mr. Hollis," Mr. Parker interjected.

"Yes," Mr. Woodcock said. "Archibald Hollis was gone to Oxford. But they never found her."

"Did they discover any evidence of what might have happened to her?" Darcy asked.

"A few days after she disappeared, her shawl washed up on the rocks at the base of the cliff. It was torn and bloodied. Some thought she had wandered too close to the cliff's edge in the misty predawn light and fallen. The village gossips whispered of self-murder, but Ebenezer vehemently rejected that notion. He feared that some vicious animal—on four legs or two—had got her. For weeks he combed Sanditon Park for evidence that she had been attacked by a wild creature or highwayman. Her body was never discovered, in the sea or on land.

"Ebenezer started going to the inn daily, meeting every coach and rider that came to the village, asking if they had seen Ivy. Old Hollis put a swift end to that. Threatened to turn him out."

"Had he no compassion?" As a mother, Elizabeth could not imagine the torment of losing her own daughter under such circumstances.

"Victor Hollis was a hard man—all the Hollises were, save Archibald. The village was relieved when Victor eventually died and his son inherited the estate. Archibald Hollis treated his tenants and servants better than his father and grandfathers had. Regardless, who ever heard of a hermit going into a village each day and talking to everyone he met? Even an inferior hermit must adhere to some essentials of the job."

"I suppose so."

"Funny thing is, after Ebenezer stopped going to the inn, he became as reclusive and peculiar a hermit as Victor Hollis could wish. When he did encounter people, he would tell them that Ivy had been spirited away by faeries, or that her ghost haunted Sanditon Park. Folks started calling him Mad Woodcock, though that didn't stop them from repeating the ghost tales—and embellishing them. Pretty soon half the villagers were telling stories of their own sightings.

"Ebenezer's brother, however—my great-grandfather—hung this tablet in a prominent location of his inn, partly as a memorial, and partly to prompt conversation with travelers who might have encountered Ivy if she were still alive. It was his hope that someday, some visitor would possess information that could restore Ebenezer's wits, or at least give him peace."

"Did that ever happen?"

"No. He lived another ten years or so, but was mad as a March hare by the end. His grave is in the churchyard, if you want to see it—says 'Mad Woodcock' right on the headstone. Of course, now so much time has passed that nobody who could have known anything is alive anymore."

"Yet you still display the sign."

"When we built this hotel, we moved it from the old inn mostly out of sentiment, but it has proven a good spark for conversation, especially this season, with this year being the centenary of Ivy's birth."

Elizabeth's thoughts drifted back to the sketchbook page and the childlike handwriting upon it. A village ghost was something that captured the imagination of old and young alike.

Mr. Parker's face lit with the enthusiasm of a new idea. "We should organize some sort of observance to mark her birthday—an event that would draw more visitors to Sanditon."

"It is too late to organize anything," Mr. Woodcock said. "Her one-hundredth birthday is tomorrow."

"Dear me! It is, indeed. That is not even enough time to advertise within town." He sighed. "Perhaps in sixteen years we can plan a remembrance for the one-hundredth anniversary of her disappearance."

As they left the hotel, Mr. Parker consoled himself with the pleasure he anticipated in Lady Denham's coming dinner party. He was especially delighted by the Darcys' inclusion in it. "You must have made a very favorable impression on her ladyship," he said. "While she entertains on a scale commensurate with her station, she seldom hosts elaborate affairs, so for her to have invited you this early in your acquaintance demonstrates a particular regard."

Elizabeth could not recall herself or Darcy having said anything so amazing as to strike a great impression on the dowager. In fact, Lady Denham talked so extensively of her own concerns that Elizabeth and Darcy had not been required—nor even had sufficient opportunity—to say much at all. After they parted company with Mr. Parker and returned to their cottage to dress for dinner, Elizabeth shared this thought with Darcy.

"I suspect," Darcy replied, "that her ladyship's invitation was motivated more by the slight she would have committed had she excluded us while we stood before her, than by an intense desire for our companionship."

"Well, however we came by the invitation, it sounds like an interesting collection of guests. I am rather looking forward to it."

Volume the Second

IN WHICH THE SEARCH FOR LADY DENHAM
COMMENCES

"Her faults may be entirely imputed to her want of Education. She has good natural Sense, but quite uncultivated."
—Thomas Parker, speaking of
Lady Denham, *Sanditon*

———◦———

Ten

*"The Novels which I approve are such as display Human Nature
with Grandeur—such as shew her in the Sublimities of intense
Feeling—Such as exhibit the progress of strong Passion from
the first Germ of incipient Susceptibility to the utmost Energies
of Reason half-dethroned,—where we see the strong spark of
Woman's Captivations elicit such Fire in the Soul of Man as leads
him—(though at the risk of some Aberration from the strict line
of Primitive Obligations)—to hazard all, dare all, atchieve [sic]
all, to obtain her."*

—Sir Edward Denham, Sanditon

*W*hat do you mean, Lady Denham is missing?" Josiah Hollis demanded.

"I cannot find her," Miss Brereton said. "She is not in her apartment. I expected to discover her in her dressing room, perhaps taking longer to make up her toilette than usual, since this is a bigger affair than Sanditon House has hosted for some time. But she was not there. Some of the items on her dressing table are in disarray, and the seat is lying on its side—I thought perhaps she had become indisposed and struggled her way into bed, but her bedchamber is also empty."

"Did I not say she appeared unwell when I last saw her?" Diana rose from the sofa and went to Miss Brereton, where she could be in the middle of the conversation. "Lady Denham is bilious," she declared. "I did not like her color when last I saw her. I told her as much, and offered to prepare a decoction of sorrel root, but she would not hear of it—so I sent it over later, along with a phial of the sedative I regularly prepare for Susan, to ensure she gets a proper night's rest. I wager she did not take either of them." She sighed. "If only she had heeded my advice. Well, if she is feeling poorly, she cannot have gone far and must be somewhere in the house. Did you look elsewhere?"

"I checked her favorite sitting room, in case she is not ill and simply lost track of time. When I did not discover her there, I was uncertain what to do next. I do not wish to raise a panic, but—"

"No—no need to panic," Thomas Parker said.

Not yet, Elizabeth thought. Lady Denham was an eccentric old dowager, used to doing as she pleased, particularly in her own house. And elderly people, eccentric or not, wealthy or not, could become distracted, or confused, or forgetful. Heavens, Elizabeth was but five-and-twenty and only last month had forgotten an engagement herself, despite having recorded it in her diary. An appointment with one's dressmaker, however, was a far cry from forgetting about a dinner for thirteen guests, which had surely required numerous communications with her servants throughout the day. Elizabeth also did not like the image of that overturned seat.

She glanced at Darcy, hoping to catch his gaze and thereby judge whether he was of like mind, but his attention was on Thomas Parker.

"Perhaps Lady Denham stepped outside for some air," Mr. Parker continued.

"This house is so drafty, there is no need to step outside for air," Mr. Hollis said. "Just stand near a window—open or closed."

"It is not drafty," Sir Edward said.

"I feel a draft right now," Mr. Hollis claimed.

"You are not anywhere near a window," Miss Denham said. "If you feel moving air, it is your own bluster." She gathered her shawl, which had been hanging loosely at her elbows, more tightly against her arms. "Even if Sanditon House did suffer drafts, at least it is not damp, like Denham Park."

"Nothing is worse than damp." Arthur shuddered and looked about, as if Damp were a creature lurking in a corner of the room, waiting to pounce. "Gives me the rheumatism, damp does."

"Nothing is worse than the rheumatism," Susan said.

"Consumption," Diana trumped.

"Alas, consumption!" Sir Edward cried. "Certain death! How many poor, beleaguered heroines have succumbed to the insidious grasp of a galloping consumption—their life-light flickering until finally extinguished? What could be more tragic than the wasting away of youth, and strength, and virtue—a fate all the more heartrending for the helplessness of those who bear witness to it?"

"Oh, yes!" Diana agreed. "It is so very dreadful to observe—the coughing up of blood and other humors, the choking—"

"What blood? What choking?" Sir Edward asked. "Nay, I refer to the fainting spells of an increasingly delicate constitution overcome, the cheeks flushed against the angelic paleness of the skin—

'If this be dying . . . there is nothing at all shocking in it. My body hardly sensible of pain, my mind at ease, my intellects clear and perfect as ever.'

—the slow, peaceful decline," concluded Sir Edward, "of a beautiful death."

Diana and Susan launched into an extensive exchange on the most effective treatments for consumption, to which Sir Edward attended closely in the event that he should ever wake up and find himself in a sentimental novel.

Sidney Parker turned to Charlotte and Mrs. Darcy. "Other ladies spend their evenings reading popular novels; my sisters read aloud from Culpeper's *Herbal* and the *Pharmacopœia of the Royal College of Physicians*."

Charlotte offered a small smile in return. Though not disinclined to receive attention from the most charismatic gentleman in the room, she appeared uncertain as to whether he jested about his sisters' reading material. Given their obsession with all things bodily, Elizabeth was uncertain herself.

"Now, Sidney," Diana said, "you know we are so familiar with Culpeper that we scarcely open the book anymore, and the *Pharmacopœia* we consult only as needed. In the evenings, we have lately been reading the latest volume of *The London Medical Repository and Review*."

"I stand corrected. My apologies for having misrepresented you." Sidney's mouth quirked. "I cannot help but think," he murmured in a voice low enough that only those beside him could hear, "that perhaps faced with the prospect of an entire evening of conversation such as this, Lady Denham decided she preferred the silence of her own company."

"You say that lightly," Miss Heywood replied. "Are you not concerned for her well-being?"

"I assure you, Miss Heywood, though sometimes I may speak with more levity than I ought, tonight I have Lady Denham's best interests at heart."

Elizabeth hoped someone in the room did, for most of the others seemed to have forgotten about Lady Denham, and poor Miss Brereton was at a loss to redirect the discussion back to the missing dowager. Mr. Hollis complained of drafts again, earning another peevish response from Miss Denham. Arthur, noticing the darkening sky, advocated the lighting of a preemptive fire before Damp arrived along with the rain.

Darcy and Thomas Parker commenced a side conversation of their own—which Elizabeth was fairly confident contained the only words of substance presently being spoken in the room. She excused herself from her current companions and moved toward the pair. When she reached them, she was surprised, though not unpleasantly, to realize that Sidney had followed her.

"Tom, I am curious as to your and Mr. Darcy's thoughts regarding this situation," Sidney said.

"It is unlike Lady Denham to keep people waiting with no explanation," his brother replied, "let alone to leave an article of furniture in an upended state."

Darcy's countenance reflected Thomas Parker's apprehension. "I was just asking Mr. Parker who among the present company is the most appropriate individual to initiate an effort to locate Lady Denham."

"Unfortunately," Mr. Parker said, "nobody in this room holds clear authority or responsibility to take command of Sanditon House or its staff. Lady Denham has no children of her own. Her only blood relations are cousins once or twice removed; of these, Miss Brereton alone is present, but her status in Sanditon House is that of an impoverished dependent charitably taken in as a companion—not quite a servant, but also not fully a member of the family."

"What of Sir Edward?" Elizabeth asked.

"Sir Edward and Miss Denham are Lady Denham's nephew and niece by her second marriage. They have no legal claim upon her or Sanditon House."

"And yourself?" Darcy asked.

"Although I am her business ally, I have only the sanction of friendship to act on her behalf in personal matters—which of course I will do if called upon, and if my doing so is acceptable to those with even slight family connections." Mr. Parker nodded almost imperceptibly toward Josiah Hollis.

They all exchanged glances. Whatever that unpleasant man's connection to Lady Denham might be, nobody wanted him to develop any ideas about taking charge.

"Someone needs to take action to determine whether Lady Denham's absence is intentional, accidental, or involuntary," Darcy said. "I suggest that Miss Brereton, because she is a resident of the household and therefore most familiar with the staff, find and speak with Lady Denham's maid."

"That does seem the obvious place to start," Elizabeth said. Lady Denham's personal attendant would have helped her dress for tonight's engagement and would have been conscious of the time at which her mistress needed to be ready to greet her guests. That hour having come and gone, her maid was more likely than anyone else to know her mistress's whereabouts, or was herself with Lady Denham at this moment.

She glanced about the room. Restlessness had seized its occupants, most of whom engaged in rampant speculation and vacuous statements of self-confident authority. Even Mr. Hollis had risen from his chair to mill around. "I do not think the maid should be summoned here," Elizabeth continued. "The number of people might overwhelm her. Miss Brereton should speak with her elsewhere."

"Agreed," Darcy said, "and you should accompany her. If the maid's report suggests that anything out of the ordinary has happened, Miss Brereton might not know what questions need to be asked."

Sidney looked at Darcy. "Do you also wish to participate in the interview with the maid?"

"I have learned from my wife that women are often more forthcoming among themselves."

Sidney laughed. "So they are. Well, let us extract Miss Brereton from the scintillating discourse enveloping her, and send her with Mrs. Darcy to find the maid and relieve our collective suspense."

Miss Brereton was easily—and willingly—disengaged, not to mention grateful for guidance on how to proceed. She thought talking to Lady Denham's maid was a wise suggestion—regretted not having thought of it herself—and accepted without question Elizabeth's offer to accompany her. With a signal to the footman to follow them, and an opportunely spirited moment of discussion among the larger company as a distraction, the two ladies slipped out of the room unnoticed.

Or so they thought.

Eleven

"I do beleive [sic] those are best off that have fewest Servants."
—Lady Denham, Sanditon

*O*nce in the hall, Miss Brereton sent the footman to the servants' hall with a message for the housekeeper. "Tell Mrs. Riley to send Rebecca to us in the blue room, and to continue to hold dinner." As he departed on his commission, Miss Brereton's gaze followed him. "I pray there is a simple explanation."

"I am sure there is." Elizabeth's conscience pricked her only slightly at the venial lie. She was not sure of anything at present, but she saw no reason to increase Miss Brereton's anxiety. The somber cast of Clara's countenance and the way her eyes scanned the hall and doorways for a sign of Lady Denham, bespoke a young lady already altered from the blithe Miss Brereton who had greeted Elizabeth and Darcy an hour earlier. "However, if there is not," Elizabeth added, "hearing in private whatever information the maid imparts enables you to determine what would be appropriate to disclose to the other guests."

Miss Brereton led Elizabeth down the corridor. The blue room was on the ground floor, round a corner from the portrait room. It was a small sitting room, less formal than the one they had just quit; its upholstered furniture looked softer and more inviting—if the sunlight invading from the southwest windows did not drive one away. It was an eerie light, with a greenish cast emanating from where it met the dark clouds advancing from the west.

Miss Brereton crossed to one of the windows and drew closed the heavy draperies.

"We seldom use this room in the evenings, though sometimes I come in here by myself when the light is fading, to watch the sun set."

Elizabeth imagined Miss Brereton must lead a rather lonely existence, living with an elderly dowager and without the regular friendship of girls her own age. Such a state would explain—though not excuse—her stealing away to indulge in the sympathetic companionship of Sir Edward. "Do you miss Gracechurch Street?"

"I miss my aunt and uncle, and my cousins. They are kindness embodied, and I am grateful to them for taking me in when my parents died, despite the additional burden I placed on their household." She closed another pair of draperies, but left the remaining windows uncovered so as not to cloak the room in darkness. The approaching clouds would accomplish that soon enough. "Yet even had I not come to Sanditon House, I would no longer be living with them by now. At the time I met Lady Denham, I was preparing to take a position as a nursery maid."

Elizabeth wondered whether Lady Denham often reminded Clara of her dependency. "How long have you lived at Sanditon House?"

"Since shortly after Michaelmas." She rejoined Elizabeth in the center of the room. "Lady Denham originally invited me for a stay of six months, intending that one of my cousins would then have a turn. When April came, however, she did not make any arrangements as to my leaving."

"You are here permanently, then?"

"I do not know. Neither of us has spoken of it. I dare not broach the subject, for if Lady Denham has forgotten that my residency here was to have ended long before now, I do not wish to remind her."

Elizabeth pitied Miss Brereton her state of uncertainty. To be perpetually at the mercy of the dowager's disposition—to wake every morning wondering whether this could be the day she forever went from a condition of gentility to one of servitude! Was she attempting to secure Sir Edward's affections—and thus, her station in life—before that happened?

Rebecca arrived. Lady Denham's personal attendant was an older woman, with a tall, trim figure and dark eyes whose gaze shifted uncertainly between the two ladies. "You sent for me, miss?"

"Lady Denham has not yet joined her guests in the portrait room, nor is she in her apartment. Have you any notion where she might be?"

"No." The creases between the servant's brows deepened. "I thought she had gone to the portrait room."

"When did you last see her?" Elizabeth asked.

Rebecca regarded Elizabeth warily and did not immediately respond. After a few seconds her lips parted as if she were about to speak, but then closed once more. Elizabeth suspected the cause of her hesitation—and respected it. Rebecca was a loyal servant, and Elizabeth a stranger.

Miss Brereton recognized it, too. "Mrs. Darcy is a friend of Lady Denham's, albeit a new one," she assured Rebecca, "and I know her family well. You may speak to her as you would to me."

At this, Rebecca's expression relaxed, though not completely. "I last saw her at about half past three, when I helped her dress for dinner."

"Did you see her leave her apartment?" Elizabeth asked.

"No, ma'am. We finished early, and I began tidying her things—clearing the dressing table, hanging her dressing gown, and so on. She said to simply leave everything and come back later—she wanted a few minutes to herself before her guests arrived."

Elizabeth supposed that could explain the disarrayed items atop the dressing table that Clara had reported—though not the upset seat, which suggested a hasty departure.

"Did she mention anything else she planned to do before the party? A task that might take her to another room of the house?"

"No, ma'am."

Rebecca's manner became anxious again, and Elizabeth realized she was firing questions at too rapid a rate. She slowed down and took a less direct approach.

"From the way in which you speak of her, I sense that you have a good relationship with your mistress."

"I have served her ladyship a long time."

"How long?"

"Over forty years, ma'am, since before she married Mr. Hollis. She brought me to Sanditon House with her, and when she married Sir Harry, I went with her to Denham Park."

"My own maid, Lucy, has not served me nearly so many years, but she is adept at anticipating my needs and reading my moods," Elizabeth said. "I imagine that in four decades of service, you have come to know Lady Denham very well. Was there anything unusual in her manner today?"

Rebecca contemplated a moment. "She was distracted by the dinner. Indeed, she talked of little else—how she looked forward to having everyone assembled under her roof, how she had carefully planned everything, and how she hoped the evening would prove a success."

"So she seemed to be feeling quite well?"

"Perfectly well. In fact, I would say she was in higher spirits than she has been in some time—reminded me of the young woman she was when I first started working for her."

"Can you think of anything that would have drawn her away from the party that she had been so happily anticipating? Perhaps something that might have caused her to leave her chamber in a hurry?"

"No, ma'am."

"When Miss Brereton went to Lady Denham's apartment just now, she found the seat at the dressing table overturned. Have you any idea how it came to be so positioned?"

Rebecca's eyes widened. She turned to Miss Brereton. "Is Lady Denham hurt? Is she in trouble?"

"That is what we are trying to determine," Miss Brereton said. "Do not become alarmed—there may yet be a perfectly ordinary explanation for her absence."

"Her ladyship was sitting on the seat when I left the chamber."

"And where did you go when you left?"

"Down to the servants' hall to report to Mrs. Riley. The party has the staff so busy that everyone's help is needed, even for tasks that don't normally fall under my duties."

"To your knowledge, have any of the other servants seen or heard from Lady Denham since you last saw her?"

"I don't believe so. There was a bit of speculation about why dinner was being held so long, but—come to think on it—nobody said anything about having spoken to Lady Denham herself. Perhaps Mrs. Riley knows more, but she and the cook have all they can do simply trying to keep the food at the right temperatures and everything else ready the moment it is called for."

Elizabeth looked to Miss Brereton. "Have you any more questions?"

Miss Brereton shook her head. "Thank you, Rebecca. You may return to Mrs. Riley."

"And send her to us," Elizabeth added.

Elizabeth and Miss Brereton had not been long from the portrait room before Darcy determined that, in going to speak with the servants while he stayed behind with the other guests, his wife had gotten the better end of the arrangement.

After an exhaustive discourse on consumption, complete with citations from leading authorities—in Diana Parker's case, the most current medical journals; in Sir Edward's, the most melodramatic novels of the previous century—the conversation had wended from sentimental heroines to gothic ones, and hence, in a roundabout manner, back to the subject of Lady Denham.

"This is all so very perplexful," said Sir Edward—"'not to see the lady of this castle . . . who disappeared so strangely.' A mystery worthy of Mrs. Radcliffe's pen! A large, ancient house, a lady vanishing into thin air—"

"People do not vanish into thin air," Diana said. "Now, I *have* read cases of spontaneous combustion—a most extraordinary demise! But people do not simply vanish. They, or their remains, exist somewhere."

"I believe Diana has the right of it," Susan said. "Lady Denham cannot have evaporated. She either left Sanditon House, or she is still inside it."

"Then we should search the house." Josiah Hollis's abrupt declaration drew all eyes toward the front of the room. He stood beside the pier table nearest the doors, a rather expensive-looking vase in his hands. He restored the vase to its place on the table and turned to face the others. "If you are all so concerned about her, quit yammering and go look for her."

"Miss Brereton is even now asking the servants if they know Lady Denham's whereabouts," Thomas Parker said.

"If the servants do know, then by now one of them ought to have delivered a message to us from Lady Denham explaining this interminable delay," Josiah said. "I will search for her myself, if it means dinner might be served sometime this week."

Darcy suspected Mr. Hollis would prove only too happy to assist a search effort. During the others' conversation, he had quietly walked a circuitous path through the portrait room. Though his pace gave the appearance of idle wandering, anyone watching him—which Darcy had been—could see that his movements were methodical, taking him to every part of the room, where he examined and appraised its contents—a painting here, a bust there, the marble mantelpiece, the crystal decanter resting on a mahogany sideboard. There, he had paused to pour himself the last of the wine it had held, the rest having been consumed by other guests during their extended wait for Lady Denham. He sipped sullenly, regarding the portrait of Sir Harry with open disgust, before leaving the empty glass on the sideboard to continue his casual inventory.

The only corner Mr. Hollis did not reach was the one in which the miniature portraits were displayed, and that, only because Mr. Granville had taken an interest in the likenesses—or perhaps, an interest in Esther Denham, who stood with him near the glass-fronted case, speaking with the well-dressed young bachelor in a far more amiable manner than she had accorded anyone else in the room. Whether Mr. Granville shared her interest in continuing their conversation was another matter, one that could not be determined at present: To Miss Denham's obvious vexation, Mr. Hollis now commanded Mr. Granville's attention along with everybody else's.

"Tom, I believe I have been remiss in not recognizing this call to action before now," Diana said. "If we all look for Lady Denham, I am sure we would find her in short order—more quickly still, if we divide the house." She grew quite animated as the missing dowager became her newest project. "I will take the top floor—though the climb may fatigue me, it is for the best of causes. Tom, you should stay on the ground floor—there is no sense chancing your ankle on the stairs. Sir Edward and Miss Denham, perhaps you—"

"My dear sister," Thomas Parker interjected, "let us first hear what the servants report."

"But Tom, what if Lady Denham is in need of help? Think of all the time we have already lost."

"And if she is not?"

"Then it's about time she told the housekeeper to serve dinner," Mr. Hollis said. He started toward the doors. "I will take the study, library, and Archibald's former apartment."

Darcy balked at the very idea of Josiah Hollis let loose in Sanditon House unattended. Lady Denham would be the last object he sought.

"I do not think Lady Denham would appreciate thirteen people roaming through her home without having been invited to do so," Darcy said. "If it turns out that the servants do not know where she is, they ought to be the ones who conduct a sweep of the rooms. They are most familiar with the house."

"I am familiar with it, too," Josiah said. "I lived here for a time, before Miss Philadelphia Brereton—pardon me, *Lady* Denham—ever became mistress of it."

In the distance, thunder rumbled, and Darcy realized the room had grown darker as they debated. His gaze went to a window. There was no rain yet; in fact, part of the sky was still clear. But it was coming.

Mr. Granville cleared his throat. "May I be so bold as to offer an opinion in this discussion? If a search for Lady Denham is likely to include the grounds, perhaps it ought to be commenced sooner rather than later, no matter who undertakes it."

Darcy could not deny the wisdom of Mr. Granville's statement. If an outdoor search eventually needed to be conducted, they would regret not having started it earlier, with as many men as possible, before the light grew dimmer and evidence washed away.

And it would take Josiah Hollis out of the house, where he could appraise the shrubbery as much as he liked.

Darcy turned to Thomas Parker. "I will go see whether Mrs. Darcy and Miss Brereton have learned anything from the servants. If not, I concur with Mr. Granville—the men should start a search of the grounds."

Mr. Parker nodded. "There are seven of us, plus the male servants.

We will need to spread out if we are to cover as much of the park as possible before the rain comes."

"The air already smells damp," Arthur said. "Miss Heywood, can you smell it?"

"I am afraid I cannot," Charlotte replied. "The windows are closed."

"Must be the draft none of you seem to feel," Mr. Hollis muttered.

"Tom, I hope you do not plan to lead this search," Diana said. "You should not be walking far on that ankle."

"My ankle is perfectly fine."

"It will not remain that way if you are treading about over uneven ground. Let the younger gentlemen rush off to the farthest reaches of the property while you explore the paths."

"You say that as if I am elderly!"

"You are not elderly—though next to Mr. Hollis you *are* the oldest gentleman here—but you have an injured ankle whether you choose to acknowledge it or not. Besides, if Lady Denham left the house, she is most likely walking on one of the paths, not traipsing through the pines."

"Diana, I haven't the inclination to argue with you. Very well. Sidney, will you organize us?"

"I?" Sidney seemed surprised by the request. "Well, I suppose I could, though surely Sir Edward is more familiar with the property—"

"As am I," interjected Mr. Hollis.

"I am gratified, sir, by your faith in me," Sir Edward said, "but I fear I am too overcome by dread for Lady Denham to lead this enterprise. Send me wheresoever on this quest you wish, but pray, do not ask one with such an emotional stake in the outcome to direct it."

As Sir Edward had yet to impress Darcy as a man of strong intellect, he thought it just as well that the baronet declined to take charge. He glanced at the remaining men for the most promising alternative. Arthur even now had a look of anxiety as he watched the clouds advance. If the rain arrived while they searched, he would probably fall to pieces. That left Mr. Granville, who knew the property no better than Darcy did, and—

Josiah Hollis coughed. "Well, if *you* don't want to take charge—"

"—then I volunteer," Darcy said quickly.

Mrs. Riley was even older than Rebecca. While Elizabeth understood and appreciated the value of senior servants, she was begun to wonder whether it were age, rather than laziness, that caused the perceived lack of motivation of which Lady Denham had complained. If Lady Denham was seventy, her housekeeper had to be nearing that milestone if she had not already surpassed it. Her hair, mobcap, and apron were all the same shade of white, and the hand that rested on the large ring at her side, attempting to silence its clinking keys as she entered the blue room, exhibited swollen knuckles suggestive of the arthritis that plagued other elderly people of Elizabeth's acquaintance. Were Diana Parker to catch sight of them, she would probably insist on following the housekeeper back to the offices and concocting a salve in the stillroom.

She was a round woman, not only in face and figure, but also in speech: A few minutes' conversation with her revealed a circularity of thought that resulted in looping rather than forward-moving discourse. After a simple question from Elizabeth led to a five-minute response, four and one half of which was the recipe for tonight's soup and where each of the ingredients had been obtained, she returned to the main subject.

". . . so I last saw her ladyship at about two o'clock."

With some hesitation, lest she inadvertently prompt a geographical discussion requiring an atlas, Elizabeth asked where.

"In her morning room. We generally meet there after breakfast to discuss the day's schedule, but today she wanted to meet later to review arrangements for the party one final time. Guests were to gather at four o'clock; dinner at half past; gentlemen left in the dining room only a short time while the ladies withdrew—Lady Denham did not want the men drinking up all her wine—we just received a fine shipment of port. Then tea in the drawing room—black tea for all. Her ladyship has no liking for the green tea the misses Parker drink, and won't have it in the house—"

"It sounds as if Lady Denham had a rather precise plan," Elizabeth said. "When she did not adhere to it and you were told to hold dinner, did you wonder at that, or is it not unusual for her to stray from previously discussed arrangements?"

"To be honest, ma'am, we were behind schedule downstairs— being out of practice for a dinner with so many removes, many of the dishes were not ready yet—so the delay came as a relief. When Miss Brereton sent word that her ladyship had not yet joined her guests, and to hold dinner until further notified, I did not question it, just took advantage of the extra time to prepare. Besides, it is not for me— or any of the staff—to question her ladyship's wishes or whims. If she wanted to stay in her apartment all night, that is not my business."

"Of course. Other than preparing for so elaborate a dinner, has anything uncommon happened today—not necessarily involving Lady Denham directly?"

"Nothing out of the ordinary. I thought I heard one of the footmen arranging the chairs in the dining room as I passed by earlier today, but when I went inside to give him additional instructions, it was only Mr. Hollis."

"You found Josiah Hollis in the dining room?" Elizabeth thought he had arrived after everyone else.

"No, Archibald Hollis."

Archibald? Was that not the name of Lady Denham's late husband? Mrs. Riley must have confused her Hollises. "I beg your pardon?"

"Mr. Archibald Hollis," Mrs. Riley repeated in a louder voice, apparently thinking it was her volume, not her statement, that impeded Elizabeth's understanding. "He was probably feeling left out of the party."

Elizabeth cast a sideways glance at Miss Brereton, who appeared as confounded as she.

"Mr. Hollis died five-and-thirty years ago," Miss Brereton said.

"Yes, miss."

Elizabeth and Miss Brereton waited for some explanation, but Mrs. Riley seemed to think the logic of her statement was self-evident.

"So . . . would you not consider his appearance in the dining room unusual?" Elizabeth asked.

"I would indeed, ma'am, for I have never actually seen him—since he died, I mean."

"Then what makes you believe he was in the dining room today?"

"Why, Archibald Hollis has been visiting Sanditon House off and on since crossing to the hereafter, as did other Mr. Hollises before him. The masters of this house seem to have trouble letting go of it."

"You are telling me that Sanditon House is inhabited by the spirits of all the Hollises who have ever owned it?"

"Oh, heavens, no!" She laughed. "That would be the talk of a dotty old woman, wouldn't it?"

It certainly would.

Elizabeth managed a forced laugh in response and stole another glance at Miss Brereton. The younger woman still appeared bewildered. But wherever this conversation was going, at least Mrs. Riley did not believe Sanditon House was haunted.

"Of course all the misters Hollis are not here at once. The previous spirit leaves when the next master moves on to the afterlife."

"But I thought you just said you have not seen Mr. Hollis— Mr. Archibald Hollis—since he died?"

"I have not *seen* him. I have heard him. And seen evidence of his visits. He visited regularly during the years Lady Denham lived at Denham Park with Sir Harry. Sanditon House had no master or mistress in residence for more than two decades—he probably felt it his duty to check on the place periodically."

"The house sat vacant for twenty years?" Elizabeth asked.

"More like twenty-five, I would say."

"Was it completely shut up?"

"Partially. Her ladyship kept me and a greatly reduced staff, and we had a limited number of rooms to take care of."

"Why did she not lease the house to tenants?" Given Lady Denham's strict governance over her money, Elizabeth expected she would have welcomed the opportunity to add rental income to her fortune.

"Her ladyship has always been independent by nature, even during her marriages," Mrs. Riley said. "I think she wanted the security of a place to retreat to if she had need of it, or if she quarreled with Sir Harry. But she and the baronet got along well—not at all like the Prince Regent and Princess Caroline, living separate all these years— so she rarely came to Sanditon House while Sir Harry was alive, which is why I think Mr. Hollis visited so often. Since her ladyship's return about five years ago, he still visits every once in a while. He never causes any trouble, unless you count not tidying up after himself. But then, I suppose it's not easy for a spirit to set objects to rights that he has knocked down, being disembodied and all."

Elizabeth decided that it was probably best to forgo a discussion of how a disembodied spirit could knock over an object in the first place. "Do others know of these . . . visits? Does Lady Denham?"

"Oh, certainly! In fact, she told me this morning that she suspected he might be drawn to this evening's party, so I was to leave a tray out for him after the other gentlemen left the dining room."

"A tray of food for an incorporeal spirit?"

"Oh, it would not be the first time unattended food disappeared. Zebediah Hollis—Archibald's grandfather—was famous for that. I remember when I first came to work here, the older servants used to leave pots of chocolate for him. They said if we took care of the Hollis ghosts, they would do us no harm, and that has proven true. We have gotten used to them, actually. They are rather like pets."

Doubting the profitability of continuing the interview, Elizabeth thanked the housekeeper for her information.

"Yes, ma'am. I hope you find her ladyship soon." She turned to Miss Brereton. "In the meantime, miss, what should I do about dinner?"

Miss Brereton, her expression full of uncertainty, in turn looked to Elizabeth—who wished she herself had someone with whom to confer. The meal could not be held indefinitely, becoming increasingly inedible and occupying staff whose effort and attention were needed for more important matters, while everyone—guests and servants—went hungry on what could prove a long night. Yet they could hardly sit down to an elaborate dinner with their hostess's whereabouts and safety unknown.

As she pondered, Darcy appeared in the doorway and beckoned her. She was relieved to see him—perhaps he brought news.

"Have you learned anything from Lady Denham's maid?" he asked.

As quickly as it had arisen, hope of an easy resolution fled.

"Nothing of substance," Elizabeth replied. "She left Lady Denham in her apartment at about half past three, after helping her dress. The housekeeper"—she nodded toward Mrs. Riley—"last spoke with her even earlier. Neither has any idea where she might be. We will have to question the rest of the servants to determine if *anyone* has seen Lady Denham."

"We do not have time to talk to them individually—at least, not at present. There is a storm approaching, and the men are going out to search the grounds before the rain comes. Tell the housekeeper to assemble the staff. We will ask them as a group whether anyone has information; if not, then the male servants will be enlisted to help with the search."

"Are all the gentlemen going?"

"Sir Edward has volunteered to take the stretch of property between the house and his own estate. Sidney Parker and Mr. Granville offered to head out in the other direction, toward the hermitage. Arthur Parker is walking the garden paths closest to the house, and I am taking the outer ones. We all agreed that the hedge maze is best left to the gardener, who knows all its turns and ends. The outbuildings and the remainder of the grounds will be divided among the other servants. Thomas Parker will ride into the village and enquire at the shops and other places that Lady Denham frequents."

"What is Josiah Hollis doing?"

"I knew you would ask about him." Darcy's businesslike expression softened, reflecting the relief she felt at being able to snatch a few minutes' private conversation with each other. "Have you the same impression that I do of the man?"

"Unpleasant? Without doubt. And clearly antagonistic toward Lady Denham, even were she not keeping him from dinner. I am at a loss to understand how he came to be invited."

"As am I. He is accompanying me on the garden paths. I would like to have been assigned with him to the section of property between here and the entrance gates, in hope that he simply continued through them and hied himself home, but given his age, that is too great a distance for him to cover as quickly as must be done."

"Lucky you, to have drawn the lot of being yoked to him. I confess myself surprised that he is assisting the search at all."

"He was agitating to search the interior of the house, and offered to lead such an exploration himself, but I do not trust him."

"Nor do I. Who *is* directing this effort?"

Darcy's hesitation was answer enough.

Elizabeth could not stop the wry smile that formed on her own lips. "Why am I not surprised? You will have to regale me later with the tale of how that came to be. For now, simply tell me what the ladies ought to do while the men are out of doors."

"Devise a way to salvage dinner—our fellow guests are already growing cross, and the gentlemen will be even more in need of sustenance when they return. Whichever maids can be spared should commence a search of the house, under Miss Brereton's supervision—and yours, if you can effect it without overstepping. My sense of Miss Brereton is that she is sensible but inexperienced in managing servants?"

"Yes, even more than I was when I first came to Pemberley. She possesses sense and good instincts, but wants guidance."

"Mr. Parker's sisters will happily assist if asked; I believe Diana Parker would organize a search for the Holy Grail given the opportunity. However, if you will forgive my saying so—" Though he was already speaking in a tone too low for Miss Brereton and Mrs. Riley to hear, his voice dropped lower. "I feel allowing certain of our fellow guests to roam freely through the house is akin to inviting lunatics to run the asylum."

Elizabeth's gaze drifted to Mrs. Riley.

"I think one already is."

Twelve

The wind had been rising at intervals the whole afternoon; and by the time the party broke up, it blew and rained violently.

—Northanger Abbey

*D*arcy and Josiah Hollis made their way through the pleasure grounds of Sanditon House, their progress slowed not only by their departures from the paths to search for evidence of Lady Denham in the gazebo, pavilion, walled garden, and various follies, but also by Darcy's surreptitious monitoring of Mr. Hollis's movements. What trouble the man could possibly cause outdoors in the park, Darcy did not know, but he *did* know that he trusted Hollis only as far as he could see him. Hollis's movements were in turn slowed by the older gentleman's lumbago, which had suddenly manifested without ever having shown signs of its existence before Hollis was enlisted to assist the outdoor search.

"Always acts up when it rains," Hollis had said, then made another bid to stay behind and conduct a search of the house while the rest of the gentlemen roamed the grounds. But Darcy was having none of that, nor would he leave Hollis in the house to burden Elizabeth and the other ladies with the responsibility of monitoring him—the work of ensuring the man did not commence an unofficial tour of the house would be worse than minding a toddler.

"Then we had better move quickly," Darcy had replied.

They conducted their sweep largely in silence, united in mutual disinclination for conversation. Grumbles about his lumbago and dire weather predictions formed the main content of Hollis's discourse, and required little in the way of response on Darcy's part. However, a greater, eerier silence hung over the grounds—the quiet of a park in which the wildlife have taken cover in anticipation of a coming storm, broken only by intermittent rumbles of thunder and the *shush* of swaying pine boughs dutifully breaking the shifting winds and shielding the house from the worst of their fury, their whispers blending with the sound of the unseen but ever-present tide crashing against the shore. There was no more sunlight now; clouds entirely obscured what little illumination penetrated them, and Darcy was grateful for the lanterns with which they had equipped themselves upon leaving the house.

One garden building remained to be visited before their path curved back toward the house. It stood far off the path, and so much ivy covered the exterior that in the rapidly diminishing light he had difficulty discerning exactly what it was.

"Do you know what that structure is, over there?"

"Just an old grotto," Hollis replied. "No reason to bother with it."

Darcy doubted Lady Denham—or anybody, for that matter—had visited the overgrown grotto in years, let alone today. Further, he doubted the dowager was anywhere outside at present. But the possibility, however slim, that she had gone for a walk before her guests arrived and become injured, coupled with Darcy's aversion to leaving unfulfilled any responsibility to which he had committed, rendered him reluctant to turn back without examining the grotto's interior.

"We have come this far," he said. "It will not take much longer to look inside."

"It is only an empty cave—of use to no one but children playing hide-and-seek, and Sanditon House has seen few of those since I was a boy."

"Then it is time you made a return visit. We will be quick about it." Darcy started toward the grotto.

"I am going back to the house," Hollis declared. "You can fool around out here longer if you wish, but I have not seen a sky like this in twenty years at least, and I won't get caught in this storm for anybody—least of all Lady Denham."

Darcy had experienced one other major coastal storm—two summers ago in Lyme, where a single bolt of lightning destroyed a ship as he and his family watched in helpless shock. That disaster and other casualties of the day had left him with a healthy respect for the violence of sea storms and the warnings of local residents—even someone as unpleasant as Josiah Hollis—who knew them firsthand.

He looked to the sky. In the distance, rain already drove down. It would be upon them within minutes, and Darcy was not properly dressed for inclement weather; the sun had been shining when he and Elizabeth set out for Sanditon House from their lodgings. The servants had scrounged up a few spare oilskin coats for the gentlemen, but wearing borrowed servants' togs was not the same as wearing one's own overcoat.

Perhaps Hollis was right. Darcy turned to speak to him, but he had already commenced his retreat—at a much more rapid pace than he had exhibited earlier. Lumbago, storms, grotto . . . could the man's word be trusted on anything?

Lightning flashed. In the momentary illumination, he thought he saw movement at the entrance to the grotto, behind the curtain of ivy. An injured Lady Denham who had sought shelter within? Or merely a trick of the light?

He strode to the grotto. Pulling aside the ivy curtain, he thrust his lantern forward.

It was not a large space—a half-sphere perhaps eight feet in diameter, constructed of rough-hewn stones to create the illusion of having been naturally formed.

And it was far from empty.

After canvassing the domestic staff only to learn that no one knew Lady Denham's whereabouts, Miss Brereton, under Elizabeth's guidance, initiated a full search of Sanditon House. The gardener and other groundskeepers had already been enlisted to aid the gentlemen's search of the grounds, and now those servants such as the coachman, stable boy, dairymaid, and others whose duties utilized the outbuildings were sent to those locations to look for signs of anything unusual. Within the house itself, all maids not essential to kitchen duty were dispatched with instructions to check each room of the house, looking not only for Lady Denham, but also anything unusual or out of place.

"While we await their reports," Elizabeth said to Miss Brereton, "may I see Lady Denham's chamber? I do not mean to intrude upon her privacy, but I would like to see the dressing table and upset seat for myself."

"Certainly," Miss Brereton replied. "In fact, I was about to ask whether you would return there with me and have a look about the whole apartment. The longer she remains missing, the more anxious I become."

Miss Brereton led her to the suite. Elizabeth was somewhat surprised to discover that Lady Denham's apartment was on the ground floor, while Archibald Hollis's apartment was on the floor above.

"When Mr. Hollis was alive, she used an apartment upstairs adjacent to his," Miss Brereton explained. "From the time Sanditon House was built, the mistress of the house had an antechamber, dressing room, and bedchamber of her own, with a shared sitting room between her apartment and the master's. This"—she opened the door—"was a state apartment, reserved for only the most noble of guests. Who was ever received here, I have no idea. I do not get the impression that the Hollis family regularly consorted with dukes and royalty."

"When did Lady Denham move to this suite?"

"After Mr. Hollis passed away. She told me that the change was for economy—as a widow, most days she had no need of the rooms upstairs, so it was easier to live primarily on the ground floor and close off the unused apartment and other upstairs rooms rather than heat them and pay servants to clean them daily. Of course, five years later she married Sir Harry and moved to Denham Park, leaving Sanditon House unoccupied but for a handful of servants for twenty-five years. When Sir Harry died and Sir Edward succeeded to the baronetcy five years ago, she moved back to this house and resumed occupancy of the state apartment again. Mr. Hollis's relations would probably say that Lady Denham wants to live in a grander style than her former apartment offers. I, however, think it more likely that after losing her husbands she did not want to live in rooms so close to the ones Mr. Hollis had occupied."

"Especially with his spirit about, if Mrs. Riley is to be believed," Elizabeth said.

"Oh, my goodness! I could hardly contain my astonishment when she began talking about that," Miss Brereton said. "This was the first I have heard of the former masters of Sanditon House lurking about."

"So you have not encountered Mr. Hollis since taking up residence here?"

"Nor any of his forebears."

"What, then, do you make of her tales?"

"I think the servants, not ghosts, were drinking the chocolate."

Elizabeth laughed. "So do I—or imbibing something stronger."

They passed through the antechamber, which offered little of interest beyond rich furnishings and intricately carved wooden paneling. When they reached the dressing room, however, Miss Brereton stopped suddenly.

"The seat has been moved," she said. "And the tabletop items tidied."

The seat rested under the dressing table, precisely where one would expect to find it when not in use. Elizabeth crossed to the table. The items on top also appeared in perfect order. Combs and brushes were aligned with precision that would have impressed even a military officer, with a phalanx of bottles and tins completing the formation. She opened a few of the containers; from the appearances and scents of the substances inside, they seemed to be the usual lotions and potions of a lady's arsenal—lavender water, tooth powder, cold cream, wash-balls. There were two phials, however, whose contents were less familiar. One was marked "Sorrel Root," the other, "Sleep."

"Are these the medicines Miss Diana Parker sent over yesterday?"

"I believe they are," Miss Brereton replied. "I am surprised Lady Denham even kept them, as she never takes such concoctions. Perhaps she intended to return them tonight."

A strong gust of wind drew Elizabeth's attention to the long window beside the dressing table. It was open quite wide, and the heavy breeze billowed the curtain, swelling it large enough to balloon onto the tabletop and knock over one of the phials. Elizabeth righted the bottle, lest any of its contents leak out onto the table.

"I am afraid the storm is upon us." Miss Brereton moved to the window and attempted to close the casement, but the wind was strong and created too much resistance. Elizabeth lent assistance, and together they managed to close the window.

"Let us hope the gentlemen's search proved successful, and that they return soon." Elizabeth looked at the darkening view beyond. She could see little—not only had the sky turned nearly a night-black, but the window faced a high, sculpted bank of shrubs that formed the topiary's boundary. The living green wall created privacy, shielding the apartment's windows from the view of anyone enjoying the topiary, but it also created a wind tunnel when the breeze blew from a certain angle. The open casement window had been perfectly positioned to catch the wind and channel it into the dressing room.

It was a tall window, extending from Elizabeth's knees to at least two feet above her head. A matching one flanked the other side of the dressing table, but that window was closed.

"Was the window open when you came in here earlier?" Elizabeth asked.

Miss Brereton thought for a moment. "I honestly cannot recall," she finally said. "If it was, the wind was not buffeting the curtain about as it did just now, or I would have taken notice of it." She sighed. "I am sorry—I should have paid more heed."

"Your mind was on Lady Denham, and an open window on a warm July day is hardly something extraordinary," Elizabeth replied. "Too, you had the overturned seat occupying your attention. Can you show me how it was positioned when you came in here?"

Miss Brereton slid the small padded bench from under the dressing table and pulled it toward her. Elizabeth stepped away from the window to get out of Clara's way as she tipped the stool onto its side, its cushion facing the window and its legs pointing toward the room's center.

"Do you think the wind might have knocked it down, as well?" Miss Brereton asked.

Elizabeth knew the answer, but hesitated to voice it. The sill was too high, the angle all wrong, the seat too sturdy.

Mother Nature had not upset the seat.

At Darcy's abrupt entrance, a hare darted out of the grotto. So much for the movement he had perceived. And for his hopes of discovering Lady Denham.

He did, however, discover another woman within.

Toward the back of the grotto rested an ornate fountain, dry from disuse, its copper fittings long turned green. From its center rose a marble statue of a young girl—or perhaps a wood nymph—with a garland of flowers crowning her head. Her untamed curls and simple dress adorned with leaves flowed behind her, as if her likeness had been captured while she was darting between the trees.

A flash of lightning provided brief additional illumination. The fountain's basin was full of dead pine needles, which also covered the floor. Although there was evidence of animal inhabitants beyond the lone hare that had greeted him, there was no sign of Lady Denham or any other recent human visitor.

Darcy did not enter, simply stepped back and let the ivy curtain fall back into place. As he turned toward Sanditon House, thunder clapped, and rain began to fall.

Thirteen

"Sidney is a saucy fellow, Miss Heywood."
—Thomas Parker, Sanditon

*C*harlotte, having just delivered a message to Miss Brereton, was descending a side staircase with rapid footfalls when an exterior door at its base opened to admit one very wet Mr. Parker: Sidney Parker, to be specific—Arthur already having returned to the sanctuary of the house the moment Damp attempted to overtake him out of doors, and Thomas being expected to return last, his contribution to the search effort having taken him the farthest distance from Sanditon House.

Streaming from the deluge in which he had been caught, Sidney was oblivious to both Charlotte's presence and the rainwater pooled in the brim of his hat as he stepped farther into the vestibule and removed the topper in a swift motion—inadvertently sending the water flying toward her just as she reached the bottom step.

The water splashed onto her chest, hitting her just above the neckline of her gown and eliciting a surprised "Oh!"

Startled, he turned toward her. "Miss Heywood!" He closed the space between them. "Is something amiss?"

Water and thin white muslin not being an ideal combination for a lady's modesty, Charlotte crossed her arms in front of her and en-

116

deavored to pretend that droplets were not trickling down to spread across the bosom of her gown.

He glanced at his hat, then once more at her, and realized the cause of her exclamation. "Oh," he echoed, then politely looked away, searching for a safe place to rest his gaze.

She forced what she hoped was a tone of nonchalance. "I see you were caught in the rain."

Her effort only increased Sidney's discomposure. He at last fixed his gaze on the traitorous hat in his hands and chuckled. It was not a sound of mirth; it was a nervous laugh, and she marveled to realize how disconcerted the mishap had rendered the heretofore thoroughly self-possessed Sidney Parker. "Well," he said, rotating the hat by its treacherous brim, "this is an awkward dilemma, is it not? Do we both of us stand here exchanging empty talk while acting as if I did not just shower you most regrettably, or do we defy convention and acknowledge our mutual embarrassment?"

"I think I prefer the latter."

He met her eyes, and his countenance relaxed. "So do I. Please accept my apology. I would offer you my handkerchief, but despite my coat I am so wet through that I think you would be even worse off for using it."

"There is nothing to forgive—it was an accident."

"Indeed it was. I assure you, it is not my habit to fling water at ladies I have just met. I generally wait until we have been acquainted at least a se'nnight."

"Then I shall be on my guard Saturday next."

This elicited a genuine laugh. "I like your spirit, Miss Heywood. You should display it more often—no, perhaps that is poor advice. Diana is forever telling me that my mouth will get me into trouble one of these days. At any rate, my policy is one soaking per unsuspecting lady, so having already received yours, you are safe from me Saturday next, or any Saturday, for that matter. At least, as far as water is concerned."

"I am hardly soaked—not nearly so much as you are. A few minutes' standing before a fireplace should dry me completely, and Miss Brereton ordered a fire lit in the portrait room at your brother's request."

"You must refer to Arthur. Did he get inside before the rain came?"

"His clothes got about as wet as my gown, but he is so fearful of catching the pneumonia or a putrid fever that Miss Brereton is outfitting him with some of the late Mr. Hollis's old clothes while his own dry."

"Have any of the other gentlemen returned?"

"To my knowledge, you are the second, but I have been upstairs delivering to Miss Brereton the news of Arthur's return and requests for clothing and fires."

"Should it prove necessary, I shall lure Arthur away from the fire for a time so that you can have it to yourself. If Miss Brereton will arrange a loan of dry clothes for me, I can ask him to serve as my valet while I change. Has there been any news of Lady Denham in my absence?"

"The servants have checked each room, but she was not in any of them. Dinner will be served as soon as all the gentleman have returned, at which time I believe there will be a general discussion of what to do next—that is, if none of the gentlemen have discovered Lady Denham. I take it you found no sign of her?"

"Unfortunately, my contribution to the search proved futile."

"Where is Mr. Granville? I understood that you and he set out together."

"We did, but when we realized how quickly the rain was approaching, we separated. I expect he and the others will be along soon—the rain is falling too hard for any further outdoor efforts to prove fruitful. In fact, once everyone returns, I doubt any of us will be leaving the house again tonight—I think the storm has not begun to show its true fury, and as you can see from my boots, the roads and paths are already awash in mud. That is why I came in this side entrance—so as not to track water and dirt through the house."

Recalling a conversation in which Lady Denham had expressed reluctance to have even Sir Edward and Miss Denham stay overnight at Sanditon House now that Miss Brereton was in residence, Charlotte imagined she would not be pleased to find herself hosting so many houseguests—assuming she returned. "Does Sanditon House have enough bedchambers for us all?"

"I believe so. There must be at least ten, and we are—what?—thirteen in number, including Miss Brereton? If there is a shortage, my sisters can share a chamber, as I assume will the Darcys, and I suppose Arthur can bunk with me, unless you would not mind a bed-fellow?"

Charlotte was so startled that she could scarcely utter, "I beg your pardon?"

"Oh! I was not offering myself! Though doubtless you would make a better chamber-mate than does Arthur—he snores most dreadfully. No, I meant you might share a chamber with Miss Brereton or Miss Denham. Upon reflection, however, either of them might consider a room-mate an imposition, as Miss Brereton is a resident of Sanditon House and Miss Denham wishes she were. But see how I have proven Diana right about engaging my mouth before my brain? Good heavens, what you must be thinking of me—first I douse you with rainwater, then make what sounds like an utterly scandalous proposition."

"I think only that the events of this evening have us all a bit rattled."

"You are too generous. *I* think that I had best part company from you temporarily before I do or say something even more shocking, and hope that with drier clothes comes a clearer head and more articulate speech. I have already kept you standing here an unconscionably long time when you are no doubt wishing I would end my prattle and allow you to go find the fire. Well, *that* I shall do. But only if you promise to let me make all of this up to you later."

"If you insist," she said. "In the meantime, if you wait here I will speak to Miss Brereton about room arrangements, and send a footman to help with your wet coat and boots."

"And hat." He grinned. "We cannot forget my hat."

Fourteen

Lady Denham . . . had many Thousands a year to bequeath, and three distinct sets of People to be courted by; her own relations, who might very reasonably wish for her Original Thirty Thousand Pounds among them, the legal Heirs of Mr. Hollis, who must hope to be more indebted to her sense of Justice than he had allowed them to be to his, and those Members of the Denham Family, whom her second Husband had hoped to make a good Bargain for.—By all of these, or by Branches of them, she had no doubt been long, and still continued to be, well attacked.

—Sanditon

*I*t was a wet and weary—not to mention oddly dressed—company who reconvened at Sanditon House. Darcy and Josiah Hollis returned as drenched as Sidney. Thomas Parker, despite having stopped at home for his own overcoat, regretted traveling on horseback rather than the carriage he had left behind at Sanditon House; by the time he concluded his enquiries in the village, what he saved in expedience he lost in sheltered conveyance, and returned to the Great House as wet as his brothers. Only Sir Edward and Mr. Granville managed to reenter Sanditon House as dry as when they left it, though their respective quests proved as unsuccessful as those of the other gentlemen.

The need for dry clothes to temporarily outfit the three Parker brothers, Josiah Hollis, and Darcy led to the plundering (authorized by Miss Brereton) of a large trunk wherein was stored attire that once belonged to Archibald Hollis. As Mr. Hollis had died thirty-five years ago and had not exactly kept up with the newest fashions during the final decade or two of his life, the garments available to the gentlemen were a parade of styles spanning half the previous century.

Owing to a brief detour to Lady Denham's dressing room that Darcy and Elizabeth had made upon his return to the house, Darcy was the last gentleman to change clothes, and therefore was left with the narrowest choice. He tried on several ensembles before selecting one he had found at the very bottom of the trunk, beneath less-desirable garments and a few random objects that had also been stored within—a fob chain, cuff links, a small hinged trinket box containing a blond curl of baby-fine hair, a tattered shawl, a miniature portrait of a young woman, a worn pair of mittens, a snuffbox.

"You look good in that attire," Elizabeth said, "even if you are eight decades out of fashion."

Darcy consulted the dressing-glass one final time. Of all the clothing the trunk had offered, this ensemble was probably the oldest—from its style, Darcy speculated that Archibald had worn it while a student at Oxford—but it fit him the best. The dark blue frock, waistcoat, and breeches, modestly trimmed in white lace with gold buttons, were well made and had survived their eighty-year interment in good condition. He adjusted the wide skirt of his coat, unused to its length. It fell nearly to his knees, with two large buttoned pockets at the hem embroidered in a pattern that matched the elaborate oversized cuffs.

"I would be happier about wearing it if the sacrifice of my own clothes had produced a worthwhile result. Between the gentlemen's outdoor search and yours within, we know no more regarding Lady Denham's whereabouts than we did three hours ago."

Darcy was counting the minutes until his own clothes were dry and returned to him. In the meantime, however, he was glad to be finally about to eat. Though accustomed to later dining hours at Pemberley, and almost ridiculous ones when in London, those meals generally did not follow tramping about in the rain seeking a dowager he barely knew, on an unfamiliar estate, in the company of a human rodent. He could feel himself growing tetchy.

"We know where she is *not*. I suppose that is a start," Elizabeth replied. "But that overturned seat . . ."

"It disturbs me, too." Before coming to Archibald's apartment for dry clothes, Darcy had asked to see the seat and window for himself. "You voiced your suspicion to no one else?"

"I wanted to discuss it with you before disclosing it to the others, even Miss Brereton."

Darcy shared her reserve. He did not trust Josiah Hollis, several of the other guests seemed loose cannons, and he did not want to unnecessarily alarm anybody.

"I concur that at this point we are no longer seeking an elderly lady who took ill, or who became confused and wandered off, as some old persons are known to do," he said. "That means Lady Denham either left this house intentionally under her own power, or involuntarily. Since no one saw her leave, it is possible Lady Denham left her apartment through the window, which certainly suggests an involuntary exit. However, having just traversed Sanditon Park, I find it hard to imagine that she was forcibly conveyed off the grounds in the middle of the day, while all her guests were converging, without anyone's noticing."

"Perhaps one of them did notice something," Elizabeth replied, "but does not realize it."

Dinner was surely a caricature of the affair Lady Denham had envisioned. In the confusion of her disappearance, the servants had apparently forgotten to set out placecards, although with no hostess to preside at the head of the table, the privilege of precedence meant little. Left to take their own seats, the primary principle governing each guest's choice was that nobody wanted to sit near Josiah Hollis.

By agreement, Darcy and Elizabeth gravitated toward opposite ends of the table. A party so large was bound to break into smaller conversations; separating would enable them to hear more of these side discussions, and to learn more about their fellow guests—one never knew what information might serendipitously come to light. Elizabeth especially wanted an opportunity to converse with the gentlemen, and Darcy with the ladies, before custom split the sexes into different rooms after dinner for an hour or more.

Darcy should have known better than to be among the first to choose a seat; doing so left one powerless to control who would occupy the chairs next to him. He had not fully committed to one beside Miss Denham, but had his hand on its back, when Josiah seized the chair on the other side of him. Apparently, their sojourn to the grotto and back had created some sort of bond between them. A shackle.

"It's about time dinner is served." Josiah settled himself into his seat, unfolded his serviette, and lifted the cover of the corner dish. "Mmm . . . one of my uncle's favorite dishes—buttered prawns."

Josiah had claimed for himself not only the closest thing to a seat of honor, next to where their hostess would have sat were she present, but also the newest of Archibald's clothing—a mere forty or so years old. Apparently he was of similar build to his kinsman, for the costume fit him well. If only his disposition were as tailored.

Josiah's hand strayed toward the serving utensil, and for a moment he looked as if he might help himself to a wedge before the entire company was even seated. However, noticing Darcy's disapproving expression, he replaced the cover. "The toast underneath is probably soggy," he said, then commenced thrumming his fingers on the table.

Thankfully, Miss Brereton and Thomas Parker sat within conversational range of Darcy. Thomas, the tallest of the gentlemen, had been forced to make do with a borrowed suit that fit him ill. So, too, had Arthur, the stoutest. Both men had wound up with clothing from what Darcy guessed was the 1750s, and poor Arthur was particularly disadvantaged. Though apparently broader during his middle years than in his youth and old age, Archibald had possessed a smaller frame than Arthur's, and his frock stretched tightly across Arthur's shoulders. Arthur did, at least, benefit from the wide skirts at its bottom. The waistcoat had to go unbuttoned, but its extra length—it would have fallen mid-thigh on its original owner—was a blessing. Both Arthur's and Thomas's breeches ended above their knees, shorter than was fashionable even when the garments were designed.

At last, all were seated and the servants uncovered the dishes. It was a generous first course: nine dishes on the table, plus a remove for the soup.

Unfortunately, if many of the diners' clothing was out of date, the food upon which they dined also had lost its freshness long ago. None of the meal was hot, any attempt at keeping it so having been abandoned after several dishes had been ruined in the attempt. Although the guests partook of the meal with appetite fueled by hunger and damp, their gastronomical experience was less than satisfying.

Conversation was minimal at first, the diners focusing more on their food than anything else, tasting each dish in hopes of appeasing their appetites, if not their palates. But Lady Denham's disappearance weighed on their minds, while the wind moaned and drove rain against the windows.

"That is an eerie sound," said Sir Edward. "Like a ghost howling to come inside. Reminds one that today is not the first time a woman has disappeared from Sanditon."

"I suppose you refer to Ivy Woodcock," said Diana. "That old tale, however, can have nothing to do with our present crisis. It must have happened a hundred years ago."

"She was born a hundred years ago," Thomas Parker said. "One hundred years ago today—and disappeared on the night of her sixteenth birthday,."

"Who was Ivy Woodcock?" Mr. Granville asked.

"Did you not see the memorial tablet in our hotel?" Sidney replied. "She was a distant relation of the current innkeeper. Her story has become a cautionary tale for local children." He turned toward Charlotte with a lively look in his eye. "Do not wander off after dark, Miss Heywood, for if Ivy Woodcock does not find you, the faeries who snatched her might."

"Sidney, you will spook poor Miss Heywood." Arthur turned to Charlotte. "He told me the same thing when I was six, and I do not think I slept a single night all that summer."

"I have already advised Miss Heywood that she should listen to only half of what I say." Sidney returned his attention to Charlotte.

"I do not scare easily," Charlotte responded.

"I am glad to hear it, for I would hate to be the cause of your losing even a moment's rest," Sidney said. "But should Ivy Woodcock rap upon your window tonight, you can rely upon me to come to your rescue. My offer extends to you, too, Arthur."

"I am no longer six," Arthur replied peevishly. "I know Ivy Woodcock is not going to come calling."

"Even on her one hundredth birthday? The anniversary of her disappearance?"

"I think it such a poetic coincidence, that Lady Denham should disappear today," Sir Edward said with delight. "And you cannot deny the similarities between her and Ivy."

"What similarities?" Diana asked. "Ivy Woodcock was a wild young girl, not a rich old dowager."

"They were both women," Sir Edward said, "and they both disappeared."

Diana simply rolled her eyes ceilingward.

"I understood Ivy lived an isolated existence, but I had not heard she was wild," Elizabeth said.

"She must have been utterly uncivilized, living as she did in the hermitage," Miss Denham declared. "It is such a *rustic* dwelling."

"I find the very idea of a hermitage enchanting!" Sir Edward declared. "The more rustic, the more picturesque. In fact, I may erect one at Denham Park when the cottage ornée is finished."

The servants cleared the first course from the table, removed the first tablecloth to reveal the fresh one beneath, and brought in the second-course dishes. A footman removed the cover of the dish closest to Darcy.

"What *is* that?" Josiah Hollis blurted.

"Ragoo of celery with wine," the servant replied.

"Looks like infant food," he muttered.

Darcy privately agreed. He had eaten the dish many times; it was one occasionally served to guests at Pemberley. Although he knew no particulars of its preparation, the thick sauce normally contained whole bread rolls and hard egg yolks—all of which appeared to have disintegrated, turning the sauce into a thick paste surrounding celery that barely held its form.

Josiah's declaration also drew the notice of both Susan and Diana. They, however, considered his pronouncement a recommendation.

"The texture is optimal for digestion," Diana said.

"Oh, yes!" Susan exclaimed. "Soft-cooked vegetables are most agreeable to the stomach and intestines."

"Well, you can have my portion," Josiah said. "Just stop talking about intestines."

The sisters, being in the habit of not eating much, restricted themselves to modest servings, but Arthur enthusiastically helped himself to Josiah's share along with his own.

"No sense in letting food go to waste," he said. "Especially a dish that is easy on the coats of the stomach. A full stomach is good defense against the Damp." As he spooned from the dish, the cuffs of his shirt and frock coat slid up nearly halfway to his elbow, straining against his forearm.

"Arthur, how can you complain of the damp when it has inspired such an entertaining fashion display among us?" Sidney had cheerfully claimed the most ostentatious ensemble available to him—a 1740s gold-trimmed red velvet frock coat with matching knee breeches and a waistcoat that extended nearly to his knees. He sported the attire with great flair. "Why, the rain has turned an ordinary dinner into a *bal masqué*—except it is the dishes rather than the guests that are keeping their identities a secret. Truly, we all cut such fine figures in this garb that when Lady Denham returns, we should ask whether we might keep it. Look at Granville—one would think we were in the company of Archibald Hollis himself."

Though not in need of dry clothes, in the spirit of good sportsmanship Percy Granville had decided to participate in the impromptu costume party. In doing so, he had unknowingly adopted what appeared to be the clothing Archibald had worn in a portrait hanging on the wall behind him.

Mr. Granville twisted to study the wigged figure of the portrait. "I do not think I look at all like him." He turned back to the others with a lively expression. "Archibald Hollis had much better hair."

Sidney laughed. "Next time, you must remember to bring powder."

"You make sport, Sidney," Diana admonished, "but if that portrait is accurate, Mr. Granville and Archibald Hollis exhibit similar constitutions, and is that not the essence of any man? Mr. Granville, I imagine, would like quite well to live to nearly seventy. Why—"

She suddenly stopped and tilted her head to one side. "Did you hear that?"

"Hear what?" Sidney asked.

"That scraping sound."

"I don't know how anyone could hear a scraping sound or anything else, you talk so much," Josiah said.

"I heard a noise." She looked around. "But I cannot determine where it might have come from."

"Perhaps it is Ivy Woodcock," Sidney said impishly.

"They do say this house is haunted, you know," Josiah said. "But it is probably my uncle, taking umbrage at everybody's appropriation of his clothes."

"*They* say?" Miss Denham repeated. "Who are 'they'? I have lived in Sanditon my whole life and never heard such a thing. Ivy is the only local ghost I know of."

"Well, now, you are not a Hollis, are you? This is the house of my ancestors—the house that right now ought to be occupied by Uncle Archibald's blood kin, not that interloper who drew in my uncle for his fortune. Actually, perhaps that is why Lady Denham has disappeared—my uncle wants to see his estate pass to his rightful heirs."

"I suppose by 'rightful heirs,' you refer to yourself?" Miss Denham asked, rather snidely.

Josiah made no reply.

"A gentleman can leave his property to whomever he chooses in his will, provided the estate is not entailed," Thomas Parker said.

"And he was going to leave it to me. From six to sixteen I lived here, being groomed as his heir presumptive. The ink recording their marriage in the parish register was scarcely dry before she persuaded him to oust me from the house. Well, now that her *ladyship* has enjoyed control of it for five-and-thirty years, it is time she gave it back to his relations. It is not as if she has any children of her own to whom to leave it."

"She has a niece and nephew." Miss Denham's tone lowered the room temperature by several degrees.

"From a second marriage that did not contribute a farthing to what she has to bequeath. The only reason Sir Harry married her was in hope that her fortune would replenish the Denham family coffers. But she duped him as thoroughly as she duped Archibald Hollis. She got a title, and you and your brother got nothing."

"I inherited a baronetcy," Sir Edward said, "passed down through generations. That is hardly 'nothing.'"

"Well, good luck to you, trying to live off your title after your dwindling fortune runs out, while her *ladyship* sits on hers."

"Lady Denham is sympathetic to my plight. She hopes to see me marry well."

"Isn't that generous of her? She hopes to see you live off someone else's fortune. You, meanwhile, no doubt hope to see yourself remembered in her will. Ha! I am right—I can read it in your face."

Sir Edward shifted in his seat. "You have no idea how costly it is to be a baronet—to maintain a commensurate style of living, and an estate with tenants who are always needing something."

Josiah smirked. "So you *are* hopeful. As hopeful as your sister is of inheriting enough money to catch a husband. Tell me, do you think Lady Denham's will names either of you as her heirs? Or has Miss Brereton over there quietly worked her way in and replaced you?"

Miss Brereton regarded him in astonishment. "I—I would never . . ."

"Mr. Hollis, that was a most ungentlemanly remark," Thomas Parker said.

"It is only what everyone here is wondering, but has not the boldness to say aloud," Josiah responded. "And do not presume to admonish me, when you yourself also have cause to covet Lady Denham's fortune. A bequest from her would fund any number of the plans you have for Sanditon, would it not? With money to spare for your sister's charitable projects and an unlimited supply of remedies for your invalid siblings? The entire Parker family could benefit."

"What are you suggesting?"

"Nothing. Nothing at all. I am merely observing that there are very few people at this table who do not have an interest in Lady Denham's will—and for all I know, they may hold a stake, too, that we just have not realized yet. Mr. Darcy seemed terribly eager to lead the search of Sanditon's grounds."

"My motives were entirely disinterested," Darcy said.

"As, I imagine, was the nice, long tête-à-tête your wife had with Miss Brereton while you ensured half this company were out of the house."

"Miss Brereton and I are concerned for Lady Denham's welfare, and that subject formed the entirety of our conversation," Elizabeth said.

"I expect everybody here is concerned for her welfare," Josiah said, "or ought to be. If she is found dead, whatever her will states right now are the terms we must all live with."

"What if, like Ivy Woodcock, she is never found?" Sir Edward asked.

No one immediately answered.

"Granville, you read law at Oxford," Sidney said. "Do you know?"

"The will would stand," he replied, "but Lady Denham's heir would have to wait until the court declares her legally dead—usually seven years—before coming into the bequest."

The company fell silent as the servants cleared the table and removed the cloth to set out the dessert course. Only the sound of plates gently placed on the bare wood, accompanied by the ceaseless wind and rain, filled the room while the guests digested both their dinners and what this information meant to them.

And contemplated each other with gazes more suspicious than before.

Darcy's own thoughts tumbled rapidly. As much as he disliked Josiah Hollis, the disagreeable little rodent had raised questions Darcy had not previously considered. Since looking at the overturned seat and open window in Lady Denham's apartment, he had not really had time to fully consider their implications, but the few images he had of a potential involuntary exit had featured an unknown kidnapper—not one of the individuals with whom he now dined. Now, however, he wondered: Did one of them know what Lady Denham's will contained . . . and had he—or she—taken steps to prevent its being changed?

A boom of thunder powerful enough to make the candles flicker jolted them all from their private reflections.

"Well, of course Lady Denham will be found long before seven years pass," Diana declared. "In fact, I think we ought to forgo dessert and recommence our search for her."

Both Arthur and Josiah looked rather reluctant to relinquish dessert. As the nuts, fruits, and cakes had suffered no ill effects of the dinner's delay, it was the most appetizing of the courses. Arthur regarded a nearby gooseberry tart with particular regret.

"The house has already been searched, and she is not inside it," said Miss Brereton. "Where else are we to look?"

"It is not *where* to look," Elizabeth said, "but what must be sought—evidence of when, how, and why she might have left Sanditon House."

Diana placed her serviette on the table. "Then let us begin directly."

"Before everybody takes off helter-skelter, I think our efforts are better served if someone guides them," Thomas Parker said. "Someone free of self-interest and emotional entanglement, who can see things clearly and provide the direction this situation needs. Mr. Darcy, do you agree?"

"Absolutely. This is a matter that should be turned over to the parish magistrate."

"Unfortunately, our magistrate is in London at present," Sir Edward said.

"Even were he at home, I doubt he would brave the weather to come here tonight," Thomas Parker added. "He is not the most conscientious administrator of justice to begin with, so there is no way he would venture out into this storm—indeed, this tempest is so violent that we all ought to consider ourselves detained here for the night. Should he decide to return to Sanditon upon learning of Lady Denham's disappearance, it might be days before the roads are safe enough for him to travel. It is up to us, therefore, to initiate the investigation in a timely manner."

"And I suppose you mean for yourself to conduct it," Josiah Hollis said, "so that it ends in your favor. I knew you wanted a place in Lady Denham's will; if you find her, you hope she might give you one if she has not already."

"Actually," Mr. Parker replied, "I did not intend to volunteer myself."

"Whom, then, do you have in mind?" Darcy asked. His gaze drifted around the table. Sir Edward, Miss Denham, Clara Brereton, and Josiah Hollis could all be accused of the same self-seeking motive, and Hollis had already accused Thomas Parker's siblings of interest by family association. That left Miss Heywood . . . Mr. Granville . . . and—

Sidney chuckled. "Mr. Darcy, I believe he means you."

Darcy had been afraid of that.

"Of all the people present, I have the least connection to Lady Denham, and no familiarity with her habits, her history, or her house," Darcy said. "Moreover, I have no connection whatsoever to the parish."

"You already directed the search of the grounds," Arthur said.

"For all the good that accomplished," Josiah said caustically. "Half of us soaked, all of us starved, and still no Lady Denham."

"I understand from allusions made by Colonel Fitzwilliam before we met you in Willingden," Thomas Parker said, "that you and Mrs. Darcy have experience in matters such as this."

"What's this?" Josiah said. "The Darcys have been associated with other missing dowagers?"

"No." Darcy became defensive. What, exactly, had Colonel Fitzwilliam said? Moreover—why? Beyond a very circumscribed set of friends, he was reluctant to discuss particulars of the investigations into which he and Elizabeth had become drawn on behalf of acquaintances who had found themselves in spots of trouble they could not navigate alone. He was not by nature a person given to nosing about in the affairs of others—but nor was he one to suppress his innate sense of justice and social responsibility when circumstances demanded his involvement, particularly in the aid of people close to him, or who were unable to act for themselves. He entered into such investigations with discretion, and maintained it long after they were resolved. He did not want to discuss them with a roomful of near strangers, Josiah Hollis least of all.

"My wife and I have solved a few puzzles," he finished dismissively.

"Indeed?" Sidney said. "I am all curiosity, for I sense that you refer to more than a game of twenty questions. That, however, is a conversation for another time. For now, I will merely point out that you are not the person with the least connection to Lady Denham—Mr. Granville has never met her at all—and that if you and your wife indeed have experience in working out 'puzzles' of a critical nature, then you are more qualified than anyone else here to direct us."

"As for familiarity," Thomas added, "my siblings and I have known Lady Denham all our lives. Consider us at your disposal. I am certain the Denhams and Miss Brereton also will provide any assistance they can."

In truth, there was no one Darcy trusted more than himself and Elizabeth to properly handle the matter. Sir Edward lacked sense; Arthur, drive; Sidney, seriousness. Josiah Hollis lacked any social graces whatsoever—while exhibiting an abundance of hostility toward the very person they were trying to find. Even Thomas Parker was at times so fixated upon Sanditon's future that he could not see what was in front of him. Among the women were one rational but unworldly young girl, two irrational spinsters, and two ladies dependent upon the contents of Lady Denham's will to maintain the social status to which they had grown accustomed.

Attempting to control this group would be akin to herding cats. Yet standing back and watching any of the rest of them manage the inquiry would prove a still greater exercise in frustration. At least if he consented to lead the investigation, he would have the authority to ensure it was done well, and that no one with an interest in the matter would be able to exploit the proceedings for his or her own benefit.

He met Elizabeth's gaze. Her slight nod revealed her opinion.

"All right, then," Darcy said. "Here is how we will proceed."

Fifteen

Miss Denham was a fine young woman, but cold and reserved, giving the idea of one who felt her consequence with Pride and her Poverty with Discontent. . . . The difference in Miss Denham's countenance, the change from Miss Denham sitting in cold Grandeur in Mrs. Parker's Drawing-room to be kept from silence by the efforts of others, to Miss Denham at Lady Denham's Elbow, listening and talking with smiling attention or solicitous eagerness, was very striking—and very amusing—or very melancholy, just as Satire or Morality might prevail.

—Sanditon

"*L*et us start by pooling our knowledge," Darcy said. "When was the last time each of you saw Lady Denham, and what transpired?"

"As my reply is the simplest, I might as well answer first," Mr. Granville said. "I have never met Lady Denham at all. When I arrived in Sanditon yesterday, Sidney told me she had extended a dinner invitation to us both, so here I am."

"I am afraid I gave Granville little choice in the matter," Sidney said to Darcy. "As you will recall, the idea of this dinner party was conceived rather quickly when we all happened to meet at the hotel yesterday, and I accepted on our mutual behalf."

"Is that when you last saw Lady Denham?" Darcy asked.

"I left to retrieve Miss Brereton from the library, and on our way back to the hotel she and I met Lady Denham. Miss Brereton joined her, we parted ways, and that was the last time I saw either of them until I came to Sanditon House today."

"You and Lady Denham were in conversation when we met you in the hotel lobby," Darcy said. "What were you discussing?"

"We were merely exchanging the usual pleasantries that pass between acquaintances that have not seen each other for some time," Sidney said. "How was my journey, how long was I staying, why on earth was I paying good money to lodge at the hotel when I could be staying with Tom? I enquired after her health, and whether Miss Brereton was yet with her at Sanditon House. That sort of thing. Nothing of consequence."

"That meeting at the hotel was also the last time I saw Lady Denham," Thomas Parker said.

"I have not seen her since the evening before last, when she and Miss Brereton called at Trafalgar House after dinner," Diana said. "Nor, I believe, has Arthur."

At the mention of his name, Arthur, who had embraced Darcy's methodical inquiry as an opportunity to partake of dessert after all, paused in the midst of lifting a slice of gooseberry tart from its serving dish. The wedge, the first to leave the tart, had not come out quite cleanly, and it balanced precariously on the pastry server. Plump berries dropped back into the pan, much to Arthur's noticeable sorrow.

"I have not," he confirmed. "Would anybody care for a slice of tart?" He glanced at Charlotte, seated beside him. "Miss Heywood?"

"I will have one," Josiah said.

Arthur, happy for a conspirator in indulgence, served the first two slices to himself and Miss Heywood—whether she wanted one or not—then reached for the cream while the footman carried the tart dish to Josiah.

"Now, Arthur," Diana said, "take care that you do not—oh, there you go again! You always pour too much cream."

"The jug was more full than I anticipated."

Diana rolled her eyes and turned back to Darcy. "As I was saying, my most recent meeting with Lady Denham was at Trafalgar House on Tuesday evening, when you and Mrs. Darcy had dinner with us, so you know what transpired. Susan has not seen Lady Denham since then, either—she did not feel up to going out at all yesterday following the leeches."

"Leeches always leave me faint-headed," Susan said. "In fact, I am still fatigued, and may need to retire before the rest of you. Since we all must remain here until the storm has passed, I would be much obliged if following this discussion I could be shown to whatever chamber I am to sleep in."

"Miss Brereton, have you made arrangements for our accommodation?" Darcy asked.

"The bedchambers are being prepared," she replied.

"I should like the room I occupied last summer," Miss Denham said, "when my brother and I were Lady Denham's guests for an *extended* visit. Do you know the one? You had not yet met Lady Denham at the time."

"I will convey your request to the housemaids," Miss Brereton replied. "I am sure they remember."

Darcy's gaze shifted to Esther Denham. "Miss Denham, when did you last see Lady Denham?"

"It has been a full se'nnight since I enjoyed Lady Denham's society—unusual for us, as Edward and I are so close to our aunt. We met her and Miss Brereton as we were leaving the library, and we all lingered a while on the Terrace, sitting on the benches and observing passersby. Lady Denham and I had a delightful conversation—we always do, when we are together."

"On what subject did you converse?"

"Oh, everything and nothing. You know how it is when one is with *family*." She cast a superior look at Josiah Hollis. Fortunately, he was too deep in enjoyment of the tart to rise to her bait. "We did spend considerable time fondly recalling last summer's visit."

"And you, Miss Heywood—when did you last see our hostess?" Darcy asked.

"Yesterday morning, when I called upon her here with Mrs. Darcy, Mrs. Parker, and little Mary."

Though Elizabeth had shared with Darcy some details of that visit, Darcy wanted to hear Miss Heywood's account of it. "What did you discuss?"

"The past, mostly. She spoke of the late Mr. Hollis quite a bit. When we arrived, we were shown to the same sitting room where we all gathered tonight—the one they call the portrait room, with the painting of Sir Harry over the fireplace and the miniature case in the corner. Mrs. Parker was identifying Mr. Hollis's miniature to me when Lady Denham joined us, which led to her talking about him and his family. Then later, when Sir Edward called, they told us of the long connection between the Hollises and the Denhams."

"Alas! Had I known that would be the last time I beheld Lady Denham before her disappearance, I would have settled myself in the foyer to stand guard," Sir Edward declared.

"Well, that would surely make *me* feel better," Josiah said. He had finished his sweet and now leaned back in his chair, returned to his acerbic self. "I should like to know what her ladyship had to say about Uncle Archibald's family," he said to Miss Heywood.

Charlotte hesitated. "She said that since Mr. Hollis's death, there had been an estrangement between herself and his family." She spoke slowly, as if choosing her words with care. "But that recently his relations have been seeking a reconciliation."

"Is that true?" Darcy asked Hollis.

"Perhaps."

Was a straightforward response truly too much to expect? Darcy regarded Hollis with the withering expression he reserved for people who tested his patience dangerously close to its limit. His brother-in-law Wickham was immune to the look, but it generally worked on gentlemen who possessed at least a shred of prudence. "And how did Lady Denham receive your overtures?"

"Reconciliation was not *my* idea—it was my sister's! I resigned myself a long time ago to the provisions of Uncle Archibald's will, and was perfectly happy to never have anything to do with that woman again. But my sister went and wrote to her, saying that maybe we had been unfair to her back when our uncle died. The letter must have appeased her vanity, because last night, Lady Denham's servant delivered an invitation to this ill-conceived dinner party. It was the first communication between us in fifteen years, at least."

"Did she say what prompted the invitation?"

"No. And I was pretty darn suspicious of it, let me tell you."

"Then why did you come?"

"Curiosity," he said. "Plain and simple. Curiosity about whether the house had changed during her possession. About the young woman who has come to live here with her. About Lady Denham herself—what that calculating woman is up to now that she is too old to entrap rich bachelors into marrying her."

"And what have you concluded?"

"That I have had enough of Lady Denham—and all of you—for one evening." He tossed his serviette on the table and stood. "If this deuced storm is imprisoning us all here for the remainder of the night, I say we retire to our separate quarters."

Darcy consulted his watch. It was nine o'clock, but weariness from the search outdoors—and several of the personalities indoors—made the hour feel later. He had more threads of investigation he wanted to follow, but not with the group as a whole.

"Does anyone have additional information that might prove germane to the present situation?" he asked. "Anything—no matter how insignificant it may seem."

The howling wind offered the only response, which came as no surprise to Darcy. He sensed that he had learned what he could in this context; that anyone in possession of new details was more likely to reveal them in private conversation with him or Elizabeth, than to the company at large.

"Then let us adjourn. Miss Brereton, how soon do you anticipate all the bedrooms will be ready?"

"The housemaids should be able to finish while we have tea."

"We gentleman shall keep the interval short and join you ladies in the drawing room in a quarter hour or so. I am sure Mrs. Darcy will be happy to assist you with room assignments or any other matters involved in accommodating so large a company on short notice."

While the party broke up, Darcy went to Elizabeth and pulled out her chair for her. As she rose, he leaned close to her ear. "Find out which room each guest will occupy," he said, "and try to keep Josiah Hollis as far away as possible from Lady Denham's or Archibald Hollis's apartments." Darcy did not want to give the man an easy opportunity for snooping.

"I had already planned on it," she replied in an equally muted tone.

"Shall I also ascertain whether Miss Brereton or Miss Denham knows where Lady Denham might keep her will?"

Darcy wished he could speak with Elizabeth more freely, and at greater length, about the course the investigation ought to follow, but such a conversation would have to wait until they obtained privacy. For now, they had to simply use this time and the presence of the other guests to best advantage.

"If you can. Preferably in a manner that does not put the idea in their heads to go looking for it themselves. We do not want it disappearing along with Lady Denham. I will similarly try to determine whether Thomas Parker or Sir Edward know the document's whereabouts. The more I hear of Lady Denham, however, the more I doubt she confided such information in anybody."

Elizabeth glanced from the caustic Josiah, to the haughty Miss Denham, to the absurd Sir Edward.

"I cannot say I blame her," Elizabeth responded. "But do you truly believe Miss Brereton's motives are suspect?"

"You have spent more time in the young lady's company than I, and are better able to judge her character," he said. "However, at this point I am making no assumptions about any of our fellow guests."

Elizabeth moved toward Miss Brereton, hoping to draw her aside to discuss chamber arrangements while the other ladies proceeded to the drawing room. She was thwarted, however, by Mr. Granville, who reached Clara first and, in a most gentlemanly manner, declared himself at her disposal should she require any assistance during this anxious time.

"I realize I am all but a stranger to you," he said to Miss Brereton. "There are others here with whom you are better acquainted, and to whom you are more likely to turn. Please know, however, that I sympathize with the apprehension you must feel over the disappearance of your cousin. If there is any service I can perform that would alleviate your distress in even the slightest measure, you have only to name it, and it shall be done."

There was an earnestness in his offer that, to Elizabeth's eye and ear, hinted at the beginnings of a more personal interest in the state of Clara Brereton's emotions. However, Miss Brereton herself—distracted by anxiety and the unfamiliar duties pressing upon her—seemed unconscious of any motive beyond simple goodwill in Mr. Granville's address, and answered him with the same degree of cordiality she had extended to all the other guests.

"Thank you, Mr. Granville. It is kind of you to make such an offer to someone with whom you have so slight a connection, and you have already been of assistance in searching the grounds. This surely is not the evening you anticipated when you accepted an invitation to dine at Sanditon House."

"Indeed, but I would not have missed it for the world, if my presence here can be of use, or perhaps even comfort, to you."

This overture, Clara did recognize. A self-conscious expression revealed her surprise, but the hint of a smile that replaced it indicated that Mr. Granville's attentiveness was not unwelcome.

"The support of any friend at this time is a comfort," she said.

Elizabeth was not alone in observing their exchange. It had been noticed by Miss Denham and Sir Edward—neither of whom appeared pleased by the solicitude with which Mr. Granville had tendered his offer. From opposite sides of the room, the Denham siblings converged upon the unsuspecting couple.

Sir Edward reached them first. "My dear Miss Brereton—" He offered a deep bow to Clara, a civil nod to Mr. Granville. "Pardon my intrusion, but I must impose upon your attention in a matter of some urgency—that is, I require a word—a private word—with you, if you would spare a moment for an *old,* or shall I say *longtime*"—he cast a pointed look at Mr. Granville—"friend."

Miss Brereton turned to Mr. Granville with an apologetic expression. "Pray excuse me, sir."

"Of course." Mr. Granville appeared about to say more, but at that moment Miss Denham swooped upon him.

"Mr. Granville, I see my brother is abandoning me. I am left, then, to find my own way to the drawing room . . . unless another gentleman offers to escort me."

"I—" He glanced at Clara, but a sidestep by Miss Denham quickly blocked his view. Thus cornered, he had little choice but to offer her his arm. "I would consider it an honor."

Mr. Granville and Miss Denham followed the Parker sisters and the rest of the guests who were quite capably making their way to the drawing room without the need of an escort. Sir Edward, meanwhile, had drawn Clara aside to a doorway on the opposite end of the room. Lit only by residual candlelight from the dining room, the adjacent chamber was cloaked in shadow. Elizabeth thought she could make out the form of a pianoforte lurking within.

Miss Brereton paused in the doorway, but Sir Edward urged her to enter the dim room. She acquiesced reluctantly. Given the clandestine interview Elizabeth had witnessed between the two yesterday morning—had the tête-à-tête truly been only yesterday? Interim events made it seem much longer ago—Elizabeth ascribed the young lady's affected indifference to an attempt at concealing from casual observers the true extent of her relationship with Sir Edward. Though Sir Edward went far enough into the music room that the door frame blocked Elizabeth's view of him, Clara's profile remained visible through the doorway.

Sir Edward's maneuvering left Elizabeth in a quandary. She, too, needed to speak to Miss Brereton privately, before they rejoined the other guests, but to simply wait in the dining room risked giving the couple the impression that she was intentionally spying on them. She elected to migrate to the drawing room doorway, where she could observe the proceedings of the other guests—many of whom were engaging in small conversations of their own—while surreptitiously continuing to monitor Miss Brereton and Sir Edward.

Miss Brereton regarded the baronet attentively at first, but after a moment her chin dipped toward the floor. Her countenance was difficult to read from this distance, but from what Elizabeth could discern of Miss Brereton's expression, it seemed one of surprise, followed by uncertainty. One of her hands moved to her chest. She shook her head slowly and spoke something Elizabeth could not hear, then raised her gaze once more.

Had she received bad news? Sir Edward drew nearer; Elizabeth now could see his hand, which took Miss Brereton's. The young woman said something else. The baronet stepped fully into view— dropped her hand—struck his own breast. While Elizabeth awarded him credit for dramatic presentation, Miss Brereton suffered his theatrics patiently.

Tea arrived in the drawing room, an event that wrested Elizabeth's attention from the baronet to his sister. In Miss Brereton's absence, there was no clear hostess to serve the tea. Miss Denham smugly appointed herself acting mistress of the house, citing her close connection to Lady Denham and her previous se'nnight's stay at Sanditon House. Nobody objected, everyone interested more in receiving their tea than in who poured it, but Esther seemed to want to exploit the occasion to impress Mr. Granville with her superior handling of a teapot.

By the time Elizabeth had her own cup in hand, Miss Brereton was at her side. Some vestiges of discomposure hung about her, but Elizabeth could not tell whether they were hallmarks of the anxiety Clara had already been feeling, or new disquiet brought on by her conference with Sir Edward. The baronet was nowhere in sight.

"Is all well?" Elizabeth asked.

Miss Brereton, lost in her own thoughts, made no reply.

Sixteen

"I have no fancy for having my House as full as an Hotel. I should not chuse to have my two Housemaids Time taken up all the morning, in dusting out Bed rooms. . . . If they had hard Places, they would want Higher wages."

—Lady Denham, Sanditon

*S*hortly after receiving word that the bedchambers were ready, the party broke up. Susan was the first to announce her intention to retire, citing fatigue from the evening's events.

"Not that I expect to get much rest," she said. "I never do—if it is not one complaint keeping me awake at night, it is another. And tonight, anxiety over poor Lady Denham will be an additional bedfellow."

"Oh, dear! Susan, however could I be so neglectful?" Diana exclaimed. "I did not consider that our unanticipated stay here means you are without your usual sedative. Allow me to prepare it—I am sure the components can be found in the stillroom. Miss Brereton, if someone will direct me there, I can make up a phial within minutes."

Rebecca was summoned to escort her, and Diana happily sallied forth, delighted to have a medical crisis to give her purpose.

The rest of the guests climbed the central staircase to the first floor, where the bedchambers were located. All available bedrooms—save Lady Denham's—had been pressed into service, including Archibald Hollis's former apartment. The single ladies were clustered in one part of the wing; the gentlemen, another farther down the corridor. Miss Denham's request for her previous bedroom had not been honored—

much to her obvious vexation. Apparently, it was the same chamber that Miss Brereton had been given when she moved into Sanditon House, and even Miss Denham had to concede—albeit not graciously— that expecting Clara to relocate from the room she had been occupying for the better part of a year was asking a bit much. Miss Denham was, however, determined to find evidence of some social slight in the sleeping arrangements, and therefore fixated upon the distance be- tween her assigned chamber and Miss Brereton's.

"In this house, we are as much family as is Miss Brereton," she com- plained to her brother after everyone except themselves, the Darcys, Miss Heywood, Miss Brereton, and Sidney Parker had retired to their chambers, "and therefore should be lodged nearer the family quar- ters. Yet Miss Heywood has the chamber next to Miss Brereton's, with the misses Parker on her other wall. I am not even on the same side of the corridor as them, but opposite the sisters."

"That arrangement was made upon my recommendation," Eliza- beth said, "in the interest of propriety. Your chamber is adjacent to your brother's, and Thomas Parker is next to his sisters. That puts the other single gentlemen farther down the corridor from the ladies."

"Surely you do not expect anything untoward to occur during the night?" Miss Denham's tone was cold, back to its usual temperature when Mr. Granville was out of hearing.

With airs like hers, Elizabeth doubted Miss Denham stood in per- sonal danger of something untoward occurring tonight or anytime soon.

"As the sole matron among us, Mrs. Darcy is merely fulfilling her duty to protect all the ladies' sensibilities," Sir Edward said.

Though Elizabeth appreciated his defense, part of her bristled slightly at being referred to as a matron. Yes, her marriage had made her one in the eyes and parlance of society, and motherhood had heightened an instinct to unofficially safeguard the well-being of younger friends such as Miss Heywood, yet hearing the word applied to herself made her sound so . . . old.

"O modesty, fair and fragile as a flower—" the baronet continued, his discourse wandering off on some inflated, convoluted tangent until his sister cut him off.

"Edward, did you not notice that in the process of 'protecting' everyone's modesty, our sole *matron* managed to seize the best chamber for herself?" Miss Denham relished the word. "By rights, it should have gone to you, as the sole person of *rank* among us."

"Mrs. Darcy is innocent of any such maneuvering," Miss Brereton said. "I offered Mr. Hollis's former apartment to her and Mr. Darcy because they are the only married couple among us, and his chambers are the most spacious."

Elizabeth had readily accepted Miss Brereton's offer of the former master's quarters not out of a desire for expansive or luxurious accommodations, but because the arrangement met an unexpressed objective of her own: the Darcys' occupation of the apartment enabled them to guard against anyone nosing through the late Archibald Hollis's possessions during the night. Now their primary concern lay in preventing potential prowlers from accessing Lady Denham's apartment. As a precaution, Darcy had, through Miss Brereton, ensured that Mrs. Riley locked the apartment's doors. Miss Brereton had then acquired the key, along with those that opened the study and Archibald's apartment, and surrendered them all to Darcy. They now rested in one of the large flap pockets of his borrowed coat.

"I commend Miss Brereton's judgment," Sir Edward said. "What need have I to ensconce myself in grandeur? It is meet that Mr. and Mrs. Darcy, our honored guests from the majestic Peaks, occupy the apartment. I assure you, I am perfectly content with the present arrangements."

Miss Denham sniffed and retreated to her inferior chamber, too out of sorts to spare any of them another syllable. Her haughty exit was, unfortunately, marred by a huge crack of thunder that startled her into a less-than-dignified jump as she passed through the doorway. She gripped the frame to steady herself. After a moment, without another glance at the others, she continued into the room and closed the door forcefully.

"Well." Sir Edward cleared his throat. "It has been rather a long day for us all. Without further ado, I shall withdraw to my own chamber, wherein I hope to be visited by slumber, if the storm will but abate—unless, Miss Brereton, there is any service I can perform on your behalf before I retire?"

"Thank you, Sir Edward, but I believe all is well in hand—at least, as much as is possible given the circumstances."

"Yes—we shall resume our search for Lady Denham upon the morn. In fact, I intend to rise early so that I may get right to it."

"What is it that you propose to do?" Darcy enquired, his tone wary. Elizabeth herself was suddenly possessed by dreadful visions of the baronet running amuck through the house.

"I—well . . . I am not altogether certain. Perhaps something will come to me during the night." He offered a cavalier bow. "For now, I bid you all good eve."

As he strode down the corridor, Miss Brereton and Miss Heywood took leave of the Darcys as well.

"I do not think I shall sleep a minute all night," Miss Brereton said. "Please come to me with any news—no matter how late the hour."

"I shall," Elizabeth promised.

"Do you think we will indeed find Lady Denham in the morning?" Charlotte asked Elizabeth.

Elizabeth wished she had an answer to that. "I think once the storm ends and the sun rises, we will all gain new perspective."

"In the meantime," Sidney said, "try to get some rest. Good night, Miss Heywood."

The two girls retired to their respective rooms; Sidney lingered.

"Have you a plan for tomorrow?" he asked Darcy.

"Not yet," Darcy replied. "I need to contemplate the day's events in the quiet of my own chamber and consider what we have learned so far."

"Do keep me apprised of your thoughts on the matter, and call upon me with any need that arises. I assure you of my discretion and dependability. Although I no longer reside in Sanditon, and therefore do not see Lady Denham often, I have known her as long as I can remember, and am deeply concerned for her."

Darcy acknowledged him with appreciation. "In turn," he added, "I assure you that although Mrs. Darcy and I have known Lady Denham for only a brief time, we, too, are genuinely concerned for her welfare, and will work toward her discovery with as much diligence as we would exert on behalf of our oldest acquaintance."

Sidney headed to his own chamber. Elizabeth was relieved to have Darcy to herself at last, for she longed to freely discuss the day's events with him. They spoke little until they reached the privacy of Archibald Hollis's apartment. There, they found loaned nightclothes laid out for them.

"I was hoping to find my own suit also waiting for me here," Darcy admitted, "although I knew the wish was unreasonable."

"Now that dinner is over, the servants can give proper attention to the gentlemen's clothing. I am sure it will be ready in the morning," Elizabeth replied. "Besides, I am growing used to seeing you in Mr. Hollis's attire."

"I much prefer my own. I do not feel quite myself in these garments."

Elizabeth's gaze drifted around Archibald's bedchamber, taking in the room's appointments—the wardrobe, four-poster bed, side tables, chairs, looking glass, draperies, paneling. She attempted to form an impression of the gentleman who had once occupied these quarters as his own. However, could any such assessment be accurate? How many of these furnishings reflected Archibald's taste, and how many had he inherited from previous generations? The only piece she knew with certainty to be his choice was the chamber horse, and she did not want to pass judgment on him solely based on his ownership of that odd contraption.

Her lips formed a half-smile. To hear Mrs. Riley talk, they might be visited by the man himself tonight.

Darcy caught her expression and regarded her with curiosity.

"If the housekeeper is to be believed, Archibald Hollis might decide to visit his former apartment before evening's end. I tell you, I hardly knew what to say when she started talking about the former masters of Sanditon House roaming its rooms."

"And you said she was serious?"

"Quite! She spoke of them as matter-of-factly as she did the dinner arrangements."

Lightning flashed, illuminating a window so splattered with raindrops that one could not see clearly through the glass. "I think we have more to fear from the storm than from any lingering spiritual presence within these walls," he said.

"At least the ghosts can be tamed with chocolate. I would welcome Mr. Hollis's appearance if he brought news of Lady Denham's whereabouts." Thunder boomed, dashing any hope she harbored about the storm blowing itself out anytime soon.

"No one else is likely to appear with such tidings in this weather." Darcy removed his cravat, folded the long strip of cloth in half, and draped it over the back of a chair. "Except, perhaps, Ivy Woodcock, if we are to give Sir Edward's words any credence—which I do not."

"I wondered what opinion you had formed of the baronet."

"That he reads too much—an indictment I never thought I would make against any gentleman, but he seems to recite rather than comprehend what he reads."

"You are kind in your criticism. I would describe his discourse as regurgitation—wholesome passages of prose and poetry returned all jumbled together in half-digested, scarcely recognizable form."

"Thank you for that lovely image to cap off our evening."

She laughed. "Perhaps prolonged exposure to the Parker sisters is influencing my own discourse, though motherhood has a way of making one less squeamish about such subjects in general. I assure you, however, I would never express so indelicate a comparison in polite company."

His brow rose in mock indignation. "So what does that make me?"

"The man who has seen me at my worst, and loves me despite it?"

"And who shall continue to do so always, though if we could confine talk of regurgitation to the sickroom, I would rather engage in more pleasant topics of conversation with you." He sighed. "Even those, however, will have to wait until I hear your thoughts on the more urgent matters at hand."

"As regards our discussion of Sir Edward, I will simply say thank goodness he did not attempt to assert authority over this investigation, which, as Lady Denham's nephew and—as Miss Denham is quick to remind everyone—a gentleman of rank, he could by rights have done."

"Agreed. Nothing would come of an enquiry under his direction, if indeed it ever even got under way. We would still be sitting in the dining room talking about Ivy Woodcock, or some other nonsense that has nothing to do with the present crisis."

Elizabeth's gaze drifted to the chamber horse once more, her mind recalling the slip of paper little Mary had found wedged within its coils. For a woman no one had seen in nearly a hundred years, Ivy Woodcock's presence in Sanditon certainly remained strong—even if only in the number of times her name had come up in the past four-and-twenty hours.

She rose and crossed to the chamber horse. Darcy regarded her curiously.

"Do you suddenly fancy a trot?"

"Not at this hour. And not on a mechanical horse." Another boom of thunder punctuated her reply. "However, if the rain continues to confine us in Sanditon House through tomorrow, I might reconsider getting better acquainted with old Tilly here."

Elizabeth reached for the drawer pull above the footrest. "When little Mary rode the chamber horse yesterday," she continued, "her movements loosened a page of paper that had been caught in the seat coils. 'Ivy' was written on it multiple times, and 'woodcock' once, along with simple illustrations of ivy vines and birds. There were roses on it as well. I thought little of it at the time, taking it to be a page from a child's sketchbook, but now that we know there was a woman by that name, and have heard her story, I want to take another look at it." She opened the drawer, its runners scraping the cabinet floor.

It was empty.

She stared into the bare drawer. She and Mary *had* put the paper into the drawer—had they not?

"Well, do not keep me in suspense," Darcy said. "Bring it over here and let us examine it together."

"I cannot." She did not turn as she spoke; rather, she continued gazing into the empty drawer as if doing so could make the page materialize. "It is gone."

She pulled the drawer all the way out, felt inside the cavity with her hand, stooped to look within. There was no sign of the page ever having been in there—no crumpled wad or even a torn scrap from having been caught between the drawer and its housing.

"Are you certain you put it in the drawer?"

"Yes." As soon as she said the word, however, doubt crept into her mind. Had she misremembered?

"Perhaps Mary moved it afterward?" Darcy offered. "Or took it with her?"

"She could not have taken it home with her—someone would have noticed her possession of it during our visit with Lady Denham, or during the walk home. As for moving it, I do not think she had an opportunity, as we departed this room immediately after putting it in the drawer."

Elizabeth knew from experience, however, that children could move quickly when they wanted to. She went to one side of the chamber horse, slipping her hand through each slit in the leather to feel around the coils. Darcy came forward and examined the other side.

Each time her hand brushed the internal wooden boards separating the layers of coils, Elizabeth felt dust and a couple of small, hard, dry objects; she suspected the latter were dead flies but decided she would rather not contemplate their nature too closely. What she did not feel, was anything resembling paper.

"It is not on this side," Darcy said.

She released a frustrated sigh. "Nor this one."

"If you are sure that you put it in the drawer, then—"

"Someone else has taken an interest in it," she finished. "But whom? The paper appeared to have been caught in the coils a long time. I would venture that no one even knew of its existence before Mary discovered it."

"Was anyone else with you while she rode the horse?"

"Miss Brereton initially assisted her. However, Mrs. Parker and Miss Heywood were in the next room, and summoned her with a question about one of the sketches on the wall. She left to attend them and I stayed behind with Mary, so the two of us were alone when she found the paper and put it in the drawer."

"Miss Brereton could have returned any time between then and now, and discovered it for herself. Do you know whether she ever takes exercise on the chamber horse?"

"She said she does not, nor does Lady Denham. The dowager claims the horse is good as new, so my impression is that it sees little use at all. From the creaking of the springs when Mary rode, I would not be at all surprised to learn it was Mr. Hollis himself who last used it. So it is highly unlikely that the paper was discovered by anyone in the course of simple exercise. Whoever removed it either came here looking for it, or entered for another purpose and took advantage of the opportunity to rifle Archibald Hollis's belongings. Although I know that Miss Brereton *did* return to this room earlier today, to inspect the clothing brought down from the attics before it was loaned to you and the other gentlemen, with that matter to occupy her, I doubt the chamber horse would have drawn her attention. Why should it today, when it never has before?"

Darcy acknowledged her point with a nod. "Well, then—that merely leaves as suspects all the servants and every gentleman who borrowed Mr. Hollis's attire. Were the ladies left to roam about the house while the gentlemen were searching the grounds? If so, we can add them to the list, as well."

A sudden bang on the window caused them both to jump. Elizabeth's gaze flew to the glass. The wind had torn a large twig off one of the trees and driven it against the pane. The force held it to the glass another half-minute before subsiding enough to let it fall.

Elizabeth released breath she had not realized she was holding. "Perhaps we ought to include Ivy Woodcock on the list."

"You have been listening to Mrs. Riley too much."

"I was jesting." She did not truly believe Ivy's spirit haunted Sanditon, this night or any other. Her heart, however, yet raced from the start the flying twig had given her. "We have ample cause for anxiety without anything supernatural contributing to it. I doubt any of us will find much sleep tonight."

Another bang sounded—this one louder, from the chamber door. "Mr. Darcy!" Another series of raps sounded. "Mr. Darcy!"

It was a woman's voice, its owner not immediately identifiable through the heavy wooden door and the noise of the storm outside. Darcy crossed quickly to the door, Elizabeth right behind him.

He opened it to reveal a darkened hallway, lit only by the glow of the candle being held by an utterly distraught Diana Parker.

"Susan is missing."

Seventeen

"I hate to employ others, when I am equal to act myself—and my conscience told me that this was an occasion which called for me."
—*Diana Parker,* Sanditon

*T*hough Diana strode into the apartment with as much force and purpose as ever, the hand in which she held her candle trembled. Fearing Miss Parker might upset the taper and set fire to the carpet, Elizabeth took it from her and placed it on a table near the door as Darcy attempted to usher her toward a chair.

"Please, sit down," he said calmly.

"Sit down? My sister has disappeared! I cannot possibly sit down. We must find her without delay!"

"Of course we must," Darcy said. "However, we can search in a more productive manner if first you tell us how she came to be missing."

"I have not the faintest idea! As you surely recall, I left Susan in our bedchamber while I went to the stillroom to prepare a sedative for her. Assembling it was a frustrating business—though Lady Denham makes a great point of eschewing elixirs, Mrs. Riley ought to keep the house better stocked with basic medicinal components— she lacked at least half the ingredients I needed. Fortunately, I knew of substitutions that could be made. When I returned to the bedchamber, Susan had already changed into one of the nightdresses that

had been laid out for us—I think they must belong to Miss Brereton—
at least, the one Susan donned. My sister eats so little, you know, that
she is about the same size as the younger miss. She was grateful that
I had managed to prepare the draught—she anticipated difficulty in
falling asleep because at dinner she had bit down incautiously on her
gum, which is still tender from her tooth extraction. 'My poor sister!' I
exclaimed. 'Why did you not tell me your gum is agitated? I would
have made up a poultice as well.' I left the sedative on the night table
and then went back downstairs to prepare the poultice. Mrs. Riley offered to make it up, but I insisted on doing it myself—the kitchen and
offices are all still at sixes and sevens following the dinner party, so
who knows whether any of the staff could be trusted to give the task
proper attention? They certainly do not have my experience in such
matters. Even so, the process took far longer than it ought to have,
and by the time I returned upstairs, I wondered whether I would
find Susan asleep without the poultice and all my efforts in vain.
When I entered our chamber, however, I did not find her at all."

Darcy sorted through the barrage of detail to isolate the essentials.
"Is the room still in order?"

"The bedclothes on one side of the bed are rumpled. All else looks
as it did when I left her. The phial containing the sedative is still full."

"Might she have grown impatient and gone downstairs in search
of you?" Elizabeth suggested.

"Susan would not wander around in the dark by herself. She knew
I would return as soon as possible."

"Have you spoken to any of the others since we all parted?" Darcy
asked.

She shook her head. "I came to you immediately. But of course we
must rouse them without delay!" She picked up the candle and opened
the door. "We must comb every inch of the house!"

"Do not succumb to panic yet. Let us start by determining whether
anyone heard her leave your chamber," Darcy said. "Perhaps she is
merely in one of the other ladies' rooms, having a late conversation."

Diana, however, was already striding down the hall.

"Do you truly believe that is where we are likely to find Susan
Parker?" Elizabeth asked Darcy as they hastily seized candles of their
own and followed her. "In a quiet tête-à-tête with Miss Denham?"

Despite the calm assurance he had tried to offer Diana Parker, Darcy was uneasy. An absent elderly dowager was one matter; an additional missing middle-aged spinster, unrelated to her, transformed the situation disturbingly.

"That is where I hope to find her," he said at last.

In the short amount of time it took Elizabeth and Darcy to catch up with Diana, she had collected Thomas and Sidney Parker in the corridor outside the sisters' bedchamber. Like Darcy, they had removed their coats and neckcloths but were otherwise still dressed. Arthur, whom Diana had also wakened, emerged a couple minutes later from his chamber in a nightshirt, dressing gown, and nightcap, neither the storm nor anxiety over Lady Denham's disappearance apparently having interfered with his ability to rest.

"Now, what is this about Susan?" Arthur asked, blinking sleep from his eyes.

"I told you, she is missing!" Diana released a sound of exasperation. "Did you not hear me say so?

"Spare him a little mercy, Diana," Sidney said. "He looks as if you woke him from a sound slumber."

"She did!" Arthur replied defensively. "I had just fallen asleep. One cannot expect a man to be in full possession of his faculties the instant he wakes up. The brain needs time to rekindle."

Diana rolled her eyes.

"Well, it *does*," Arthur said. "And you were pounding on the door as you said it."

"We are wasting precious time," Diana replied. "Susan is missing. Unless you know where she might be, we must rouse the others."

"If your pounding has not already?"

Ignoring Arthur's question, she turned toward Miss Brereton's chamber. Before she reached it, the door opened. Clara, too, was dressed for bed, though did not appear to have been sleeping. A dressing robe covered her nightgown, and she had not yet donned a nightcap. An expression of anxiety clouded her face.

"Miss Brereton, summon the servants!" Diana said. "We must search the house for my sister—she has disappeared."

Clara nodded. "I could not help overhearing."

Indeed, Diana spoke at such a volume that the remaining guests emerged from their chambers one by one, in various states of dress, to assemble in the corridor. Sir Edward strode up the hall; still fully attired, he also wore an expression of great concern.

"Miss Parker—missing!" His words, delivered more as a statement than a question, were punctuated by a crack of thunder that made Arthur jump. "I wonder where she could have gone? She must be somewhere in the house—no one could leave here without becoming wet through. Utterly wet through! No one!"

Josiah Hollis appeared last, grumbling about "a man's right to peace and quiet in his own family home." Nobody had seen Susan since the elder Miss Parker had retired to her room.

"I am sure she is around here somewhere." Miss Denham waved her hand dismissively before crossing both arms in front of herself in a stance that radiated boredom. Though not indecently exposed, she appeared in a greater condition of dishabille than the other ladies. Where the hair of the misses Brereton and Heywood was gathered in long braids, Esther's dark tresses hung loose, softening the disdainful expression that so often dominated her countenance. Also unlike Clara and Charlotte, whose nightgowns were completely covered by their robes, Esther's loosely tied wrap gave the impression of having been hastily donned. "No doubt Miss Parker will return momentarily, and all of us disturbed for naught."

"I would be grateful for the false alarm if it means we find her well," said Mr. Granville. Like most of the other gentlemen, he had shed his cravat, but was otherwise still attired in his full eighteenth-century finery.

"Oh—I, too—of course!" Miss Denham added quickly, her tone warmer. She smiled at Mr. Granville as she pushed back a lock of hair that had been perfectly content where it was. The motion resulted in her robe slipping slightly off one shoulder. "I only meant to reassure Miss Diana that this whole incident will be resolved happily."

Mrs. Riley was summoned, then dispatched to direct the rest of the staff in their second search of the house that night. Diana was all nervous energy as she watched the housekeeper depart. She shifted from one foot to the other, then commenced full-fledged pacing. "The servants could not even locate their own mistress earlier tonight," she said. "How can we trust them to do a thorough exploration for Susan?"

"They know the house better than we do," Darcy replied.

"True as that might be, I know my sister better than they do, and I cannot stand here idle while Susan is missing." Diana started down the corridor.

"Where are you going?" Thomas Parker asked.

"Where do you think, Tom?" she replied without turning around. "I am going to look for Susan."

Sir Edward struck his hand to his breast.

She walks in beauty, like the night
Of cloudless climes and starry skies;
And all that's best of dark and bright—

A boom of thunder cut short his oration. So much for cloudless climes.

This was exactly what Darcy had hoped to avoid—everyone running off half-cocked, with the cause of the two ladies' disappearances yet unknown. What if the incidents were related? Yet preventing Diana Parker from embarking on a course she had settled upon seemed futile. "At least allow someone to accompany you," he said to her.

"A companion would only slow me down."

"That might not be a bad idea," Thomas said under his breath. Then he called after her, "Take Arthur with you."

Arthur looked as if Thomas had suggested he capture a running stag. "Me?"

Diana, either unaware or unmindful of her eldest brother's directive, continued striding down the corridor.

"One of our sisters is already missing—we cannot risk losing the other."

"Come, now, Tom," Sidney said. "Do you not think such panic premature? I doubt some general threat lurks in the corridors. More likely, Susan has taken some notion into her head and is acting upon it. Given both our sisters' propensity for self-doctoring, I would not be at all surprised to discover her collecting rainwater from the cistern for one of their concoctions, or before a large window attempting some newfangled remedy that can be performed only by the illumination of a lightning bolt in a summer storm."

"It is precisely such possibilities that require us to protect our sisters from themselves." Thomas cast an imperative look at their youngest brother.

Arthur heaved a reluctant sigh and set out in pursuit of the stag.

The sigh Sir Edward issued as he turned his gaze to Clara Brereton was still more dramatic, augmented by a sweeping bow. "Miss Brereton, if you, too, wish to take part in the search for Miss Parker, it would be my honor to serve as your escort and protector through the darkened house."

Clara flushed and appeared at a loss for a reply. Elizabeth felt her discomfort. Regardless of whether Miss Brereton welcomed the baronet's advances, his suggestion put her in an awkward position.

"That is a most gallant offer," Elizabeth interjected, "but if we are undertaking our own search of the house, should you not escort your sister?"

Now it was Sir Edward's turn to appear embarrassed. "I meant for the three of us to search together, of course."

Miss Denham's expression froze in obvious dislike of her brother's proposal. "We can search more quickly if we divide into pairs rather than threes," she said. "And, Edward, you and I should separate. After all"—she turned to the others—"we practically grew up in this house. We know it intimately, and so should partner with others less familiar." She pushed back the same lock of hair she had before, resulting in the same slippage of her robe. "Perhaps Mr. Granville could accompany me."

Mr. Granville appeared surprised by the suggestion, but responded graciously. "If that is your wish, it would be my privilege."

"Miss Denham, would you like help changing back into your gown?" Elizabeth asked.

"What? Oh!" She laughed. "My thoughts were so much upon Miss Parker that I had forgotten my state of dress. No—I thank you, but I can manage." With a look at Mr. Granville and a promise that she would return in but a moment, she reentered her room.

"Miss Brereton," the baronet prompted, "I stand ready to escort you at your command."

"You are most kind, sir," Miss Brereton replied, "but I have been thinking—I also know the house well, so perhaps you and I ought to separate, too."

"I would not have you go alone!"

"Nor I," Darcy said. "In fact, I do not think any of the ladies ought to be wandering about by themselves."

"I did not intend to search alone. Mr. Parker, I can see that you grow more anxious for Susan with each passing minute. Shall we go at once?"

Thomas Parker seized upon Miss Brereton's offer. "I feel a great need to be doing *something*," he confessed.

"Before everybody scatters," Darcy said, "let us agree to reconvene in one hour's time, if Miss Parker is not discovered sooner."

"Where?" Mr. Parker asked. "Here?"

The corridor was not an ideal location for a conference, should an unsuccessful search prove one necessary.

"The morning room is behind that door." Miss Brereton nodded toward a room near the top of the staircase.

Darcy shook his head. "Miss Diana and Arthur Parker have already left us, and might not know where the morning room is. Let us meet in the portrait room, where we gathered before dinner. Apprise your siblings if you see them."

"I shall," Mr. Parker said.

"We will also inform Mrs. Riley that we are looking for Susan," Miss Brereton added. The pair headed off in the direction Diana had taken.

Sir Edward at last broke his cavalier stance. "I, too, will start my quest," he said. "Miss Heywood, if you intend to join the search, I volunteer myself as your companion."

"Should not someone remain here, in case Miss Parker returns by herself?" Charlotte asked.

"I would as soon see everybody unfamiliar with the house return to their own rooms," Darcy said. "There is no sense in risking someone else becoming lost or stumbling in the dark."

"I, for one, have no intention of wandering about these passages at midnight," Josiah Hollis declared. "If you ask me, we are more likely to come upon Uncle Archibald or Ivy Woodcock than Miss Parker. I am going back to my bed."

He lurched down the corridor, the limp from his lumbago more pronounced than it had been earlier. Darcy wondered whether it were an intentional exaggeration.

While Sir Edward lauded Charlotte's wisdom in staying behind, offering examples from half a dozen gothic novels to illustrate the perils of young ladies exploring large old mansions after dark, Mr. Granville stepped closer to the Darcys and Sidney Parker.

"My chamber adjoins Josiah Hollis's. There is an interior door through which I can hear him move about." Mr. Granville spoke softly, his statement unheard by the baronet and Charlotte, but accompanied by a meaningful look at the others. "If you like, rather than search with Miss Denham, I could return to my room."

Darcy understood the unspoken half of his offer: *and monitor whether Hollis stays where he claims he will.* Darcy nodded. "I would appreciate that."

Elizabeth doubted Esther Denham would.

"How will you explain the change of plans to Miss Denham without her perceiving it as a slight?" Elizabeth asked.

"I have not worked that out yet," Mr. Granville said. "I do not think I can suddenly claim indisposition." He turned to Sidney. "I scarcely know the lady. Have you any suggestions?"

Sidney thought a moment. "Allow me to bear the burden of blame," he finally said. "Leave with me now, before she emerges from her room. We will commence a search of our own. Then as soon as both Denhams clear this corridor, you can return to your chamber. Mrs. Darcy, if you would, kindly inform Miss Denham that I grew impatient to seek my sister—which is true—and that I insisted Mr. Granville come with me—also true."

"And convey my regret at being deprived of the opportunity to accompany her tonight," Mr. Granville added, "along with my earnest anticipation of enjoying her company sometime tomorrow."

Elizabeth agreed to the scheme, but Darcy frowned. "This feels disingenuous."

"I assure you, on my part, it is not," Mr. Granville said.

"Nor on mine," Sidney added. "I am indeed wanting to have a look about the house myself. Despite my belief that Susan is perfectly fine, I will not be able to rest tonight until she is discovered."

Elizabeth shared Darcy's abhorrence of deception in any form, but pronounced her own conscience clear in this matter. The excuse and its effect on Miss Denham would be more an instance of disappointed hopes than deceit, and as she found Miss Denham a bit duplicitous in her own dealings with people—charming toward individuals of use to her, dismissive (or altogether disdainful) of those who were not— she had little doubt that the woman's interest in seeking Susan Parker was motivated by the opportunity to spend time with Percy Granville rather than deep concern for Miss Parker's whereabouts.

"Consider, too, Darcy," Elizabeth said, "that with Mr. Granville otherwise occupied, if Miss Denham remains inclined to search for Miss Parker, her brother can escort her—a more proper arrangement. And Sir Edward will delight in being of use." She glanced at the baronet, still engaged in rambling monologue directed at a very patient Miss Heywood. "He does seem rather keen on escorting *somebody* this evening."

Sidney and Mr. Granville made good their escape, disappearing round the corner just as Miss Denham emerged from her chamber. She glanced about, her countenance and mien rapidly transforming from amiability to pique. Her eyes narrowed as she addressed the Darcys. "Where is Mr. Granville?"

Elizabeth delivered the agreed-upon excuse. Before she could also tender Mr. Granville's regrets, Miss Denham cut her off.

"What need of Mr. Granville has Sidney Parker? Mr. Granville was engaged to escort *me*."

"Mr. Granville was exceedingly reluctant to alter the arrangement and sacrifice his pleasure in your company," Elizabeth assured her. "In fact, I rather imagine he would like to dine beside you tomorrow, if we are all still detained here at dinnertime." She hoped the gentleman in question would not mind this little augmentation to the message she had been entrusted to deliver. While Mr. Granville had not explicitly stated any such desire, if they all were to work together to find the two missing ladies, and if the weather continued to confine them all at Sanditon House for an indeterminate amount of time, keeping everyone in an agreeable temper, including Miss Denham, served the greater good.

The suggestion softened but did not obviate Miss Denham's

vexation. "And what am I to do in the meantime? Search for Miss Parker by myself?"

"Your brother is still here and able to escort you."

"My *brother*?" She cast a derisive glance at the baronet and Charlotte. "I think not. He can accompany Miss Heywood if he likes. It matters little." She turned her gaze back to Elizabeth; a lesser woman might have withered under it. "If Sidney Parker required Mr. Granville's assistance so badly, his friend must be such a talented searcher that the rest of us need not bother. I am retiring for the night."

For the second time that evening, Miss Denham donned her mantle of injured pride, swept through her doorway, and shut the door with resounding force.

The sound startled Sir Edward, who had been too engaged in his own discourse to attend his sister's. "Whatever was that about?" he asked.

"Miss Denham has elected not to participate in the search for Susan Parker after all," Elizabeth said.

"Oh? Well—I suppose I ought to be getting on with mine," Sir Edward said.

With a final invitation to Miss Heywood—politely declined—he headed off. Miss Heywood withdrew to her own chamber, leaving Elizabeth and Darcy alone in the corridor.

"What now?" Elizabeth asked. "Do we join the others in searching for Susan Parker? Find Mr. Granville and tell him the coast is clear to return to his chamber?"

"No," Darcy replied. "We are going to Lady Denham's apartment—by way of the study—to ensure no one is using the search for Miss Parker as an opportunity to search for something else entirely."

Eighteen

To close her eyes in sleep that night, she felt must be entirely out of the question. With a curiosity so justly awakened, and feelings in every way so agitated, repose must be absolutely impossible.
—Northanger Abbey

*C*harlotte stared at her chamber walls.

She had volunteered to stay behind out of the belief that she could be more useful to Susan by attending to whatever Miss Parker might need if she returned on her own, than by wandering around the house looking for her—particularly with Sir Edward as her guide. She still believed that, but regretted not having considered how she would occupy her time while waiting. At the moment she did not feel of use to anybody, including herself.

The bedroom was a fine chamber, certainly the finest in which she had ever slept. Layers of fabric swathed the canopied bed, and elaborate carvings adorned the solid old furniture. But the quarters offered little in the way of diversion. Hastily prepared along with so many other rooms for the unexpected guests, the chamber had been supplied with essentials but not amenities—no books or magazines, no writing paper or drawing pencils, no means of activity, let alone amusement. She would have been grateful for an outdated issue of *The Spectator* or *Ackermann's Repository,* or even old Mr. Hollis's chamber horse. Heavens, she would have been grateful for a needle and the household mending.

Charlotte was not a young lady who required constant stimulation to ward away boredom. Under normal circumstances, she welcomed quiet moments and opportunities for reflection. These, however, were not normal circumstances, and she wanted distraction from the thoughts tumbling through her mind. As if Lady Denham's continued absence were not disturbing enough, Susan Parker's disappearance added to her apprehensive musings. Charlotte believed Susan would be found somewhere in the house; it was merely a matter of where and the motive that had led her there. She thought the possibility Mr. Darcy had presented—that Miss Parker had gone down to the stillroom in quest of an additional remedy—the most probable scenario. However, until Miss Parker was discovered, Charlotte could not be easy, nor banish from her thoughts the worry that Susan, still weak from yesterday's leeching, had become disoriented or fainted before reaching her destination.

She went to a window and drew back the drapery, but could see little beyond the dim reflection of candlelight on the rain-spattered glass. Clouds obscured any trace of the moon, and the storm's lightning strikes appeared to have moved to the east, leaving the house enveloped in darkness and the drum of gentler yet steady rainfall. Whether the storm was abating or simply gathering new energy for another furious display remained to be seen.

Between the weather and the missing ladies, heaven only knew what the morrow would bring. Even were Susan found, Charlotte could not imagine ever being able to fall asleep tonight. Perhaps, however, she ought at least try to rest.

She decided to lie down, remaining alert to any sounds that might come from the corridor. She removed her slippers, setting them beside the dressing table, then took off her robe and draped it on the bench seat. As she climbed into the high, ornate bed, she pushed aside the heavy counterpane. The sheet would suffice; with the windows closed against the rain, the room was close and humid—yet another safeguard against accidental slumber. Out of habit, she turned to blow out the candle, but paused. Were she needed quickly, how would she relight it? On the other hand, she did not think Lady Denham would be very well pleased to learn upon her return to Sanditon House that a considerable quantity of candles had been depleted. The expense would give the old dowager apoplexy. No—'twas better to conserve the candles for those moving about the house, who had a real need for light. If someone summoned Charlotte, she could reignite her candle from their flame.

She extinguished the taper, immediately plunging the room into darkness so complete that the chamber seemed empty of anything but the sound of her own breathing. Darkness did not typically bother her, but the unfamiliar surroundings, coupled with the evening's events, combined to increase her already-present disquiet. She settled into a supine position, drawing reassurance from the sensation of something solid at her back.

She lay thus for she knew not how long, when a noise in the corridor caught her notice.

It was the sound of a nearby door opening. Unlike Miss Denham's earlier dramatics, it was a muted sound, as of one attempting to enter without disturbing others. Moments later, it was followed by the soft tap of the door being closed with equal care. The sound was very near; in fact, Charlotte believed it came from the chamber adjacent to her own. The Parker sisters' room.

Had Susan returned, unaware that with the entire household seeking her, a cautious entry was unnecessary? She doubted it was Diana. Susan's sister would not have given up the search this soon, before any of the others—unless she had learned something, or brought Susan back with her.

Charlotte sat up. Whether it were Susan, Diana, or both who had just entered the chamber, they might be in need of assistance.

She left the bed and cautiously moved in the direction of the dressing table, bending with arms extended so that her hands would find the seat before her knees encountered it. She reached the bench and immediately felt the robe beneath her fingertips. As she reassumed the garment, her right foot brushed against one of her slippers, sparing her the trouble of groping around the floor to find them. She donned the shoes and carefully moved toward the door.

The distance seemed longer than she remembered, and she had begun to fear she was shuffling in the wrong direction, when her hands touched the wall. She moved along it until she felt the door frame.

She opened her door to an empty corridor, faintly lit by a single candle that had been left burning in a sconce farther down the hallway when the search for Susan began. She went to the neighboring door and knocked softly, so as not to startle its occupant.

"Miss Parker?"

There was no response, no sound of movement within.

"Miss Parker?" Charlotte repeated. "It is Miss Heywood. Is everything all right?"

Again, her words elicited no reply.

Hesitant to intrude, yet anxious for Miss Parker's welfare, she grasped the door handle and gently released the catch. Why she felt the need to maintain silence with this part of the house all but deserted, she was unsure, but the atmosphere of the darkened wing seemed to discourage noise.

The Parker sisters' chamber was as black as her own, so dark that in the weak ambient light penetrating from the corridor she could scarcely make out the shapes of the furniture. She had expected to find the room illuminated by the taper of the returned Susan Parker, but no spinster greeted her, and the closest thing to candlelight that she observed was the lingering scent of burning wax left behind from Diana's earlier visit. Long, heavy draperies covered the windows but could not completely muffle the sounds of the now-raging storm. Only the great bed that dominated the far wall boldly asserted its presence, and even that hid more than it revealed. Curtains hung from its canopy, enshrouding the interior.

Charlotte contemplated the bed. Had she spent so long fumbling her way out of her own room that Miss Parker had not only returned but already retired? She considered retrieving her candle, left behind in her haste to reach Miss Parker. However, a sense of urgency propelled her into the unfamiliar chamber rather than take time to find the candle, travel down the hall to light it from the sconce, and return.

"Miss Parker?" Charlotte moved toward the bed and attempted to draw aside the veiling, but had difficulty finding an opening between panels. "Miss Parker, it is Charlotte Heywood, come to check on you. The entire household is concerned for your well-being." At last, her fingers discovered the fabric's edge. She pulled the curtain to one side, peering into the enclosed space—and saw nothing. Nothing that looked like a person, anyway; only rumpled bedding . . . or what looked like rumpled bedding.

Charlotte recalled, from childhood games of hide-and-seek with her siblings, that it was possible for a bed to appear empty while actually concealing an occupant. Where her younger sisters inevitably betrayed their presence with insuppressible giggles, no telltale sounds issued from these bedclothes, and she doubted Miss Parker would deliberately disguise her presence in such a manner—what reason had she? However, if she were sleeping, she might have unconsciously wrapped herself well enough to hinder detection in the dark.

"Miss Parker?" She grasped the thick counterpane and pulled it back, prepared for a startled cry from a rudely awakened Susan. However, only linens lay beneath, and only her own heartbeat sounded in her ears.

She wondered at her accelerated pulse. Why should an empty chamber set her heart racing?

Because it *was* empty.

She had been so certain of having heard stirring in here, of having heard the door open and close. Now she doubted her own senses. Had the noise come from elsewhere? She had not detected other sounds of motion from nearby rooms when she was in the corridor. Nor did any break the stillness now.

While lying in her bed, had she unknowingly drifted into a state of half-dream and simply imagined the sounds?

Regardless of the explanation, she now felt her own presence to be an invasion of the absent Parker sisters' privacy. With neither Susan nor Diana in the room, Charlotte had no business being in there, either. She was an unwelcome intruder.

She let fall the curtain and turned away from the bed, casting her gaze about the room one last time. The shadows seemed darker and somehow more sinister than they had when she entered. Despite her robe, she shuddered as an uncomfortable self-consciousness crept over her.

It was more than a sense of having trespassed.

It was a sense of being watched.

Nineteen

She took her candle and looked closely at the cabinet. . . . her quick eyes directly fell on a roll of paper pushed back into the further part of the cavity, apparently for concealment.
—Northanger Abbey

"So you *do* believe that Susan Parker's disappearance is related to Lady Denham's?"

"Not necessarily." Darcy kept his voice low as he replied to Elizabeth's query. They were en route to the study, the location of which he had obtained from Miss Brereton earlier and was fairly confident of being able to find without escort. Their path took them past and through numerous other rooms, and he did not want to risk being overheard by any of the guests or servants seeking Miss Parker. "I do, however, believe that enough of our fellow guests hold a stake in Lady Denham's affairs that one or more of them might employ the distraction as an opportunity to determine just how great that stake is. Sir Edward, Miss Denham, Josiah Hollis, and even Miss Brereton have all in the course of this evening boasted familiarity with the house— that might extend to familiarity with where Lady Denham keeps her important papers. Any of those individuals could attempt to become even more familiar with them before the night is over."

"I confess, were I one of her potential heirs, I would prefer the last will and testament of Philadelphia Brereton Hollis Denham to any other bedtime reading tonight."

"Merely *reading* the will is the least of the potential mischief that could be occurring at this moment."

"Indeed, the document could disappear as mysteriously as Lady Denham herself. Surely, however, her solicitor retained a copy?"

"We can but hope," Darcy replied. "Yet even should her will be found here in Sanditon House, if a false document—one that purports to be a codicil—were planted among her papers, the validity of the true will would be compromised. The sooner we find and secure her documents, the better."

They entered the library, a room half the size of Pemberley's, with a fraction of the number of books. Sheets covered the furniture, and the fireplace looked as if it had not been lit in years. From his brief interaction with Lady Denham, Darcy doubted the room had seen much use since Archibald Hollis died, and doubted even further that the collection had expanded in that time. The neglect of a family library always troubled Darcy—households that did not place value on the improvement of one's mind through reading were foreign climes to him.

One bookshelf, however, appeared to have experienced recent activity. Several volumes lay stacked on their backs before a neat row of books behind them, apparently read but not returned to their proper spot. A glance at some of the titles indicated that the shelf held popular novels. Perhaps the addition of Miss Brereton to the household had restored at least some of the room's purpose.

Each end of the library held a door that led to other rooms not accessible from the corridor. He gestured toward the closed door at the east end of the room. "I believe that is the study."

The door was locked. Darcy withdrew the keys Miss Brereton had given him earlier. The first one fit into the hole but would not turn. The second produced the anticipated click of a lock disengaging. Darcy pushed open the door and stepped aside for Elizabeth to enter with the candle.

She started forward, but suddenly froze and released a startled gasp.

Darcy peered into the study. The weak candlelight barely penetrated its darkness, illuminating only the shadowy shapes of the room's furniture.

And the pair of eyes that met his.

Instinctively, Darcy stepped in front of Elizabeth, interposing himself between his wife and the study's unknown occupant.

"Identify yourself," Darcy said.

Upon receiving no reply, he repeated the command.

Again, no response. Nor did the eyes move, but challenged Darcy with their fixed, unblinking gaze. There was something unnatural, yet familiar, in the manner of their stare.

He held his breath, listening, but heard only the sound of his own heart thrumming in his chest. It was senseless to stand here in silent opposition to whoever lurked within. Better to confront the trespasser and know with whom he dealt. Darcy took the candle from Elizabeth. "Stay back."

"Darcy—"

He moved into the room, holding the candle well in front of him to cast its light as far as possible.

And released a soft chuckle.

The eyes belonged not to a human intruder, but to a bear.

A bear head, to be precise, mounted on the far wall, with fur so black that it had absorbed rather than reflected the weak candlelight that caught its eyes. The glassy gaze that had greeted him resembled those of countless game trophies Darcy had seen in gentlemen's studies, clubs, and gun rooms.

And indeed, this *was* a gentleman's room, without question. The bear was the most exotic of three trophies watching over the room: a pair of stags flanked it. Though boasting racks of ten and twelve points, the two native creatures seemed ordinary in comparison to the bear. Several paintings depicting hunting scenes also adorned the room.

He turned to Elizabeth. "I believe we are quite safe." When her brow furrowed in question, he extended his hand toward her. "Come."

With slight hesitation, she went to his side. She started upon first identifying the eyes' owner.

"Is that a bear?"

"It is."

"I have never seen one before. Have you?"

"I saw a live bear once, at a circus in London when I was a boy. That was a brown bear captured on the Continent, or so the bear keeper claimed. I believe our friend here is a black bear, which I understand inhabit North America."

"I wonder how it came to reside in Sanditon House. From what little we know of the Hollises, they do not impress me as great adventurers."

"Perhaps it was purchased as a curiosity, or received as a gift."

"If only it could tell us where to find what we are looking for."

They turned their gazes away from the bear and glanced around the rest of the study, taking in the dark paneled walls, the heavy marble surrounding the fireplace, the rug of burgundy, green, and brown. Dark green draperies closed out the night. The furnishings seemed to absorb the candle's glow.

"Somehow, I do not see Lady Denham spending a great deal of time in here, if any," Elizabeth commented. "This room might look brighter in daylight, but not by much. And as rare an ornament as the bear is, his constant stare, and those of his two companions, would unnerve me after a while."

A pair of glass-fronted bookcases stood on one wall beside a small table and two armchairs. A sturdy desk and equally solid cabinet dominated the opposite side of the study. Darcy nodded toward the desk, which, in addition to the usual small drawers and pigeonholes for pens, ink, paper, and other writing materials, had three deep drawers going down the right side.

"My guess is that any important documents stored in this room will be found there or in the cabinet," Darcy said.

He went to the desk, placed his candle on its surface, and slid open the drawers. Sure enough, letter files greeted him. He removed a handful of correspondence and began to thumb through it, skimming the close handwriting as rapidly as he could in the dim light to determine what, exactly, he had found.

Elizabeth, meanwhile, opened the cabinet. She, too, set her candle on the desk, then reached inside and pulled out a large scroll.

"What have you there?" Darcy asked.

"I do not yet know, but the cabinet holds quite a few of these." She unrolled the paper in her hands. "This appears to be an architectural plan for Sanditon House. Rather, for part of it—the ground floor." She rotated the paper a quarter turn clockwise. "It is an old one—Lady Denham's private rooms are labeled the 'State Apartment.' I wonder how often Sanditon House actually hosted nobility? This plan seems to show as many receiving rooms and servants' passages as Pemberley holds."

"The architect did take inspiration from the castle that used to stand here," Darcy replied somewhat absently as he replaced the first batch of correspondence he had perused and started on a second. "At least Lady Denham, for all the criticisms we have heard of her frugality, seems to have adopted a practical approach to managing the household. If the best apartment in the house was sitting unused, why should she not take it as her own?"

"I shall remember you said that, should I someday find myself widowed and decide to move into *your* apartment."

He looked up from the letters to meet her gaze. A teasing smile played about her lips. He returned it, grateful to her for drawing him, at least for a moment, away from the world of Sanditon and into their own. He wished they were home, instead of on a "holiday" that had turned out to be anything but.

"You may have it now, if you want it. The bedchamber is seldom enough occupied." Because he spent most nights in hers. "Whether before or after my demise, however, I would find a way to visit you after dark."

"I thought you did not believe in ghosts?"

"That was before I learned there was chocolate involved."

She laughed. "Well, do not plan to cross over to the spirit realm or pack up your belongings anytime soon, for I am quite well satisfied with our present arrangement."

They both resumed their tasks. Elizabeth rerolled the scroll and withdrew another from the cabinet. "This one is an old landscaping design." She studied it in silence for a minute. "It depicts a number of follies that I do not recall seeing in the park as we approached the house, or from the gallery window during my visit with Mrs. Parker and Miss Heywood. A temple . . . a tower . . . a grotto—"

"I did find the grotto, when I was searching the grounds with Josiah Hollis," Darcy said. "It was well hidden by overgrown vegetation—I did not even realize it was there until we were almost upon it."

"The summerhouse, hermitage, and gazebo are still extant, but I wonder whether the other structures were ever built. This does seem an ambitious scheme." She returned the scroll to the cabinet. "What have you there?"

"The majority of these letters relate to daily operations of the estate," he said. "None of them is current. In fact, all the correspondence I have seen so far is dated during Archibald Hollis's lifetime, mostly addressed to him, some of it to his father."

"I suppose it was too much to hope that we could simply walk in here and find a copy of Lady Denham's will waiting for us. Or Archibald Hollis's, for that matter. Josiah Hollis still seems to harbor a great deal of resentment over the disposition of his uncle's fortune. I am curious as to the particulars."

"The man is so abrasive that if the rest of the Hollis family are of similar temperament, it is not difficult to understand why Archibald was disinclined to leave them any bequest."

She went to the bookcases. "There are a number of bound volumes here that appear to be journals." She opened one of the glass doors, removed a random volume, and opened it. "Oh . . ." Her voice carried a note of disappointment. "This is a ledger."

"You hoped for a private diary?"

"Surely a diary would provide more interesting reading than a forty-year-old list of accounts." Her gaze swept the rest of the shelves. "These are all ledgers, from the look of them." She reshelved the ledger in her hand and withdrew several more volumes, one at a time, from the topmost shelf. "The most recent transactions are from September 1781."

"The last full year of Archibald Hollis's life." Darcy replaced the letters he had been examining. "The books that followed must be among Lady Denham's records elsewhere. It would appear that she does not use this room at all—indeed I am in some doubt as to whether she has even entered it in the past five-and-thirty years."

"I tell you, it is the bear. He is as good as a night watchman." She put the ledger back into place and bent to retrieve a volume from the lowest shelf.

"What are you seeking?"

"Nothing—this book's spine was facing the wrong direction, and its nonconformity bothers me."

"I am sure Mr. Hollis's ghost will appreciate your attending to it. Perhaps that is the reason his spirit has been unable to rest these several decades."

"Continue teasing me and *you* will be unable to rest for several decades." Despite her words, her tone was playful, and her expression belied any true vexation. She turned over the volume and opened its cover. "It is Victor Hollis who would haunt the room over this ledger. It is more than eighty years old—1732 through 1734. Shall we see what transactions occupied Old Hollis's attention on this date in history?"

"If doing so will divert you."

"Who would not find old accounting records diverting?"

She leafed through numerous pages. "Rents collected . . . servants' wages, housekeeper's allowance for stores and supplies . . . monthly pin money to Mrs. Hollis—a stingy amount, I must say. Poor woman! . . . His tailor, however, was well paid for a coat—" She lifted her gaze to study Darcy. "Perhaps the one you are wearing . . . Oxford tutorage for Trinity term—I suppose that must have been for Archibald . . ." She stopped paging and ran her finger down a column. "Here we are—one hundred years ago today. Purchase of two dozen sheep . . . a masonry bill for repairs to the dining room fireplace . . ." She broke off, her eyes narrowing as she studied one of the entries. "Hmmm."

Darcy waited in expectation. After a moment, she looked up.

"There is a fairly considerable sum deducted without any notation at all."

"How considerable?"

"Two thousand pounds."

"Considerable, indeed. Are there other entries without explanation?"

She paged through more of the volume. "None that I see. In fact, he notes individual expenditures of minute quantities, down to shillings given to the poor. He was certainly a man who monitored his money closely."

"Are you saying he would approve Lady Denham's management of Sanditon House?"

"I am not certain about that. He seems to have been willing to part with his money in order to maintain a comfortable style of living— he paid a handsome price for a desk that I believe is the one at which you are seated now. He was simply very conscious of where every penny went."

"That makes the lack of notation for a two-thousand-pound expenditure all the more curious." If there were more such irregularities, Darcy might suspect that Victor Hollis, or another member of his family, had been given to gambling or some other vice. A single outlay, however, could have been spent on anything. "Regardless, whatever he spent the money on, a purchase made one hundred years ago cannot be relevant to our present mission." He replaced the remaining letters he had been examining, closed the drawer, and stood. "We are not going to find anything in this room of help to Lady Denham or Susan Parker, and we lose more time the longer we linger here."

"I am more than ready to depart and leave behind our furry friend on the wall. This evening's events are unsettling enough without a constant sense of being observed."

They locked the study and headed to Lady Denham's apartment, where Elizabeth hoped more than expected to find the dowager's will conveniently awaiting their discovery. What she did not anticipate was detecting a slight movement in a darkened room they passed en route. Nor, upon stopping to determine its source, discovering a lone Mr. Granville in the shadows.

"Mister—"

He quickly put a finger to his lips and motioned them back into the corridor with him. "I am following Josiah Hollis," he said in a whisper. "At least, I was." He glanced with some concern at the doorway of the room he had just left. "I was hoping you would not see me and give me away."

Elizabeth regretted her imprudent tongue. Why had she not sensed the need for silence?

"What has he been doing?" Darcy asked.

"After Sidney and I parted ways, I returned to my chamber as planned, to monitor Hollis. However, upon hearing no sounds within his chamber, I could not be certain whether he occupied it, or had slipped out before I was able to double back. I knocked on his door with a pretense prepared if he answered. When he did not, I thought I had better commence a search of my own. His rancor over the disposition of Archibald Hollis's estate and his resentment toward Lady Denham led me to suspect he might try to take advantage of her absence to cause trouble, so I proceeded first to her apartment. He was indeed there—I caught sight of him with his hand upon the latch."

"Was he entering or leaving?"

"I assume he was about to enter, but I suppose he could have been leaving. Regardless, when he heard you descending the stairs, he ducked into that room"—he gestured toward the room in which Elizabeth had noticed him—"then the one beyond. I must say, for someone who claims to have not been in this house for forty years, he moves about it as confidently as if he still lived here. Fear not, however—I shan't lose him."

"Shall we come with you?" Elizabeth asked.

"Though I seldom refuse the offer of a lady's company, in this case I think our purpose is better served if I follow him alone. Three are noisier than one, and unfortunately he still hears well for a man his age."

Darcy nodded. "We will check the apartment."

"Are you not soon reconvening in the portrait room with the others?"

"We have time."

"Not much. Were I you, I would head there directly." Mr. Granville glanced at the doorway again. "As for myself, I must catch up with old Josiah before he outpaces me. I do not believe his lumbago complaints for a moment. He is a crafty one, and will probably deny this whole midnight stroll ever took place should any of us ever confront him about it. But I shall stay on his trail until he returns to his chamber. You will understand if I do not appear in the portrait room at the appointed time?"

"Of course," Darcy said. "Report back to me when you are able."

Mr. Granville resumed his pursuit of Josiah with as much haste as the need for stealth allowed. Elizabeth and Darcy continued to Lady Denham's apartment.

"It is fortunate that Mr. Granville volunteered to monitor Mr. Hollis," Elizabeth said as Darcy produced the key and opened the door. "Although Josiah must have found this door locked, we might never have known that he attempted to enter."

They stepped inside. Darcy cast his gaze about the antechamber. "If you were Lady Denham, where would you store your will?"

"I trust you mean *other* than all of the places we have already looked?" Though Elizabeth had been in the suite previously, she tried to assess its rooms and furnishings from a new perspective—Lady Denham's. The antechamber was primarily a private sitting room with a small sofa and chairs of varying degrees of comfort. Its tables offered surfaces where one could set a workbox or candle or writing materials; a few held vases of flowers heavily fragrant in the humid air; none had drawers or other receptacles where a will might reside.

"I do not see any likely locations in here," Elizabeth said. "Even if there were a writing-bureau, I somehow think Lady Denham might not keep important documents in the most public of her private rooms—the chamber through which everyone from friends to servants to her dressmaker enters the suite, or where she might sit with Miss Brereton or other intimate acquaintances. Rather, I see her storing the will—if it resides in these rooms at all—deeper in the apartment—her dressing room or bedchamber. Lady Denham impresses me as someone who might sleep more easily at night in the close proximity of a document that makes her feel in control."

"I hoped our quest would not necessitate so great an invasion of her privacy."

"I, too, do not feel entirely comfortable searching in the bedchamber, even though we do so out of anxiety for her safety. Let us first try the dressing room. We have already been in there, though not with the will in mind."

She passed into the dressing room, now noting with new interest the tallboy, a second, shorter chest of drawers, and the great walnut wardrobe. A door that she presumed opened into a closet also held promise. The room certainly hosted plenty of drawers and other places in which a will could be hidden.

Elizabeth headed toward the shorter bureau, detouring slightly around the dressing table seat, which was standing a foot or so out from its table. "Do you want to start with the tallboy while I look through the smaller chest?"

Darcy regarded both pieces of furniture warily. "I am more inclined toward the wardrobe."

"Do you think Lady Denham is more likely to have concealed her will in a hatbox?"

"No, but I would rather leave to you any accidental encounter with her"—he cleared his throat—"inexpressibles."

Elizabeth laughed. "I had not considered that. Yes—far better for you to search the wardrobe. I also grant you the closet as your province." She turned to the chest of drawers, not herself particularly relishing the thought of rifling through Lady Denham's undergarments. Perhaps, however, such disinclination would make a drawer full of shifts and stays the ideal place to secrete a will or other papers from too-curious eyes. Though a determined spy would proceed undeterred, an opportunistic busybody might not think to nose there.

The chests of drawers yielded nightdresses, stockings, and handkerchiefs in abundance, along with a generous supply of gloves and other accoutrements. Unfortunately, the only document she found was a folded advertisement for a shop in Cheapside.

JOHN FLUDE
Pawnbroker and Silversmith
No. 2 Gracechurch Street, London

Lends Money on Plate, Watches, Jewells, Wearing Apparel,
Household Goods & Stock in Trade

NB

Goods Sent from any Part of the Country directed as above,
shall be duly attended to & the Utmost Value lent thereon.

"What have you there?" Darcy asked.

"The trade card of a Mr. John Flude, pawnbroker and silversmith." She read the remainder of the text aloud, then glanced at Darcy. "I wonder how Lady Denham came to be in possession of this?"

"As her financial circumstances do not appear to necessitate pawning the china, it was probably thrust into her hand by a bill-boy sometime during her stay with her cousins in Gracechurch Street. Do not you typically return home with two or three such advertisements after a morning's shopping in London?"

"Yes," she admitted. Often the trade cards were for goods or services of which she had no need, or for which she already had a preferred merchant, but she could not bring herself to turn away the children hired to distribute them to passersby. "However, I usually discard those that do not interest me. Yet Lady Denham saved this one—for years, by the look and feel of it. In fact—"

Elizabeth studied the handbill more closely, her attention drawn to the illustration of Mr. Flude's storefront. Two entrances flanked a large bank of windows and display case filled with all manner of goods. The left entrance was a glass-paned door with signs on either side of it bearing the pawnbroker's trademark three balls and the words "Money Lent"; above the door, a large, ornate oval sign announced "Wardrobes bought in Town & Country." The other entrance was a less conspicuous solid wooden door with a small engraved plate she could not read. Near it, but above the front windows rather than the door itself, a matching oval sign stated "Unredeemed Goods sold Wholesale & Retail." A third oval sign in the center bore Flude's name in large letters.

She met Darcy's waiting gaze. "I believe I am familiar with this shop."

"A pawnshop?"

"Not as a customer—in passing. It is not far from my uncle Gardiner's house. I did not recognize it at first, for Mr. Flude is no longer its proprietor. Another broker now does business there. At any rate, there is no mistaking the dual entrances." She handed Darcy the trade card so he could see the depiction for himself.

"It appears that one is for the general public come to pledge their worldly possessions for ready money," he said, "and the other is for those of a higher class come for the same purpose but desiring more privacy in which to conduct the transaction."

"Or perhaps hoping to discover a bargain amongst the unclaimed items of their peers."

"Which do you think was Lady Denham's purpose in patronizing Mr. Flude's shop—assuming she ever entered it?"

"The latter—it is a happier thought than the former. Regardless, whether she went to buy or sell, I have no doubt that she drove a hard bargain. She prides herself on knowing the value of money—she boasted of such to me herself. She would not have left the shop without whatever it was she went there for, and some concession from Mr. Flude in the transaction."

She refolded the advertisement, returned it to the drawer with Lady Denham's reticules, and turned her attention to the dressing table. She doubted Lady Denham would keep important papers in drawers constantly being accessed by her lady's maid in search of hair combs and night creams, but she checked them nonetheless. As she shut the last drawer, her gaze scanned the tabletop. Something about the items resting on it troubled her.

"Have you found something?" Darcy asked.

"No—the opposite. I think something is missing since we were last here, but I cannot identify what." She studied the various bottles, tins, and tools—until, finally, it came to her.

"One of the phials is missing—the medicines Diana sent over." She picked up the remaining one. It was the sorrel root remedy. "The sedative is gone."

"Indeed? Perhaps Diana recalled its existence and asked for it to be retrieved for Susan's use when we find her."

"Perhaps—we must remember to ask Mrs. Riley. I believe she is the only person besides ourselves who has a key." She put the sorrel root concoction back on the table. "Have you discovered anything?"

"Nothing even half so interesting as your trade card. Certainly not Lady Denham's will." Darcy shut the closet. "Only bonnets and boots."

He approached the bedroom door, where Elizabeth joined him. She reached for the latch, but paused as a thought struck her. "That in itself is extraordinary."

"The number of hats Lady Denham possesses? I think yours exceed—"

"No, the absence of something else. Forget, for a moment, the will. We have yet to come upon any of Lady Denham's correspondence. Your mother retained just about every missive she ever received, and copies of many she authored—trunks full of letters. While Lady Denham might not keep up nearly so large a volume of correspondence, we have yet to find so much as a letter case."

She pushed open the bedroom door. Neither of them entered. They both remained transfixed in the doorway.

Upon the bed, a wooden box lay open, its contents scattered on the quilt.

Darcy found his voice first.

"A letter case such as that one?"

Twenty

"I do not know that, in such a night as this, I could have answered for my courage: but now, to be sure, there is nothing to alarm one."
—*Catherine Morland*, Northanger Abbey

*C*harlotte raced down the corridor, her gaze sweeping every corner, arch, and niche she passed. The open doorways were the worst—gaping portals of murkiness that her vision could not penetrate.

Her rational self repeatedly told her that she had nothing to fear from the darkness. Despite the stories of servants and villagers, the spirit of Archibald Hollis did *not* inhabit Sanditon House. Nor had the ghost of Ivy Woodcock come inside to escape the rain.

Her irrational self was not quite so convinced.

She had heard no further noises in Miss Parker's room, but she could not shake the sensation of being observed. It had come upon her so strongly that the thought of sitting alone in her own chamber— even with a light—unnerved her. A few minutes in the company of others would restore her courage. She most particularly wanted the companionship of Elizabeth Darcy, whom she knew best of all the party, and whose gentle nature and humor she trusted to alleviate her anxiety.

Where to find Mrs. Darcy, however, was almost as great a mystery as where to find Susan Parker. Charlotte did not expect to discover either of the Darcys in their apartment—they would be elsewhere in the house, searching for Susan like the others. However, she decided to start her own quest with their quarters anyway. Doing so made more sense than hoping to randomly encounter them, or attempting to find her way to the stillroom, the only specific location mentioned in the company's discussion of the search. The Darcys' chamber gave her a destination, the way to which she knew.

She would not think too closely about the fact that their chamber also belonged to Archibald Hollis, who could even now be haunting his former abode.

Thunder rumbled, signaling a renewal of the storm's strength, and within minutes the sound of heavier rainfall muffled that of her own steps. She was approaching the long gallery, through which she would cut to reach the Darcys' quarters—and, she hoped, their companionship.

At least, she believed she neared the gallery. She rued having left behind her candle. She had fled the Parker sisters' chamber so unsettled that she had not wanted to enter another shadowy room—even her own—to retrieve it. The sconces in the corridors would suffice, she had told herself, not realizing how widely they were scattered until she passed more empty holders and unlit tapers than dependable flames—evidence of Lady Denham's boasted frugality. At the moment, she could do with more light and less economy.

Nor had she considered that her journey would take her through a maze of interconnected rooms that opened into each other but not the main corridor. Presently unlit by fire, sconce, or sunlight, they defied easy navigation, and as she stumbled through the latest series of rooms, she began to wonder whether she had taken a wrong turn at some point. She did not remember the distance being so great. Perhaps, however, the disorientation wrought upon her senses by the darkness made both the distance and the minutes spent traversing it seem longer than they were.

After what seemed an interminable amount of time, she found the gallery and entered. Now she truly was observed—by generations of late Hollises scarcely discernible in their frames. She strode past the portraits as quickly as she dared, keeping to the middle of the narrow room. In her haste, she tripped over a buckled strip of the rug that ran down its length, and nearly pitched forward. The moment of panic before she caught her balance convinced her that she would do better to aim her gaze downward to avoid similar hazards rather than nervously shift it from side to side. Her own feet posed greater danger than barely visible images of long-dead forebears and spectres of her imagination.

As she reached the end of the gallery, she turned sharply to exit—and slammed headlong into a shadowed but unquestionably solid figure.

Her soft cry of surprise turned to a gasp of alarm as the man reached out and seized her upper arms. Heart pounding, she tried to step back, but he held her fast. His head moved close to hers as he peered at her intently.

"Miss Heywood?"

His voice penetrated her panic. He had spoken her name as a question, and sounded as startled as she. Charlotte widened her eyes in the dimness, trying to make out his features.

"Miss Heywood, you are positively shaking. Are you well?" The voice was familiar, as was the faint outline of his countenance.

"Mr. Parker?"

"Yes—Sidney Parker."

A distant flash of lightning illuminated the gallery just long enough to confirm his identity. She released breath she did not realize she had been holding, involuntarily issuing a sound of relief that was half gasp, half sob.

"Are you injured?" he asked.

Several deep breaths followed as she worked to regain her composure under Sidney's scrutinizing gaze. She was grateful for the darkness that obscured her face from clear view. "No—only rattled."

"Dear Miss Heywood! Of course you are, being knocked about and then seized by an unknown man in the dark." He loosened his grip on her arms and dropped one hand down to his side. "Forgive my catching you in such an ungentlemanlike manner—I acted instinctively, fearing our collision had thrown you off balance, or caused you to swoon." His other hand moved to her elbow, continuing to offer support. "Indeed, I fear you may swoon yet."

"I am not generally given to swooning."

"You do not impress me as the type of lady who makes a habit of it. However, I did nearly knock you down, so swooning or some other dramatic response is well within your rights."

Now that the initial surprise of encountering Sidney had passed, her nerves steadied. "I shall reserve that right for some greater occasion."

"Well, let us hope such an occasion does not arrive soon. This evening has proven eventful enough already." He paused. "Do accept my apologies for all but charging into you, and for having frightened you so. I neither saw nor heard your approach."

"Nor I yours." She did not add that she had already done a thorough job of frightening herself before he happened upon her. "Let us not argue for the greater share of blame."

"I would not argue with you, Miss Heywood, for anything. I take the full responsibility upon myself. Heavens—you started as if you had seen a ghost."

"No, only heard one."

The words were out before she considered them. Why had she said that? Now he would enquire into her meaning. She recalled Thomas Parker's statement that Sidney was a person who could say anything and get away with it. The same disarming charm that enabled him to speak freely, led others—her, at least—to reveal more than intended.

"Just one? I should think this room is full of them. Which of these dreary-looking Hollises has been haunting you?"

"None of them. I thought I heard someone enter your sisters' room, but I was mistaken."

"Indeed? What makes you think you were mistaken?"

He yet supported her forearm, and as a consequence, stood very close—close enough for them to partially see each other's faces despite the lack of light—closer than she was accustomed to standing with gentlemen not her brothers, especially after midnight in a darkened house. The proximity tipped her equilibrium in a manner different from when they had bumped into each other. She was reassured by his companionship in the gloom, yet acutely alert to his nearness.

"I went into their chamber, believing Susan might have returned in need of assistance. But there was nobody in the room at all."

Saying this aloud, to Sidney Parker, made the incident seem rather mundane, and she blushed to recall the anxiety she had experienced at the time. She had allowed her imagination to run as unfettered as those of Sidney's sisters, perceiving symptoms that did not exist, exaggerating ordinary conditions into unusual. Sanditon House was an old, drafty place; the night, extraordinarily windy. The sounds she had taken for the chamber door being opened and closed were probably nothing more than it rattling in its frame in response to the gale outside.

Another flash of lightning briefly lit Sidney's face. She had expected to read amusement or derision in his expression, but saw only sincere interest. "How long ago was this?"

"I am not certain—it is difficult to gauge time by oneself in darkness. Perhaps half an hour after everybody departed the corridor?" She remembered that Sidney had left with Mr. Granville to seek Susan. "Where is Mr. Granville, by the way?"

"We separated, to cover more of the house." He separated from Charlotte now by dropping his hand from her forearm. He did not, however, increase the distance between them.

"That explains why you have no candle," she said. "Otherwise, I would have seen its glow and avoided our collision."

"I am glad, then, that I gave it away, for I confess to enjoying this opportunity to converse with you despite the circumstances that brought it about."

In truth, she was beginning to enjoy Sidney Parker's conversation and companionship rather more than might be wise. She wished for another flash of lightning, to better read his countenance, but all night long the storm had blown contrary to the preferences of any occupant of Sanditon House, and it continued its willfulness.

"The sounds you heard in my sisters' room—" Sidney continued. "Have you reported them to Mr. Darcy?"

"Not yet—I was seeking him and Mrs. Darcy just now."

"I would not trouble him with the information, since it came to naught."

"All the same, I would like to speak with Mrs. Darcy before returning to my chamber." She did not wish to reenter the deserted wing alone. "Have you encountered the Darcys, or any of the others who are searching for your sister?"

"I have seen Diana and Arthur—though fortunately for them, not as closely as I encountered you just now."

"I take it they had not found Miss Parker yet?"

"No, but I believe Diana intended to explore the entire house in the space of an hour, for Arthur was struggling to keep up with her. If they have not found Susan, perhaps someone else has by now. We are all to reconvene very soon; in fact, I was heading back when you waylaid me. Everyone has probably gathered while we have been talking." He offered his hand. "As we are both without lights, shall we navigate together this labyrinth of a house? I volunteer to pioneer the way and fend off any other inmates—corporeal or not—who come at us."

She accepted his hand. His grip was firm but gentle, and she had not realized how cold her fingers were until she felt the warmth of his. They set off in the direction from which she had just come, he leading by two paces to guard against any rogue floorboards, furnishings, or buckled carpets that might suddenly emerge to menace them.

"And how is it that *you* came to be wandering the house with no candle?" Sidney asked as he guided her along a route so circuitous that she utterly lost her orientation. "Or did you deliberately contrive to plough through me as repayment for the earlier misbehavior of my hat?"

"I left it behind in haste," she said. "In hindsight, that was not a prudent decision."

"Indeed not." They entered a corridor new to her, one so black that she could only follow him in blind trust.

"You never know whom you might run into, in the dark."

Twenty-one

The window curtains seemed in motion. It could be nothing but the violence of the wind penetrating through the divisions of the shutters; and she stepped boldly forward, carelessly humming a tune, to assure herself of its being so.

—Northanger Abbey

*D*arcy's mood as he and Elizabeth approached the portrait room was as gloomy as the house itself. The letter case they had found open on Lady Denham's bed contained numerous items of business correspondence—but no will. He could only hope that whoever had rifled the box had also failed to find the will among its contents. The alternative—that the document was now in the intruder's hands—would compound the difficulties of an already challenging investigation.

"Let us keep the discovery of the ransacked papers to ourselves for the time being," he said. "Mr. Granville's report of Josiah Hollis's movements casts him in greatest suspicion, but nearly every guest has been roaming the house this past hour. Any one of them could have rummaged through that letter case."

"Any one of them who found a way to penetrate the apartment's entrance," Elizabeth corrected. "How does one pass through a locked door?"

Darcy had been pondering that very question the whole of their walk from Lady Denham's bedchamber to the portrait room. Along the way they had stopped in their own quarters to hide the box and its remaining contents—not that he harbored illusions about the locked door of Archibald Hollis's former apartment offering any greater security than that of Lady Denham's. At least, however, Archibald's apartment was above the ground floor, reducing the potential of entry through a window.

"Several of the guests could know where a key might be surreptitiously borrowed. Josiah Hollis did, after all, tell us earlier this evening that as a boy he freely roamed all over this house, and judging from the age and demeanor of the housekeeper, I venture to say very little has changed around here in the past half century."

"If it has, Sir Edward and Miss Denham possess more familiarity with the current state of the house."

"As does Miss Brereton."

"Surely you do not believe Miss Brereton would so violate the privacy of her benefactress?" Elizabeth asked.

"No, but we cannot rule her out solely on instinct. I expect that when we reach the portrait room, her report, corroborated by Thomas Parker, will remove her from suspicion. The Denham siblings, on the other hand, have to the best of our knowledge each spent this hour solitarily, and have only their own word to vouch their whereabouts."

"And Josiah Hollis?"

"I think it goes without saying that I am particularly impatient to question Mr. Hollis about his nocturnal wanderings."

"Mr. Granville cautioned us that Josiah would likely deny leaving his room."

"Then we shall have to catch him in the lie."

"What of the other guests? We are assuming that because you and I were searching for Lady Denham's will, the intruder entered with the same motive. Have you considered that he or she might have been seeking something else entirely?"

"I have." He believed he had considered all possibilities, even Susan Parker as the intruder—however unlikely, that would explain where she had disappeared to—but immediately dismissed the notion as utterly improbable. "In my opinion, expanding the list of possible motives increases our pool by only one legitimate suspect: Thomas Parker. He could have a business interest in examining Lady Denham's papers. As for the rest of the Parkers and Miss Heywood, I do not think any one of them possesses a motive or the means to access those documents."

"If Diana Parker believed there was something in Lady Denham's apartment that would lead her to Susan, I think she would find a way to obtain it even if doing so required breaking the door down herself."

"But it was not broken down; the intruder acted covertly. This was not a casual, opportunistic glance at something left in one's path. Gaining entry to a locked suite requires work and forethought, especially if done in secret."

Their arrival at the portrait room ended their conversation for the present, for they entered to find Miss Brereton and Thomas Parker waiting within. Though the pair's candles struggled valiantly to illuminate the space, the atmosphere of defeat that hung over them created its own darkness.

"We discovered no sign of Susan," Mr. Parker reported, his voice and manner a subdued echo of his normal exuberance. "We searched the entire ground floor, and also looked into my sisters' bedchamber just now. It remains empty—Diana is not there, either."

"The others will join us soon," Elizabeth said. "Perhaps they had better luck."

"I certainly hope so," Mr. Parker replied. "This is entirely unlike Susan—going off somewhere without telling anybody. Diana ofttimes will get a notion in her head and fly away in pursuit of it with such urgency that she does not pause to communicate her intentions, but Susan's determination does not manifest itself quite so impulsively."

"All the more reason to believe that there is a perfectly reasonable explanation for her absence," Elizabeth reassured him, "just as we hope there is one for Lady Denham's. By chance, did your exploration of the ground floor happen to include Lady Denham's apartment?"

"It would have, if we could have entered it."

"The door was locked," Miss Brereton said, "just as you left it earlier tonight, so we assumed Miss Parker could not have entered the apartment, either, and continued on."

"I cannot think why Susan would have had any reason to go in there, anyway," Mr. Parker added.

"Nor can I," Elizabeth said. "I enquired in hope that perhaps something within sparked your or Miss Brereton's memory of a clue to either of the ladies' whereabouts."

"Did you encounter anybody else in that part of the house?" Darcy asked. "The search for your sister was, as a whole, not undertaken in the most organized manner—we should have assigned areas of the house more specifically, so as not to waste time duplicating efforts or neglecting some areas altogether on the assumption others were exploring them."

"We saw Sidney, but he reported no better luck than ours."

"While you were in the corridor with all the bedchambers, did you speak with Miss Heywood? As her room adjoins that of your sisters, she stayed behind to watch for Susan's return."

"We were unaware that she remained," Miss Brereton said. "I heard no sounds within her chamber."

"Nor did I," said Mr. Parker.

"I am surprised she did not hear you and emerge," Elizabeth replied. "Perhaps she fell asleep. I will look in on her."

Elizabeth had not been long gone when Arthur Parker appeared.

"There you are!" Thomas crossed the room to greet his brother, then glanced toward the doorway in expectation. It remained empty. "Diana is not with you?" His expression clouded for a moment, but optimism rapidly overtook his countenance. "Did you find Susan? Is Diana with her?"

Arthur shifted uncomfortably. Still stuffed into Archibald Hollis's too-small frock coat, he tugged at its sleeves. "We became separated."

"Separated? How could you have allowed that to happen? Your sole duty was to accompany her."

"I tried! Truly, Tom, I did—despite her constant complaint that I was slowing the pace of her search. But when we entered the morning room—"

"The morning room? Whatever would Susan be doing there?"

"I asked Diana that very thing, but she insisted that she heard someone moaning inside. Once she drew my attention to it, I heard the moaning, too. However, when we entered, we did not find Susan, nor any living creature—only the continued sound of moaning. I was certain it must be the ghost of Ivy Woodcock and wanted to leave at once, but Diana scoffed, and strode to the far side of the room. 'Here is your ghost,' she said. 'The window is not quite shut.' The wind howling through the casement *did* sound like someone moaning, but even worse—the air was so damp I thought it would surely prove the death of us both!

"I tried to close the window," Arthur continued, "but the wood was so swollen by the damp that it did not want to shut, and the wind kept driving against it from all the wrong angles. Diana lost patience and told me to step aside so she could close it herself, but then a sudden gust extinguished both our candles. So now the room was damp and dark! I said we should just forget about the window and move on to another room—any other room! But by then Diana was determined to conquer that window, and you know, Tom, how resolute our sister is once she sets her mind to something."

Thomas Parker replied with an exasperated sigh and resigned nod. "So, come to the point. If you were left in the dark, why on earth did you and Diana part?"

"We had passed a lit sconce in the corridor some way back, and she told me to go relight our candles while she shut the window. When I returned, she was gone. I—" His face flushed and he dropped his gaze, unable to meet his brother's eye. "I think she cast me off so she could continue searching without me."

While Darcy could easily imagine Diana Parker losing patience with Arthur, he thought even she would not have sent off her candle along with her brother if she intended to continue searching alone.

Thomas looked as if *he* would like to cast off his youngest brother, but held his ire in check. "It would not be the first time she diverted one of us so that she could carry on some scheme unhindered," he conceded. "Did you look for her in nearby rooms?"

"I did, but failed to find her in any of them. I knew it was almost time for us all to meet here, so I came hoping that she had made her way back on her own."

"Well, she has not, has she? And now thanks to you, both our sisters are missing."

Arthur reddened and busied himself in trying to tug his too-short cuffs over his wrists. After a minute of charged silence, Darcy attempted to defuse the fraternal tension.

"The window in the morning room—was it closed when you returned?"

"No," Arthur said. "In fact, I think the wind pushed it open even farther after Diana left."

A movement at the edge of his vision prompted Darcy to look toward the door. Mr. Granville entered. Diverted by Arthur's report, Darcy had not heard him approach the portrait room. His eyes looked past the gentleman to the corridor beyond, impatient for Elizabeth's return. How long could it take to rouse a sleeping Miss Heywood? Diana's unexplained absence made him anxious for his wife's presence, as proof that she, too, had not mysteriously disappeared. His gaze, however, met only disappointment.

Mr. Granville stopped short just inside the room, conscious of the many eyes suddenly upon him. "I must say, none of you looks happy to see me."

"We were hoping you were Diana," Arthur said.

"I might not appear quite myself in Archibald Hollis's clothing, but I draw the line at petticoats." His attempt at humor falling upon a less-than-jovial audience, Mr. Granville cleared his throat. "I see we are but partially assembled. Is there any news?"

"Susan still has not been discovered." Thomas directed a stern look at Arthur. "And now Diana is missing."

"We do not know that!" Arthur said. "She will probably walk in here any minute—maybe even with Susan."

Mr. Granville regarded Arthur with surprise. "She was with you when Sidney and I crossed your path earlier. Did you accidentally misplace her?"

Arthur's countenance settled into a sulk as he looked from his brother to Mr. Granville. "It is a long story."

"Well, I am sure she is fine," Mr. Granville said. "Your sister seems a lady quite capable of taking care of herself. My guess is that she merely lost track of the time, which is easy to do in the dark. Or perhaps she is with Sidney, as he, too, has not yet returned."

Arthur brightened somewhat at this suggestion. "There—you see,

Tom? That makes sense. Diana would not object to Sidney as an escort, and he is much better suited than I to manage her. We have only to wait patiently for them to finish their exploration. At the pace she was going, they cannot be long." He took a seat—the first among them to do so—thus demonstrating the ease of his now-pardoned conscience.

Darcy, however, was troubled by Arthur's earlier report, particularly because the morning room was on the first, not the ground, floor. "Mr. Parker," he said to Arthur, "is the window large enough that when your sister continued to struggle with it after your departure, she might have fallen *out* of it?"

"Good G—d!" Thomas exclaimed before Arthur could reply. "I had not even considered that possibility." He turned to Arthur. "Upon your return, did you look out the window—down below?"

"No." Arthur's complexion turned a pasty shade, with beads of perspiration that had nothing to do with the fire in the hearth. "But even if I had, it is so dark outside that I could not have seen—"

Thomas was halfway out the door. Arthur leaped off the sofa and followed him, moving with more rapidity than Darcy had heretofore witnessed or even believed him capable.

"Well!" Mr. Granville exclaimed. "Odd as it sounds to say, I hope they do not find her."

Twenty-two

Miss Denham's character was pretty well decided with Charlotte.

—Sanditon

*A*s Elizabeth approached Charlotte's room, she met Sir Edward coming down the hall. His rapid strides ceased abruptly when he reached her.

"Mrs. Darcy." He offered a courtly bow. "You appear to be a lady with a mission. Is it I you seek?" His gaze searched her countenance with intensity.

"No—I am on my way to Miss Heywood's room."

"Miss Heywood! Is all well with her?"

"So far as I know."

"And Miss Brereton?"

"I left her but moments ago in perfect safety, with Mr. Darcy and Mr. Parker in the portrait room."

"Thank heavens! It would not do for another lady to go missing. We have lost too many as it is. What have you learned of Miss Parker?"

"Nothing yet, but we are still awaiting the return of the others. Perhaps one of them will bring news, or better still, the lady herself."

"We can but hope!" Sir Edward lifted a hand to his head, gripping his hair at the crown before sliding his fingers through to the back.

"This is all so very perplexive—first Lady Denham, and now Miss Parker. Whither can those ladies have wandered?"

The baronet's fingers left a thin white string trailing from his hair. Elizabeth noticed a similar one clinging to the cuff of his coat.

"Sir Edward—"

"What an extraordinary course of events. A series of missing women! The stuff of novels—"

"I would not call two a series. But Sir Edward—"

"Only two—of course! Of course you are right! Two is not a series. There must be three—or more—for a series, and we have only two. *Thankfully,* only two—"

"Sir Edward!" She forced her voice above his, earning a startled reaction and a blessed moment of silence. "You have something caught in your hair." She gestured toward the side of his head.

"I— Oh? Oh! Dear me!" He reached up to brush it away, but the effort resulted only in its being caught more firmly between strands of his hair. "Is it gone?"

"I am afraid not." She extended a tentative hand. "Would you like me to—"

"Yes, please." He leaned his head toward her.

The thread clung to his hair, but she loosened it and pulled it free. It was a fine, delicate strand, the end of which floated up to touch her forearm.

"I believe this is a cobweb," she said. "My goodness, Sir Edward, whither have *you* been wandering?"

"A cobweb!" He brushed the sleeves and lapels of his coat so vigorously that Elizabeth wondered whether the would-be cavalier harbored a fear of spiders. "I have not left the house—not at all. I have been—" He reached around, trying to brush off his back, but in the process he rotated in place until Elizabeth was reminded of a dog chasing its tail. "I have been—"

She took pity on him. "Sir, if you will but hold still." She examined the back of his coat, finding two additional strands that she silently removed and let drift to the floor.

"Thank you." He tugged self-consciously at the cuffs of his coat, attempting—not altogether successfully—to restore order to his appearance. "I have been in the attics," he said.

"The attics? Whatever took you there?"

"My search for Miss Parker, of course. All the rest of you were searching the main house—but did anybody think to check the attics? Miss Parker could just as easily have wandered up there as anywhere else. *Someone* needed to investigate, so I took the duty upon myself."

It seemed to Elizabeth that the attics were the least likely place Susan Parker would have reason to visit, but the lady displayed so many peculiarities that one could not put past her any unexpected behavior, lending a sort of convoluted logic to Sir Edward's decision. She was nevertheless a little surprised that he had chosen to search a remote area of the house, rather than one that might result in a chance crossing of paths with Miss Brereton.

"Of course," Sir Edward continued, "the attics are the most probable abode of a ghost."

Elizabeth silently and immediately retracted the credit she had given Sir Edward for demonstrating logic of any sort.

"You were ghost-hunting?"

Sir Edward laughed. "Ghost-hunting? No, no—that would be absurd."

His denial granted her a measure of relief—she could dismiss her visions of him sweeping the attics to engage in quixotic tilts at spectres.

Unfortunately, the baronet then added, "I believe it quite possible that Sanditon House's resident ghost, or perhaps Ivy Woodcock, has spirited away the missing ladies. But as I was not properly equipped to hunt ghosts, I was prepared to devise a more resourceful plan for liberating the captives."

Elizabeth was not unsympathetic to belief in spirits, or the possibility of them influencing the affairs of the living. It seemed nearly every castle and half the great houses in Britain boasted at least one. Indeed, there were times at Pemberley when she almost certainly felt the gentle presence of Darcy's late mother, and early in her marriage, she and Darcy had experienced an encounter in London that even Darcy could not deny had brought them in contact with a restless shade. Now, however, it was precisely those experiences that instinctively told her the disappearances of Lady Denham and Susan Parker

were not the work of otherworldly beings, but of something or someone very much still part of this world.

"It was gallant of you to venture up there alone. What did you
find?"

"Nothing! Nothing at all—alas, my quest was in vain. But, I hope,
no less noble for the undertaking."

"Indeed not."

"Well . . ." For one of the few times since Elizabeth met the baronet, he seemed at a loss for words. His hands flexed, then relaxed;
his gaze jumped about, seeking a place to rest that was anywhere but
upon her. After a half minute's awkward silence, he cleared his throat
and extended a bent arm. "Shall we proceed to the portrait room?"

"Actually, I was about to collect Miss Heywood from her chamber."

"Then I shall have the pleasure of escorting two lovely ladies. Do
remind me—which chamber is hers? So many doors line this corridor, all of them identical, that I can scarcely identify my own."

"Hers is this one." She knocked on the door before which they
stood. "In fact, I am surprised the sound of our voices has not brought
her out already."

Upon receiving no response to her knock, she repeated it, louder
this time—though she hoped not loud enough to disturb Miss Denham, whom she would just as soon leave hibernating through the
winter and into the following spring. "Miss Heywood? It is Elizabeth
Darcy. Are you awake? The others are gathering in the portrait room."

Still no sound from within. Elizabeth turned to Sir Edward. "She
must have fallen asleep."

Before he could reply, a different door opened.

"*What* is that pounding?"

Elizabeth winced inwardly. Forget the stuffed bear in the study;
they had wakened a sleeping one right here.

"My dear sister!" Sir Edward quickly went to her. "I am glad to find
you still awake."

"Awake?" Miss Denham stepped just outside her doorway, her wrap
pulled tightly about her and her hair loosely woven into a braid that
hung down her back. "I was not awake. Not until I heard your incessant pounding."

"It was not incessant, it was not mine, and it was not— Oh, never mind. You are awake now. We can ask you whether you heard anything this past hour that might shed light on Miss Parker's whereabouts."

"No. And I see no reason why her decision to roam about the house should prevent my obtaining a proper night's rest. Or interfere with yours, for that matter." She lowered her voice. "Cannot Mrs. Darcy's husband escort her? If the two of them insist upon inserting themselves in this affair, why must you be inconvenienced?"

Though this last sentiment presumably had not been intended to reach Elizabeth's ears, Elizabeth had already heard enough to produce an earnest desire to part company with the Denham siblings. "Pray excuse me while I check on Miss Heywood. Good night, Miss Denham." She turned to the baronet. "Sir, Miss Heywood and I will meet you in the portrait room, or see you upon the morrow, as you choose."

"I will proceed to the portrait room with all due haste the moment I have done with my sister. Should you have need of me before then, I am at your service." He bowed with a flourish.

Miss Denham rolled her eyes and sighed heavily.

Elizabeth opened Miss Heywood's door and quietly slipped into the chamber. Though she doubted Charlotte yet slept with conversation transpiring immediately outside the room, Elizabeth did not want her intrusion to startle the young woman. She soon discovered, however, that her caution was unwarranted.

The chamber was vacant.

The bedclothes had been disturbed, indicating that Miss Heywood had lain down before quitting the room. Uneasiness settled upon her as she regarded the empty bed and contemplated Susan's similarly unoccupied one in the adjacent chamber. What had caused Charlotte to rise and leave? Susan Parker's return?

Or Susan Parker's abductor?

Elizabeth had not wanted to believe that anyone but Lady Denham and Miss Parker had been responsible for their own absences. But now three ladies had disappeared from their bedchambers. Two could be coincidence. But three?

Three suggested a plan, one not of their own design.

One that was possibly not yet complete.

A sweep of her gaze revealed nothing else out of place, no evidence of struggle or forced entry. She inhaled deeply, attempting to slow her racing mind. Was she merely allowing the storm and shadows to prey upon her anxiety? Miss Heywood might have left her chamber for some perfectly mundane reason. In fact, she might even now be waiting in the portrait room with the others.

She entered the bedchamber more fully, so that her candle could illuminate its farther reaches. An extinguished candle rested on a table beside the bed, its sides and silver holder coated with hardened wax drippings. Though the half-expired taper stood unobtrusively minding its own business, something about it troubled Elizabeth. She studied it a few moments, then realized what disturbed her.

The candle itself—its very presence. Miss Heywood had quit the room without it.

Apprehension settled upon her as she contemplated circumstances under which Miss Heywood might leave the room without a means of lighting her way through the dark corridors. She did not like where those thoughts took her . . . or Miss Heywood.

She needed to return to the portrait room immediately. There, she might find Miss Heywood and rejoice to have her anxiety proved entirely unfounded, or someone else might know the young woman's whereabouts.

She reentered the corridor and firmly shut Miss Heywood's door. As she turned in the direction of the staircase, voices from Miss Denham's chamber caught her attention. Apparently, Sir Edward and his sister had moved inside to continue their conversation. Their words were muffled, but suddenly the door opened and Sir Edward stepped out.

"This whole situation is beyond my ability to remedy, and I want no part of it," Miss Denham declared from within.

"You have made your opinion abundantly clear." Sir Edward's voice resonated with the irritation only a sibling squabble can produce. "I shall now do likewise. It is unconscionable of you to sequester yourself here whilst your help is needed. You have fifteen minutes to get dressed."

"I cannot possibly dress myself in fifteen—"

"You managed it well enough earlier. Too much time has passed already. Who knows what trouble those ladies have gotten themselves into even as we stand here debating the matter?"

Sir Edward closed the door, then turned to find Elizabeth regarding him. He seemed flustered by the surprise audience, and Elizabeth regretted embarrassing him by having accidentally overheard the Denhams' quarrel. The incident, however, actually raised him in her esteem; for all of Sir Edward's absurdities, the baronet believed it not only his duty to aid in the search for the missing ladies, but to rectify his sister's neglect of the same.

"Mrs. Darcy! I thought you and Miss Heywood had returned to the portrait room already."

"I am heading there now."

"And Miss Heywood?"

"She is not in her chamber."

"Indeed? I wonder where she could be. *I* have not seen her, I assure you. Perhaps she found her own way to the portrait room. Shall we go see?" He started forward.

"Does Miss Denham intend to join the rest of us there? If you wish to wait for her, you need not feel obliged to escort me."

"She . . ." He appeared uncertain what to say, no doubt wondering how much of their squall Elizabeth had overheard. "Yes—yes, she wants very much for this confusion to end and our missing friends to return. Of course she will join us. However, she needs a few minutes to prepare. Let us—you and me—proceed to the portrait room now, to set our minds at ease over Miss Heywood. I will retrieve my sister when she is ready."

Elizabeth felt she ought to offer Miss Denham assistance—if not personally, then by the sending of a maid—but she was so anxious about Miss Heywood and so repelled by Miss Denham's insolence that she readily accepted Sir Edward's encouragement to leave his sister to herself for the time being and focus on somehow helping other ladies tonight whose need for assistance quite possibly extended beyond figuring out how to button up the backs of their own gowns. Elizabeth had promised Charlotte's mother to look after her, and the fact that the young lady's present whereabouts were unknown weighed upon her.

They reentered the portrait room to find that its population had not increased as much as Elizabeth had hoped. Though she was happy to see that Mr. Granville had joined them—if only Miss Denham knew, the knowledge might inspire her to hasten her toilette—her spirits sank at the absence of Charlotte. Diana and Sidney Parker also had not yet returned.

An atmosphere of tension pervaded. Elizabeth sensed it first from Thomas and Arthur Parker. Thomas's temper had shortened in her absence, and Arthur seemed on the defensive side of it; the younger brother's attempts at conversation met civil but terse replies from the elder. After several such rebuffs, Arthur wandered over to the hearth, evidently preferring the fire's warmth to Thomas's frost. It appeared the Denhams were not the only siblings at odds with each other as the night stretched later.

Though engaged in conversation with Mr. Granville, Darcy excused himself and crossed to her. She could tell by his manner that he, too, had grown more apprehensive. "You were gone longer than I anticipated. Is all well with Miss Heywood?"

"I wish I knew," Elizabeth replied. "She is not in her chamber."

"Miss Heywood, also missing?" Miss Brereton said. "Merciful heavens! What is happening?"

Thomas Parker shot an accusatory look at Arthur. "This does not bode well."

"It is not *my* fault! At least we did not find anyone beneath the window."

Elizabeth looked to Darcy for explanation.

"Nobody knows where Diana Parker is, either," he said.

She stared at him, the hope she had fostered of there being an unremarkable reason for Charlotte's absence ebbing away, replaced by cold dread. The population of Sanditon House was dwindling at an alarming rate.

"I do not mean to incite panic," Mr. Granville interjected, "but is anyone certain of Miss Denham's present whereabouts?"

"I just left her in her chamber," Sir Edward said, "preparing to join us here."

"Well, that is a relief." Miss Brereton's voice sounded anything but reassured. "We have only *four* ladies missing . . ." She took a deep, shaky breath and sank onto a nearby sofa.

Though as distressed as Miss Brereton by this turn of events, Elizabeth endeavored to present a composed front. She went to Miss Brereton, sat down beside her on the sofa, and placed one of her hands over Clara's. "We shall sort this out."

"There are also two gentlemen missing from this gathering," said Thomas Parker. "However, I do not harbor concern for their safety as I do for that of the ladies. Sidney can take care of himself. As for Josiah Hollis, I want to know where he is at this moment, and what he has been doing since we last saw him."

Darcy and Mr. Granville exchanged glances.

"He is in his chamber," Mr. Granville said, "and will no doubt claim to have been there the whole while. I, however, spied him in a corridor after the search for Susan commenced, and followed him on an extended tour of the house."

"Did that tour take him past the morning room?" Thomas asked. "That is where Arthur abandoned Diana."

"I went to light the candles!" Arthur retreated farther into his hearthside sanctuary.

"I believe Mr. Hollis did visit that part of the house," Mr. Granville replied. "He led me along a winding route—at times I was unsure myself where we were. I recognized this room, of course, when I passed it, but there were many more that I did not."

"How many rooms did he enter?" Darcy asked.

"I do not know. You must understand that we both traveled in the dark. A few scattered sconces provided enough illumination that I feared he might see me if he suddenly turned around, so I trailed behind at such a distance that I could see only the faintest outline of him, or—most of the time—not see him at all. When I heard his footfalls stop, I stopped; when they continued, I continued."

"So you have no way of knowing whether he entered the morning room, or whether Diana Parker was in there?" Darcy asked.

"I can say only that when I passed the morning room, I did not hear anyone within. Recall, however, that I lost Hollis's trail after encountering you and Mrs. Darcy. He could have gone there before finally making his way back to his chamber."

"I think we need to fetch Mr. Hollis directly and demand he give an accounting of himself," Thomas Parker declared.

"Do you believe he is behind all the disappearances?" Miss Brereton asked. "He has no love for Lady Denham, but what grievance can he hold against the misses Parker? Or Miss Heywood?" Her voice caught in her throat. "Indeed, what could anyone?"

Sir Edward hastened to Clara's other side and dropped to one knee. "My dear Miss Brereton! Allow me to assuage your fright by offering myself as your protector until this confusion is resolved." He reached for her hand. "Why, you tremble! You need something to calm your nerves. A glass of wine? Yes! Wine—" He leaped up and looked toward the sideboard on the far wall of the room. The wine decanter had been refilled; fresh glasses rested beside it.

Darcy, who stood closer to the sideboard than did Sir Edward, followed the baronet's gaze. "Tend to Miss Brereton," he said, starting toward the table. "I will fetch the wine."

Sir Edward stepped forward. "No, no! I am happy to serve the lady!"

"I am already here."

Sir Edward watched in dismay as Darcy reached for the decanter. He took one more step forward, but then apparently thought better of prolonging the contest. He returned to his post at Miss Brereton's side, where, crestfallen at the missed opportunity to comfort the lady by procuring wine, he resumed with increased fervor his attempts to comfort her with unceasing discourse.

"I cannot help but observe," he said to her in a low voice, "that all of the missing ladies are single."

Miss Brereton regarded him quizzically. "Lady Denham is twice widowed."

"Well, yes—of course. But that makes her *currently* single, you see—with no champion, no defender dedicated solely to her safety— as Mrs. Darcy, here, has to safeguard her."

Though Sir Edward's tone held no rancor, Elizabeth caught in his words the implication that her own "dedicated defender" had just overstepped his bounds by fetching Miss Brereton's wine. Indeed, the maneuver struck her as uncharacteristic of Darcy; while a gentleman to the core, prepared to lend aid to any lady in need, he was not one given to conspicuous displays of service, let alone elbowing out a titled nobleman for the privilege of rendering it. She could only presume that, the wine being nearest him and his mind preoccupied with unfolding events, he had acted in the interest of expedience, not considering the potential for giving offense or wounding pride.

"Mr. Darcy is concerned for the safety of us all," Elizabeth said.

"Undoubtedly. But surely you cannot deny that, as your husband, he is most concerned for yours."

She conceded the point with a nod, then glanced at Darcy, who, after being all alacrity in offering to obtain the wine, now seemed rather dilatory about delivering it. He stood with the decanter in one hand and an empty glass in the other, but both objects rested on the table and he made no movement to bring them together to pour. Instead, his gaze appeared fixed on a different target. From her vantage point, Elizabeth could see a small piece of paper lying on the table. His body blocked it from the view of most of the others.

"So, you see, Miss Brereton," continued the baronet, "why I wish to assure you that in Sir Edward Denham you have a loyal friend devoted to your protection and defense—your own Musketeer . . ."

As Sir Edward advanced his suit, Elizabeth quietly rose and went to Darcy. His back to her, he picked up the paper upon sensing someone's approach and folded it just as she reached him.

"Darcy?"

He relaxed upon realizing it was she at his side, but did not turn around. Instead, he cast her a sidelong glance, then said quietly, "When we were in this room earlier today, did you observe this lying here?" He indicated the slip in his hand.

Though they had spent considerable time in the portrait room following their arrival at the house, so much had transpired during and since then that those hours now seemed days ago. She briefly shut her eyes to better focus, but could not envision a piece of paper, nor anything other than the wine, on the side table.

She shook her head.

"I cannot recall it, either," Darcy said. "I first noticed it when Sir Edward mentioned the wine." He handed her the paper. "I believe it appeared while we were all occupied elsewhere in the house."

She unfolded the scrap. It was small, perhaps four inches square. But large enough to hold a single sentence inked in an unembellished hand.

IF YOU WANT TO SEE LADY DENHAM AGAIN, PRODUCE
SIR HARRY'S WATCH.

Twenty-three

"When [Sir Harry] died, I gave Sir Edward his Gold Watch." She said this with a look at her Companion which implied its right to produce a great Impression— and seeing no rapturous astonishment in Charlotte's countenance, added quickly— "He did not bequeath it to his Nephew, my dear . . . It was not in the Will. He only told me, and that but once, that he should wish his Nephew to have his Watch; but it need not have been binding, if I had not chose it."
—Lady Denham, Sanditon

*D*arcy met Elizabeth's alarmed gaze. His own mind still worked to absorb the import of not only the message's content, but the method and timing of its delivery.

"This confirms the worst of our conjectures," Elizabeth murmured. "Lady Denham has been abducted."

"And an inmate of this house—guest or servant—is either her captor or an accomplice to the kidnapping." Darcy glanced at the other guests to see whether any of them appeared to have noticed the slip of paper or took undue interest in their conversation, but found everyone's attention occupied by more personal interests. Arthur stirred the fire with a poker, ensuring that the rising temperature of the room would fan everyone's tempers hotter still. Thomas stationed himself in the main doorway to stand sentinel over the hall, alert for any sign that one of his sisters approached. Sir Edward continued his effusive consoling of Miss Brereton while launching aggressive looks at Mr. Granville, who had moved closer to the young lady to offer support of his own.

"However," Darcy continued, "this development is not entirely discouraging. We can now more confidently proceed on the assumption that Lady Denham is alive, which we could not do before." The grim possibility that the note's author promised only the sight of a corpse occurred to him, but he preferred to remain hopeful.

"The note makes no mention of the misses Parker or Miss Heywood," Elizabeth said.

"I have two rationales for that." Actually, Darcy had three, but only two he wanted to voice at present. "Their absences could have nothing to do with Lady Denham's kidnapping. They might simply be wandering around the house lost."

"All *three* of them?"

"I did not say that was the most likely explanation, only that it cannot be ruled out."

"Neither can the possibility that they are the ones who left the note because they jointly conspired in Lady Denham's kidnapping and are even now standing guard over her in some remote location as they plot their next move. However, I think our efforts are better spent exploring other scenarios. What is your second theory?"

"The message could have been left before the other women disappeared."

She contemplated for a moment, then nodded. "That is far more probable. We have not been in this room—at least, not as a group—since before the gentlemen's search of the grounds. Every person in the house has had opportunity to sneak in and leave the note." Her gaze swept the room, resting on each occupant one at a time before returning to Darcy.

"Have you considered," she continued in a somber tone, "that the missing ladies could have gotten too close to our culprit and been silenced?"

That had been his third explanation. "I was not yet prepared to articulate that possibility—I wanted to spare you the thought."

"After all we have been through, surely you know I am hardly missish about such matters."

"That knowledge does not remove from your husband the instinct to bear the weight of them."

"See here," Sir Edward called from the sofa. "Are you bringing that wine for Miss Brereton or not?"

"In a minute," Darcy said over his shoulder.

Elizabeth met his eyes. "Do we share this message with the others?"

As he deliberated the strategic implications of doing so, he poured wine into a glass.

"We must flush out the perpetrator somehow." He replaced the stopper and set the decanter aside. "While temporarily withholding this development would enable us to observe the behavior of our fellow guests with new perspective, their safety—particularly that of the remaining ladies—requires prompt disclosure so that they know to act with caution."

"Also, the revelation should bring this whole situation—at least, Lady Denham's portion of it—to a swift resolution," Elizabeth said. "All Sir Edward need do is relinquish the watch."

"Assuming the note's author keeps his word." Darcy was by no means confident of that assumption.

He carried the wineglass to Miss Brereton, who now shared the sofa with two occupants—Sir Edward on her left side and Mr. Granville on her right.

"At last!" Sir Edward took the glass from Darcy's hand. "Here, my dear—this will fortify you."

Miss Brereton thanked Darcy and took a small sip.

"Do imbibe a longer draught," Sir Edward urged. "Distress has afflicted your nerves still more as you waited. Indeed—I had begun to think Mr. Darcy was pressing the grapes himself."

"It is only your kind anxiety on my behalf that made the interval seem long to you," she replied. "Besides, my nerves are of little importance compared to the weightier matters occupying Mr. Darcy."

"I assure you," Darcy said to Miss Brereton, "your welfare, and that of everybody in this house, entirely occupies my present thoughts." He turned to face the room.

"Someone left us a note," he announced. "I discovered it on the sideboard just now."

"What kind of note?" Thomas asked. "What does it say?"

With a look, Darcy prompted Elizabeth. As she read the message aloud, he watched the reactions of their fellow guests. Thomas Parker blinked in astonishment. Miss Brereton gasped. Sir Edward paled. Arthur wiped a bead of perspiration from his brow. To the best of Darcy's powers of discernment, all appeared genuinely surprised.

Thomas was the first to speak. "Sir Harry's watch? Is this some sort of ransom demand?"

"It sounds like one to me," Darcy replied, "albeit an unusual request. I should think that a kidnapper who went to the trouble and risk of abducting Lady Denham would demand a higher price. Is the watch worth a great deal?"

All eyes turned to Sir Edward, who became flustered by the sudden attention. "I have no idea. Why would I ever have sought an appraisal? Its value to me is purely sentimental." He gestured toward the portrait of Sir Harry. "A remembrance of my departed uncle."

"Can you think of any individual who would take such direct interest in it? Perhaps someone else for whom it holds sentimental value?"

"My sister, naturally, treasures it as much as I do—we were both quite fond of Sir Harry. But of course Miss Denham could not have had anything to do with that note, let alone Lady Denham's disappearance!" He laughed. "Esther—an accomplice to kidnapping! I cannot imagine anything more improbable."

Neither could Darcy—it would require industry on her part.

Thomas Parker approached Elizabeth. "May I see the note? Is there any mention of *my* sisters? Or Miss Heywood? Good G–d! Whatever will I tell her parents?"

"I have been wondering that very thing myself," Elizabeth said. "I, too, promised Mr. and Mrs. Heywood to look after her." She handed the note to Thomas Parker. Mr. Granville, standing beside him, also studied it.

"Perhaps," Mr. Granville offered, "the individual is not someone who covets the watch, but resents it—or what it represents."

"I am not certain of your meaning," Darcy said.

Mr. Granville nodded toward the portrait of Sir Harry. "There is one among us who takes great offense at the late baronet's image displayed so prominently in this house."

"Archibald Hollis!" Sir Edward exclaimed. "Of course it must be he! Mrs. Darcy, did I not just tell you that I felt his spirit was restless tonight? If he is displeased with his widow, what better time to call her to account than a stormy night with a house full of guests as her jury?"

"While I agree," Darcy said, "that the late Mr. Hollis possesses a legitimate right to indignation"—(Inasmuch as a dead man could. What *was* he saying? Sir Edward's absurdity was beginning to rub off on him.)—"I think Lady Denham's deliverance would be better accomplished by our considering more corporeal suspects."

"Josiah Hollis!" Sir Edward glanced toward the vacant chair Mr. Hollis had occupied earlier. "He has not uttered a kind word for our hostess since his arrival."

"Or for anybody else," Thomas added.

"But why would he kidnap my sisters or Miss Heywood?" Arthur asked.

"Perhaps he discovered them in places he did not want them exploring," Darcy said, "or they caught him engaging in something he did not want seen."

"I suggested earlier that we should summon Mr. Hollis," Thomas said. "It is time he explained himself. I shall fetch him at once."

As he turned to go, footsteps in the hall commanded everyone's attention.

"Perhaps he comes to us," Miss Brereton said.

A moment later, Sidney Parker and Miss Heywood entered—to Darcy's immense relief. Although the discovery of the note had worsened Lady Denham's situation and the Parker sisters' whereabouts remained unknown, at least one of the missing women was not missing after all.

"Charlotte!" Elizabeth went to her immediately, the others not far behind. They closed around the new arrivals, everyone talking at once.

"Wherever have you been?"

". . . so worried for you . . ."

"Have you seen Diana?"

So overwhelming was the sudden attention that a minute passed before either Miss Heywood or Sidney had an opportunity to speak.

"I left my chamber to come find you," Miss Heywood said to

Elizabeth, "but lost my way in the dark. Fortunately, Mr. Parker ran into me, and led me here."

"Is there news of Susan?" Sidney asked.

"No," Thomas replied, "and now Diana is missing, too."

Sidney cast a questioning look at Arthur. "When I met you earlier, she was with you."

"I do not want to talk about it."

Thomas, however, did, and informed Sidney and Miss Heywood of the particulars of Diana's disappearance. Sidney received the intelligence gravely, but did not take his younger brother to task as had Thomas. Rather, he became contemplative, even as Miss Heywood exclaimed her alarm.

"Oh, dear! Where could she have gone? I thought I heard someone moving about her room earlier, but when I looked within, no one was there."

"I hear sounds like that whenever Miss Denham and I spend the night in Sanditon House." Sir Edward came forward from the sideboard, having taken advantage of the clamor at Miss Heywood's arrival to pour himself some wine. His was a small portion, not quite half a glass, and he swirled it in the wineglass as he spoke. "It is only the Hollis ghost."

Somehow, Miss Heywood appeared less than reassured by that explanation.

"Unless it was Lady Denham's kidnapper," Thomas said.

"Kidnapper?" Sidney asked. "Is there news regarding Lady Denham?"

"We have received a ransom note." Darcy handed the slip to Sidney, who held it so that Miss Heywood could read it along with him.

"Well," Sidney said when he had done, "that sounds simple enough." He passed the note back to Darcy and looked at Sir Edward. "All you need do is produce the watch. Lady Denham is returned to us—my sisters along with her, I hope—and we can call it a night."

"It is not that simple," Darcy said. "Even if Lady Denham and the others are returned to us unharmed, there is the matter of apprehending their captor and bringing him to justice."

"There is, indeed," Sidney said. "But it starts with the watch. Sir Edward, do you have it with you?"

"Alas, I wish I did! But I—" Sir Edward cleared his throat and took a sip of wine. "It is at Denham Park. I treasure it so much, you see, that I seldom carry it, for I would not want to drop it, or somehow misplace such a precious possession. It is the only personal effect I inherited upon my uncle's death. I keep it quite safe, I assure you."

"What do you think the author of this note might want with it?" Darcy asked.

"I cannot imagine! It is a handsome watch, to be sure, but—" He released a short, high-pitched laugh. "Hardly worth kidnapping Lady Denham."

"You *are* willing to surrender it, to rescue Lady Denham, are you not?" Sidney asked.

"Why, of course! If I had within my means the power to rescue any lady in distress, I would not hesitate!"

"How quickly can you retrieve it?"

The baronet hesitated. "Tonight? In this storm?"

Sir Edward's question was not a sign of cowardice; Darcy, too, would think twice before embarking on even a short journey to a familiar destination at this hour of the night, let alone under such treacherous conditions. The lightning, the rain, wind strong enough to bring down tree limbs . . . the all-encompassing darkness. The path to Denham Park was surely naught but mire. It would not do Lady Denham, nor the other missing ladies, any good for Sir Edward to leave the house now, only to suffer an accident that prevented him from returning.

And yet, time was of the essence.

"Can the errand wait until daybreak," asked Elizabeth, "when he could at least see the hazards in his path?"

It was the very question sounding in Darcy's own mind. How patient was the kidnapper? "I will leave the timing of the mission to your own judgment," he told the baronet.

"Sir Edward, you cannot be thinking of venturing out now?" Miss Brereton asked.

"Indeed," said Mr. Granville, "only the bravest of souls would attempt it."

Sir Edward straightened. "Why, of course I will do whatever is necessary to find Lady Denham—to find *all* the ladies, I mean. What hero could remain idle here with so many damozels depending upon him? I will even ward off the ghost of Ivy Woodcock if I must, to reach my destination and complete the quest posthaste." He tore his gaze from Miss Brereton to fix it on Darcy. "However, once I bring the watch back here, does the note say what we are to *do* with it?"

"It offers no such instructions," Darcy said. "I suppose we could simply leave it where we found the note, or leave a reply message for the culprit, stating terms of our own devising."

"Very well," Sir Edward said. "I shall depart at once."

"Do you wish for someone to accompany you?"

"No—I know the way well enough, and there is no sense in anybody else exposing himself to the elements. I will return as soon as I am able." He turned to Elizabeth. "Meanwhile, when Miss Denham finishes dressing and finds her way down here, I would be most obliged if you would tell her where I have gone and not to worry on my behalf."

With a final look at Miss Brereton and a deep bow to them all, he departed, carrying with him the hopes of those remaining.

"Now," Thomas said, "about Josiah Hollis . . ."

"Are you certain we ought to interrogate him?" Mr. Granville said. "Doing so would expose our suspicions."

"If he has knowledge of my sisters' whereabouts, I will expose him to more than suspicions if he refuses to cooperate," Thomas said.

"He will only deny any accusations, and then what do we do?" Mr. Granville said. "Call him a liar? Call him out?"

"What do you suggest?" Darcy asked.

"When Sir Edward returns with the watch, we leave it on the sideboard for the kidnapper to collect, then lie in wait to see who appears. I wager ten pounds that it will be Mr. Hollis—and if it is not, we will still have caught the culprit."

Darcy considered the proposal. It had merit, but he wanted to know *now* what Josiah Hollis had been about this evening. Every minute the three ladies remained missing was another minute they could be in grave danger. It nettled him to spend any of those minutes in idleness.

"We cannot possibly expect to see Sir Edward again for over an hour—likely longer," Thomas said. "What action can we take in the meantime?"

"We summon Hollis to join us, as you suggested," said Darcy. "But we make it a peaceable gathering—one in which we use ordinary conversation to learn what we can from him. In the process, we make it known that we received the ransom note and that Sir Edward has gone to fetch the watch."

"So he will know when and where to find it later, providing him every opportunity to incriminate himself," Mr. Granville said.

"And if Sir Edward returns without the watch?" Sidney asked.

"Why would he return without it?" Darcy replied.

Sidney gestured toward the rain battering against the nearest window. "What if he cannot reach Denham Park and is forced to turn back?"

"Then we are no worse off than we are now," said Mr. Granville.

"If we are in agreement, I will go invite Mr. Hollis to our assembly," Darcy said.

"I will come with you," Elizabeth declared, "and stop at Miss Denham's chamber. She is taking an overlong time to join us."

"I do wish Sir Edward had allowed someone to accompany him, rather than take the burden of his mission entirely upon himself," Elizabeth said as they approached the staircase. "I fear for his safety. Do you suppose he at least took a servant?"

"A sensible man would."

"That does not reassure me."

At the top of the stairs they turned toward the bedchambers. Elizabeth's knock on Miss Denham's door went unanswered.

"Miss Denham? It is Mr. and Mrs. Darcy. We are all gathered in the portrait room. Sir Edward said you would be joining us."

They waited in silence for a minute. "Miss Denham," Elizabeth tried again, "may I be of any assistance to you?"

The absence of sound within the chamber disturbed Darcy more than any noise might have. Postponing the acknowledgment of what every faculty of reason told him was true, he rapped on the door himself. "Miss Denham?"

His effort met with the same response Elizabeth's had: none.

"Might she be deliberately ignoring us?" he asked.

"She has certainly made no secret of her disdain for our involvement in tonight's proceedings. However, rather than sit motionless inside her chamber until we give up and leave, I think her more inclined to open the door so that she could make a show of closing it after telling us to go away."

With growing dread, Darcy made one final attempt to compel Miss Denham to open the door herself before they imposed upon her privacy by entering her chamber uninvited. "Miss Denham?" His deeper voice surely penetrated the wooden barrier between them. "Another lady has gone missing and Sir Edward has left the house on an urgent errand to Denham Park. For your own safety, he insists that you join all of us in the portrait room rather than remain alone in your chamber."

Every silent second that passed seemed to stretch eternally. He let no more than five elapse before answering Elizabeth's unvoiced question with a nod.

She opened the door. Within, they found exactly what he dreaded. No one.

A cursory inspection of Miss Denham's room revealed nothing of note—no indication of forced entry, no obvious evidence conveniently left lying around, no new ransom letter. The presence of Miss Denham's borrowed nightdress and the absence of her gown indicated that she had finished dressing before she left her chamber, but otherwise Elizabeth and Darcy found no sign of what had caused that departure.

"It *is* possible that we missed her—that she took a different route to the portrait room than the one we followed here," Elizabeth said.

"Do you believe that to be the case?"

"Not for a moment."

They hastened to Josiah Hollis's chamber, impatient to reconvene with the others, impatient to learn what Hollis knew. With another lady missing, there was no time to waste; Darcy would roust the older man from bed if he must. He had better be cooperative. Darcy was in no mood to brook resistance.

When they reached his chamber, they did not find Hollis the least bit obstinate.

They did not find him at all.

Twenty-four

The manuscript so wonderfully found . . . how was it to be accounted for? What could it contain? To whom could it relate? By what means could it have been so long concealed?
    —Northanger Abbey

*E*lizabeth's spirits plummeted as her gaze took in the empty chamber. Like Miss Denham's room, Josiah Hollis's quarters showed signs of having been slept in, but offered nothing to explain the absence of its tenant.

"Two more guests missing in less than an hour." Her hand closed around one of the bedposts as a sick feeling spread through her stomach. Mr. Hollis's unknown whereabouts were beyond her control and likely of his own volition, but she felt somehow responsible for Miss Denham's. Having seen the lady so recently, it seemed like her disappearance had occurred on Elizabeth's watch. "I knew Miss Denham was expected to join us in the portrait room. Why did I not become concerned sooner when she failed to appear?"

"Because all of us were occupied by everything else that went before."

The weight of the evening's events settled upon her all at once. Alone with Darcy, free of the need to maintain an optimistic façade before anybody else, she sank wearily onto the end of the bed. "This is the worst dinner party ever."

"Worse than the evening we met the Knightleys?"

"They lost only one guest."

"No one here has died."

"Neither of us is certain of that."

He sat down next to her. "We will do our best to make certain of that."

She leaned into his side, resting her head against his shoulder. It had been a long night, and there was no sign of its ending anytime soon. He put his arm around her and drew her closer.

"I hope it goes without saying," he continued, "that until this situation is resolved, I do not want you to leave my sight."

"I assure you, I have little inclination to roam the house by myself. I do not think Miss Heywood or Miss Brereton should be without a companion, either."

"What do you make of Josiah Hollis's absence? Do you think he has also been kidnapped, or is he responsible for all the other women's disappearances?"

"I doubt he has been kidnapped. He would not command much in the way of ransom, and without riches as a motive, who would intentionally subject himself to prolonged time in Mr. Hollis's company? No—if he is not responsible for his own absence, I think it more likely that he rubbed someone the wrong way one time too many."

"And was permanently silenced?"

"Have you yourself not wished at least once tonight that he would bite his spiteful tongue? Perhaps someone stopped it for him."

"One of our fellow guests?"

She released a heavy sigh. "I sincerely hope not. They may have their idiosyncrasies, but I dislike thinking any of them capable of violence. Although Thomas Parker was very displeased with Arthur just now, his ire is justified, and his greatest fault seems to be an overabundance of enthusiasm about Sanditon. Sidney seems the most rational of the whole Parker clan, if not the most serious; Arthur, the most indolent. Mr. Granville we have spent less time with, but for someone unconnected to any of the missing ladies, he has demonstrated admirable character in the way he has stepped forward to assist our investigative efforts in any manner he can. Ridiculous as Sir Edward might be, he is conscientious, and even now risks his own safety to perform an errand critical to Lady Denham's welfare."

"Now that you have exonerated all the other guests, that leaves us with Mr. Hollis."

"Two Mr. Hollises—let us not forget Archibald, whom Sir Edward was stalking when I came upon him earlier."

"The baronet was ghost-hunting?"

"Tilting at cobwebs to demonstrate his valor. His efforts, however, proved unsuccessful, so I believe we can safely limit our present discussion to the corporeal Mr. Hollis."

"Whom you believe to be a suspect, not a victim?"

"Perhaps tonight he is visiting revenge upon those who have rubbed *him* the wrong way—starting with Lady Denham."

He frowned. "I have difficulty imagining Hollis as the kidnapper. Even if he is feigning his lumbago—which would not at all surprise me—I cannot visualize him carrying off Diana Parker or Miss Denham without their resisting enough to cause a disturbance that *someone* would have heard. Arthur could not have strayed that far from his sister in pursuit of a candle flame."

"Unless Hollis subdued the women somehow."

"Knocked them unconscious?"

"Do you think him capable of it?"

"Physically? Yes. But for a gentleman to strike a blow to a woman crosses such a line—"

"As opposed to merely abducting her?"

The rhetorical question gave him pause. "I concede the point," he said finally. "Abduction *is* an utterly dishonorable act; it follows that if he is capable of one, he might be capable of more. However, the forsaking of some scruples does not prohibit the retention of others. I know many gentlemen who are a study in contradiction."

"I do not think Josiah Hollis possesses so complex a character. Regardless, I did not necessarily mean he subdued them with physical blows."

"What, then?"

Elizabeth was not certain. She knew only that she agreed with Darcy in not being able to imagine any of the ladies quietly acquiescing to being dragged off somewhere.

"Perhaps he won their cooperation by lying. Or by threatening them, or someone they care about," she offered. "Or perhaps he used a nonviolent means of subduing them. Diana left Susan to go prepare a sedative. Who knows what other concoctions the Parker sisters might have had in their possession? Either could carry an entire pharmacopœia in her reticule, with any number of potions and concoctions that might be used against her if administered improperly."

"What of Lady Denham? She boasted of almost never taking physic."

"Yet even she had two phials on her dressing table, one of them a sedative, courtesy of Diana. A phial that is now missing."

Darcy was silent, his expression pensive. At last he said, "No matter who the kidnapper is, after subduing the ladies, where would he take them? He cannot leave because of the storm, and the house has been thoroughly searched."

"Has it? We have not been searching in the most organized fashion, and it would not surprise me if this house contains out-of-the-way spaces that even the servants might not think to check. Perhaps we ought to take another look at the architectural plans in the study. Do you have the key?"

Darcy slipped his hand into his pocket—or rather, Archibald Hollis's pocket; he still wore the late gentleman's coat. He frowned. "Wrong pocket," he said, but did not remove his hand.

"Well, check the other one."

"In a moment." He withdrew something from the pocket. "I did not feel this before."

It was a letter, folded, the creases well worn, the paper itself cloth-like from repeated handling. The outside bore no address, only a name: "Ivy."

Elizabeth gasped. Darcy sat back down beside her and carefully opened the letter, holding it so that Elizabeth could read it along with him.

Dearest Ivy,
I never intended to fall in love with you.
In truth, I never intended to know you at all. After that day when I was eight or so, when we happened upon each other near the grotto, and played at hide-and-seek and drakes-and-ducks until the shadows grew long and my father's manservant discovered us, I received

the worst thrashing of my young life for consorting with an inferior, and swore I would never commit that error again. I put you from my mind, and if a stray recollection entered my thoughts in all the years I was at Eton, it flitted past like a ghostly impression, too fleeting to take full form.

But when we chanced upon each other again, on the eve of my departure for Oxford, I could not help but draw near, to determine whether the dark-eyed waif before me were indeed the girl of my memory, or even a corporeal woman at all, rather than a trick of the light. I did not realize, in that moment, that you would bewitch me, not with sorcery or faerie dust or the stuff of midsummer nights' dreams, but with the opposite—your unaffected, honest way of looking at the world and the creatures that populate it.

I spent Michaelmas Term immersed in my new environs, but despite all the distractions of university and the novelty of living in relative independence, every now and again my mind's eye would conjure an image of you. When I returned at Christmas, my long rambles through Sanditon Park were inspired as much by hope of another chance encounter with you, as by the need to escape the confines of my father's house and domineering presence. It is a cold house, and he a cold man. Though I had returned to the dwelling of my birth, I experienced no sense of homecoming.

Until I felt a snowball strike me squarely in the back—and turned to find you, greeting me with an impish smile that warmed me despite the frigid air.

I need not describe to you the joyful moments of those too-brief weeks before I returned to Oxford, nor when I came back to Sanditon at Easter, for you shared them. Our first tentative kiss in the grotto. The spring afternoon when our kisses led to more. The first night I sneaked you into Sanditon House whilst my father was away—and realized that its walls would not be an eternal prison if someday you dwelled inside them with me.

Dear G–d, Ivy, where are you? I learned of your disappearance only upon arriving home after Trinity Term. I came back intending to ask for your hand, to bear the wrath of my father and disinheritance if I must. Let my younger brother have what he so covets; I am *weary of his skulking about hoping to catch me in some transgression. There have been times when I wondered whether Oswald suspected my connection with you, and I looked forward to defeating that trump card by laying it before our father myself.*

Instead, you are gone, and I must guard with anguished silence what we were—nay, are—to one another, even as I fear for your safety and endeavor to learn all I can about the night you vanished. Though weeks have passed since your shawl was found, the village is yet abuzz. Even my father, unfeeling tyrant that he is, not only lends resources toward the effort to find you, but directs it. That will change in an instant should he so much as suspect what is in my heart.

Sanditon House is cold once more—colder than ever it was in winter. I refuse to believe that you are dead. I would know. I would have felt your passing somehow—over a hundred miles away in Oxford, I would have felt your death as if it were an amputation of my own limb. I keep your miniature in my breast pocket, next to my heart, at all times. Do you still have mine?

I know not where or how to reach you, so I shall leave this letter in the one place I can think of—the grotto, in the niche where we exchanged notes when I was last home. If by some miracle it finds its way to you—if you are reading this—come to me. You know how to use the old siege tunnel to enter the house without being seen. Or send me word of where you are, and I will move heaven and earth to join you. Even if you have passed from this life and haunt the woods as some villagers claim, I beg you—send me a sign. I love you, Ivy. Please do not be gone forever.

I am and shall always remain—

> *Your most devoted,*
> *A.H.*

Elizabeth read the letter twice before meeting Darcy's gaze. "Archibald Hollis and Ivy Woodcock—all those years ago! Crossed lovers parted before they even had a chance."

"They never stood a chance," Darcy replied. "These are the words of an idealistic youth who had yet to even reach his majority. Victor Hollis would never have permitted a marriage between them. The engagement would have had to remain a secret until they came of age—unlikely, with his brother already suspicious and Archibald behaving so indiscreetly as to bring his *inamorata* into the house and commission an artist to paint their miniatures. As soon as Victor learned of the affair, he would have turned Ivy and her father out of the hermitage, and likely leveled other sanctions upon Archibald. How long would their love have lasted with nothing to live on but misery?"

"I had forgotten what a romantic you are."

"I am rational, which is far more useful."

She had to grant him that, as well as the fact that Archibald and Ivy would have faced a very difficult future. Sustaining a happy marriage was challenging enough when one had a comfortable income and the support of family and friends.

"All right, then, my rational husband—I believe we can safely guess the identity of the woman in the miniature we found in Archibald's trunk, and how it came to be there. But if Archibald left this note in the grotto, how did it come to be in his pocket?"

"In any number of ways—it has had the better part of a century to find its way there. Perhaps he reconsidered and never left it in the grotto at all, lest Oswald or someone else find it. Perhaps Oswald *did* find it, and either brought it to their father or used it for extortion. Perhaps Archibald retrieved it from the grotto after so much time passed that he finally accepted Ivy's death."

Perhaps, Elizabeth speculated, Ivy was the reason Archibald Hollis did not marry until very late in life. Had it taken him that long to give up hope? "I wonder whether Lady Denham knows about Ivy."

"The grotto holds a marble statue of a young girl dressed in leaves and adorned with flowers," Darcy said. "The entrance is covered in ivy. And unlike other structures on the grounds, it has been allowed to fall into neglect."

Lady Denham knew.

"Regardless," Darcy continued, "of greater concern to Lady Denham at present is Archibald's mention of a tunnel by which the house can be secretly entered—and who else might possess knowledge of it."

"The tunnel could explain how the kidnapper managed to abduct her without anyone's seeing them."

"And how he has continued to similarly spirit away the other ladies. The question is, where does the tunnel connect to the house, and where does it lead? If it is an old sally-port, it must be a remnant of the castle on whose foundations Sanditon House was built. When you discovered the house's architectural drawings, did you notice such a tunnel?"

Elizabeth considered a moment. "I do not believe so. There were passages between and behind rooms that I took for servants' passages—quite a few, actually—but I did not note any that led outside. Nor do I recall seeing any plan that included the cellars or other subterranean areas of the house. However, I did not study the plans closely. We were looking for legal documents, not renderings of Sanditon House and its grounds."

Darcy rose and extended his hand to her. "I find myself increasingly interested in those drawings."

Twenty-five

"Wine . . . always does me good. The more Wine I drink (in moderation) the better I am."
                                        —*Arthur Parker,* Sanditon

*J*osiah Hollis entered the portrait room and scarcely acknowledged its occupants before heading for the wine decanter, ignoring the startled looks he received. Charlotte glanced toward the doorway, expecting the Darcys to have accompanied him. Her gaze, however, met only empty space.

As Mr. Hollis unstoppered the decanter, Thomas Parker was the first to find his voice. "Where are Mr. and Mrs. Darcy?"

"How would I know? I have been sleeping."

"They went to wake you."

"Well, the storm beat them to it." He splashed wine into his glass. A few dark red drops escaped the rim and trickled down the side to stain his hand. To Charlotte's astonishment, he licked them off. She was glad her own glass had been poured before Mr. Hollis got his hands on the decanter.

"Elderberry." He grimaced. "There was port in here earlier. Where is the servant who refilled the decanter?" Upon receiving no response, he shrugged and took a full sip, then replenished his glass.

Charlotte rather liked elderberry wine, but generally limited herself to a single glass. She was not even sure she would finish this one;

224

Lady Denham's wine was stronger than what she was used to at home. Mr. Hollis, however, seemed to be imposing no such limitation on himself. Another long sip and another refill followed before he carried the glass to the chair nearest Miss Brereton and sat down.

Miss Brereton regarded him with composure, but the fidgety manner in which she smoothed the skirt of her gown betrayed her unease. Mr. Granville discreetly caught her hand and pressed it. It was a forward gesture for a gentleman of such slight acquaintance, and she turned to him with a disconcerted look. He responded with one that seemed to say, "Hollis's proximity need not frighten you—a friend is near," and released her hand. The exchange occurred so fleetingly that Charlotte doubted the Parker brothers—their three pairs of eyes focused on Mr. Hollis—had observed it. Mr. Hollis surely had not. Apparently having rapidly overcome his disdain for elderberry wine, his attention had been engaged by the act of consuming half the glass.

"Where are your sisters and the Denhams?" Mr. Hollis asked. "Or have you misplaced them, too?" He drained more of his wine.

"Sir Edward is on an errand," Thomas Parker replied. "My sisters . . . we are presently uncertain. Sidney has just gone to look for them in their chamber again."

Mr. Hollis found this so amusing that he nearly spat out the wine. "Truly? You managed to lose three women and Mr. Darcy while I was napping? That does not even include Lady Denham. Seems rather careless to me."

"The Darcys are not lost," Thomas Parker said sharply. "As for my sisters, this is no humorous matter, and I would appreciate your treating the subject with the gravity it warrants."

"Yes, sir." He chuckled as he swirled the last of the wine in his glass.

Charlotte wished Mr. Darcy were present to steer the conversation with Mr. Hollis in the direction upon which they had agreed. Thomas Parker, his emotions more engaged by the disappearance of his sisters, already showed signs of vulnerability to Mr. Hollis's abrasiveness.

Fortunately, Mr. Granville intervened. In what she presumed was an effort to keep the tone of this interview amiable—or at least civil—he offered Mr. Hollis a half-smile. "Between the storm and our missing hostess, I am surprised you were able to sleep at all."

"When you reach my age, Mr. Granville, you will not wonder." Mr. Hollis ran one hand through his hair, attempting to tame it, but the grey locks demonstrated a will of their own and sprang right back into the cowlick that had formed since they had last seen him. He looked, for all appearances, to have truly dozed through at least part of the past hour. "I will point out that your staying awake does not seem to have done the missing ladies any good. If my safety depends upon the lot of you, I was better off alone in my chamber."

"If that is where you truly have been," Thomas Parker said.

"What is that supposed to mean?"

"You tell us."

"I was in my bedroom, sleeping. Anybody who says otherwise is a liar."

Charlotte was not the only one in the room who glanced at Mr. Granville following Josiah Hollis's declaration. His responding look said, "What did I tell you?"

During the exchange between Mr. Hollis and Mr. Granville, Sidney Parker had returned to the room and silently slipped into a vacant chair. At Thomas's silent question, Sidney shook his head. Susan and Diana were still unaccounted for. Charlotte was so disappointed by the news that she could only imagine what Sidney and his brothers felt.

Mr. Granville, meanwhile, continued his interview with Mr. Hollis. "I am wondering—which of the bedchambers was yours when you stayed here as a boy?"

"I did not 'stay' here, like some sort of transient guest. I *lived* here, as my uncle's intended heir—at least, until Miss Philadelphia Brereton got her hooks into him. I was shown the door within a month of their marriage, and seldom invited back—never, after Uncle Archibald's death. She planned to have a child of her own, and when she did not, claims of blood meant nothing to her as far as my uncle's estate went. I was not the only one who—"

"Yes, we heard all about this from you earlier this evening," Mr. Granville said. "You were treated most unfairly, but I did not mean to bring up that unpleasantness again. I was only curious about whether you happened to be in the same bedchamber tonight that you occupied in the old days—the familiarity could account for your peaceful slumber on a night such as this. Though I suppose, having *lived* here, you are probably familiar with every corner of this house."

"I should say so."

"Has it changed much since your time here? Surely you managed to take a little self-guided tour in all the hours we have been confined here. I know I would not be able to resist the temptation were I the rightful heir to Sanditon House."

Mr. Hollis stared at Mr. Granville, assessing him. Finally, he said, "I see what you are about, Granville, and you are not as clever as you think. If *you* were the rightful heir to Sanditon House, you very well might use this evening as an opportunity to cause mischief. I, however, have not, and no amount of verbal manipulation will make me admit that I did."

Before Mr. Granville could reply, Sir Edward entered the room. "I return triumphant!" the baronet declared. "I bear the object of a successful quest." He held up a watch for all to see. As it swung from its chain, dots of reflected fire- and candlelight danced in the room.

"Thank heavens!" Miss Brereton said. "And thank you, too, Sir Edward, for the speed at which you retrieved it. Lady Denham will be returned to us—the others, too, I am sure—and we can end this ordeal."

"It was a charge I willingly undertook," he replied. His damp hair was windblown and his clothing rumpled, but on the whole he had come through the journey rather well, given the weather. "Where are the Darcys, so that I may surrender this treasure into their care?"

"They went to collect Miss Denham from her chamber," Miss Brereton replied. "Come to think of it, they have been gone a long time."

"Oh? Well, my sister is quite good at keeping one waiting. I am sure they will be along soon."

Charlotte noticed Sidney observing Sir Edward closely—or rather, his watch. His gaze went back and forth from the timepiece in Sir Edward's hand to the one in Sir Harry's portrait, and his brows drew together.

"While we wait for them to appear, might I see the watch before we relinquish it as ransom?" Sidney asked. "I have seen it many times in Sir Harry's portrait, and recall occasions when I saw the man himself consult it. But I have never seen it closely, nor at all recently."

Sir Edward appeared somewhat alarmed by the suggestion. "I . . . well . . . perhaps later? I do not want anything to happen to it between now and when we use it in trade for Lady Denham's return, after all the trouble I suffered to retrieve it."

"We are in a *sitting room*," Josiah Hollis said. "What do you think is going to happen to it?"

"I—oh, I know not! I am just anxious for Lady Denham."

Sidney continued to frown, an expression unlike him. Charlotte studied the portrait. At full size, it provided a fairly large image of the watch in the late baronet's hand—large enough to see that its case was oval-shaped and had something inscribed on it. The round watch dangling from the chain in Sir Edward's hand did not. She caught Sidney's gaze. Realizing that she had made the same observation he had, he nodded in answer to her unspoken question.

"Sir Edward," she said, "this may seem a silly query—"

The baronet bestowed a benevolent smile upon her. "My dear Miss Heywood, no question uttered by a fair maiden is silly."

She returned the smile in acknowledgment of his compliment and continued. "Did you retrieve the correct watch?"

His smile froze. "Of course I did," he said through closed teeth.

Now Arthur looked from Sir Edward's hand to the portrait. So did others.

"No, I think Miss Heywood is right. That does not look like—"

"Sir Harry's watch is oval."

"Is the one in your hand inscribed?"

"Is that watch even gold?"

"I believe that is not even the same chain."

Sir Edward caught the watch and closed his hand around it. "Of course this is Sir Harry's watch! Do you think I would journey all the way to Denham Park in this weather and not return with the correct timepiece? What kind of nincompoop do you take me for?"

Mr. Hollis chortled. "Well, as long as you are asking the question . . ."

"This *is* his watch, I tell you! It is one of my most treasured possessions—I would know it anywhere. Would any of you?"

"More to the point," Sidney said, "will Lady Denham's kidnapper?" He crossed to Sir Edward and held out his hand. "May I see it?"

Sir Edward hesitated, then sighed heavily and stuffed it into his own pocket. "There is no point." He sighed again. "It is not my uncle's watch. I thought—well, I thought I would dupe the kidnapper into accepting a less valuable ransom, but apparently the only dupe here is me."

"You would risk Lady Denham's life over a gold watch?" Sidney asked.

"It is not that," he said. "Truly—I just thought that whomever the person is who kidnapped her, does not deserve such a reward."

Charlotte thought she heard a muffled sound behind her, as of something small dropping to the floor, but when she turned round, saw nothing out of place. She hoped the noise had been merely an invention of her own overstimulated nerves, or even the Hollis ghost— just not the kidnapper lurking nearby, eavesdropping on their conversation.

Sir Edward looked at the others with resignation. "What do you want me to do?"

"I think you should retrieve the real watch," Miss Brereton said.

He nodded. "For you, Miss Brereton—and for Lady Denham—I will. In fact, I will depart this instant."

He approached Miss Brereton and put the substitute watch in her hand, closing his own hand over hers. "Just in case," he said. Before he could make good his exit, however, Mrs. Riley entered the room.

"There is a messenger here from Trafalgar House."

"Trafalgar House!" Thomas Parker exclaimed. "It must be an urgent matter, if Mary has sent a servant at two o'clock in the morning, let alone in this weather. By all means, show him in."

"He is soaking wet, sir. Perhaps you would rather meet him in the entry hall?"

Mr. Parker immediately quit the room—and returned less than five minutes later in a state of great agitation.

"I must leave," he announced. "Our son's cold has become much worse—Mary fears it is the pneumonia. She asks for Diana's help— but Diana is not here!"

"Shall I come with you?" Sidney asked.

Mrs. Riley arrived with Mr. Parker's coat, which he donned as he spoke. "No—I need you here to look after Miss Heywood and continue to search for Susan and Diana. I will take Arthur. All those evenings spent reading aloud from the *Pharmacopœia* must have taught him something. We will go on horseback, as I did earlier, rather than take the carriage—its wheels would become mired instantly."

Minutes later, Thomas and Arthur were gone.

"Well," Sir Edward said when the bustle of their departure settled, "I suppose I must be going, too—in pursuit of the watch. Unless, Miss Brereton, you would prefer me to stay and serve as your protector?"

"We can see to Miss Brereton's safety," Mr. Granville said. "The watch carries higher priority for your attention—no one else can retrieve it."

Sir Edward looked very much as if he would rather not have so unique a commission—particularly one that required him to leave Miss Brereton in the company of a gentleman who, by all appearances, had become a rival suitor—or aspired to be. "I assure you, Miss Brereton, I shall return posthaste." He bowed with a flourish and departed.

Mr. Granville went to the wine decanter. "So," he said, his back to the room as he unstoppered the decanter and poured a glass, "we are down to five. I must say, Parker, this is by far the most memorable soiree you have ever invited me to. It will be hard to top."

"Eight," Charlotte said. "We are eight, with Miss Denham and the Darcys. Whatever could be keeping them?"

"The way people are disappearing around here, do you truly want an answer to that?" Mr. Hollis said.

No, she truly did not—at least, not from Josiah Hollis. She looked to Sidney, but he was completely lost in thought. And from his troubled countenance, those thoughts were not cheerful.

Mr. Granville rejoined the group, leaving his glass behind and bringing the decanter with him. "I am sure the Darcys and the misses Parker are fine," he said as he refilled Miss Brereton's glass. "There is no need to frighten the ladies any more than necessary."

"I was not trying to frighten anybody," said Mr. Hollis. "The kidnapper is doing a superior job of that all by himself."

"The Darcys ought to be told that Mr. Parker and Arthur have departed," Charlotte said, "and also that we are still awaiting Sir Harry's real watch from Sir Edward."

"Well, it will not be me who tracks the Darcys down to tell them," Mr. Hollis declared. "I have other things to do."

"Indeed? What sort of things?" Mr. Granville crossed to Charlotte and refilled her glass. She did not especially want more wine, but as he was thoughtful enough to provide it, she dutifully sipped.

"Maybe I will take that nostalgic tour of the house you recommended. Care to lead it?"

"I would prove a very poor guide, never having been in this house before tonight." He turned toward Sidney. "Wine, Parker?"

The question drew Sidney from his abstraction. "What? Oh—no, thank you."

Mr. Granville returned the decanter to its table, retrieved his own glass, and resumed his seat beside Miss Brereton. "Perhaps," he said to Mr. Hollis, "*you* could lead *us* on a tour."

"It is an old house, with many secrets." Mr. Hollis took a long draught. "And I know a few of those secrets. But I'll not share them with you." He drained the rest of his wine, set the glass on a nearby table, and stood. "I bid you all good night—or what is left of it."

Without another word, he departed.

"Have you noticed," Mr. Granville said after a short interval, "that Josiah Hollis has been apart from our company during each lady's disappearance tonight?"

"I have," Sidney replied, "including Miss Denham's present unexplained absence. Are you suggesting he is responsible?"

"Let me just say that I am in great curiosity regarding those secrets to which he alluded. It leads me to wonder where he has gone now."

"He obviously has a quarrel with Lady Denham, but my sisters never met him before tonight. Why would he abduct them?"

"Revenge? They are guests of Lady Denham—to harm them is to harm her. Or—I hesitate to say this—forgive my bluntness, Miss Heywood—but perhaps he has more carnal reasons. Whatever his motive, I think he is more dangerous than he appears, and should not be underestimated."

Charlotte shuddered at the thought of the disagreeable Mr. Hollis having carnal intentions about anybody. She wanted, more than ever, the reassuring presence of Mrs. Darcy. "I wish we knew where the Darcys are," she said. "They have been gone a very long time."

"Assuming they are together, I expect they are well," Sidney said. "Nevertheless, I was just contemplating going to look for them. Now I am decided." He rose.

"May I come with you?" Charlotte asked.

"Would you not rather stay here with Miss Brereton and Mr. Granville, to wait for them in comfort?"

"I will not be comfortable until I see Mrs. Darcy."

For a moment, he looked as if he preferred not to have her company, and she feared he had grown tired of it. But then he nodded and said, "She is your friend—of course you will feel more easy when you are together. Very well—let us go. Granville, I trust you will look after Miss Brereton?"

"Unless she would prefer to accompany the two of you—Miss Brereton, do you wish to seek out Mrs. Darcy's reassuring presence along with them?"

"No, I will remain here."

"Are you quite certain?" Mr. Granville asked.

"I do not want to leave this room until Sir Edward returns with the watch."

"I understand. In that case—" Mr. Granville retrieved the decanter and topped off Miss Brereton's glass. "It will be my pleasure to keep you company."

Volume the Third

IN WHICH VILLAINY IS EXPOSED,
AND ORDER RESTORED

She had been too wary to put anything out of her
own Power.
—*Sanditon*

Twenty-six

*On tiptoe she entered; the room was before her; but it was some
minutes before she could advance another step.*
                                    —Northanger Abbey

*S*idney took the stairs rapidly, forcing Charlotte to scurry to
keep up with him. She hoped his haste was motivated by impatience to find the Darcys, not to be rid of her, but she could not
help worrying that it was the latter.

"I am sorry if I burdened you with unwanted company on this
errand," she said. "That was not my intention."

He stopped and looked at her, surprise evident. "Not at all. Whatever gave you that impression?"

"You seem determined to outpace me."

"Oh! Forgive me—that was not *my* intention. I am distracted, is
all. My sisters—and now Tom gone to Trafalgar House with Arthur—"

"Of course." Charlotte reproached herself for her own vanity. Of
course with his entire family in a state of crisis, Sidney Parker's
thoughts were so focused on important matters that whether she accompanied him or not was of such insignificance that it had not
even registered in his thoughts. "Where are we headed?"

"When the Darcys left the portrait room, they were going to look
in on Miss Denham and Mr. Hollis. I thought we would start with
their chambers, and move on to the Darcys' apartment from there. If

we do not discover them in one of those places, locating them will become more challenging."

They found Miss Denham's chamber empty—which did not bode well. Charlotte had hoped to discover her ensconced there, uninterested in bestowing her presence on the inferior guests gathered in the portrait room. Her absence made it all the more likely that she, too, had fallen prey to the kidnapper.

Mr. Hollis's chamber was also empty.

"After bidding us all good night, he is anywhere but retired," Charlotte said. "What do you suppose he is up to?"

"No good."

"Do you think Mr. Granville is correct—that Mr. Hollis is dangerous?"

Sidney met her gaze squarely and said to her, with more seriousness than she had yet witnessed in him, "Until we get to the bottom of this, Miss Heywood, do not allow yourself to be left alone with anyone you do not absolutely trust. Especially Mr. Hollis."

They proceeded to the Darcys' quarters. Charlotte recalled that their rooms were Archibald Hollis's former apartment. As they neared, they saw a figure turn the corner at the far end of the corridor to approach the apartment from that direction.

Sidney quickly pulled her into an alcove. There was very little light in this part of the hallway; the few sconces that had been lit earlier had sputtered out in the course of the night, leaving them in such dimness that they could barely see each other. The far end was better illuminated; there, a single sconce resolutely soldiered on, holding out until the bitter end after its companions had fallen. By its light, before they took cover, she had managed to identify the approaching figure: Josiah Hollis.

Sidney leaned out of the alcove just enough to peer down the hallway. "I do not think he saw us," he whispered.

Charlotte slowly released her breath. "What is he doing?"

"He just entered the Darcys' apartment. With a key."

He took her hand again, and together they quietly crept down the hallway. When they reached the apartment, the door stood slightly ajar.

Sidney slowly pushed it open as Charlotte silently prayed that

Mr. Hollis was not in the antechamber immediately behind the door—and that Lady Denham's servants kept the hinges well oiled. Mercifully, the door swung without sound, enabling them to see the glow of candlelight coming from the chamber beyond—the dressing room. Unfortunately, Mr. Hollis was not visible through the dressing room doorway directly opposite. If they wanted to observe the business that brought him here, they would have to enter the antechamber and look through the doorway from a more advantageous angle.

Sidney gestured toward a corner of the antechamber, indicating that she should move there while he completed the more daring mission of going to the interior doorway to peer inside the dressing room. Charlotte held her breath as he proceeded. The only noise was that of Mr. Hollis rummaging through something in the next room—and her own heartbeat, which thumped so loudly in her ears that she could hardly believe it went unheard by Sidney and Mr. Hollis.

Thankfully, Sidney did not have to enter the dressing room to view Hollis. Whatever the unscrupulous gentleman was doing, Sidney could observe by remaining in the antechamber and looking through the doorway at an angle. Thank heavens—she did not think her nerves equal to anything riskier than what the two of them were already doing.

After what seemed an eternity, but was probably no more than a minute or two, Sidney stepped back from the doorway and came to her side. From within the dressing room, she heard the sound of wood meeting wood—as of a lid shutting. Hollis was leaving—heading for the only door by which they could escape.

Sidney dropped to the floor, gesturing her to do the same.

Hollis emerged. Without so much as a glance to either side, he passed straight through the antechamber and looked into the corridor. Apparently satisfied that he could leave unobserved, he exited, quietly closing the door.

Charlotte waited for the sound of a key turning the lock. But it never came . . . only the sound of receding footsteps.

"Is he gone?" she whispered.

"Unless those footsteps belonged to someone else, I believe so." He stood and offered his hand to help her up from the floor.

"Why did he not relock the door?"

"Not being privy to his thoughts, I can only suppose he either forgot or does not care whether the Darcys know someone has been here." He pulled her to her feet. Though they stood but inches apart, without the glow of Hollis's candle, they could barely see each other.

"What was he doing in the dressing room?"

"Pawing through the trunk that contained these fine garments we all borrowed from the late Archibald Hollis this evening. He removed something small enough to put in his coat pocket, but I could not see what it was. Come—let us follow him and find out what he does with it." He led her toward the door.

Charlotte was not altogether certain that continuing to follow Mr. Hollis was a good idea, but if they had it within their power to learn something that could enable them to rescue Sidney's sisters and the other missing ladies, she felt they ought to attempt it. Were she being held captive, she hoped someone would do the same for her.

Sidney slowly opened the door and looked out. Mr. Hollis was not in sight.

"From the sound of his retreating footsteps, I believe he went in the direction whence he came," Sidney said.

Charlotte concurred. They walked to the end of the corridor and rounded the corner, leaving behind the illumination of the stalwart sconce and entering darkness once more. Sidney offered his hand again, which she readily accepted.

"Someday," he said, "I shall have to take you for a stroll in the daylight."

They passed numerous rooms until they reached the one that opened into the long gallery—the scene of her earlier collision with Sidney. From this anteroom they could see candleglow emanating from the gallery. They slowed their strides to the smallest of steps and ever so cautiously peeked through the doorway.

Josiah Hollis stood about halfway down the length of the room, studying one of the portraits. From her angle of vision, Charlotte could not be entirely sure, but she was fairly certain that it was the watercolor of Archibald Hollis in his youth. As they watched, Josiah reached into his coat pocket and withdrew a small object that he held up to the painting. It was about the size of the miniatures in the portrait room case.

Mr. Hollis remained there some minutes, contemplating the juxtaposed images. Then, nodding, he returned the miniature to his pocket.

Charlotte and Sidney backed away from the doorway. Footsteps commenced in the gallery. Thankfully, they sounded like they were heading toward the opposite end, but the two would-be spies were not about to linger. They turned quickly to exit the anteroom.

However, in the nearly nonexistent light of Hollis's retreating candle, neither of them realized how close they were to the small table holding the delicate bud vase that had captured little Mary's attention during Charlotte's first visit. The skirt of her dress caught one of its corners—

Disturbing it just enough to send the vase crashing to the floor.

Twenty-seven

[She] had expected to have her feelings worked, and worked they were. Astonishment and doubt first seized them; and a shortly succeeding ray of common sense added some bitter emotions of shame.
—Northanger Abbey

*A*s the sound of shattering glass pierced the silence, the sound of Mr. Hollis's footsteps ceased.

Charlotte thought her heart would surely stop along with them. She looked at Sidney; even in the near darkness his face reflected every bit of the horror spreading through her.

As abruptly as they had lapsed, the footsteps resumed—now coming in their direction.

They glanced frantically about, seeking a hiding place. Sidney caught her hand and hurried them to the nearest window. The heavy draperies had not been drawn across it, but hung to either side, and he pulled her behind the nearest drapery panel. It was not wide enough for them to stand side by side, but there was no time for them to adjust it or for one of them to move behind another panel. The increased volume of Hollis's footsteps announced that he had entered the room.

Charlotte flattened her back against the wall. Sidney leaned into her, both of them trying to take up as little space as possible lest from the outside the unusual fullness of the drapery panel reveal their presence to Mr. Hollis. It was so dark behind the panel that she could not see Sidney, only feel his chest against hers, his cheek against her temple, his arms on either side of her. They struggled to control their breathing, fearful that the sound of accelerated exhales or the rise and fall of the drapery fabric hanging against Sidney's back would draw Hollis's attention. Sidney's short, shallow breaths warmed her neck; she could feel his heartbeat as strongly as her own.

The footfalls ceased midway through the room. Mr. Hollis had stopped.

Sidney held his breath. So did she. Why—why did Hollis not simply continue on his way, thinking they had fled the room? Had he noticed them? Dear G–d, he must have noticed them! She willed him to quit the room. Willed the darkness to shroud them from observation.

The footsteps resumed. Quickly. Moving toward them.

Charlotte inhaled sharply.

"Trust me," Sidney whispered.

And kissed her.

She was so startled that she hardly knew how to respond. It was a long kiss—long enough for her to wonder what on earth Sidney was thinking, kissing her without any sort of understanding between them, having known each other not even two days—and at a time like this! Long enough for Sidney to move his hands to hold her face between his palms. Long enough for her to know that she ought to raise one of her own hands and slap his presumptuous cheek. Long enough to realize that she did not want to slap his cheek, because she was kind of, sort of, maybe just a little bit enjoying the sensation of Sidney Parker softly kissing her.

Long enough that, heaven help her, she began to kiss him back.

In truth, the kiss probably did not last all that long. Time seems to slow down during moments of great apprehension, such the seconds before an unavoidable accident, or when one is about to be discovered by an ornery and possibly dangerous old man roaming suspiciously through a darkened mansion in the middle of the night. But it lasted long enough that the kiss was still in progress when the drapery panel was unceremoniously yanked back to expose them.

Sidney immediately broke off the kiss, turned Charlotte's head so that she faced away from him and Josiah, and moved his own head so that it blocked Josiah's view of hers as he regarded Mr. Hollis.

Josiah chuckled. "Well, now, Mr. Parker. I thought I heard somebody skulking about in here, but I did not expect to find you, let alone *two* somebodies."

Sidney stepped away from Charlotte and drew the panel so that it concealed her as they spoke. Her heart yet raced—in response to what had just transpired between her and Sidney, and in dread of what was about to transpire between Sidney and Josiah Hollis.

"We did not realize anyone else was in this part of the house," Sidney replied.

"Obviously." A pause followed, then Josiah spoke again. "I seem to have interrupted a tête-à-tête between you and Miss . . . ?"

Charlotte released her breath. Apparently, between the darkness and Sidney's strategic movements, Josiah had not been able to identify her.

"Miss Never-you-mind," Sidney said. "You may embarrass *me* all you like, Hollis, but surely we can agree to allow the lady her privacy?"

"Women are disappearing from this house left and right, Mr. Parker; you will understand if I am not sure what I just discovered. Is that lady with you willingly?"

"Most willingly. I give you my word as a gentleman."

Most willingly. Charlotte's face flushed so hot with embarrassment that she could barely listen as the conversation continued.

"I could observe that a gentleman would not have put the lady in such a compromising position."

"I likewise could say that a gentleman would not be roaming the house at this hour in the dark without a purpose. You witnessed mine—what is yours?"

"Never *you* mind."

"Come, now—you bade us all good night when you left the portrait room only a short while ago, and now, just when my friend and I thought we had found an empty corner of the house, you appear. Did you decide to follow Mr. Granville's suggestion and take a sentimental tour after all?"

"In a manner of speaking. Mr. Granville's words inspired me to visit my uncle Archibald's portrait before retiring for the night. Unfortunately, two careless lovers broke a vase and interrupted me, and now I suddenly find myself so sleepy that I believe I will barely make it to my chamber. So once more, I bid good night to you—and your *friend*."

"Good night to you, as well, then." Sidney paused. "Mr. Hollis, I—*we*—appreciate your discretion."

"Believe it or not, Mr. Parker, I was young once, too." He chuckled. "For that matter, so was my uncle Archibald. Yours is not the first stolen kiss within these walls."

A long silence followed. Charlotte spent the time trying to collect herself before facing Sidney again.

For him, the kiss had been a performance—a means of diverting Mr. Hollis from realizing they had been spying on him. It had been a desperate, last-second gambit, clever in its simplicity, successful in its execution.

Too successful, for it had misdirected her, too; had led her to act in a manner inconsistent with her principles and upbringing.

The kiss itself she could blame on circumstances. On Sidney. It certainly was not something she herself would have initiated, with any gentleman, ever. But she had returned the kiss—and for that, she could indict no one but herself.

A gambit requires a sacrifice. Was that sacrifice to be her reputation?—If not her reputation among society in general (and she shuddered to think that she now was dependent upon not only Sidney Parker but Josiah Hollis for the preservation of that), then the esteem (or, now, lack thereof) in which Sidney Parker himself regarded her?

At the very least, her own self-regard suffered. She was embarrassed. Ashamed. *Most willingly.* What did he think of her? At best, he believed her to be a naïve country girl, momentarily deceived by her own wishful thinking that the kiss was real, that the worldly Sidney Parker could possibly have developed romantic interest in her *ever,* let alone in the space of a day. At worst, he thought her a lightskirt, willing to sacrifice propriety for pleasure. Or would he simply take her for that too common of drawing-room denizens—a calculating husband-hunter who seized any opportunity to employ feminine wiles in hopes of catching a wealthy bachelor?

Alternatively, had it been Sidney who was the opportunist, drawing

her into a kiss that she could not resist without exposing their presence to Hollis? *Trust me,* he had said—but could she? Dare she? He
was worldly—far more so than she. Was he in the habit of using his
charm to seduce less sophisticated young women?

She realized that she did not really know much about Sidney
Parker—only that he was the brother of Thomas Parker, a man whom
both she and her parents trusted, and who spoke well of Sidney. That
connection ought to provide sufficient recommendation, but scoun-
drels could come from respectable families as well as disreputable
ones, and kinship could blind one to a sibling's faults. Even Thomas
Parker had said that Sidney "lived too much in the world to be settled." She now wondered exactly what he had meant by that.

One thing she knew for certain: There could be no happy result
of that kiss. Sidney had possibly revealed himself as a rake, she had
proved herself a fool, and her reputation now lay at the mercy and
discretion of Josiah Hollis.

Her thoughts whirling thus, she had worked herself into an advanced state of mortification and misery when Sidney at last pulled
aside the curtain.

"Hollis is gone."

Another round of lightning had arrived outside and its intermittent flashes offered sufficient illumination for them to see each other's
faces once more. She searched his, hoping to find in it some hint of his
thoughts. Unfortunately, his expression revealed little, beyond the impression that he studied her with the same goal in mind. She dropped
her gaze, unable to bear his scrutiny.

"I watched him walk down the corridor as far as I could see," he
said, "to ensure he did not linger outside the doorway to eavesdrop
on us. I think he is indeed sleepy, or perhaps had too much wine—
he wove a bit as he walked."

She nodded in acknowledgment, but said nothing. She did not
trust her voice to remain steady, even if it managed to find its way
around the enormous lump in her throat that defied every attempt to
swallow it.

"Miss Heywood—" He paused. "Pray forgive me. I thought only of
thwarting Hollis, to embarrass him into overlooking any other
purpose we might have had for being here. It was the decision of

an instant, motivated, I assure you, by well-meant—if flawed—intentions. In the clarity of hindsight, I realize my failure to adequately consider all the repercussions."

There—it was confirmed. The kiss had indeed meant nothing to him. Her humiliation was complete. Now it was merely a matter of how many people would know of it.

"Do you honestly believe he will keep his discovery of us to himself?" she asked.

"I cannot say for certain. I am more inclined to think so than I would have been an hour ago, but we all distrust him. Fortunately, he could not identify you—only me."

"There are six ladies among the guests. Two of them are your sisters, Miss Denham is missing, and Mrs. Darcy is happily married. That leaves me and Miss Brereton. My identity cannot be difficult to puzzle out, even for Josiah Hollis."

"Perhaps he took you for one of the housemaids?"

She had been wrong—*now* her humiliation was complete. She struggled to maintain her composure. And to think of something to say that would not expose the mortification consuming her.

"Did *you?*"

The blunt question startled him. It startled her.

"I meant that in a hopeful way," he said. "If Hollis thinks I was with a servant, that is hardly a matter worth spreading tales about."

"Why? Are you in the habit of dallying with servants?"

"No." He seemed about to add something else, but stopped. She wondered what it had been. *Only deluded daughters of country squires?* The awkwardness between them was palpable, more than she could bear any longer.

"I am returning to the portrait room," she declared.

He nodded, looking relieved. "I will escort you, then attempt to catch up with Mr. Hollis again."

"I can find my own way."

"Miss Heywood, whatever your feelings toward me at this moment, I implore you to reconsider. Four ladies have gone missing tonight—pray, do not render yourself vulnerable to becoming a fifth. I will see you there safely. My conscience will not permit me to do otherwise."

"I have seen what your conscience permits. Mine dictates that we part company."

"I cannot allow you to do that." He spoke with intensity that made her nervous.

"You cannot *allow* me? Who are you to determine what I am *allowed* to do?"

"I am your friend, whether at this moment you believe me to be or not. The man you entrusted with your safety earlier this evening, when I found you alone in the dark."

A defensive shiver ran down her spine. Indeed, he had been cultivating her trust all evening, using his charm to disarm her. And yes, she *had* trusted him when they encountered each other in the gallery—despite his never having fully explained what had brought him to that room, of all places in this vast house. Or why he, too, had been wandering the house past the appointed time at which all the guests were to reconvene. Or where he had gone after parting ways with Mr. Granville.

He had found her after she fled Susan Parker's chamber, spooked by a sense of being watched. He had dismissed the significance of her experience—indeed, had outright discouraged her from mentioning it to the Darcys. How could he have been so confident that she had nothing to fear? When people were missing and everybody was trying to piece together what was happening?

A terrible thought took possession of her. What if his discovery of her in the gallery had not been a coincidence—because it was he whom she had sensed in his sisters' chamber, and he had followed her?

"Miss Heywood?" His voice penetrated her disturbing reverie, and she realized she had not spoken for several minutes. "Is there anything I can do to regain your trust?"

Another shiver passed through her. "Answer one question."

"Ask it."

"Do you know more about tonight's events than you are letting on?"

The moment she uttered the words, she regretted them. If he were indeed involved in the disappearances, she had just betrayed her suspicion to him. And at present she was once more alone with him in the dark. *Do not allow yourself to be left alone with anyone you do not absolutely trust.*

He paused before answering—too long. Long enough for his hesitation to condemn him. Long enough for her to wonder whether Mr. Hollis was still close enough to hear her scream if she had need.

"My own sisters comprise half the missing ladies," he finally said. "Why would I keep secret any information I might possess?"

To use the circumstances to take advantage of her? Even if he had nothing to do with the other ladies' disappearances, Sidney Parker could still be a rake. Her heart pounded; her head began to ache as thoughts came in such a rushed jumble that she could not sort the sensible ones from the panicked.

"I do not know you well enough to speculate," she replied. "Indeed, I realize I do not know you at all."

"Surely you know enough about my character—"

"It is your character about which I am particularly in doubt after what transpired behind that drapery."

He looked as if she had just delivered the slap she had contemplated earlier. She had injured him. To impugn a gentleman's honor was a matter as serious as his offense against her; were she a man, they might have gone so far as to settle their differences on a remote field at dawn. Then again, were she a man, he would not have kissed her behind the drapery.

"I suppose I deserve that," he said quietly. "My transgression was great. Again, I offer my most sincere and humble apology for my poor decision. But Miss Heywood, if you are unable to forgive me—and I do not deny your right to withhold your forgiveness—can you at least agree to a tentative truce long enough for me to return you to your friends the Darcys? There is a kidnapper loose in this house. I fear for your safety should you walk these corridors alone. I have enough on my conscience tonight; were your disappearance added to it, I could not forgive myself."

Charlotte wanted to trust him. She did not want to believe Sidney Parker capable of treachery against her or anyone else. But this had been the longest day of her life, one so fraught with confusion and anxiety that it now left her too physically and emotionally weary to trust her own judgment. Was it more dangerous—in any number of ways—for her to remain alone with him, or to venture through the house without him?

She wondered what he had meant about having enough on his conscience; then wondered whether she truly wanted to know. Her pulse still raced. She felt like a mouse befriended by a cat, unsure whether he was toying with her before pouncing. She needed to remove herself from him, needed to think clearly.

"I will return to the portrait room by myself," she said.

"If you are going anywhere, it is with me. Do not resist me on this, Miss Heywood. I will pick you up and carry you if I must. You leave me no choice."

She recalled how strongly he had seized her in the gallery when they had collided . . . how completely his arms had surrounded her behind the drapery panel. Fear overwhelmed her—along with a primal urge to flee.

He advanced a step toward her. She flinched and instinctively retreated several steps back.

"If you are a gentleman, Mr. Parker, you will not force me into a situation I do not want to be in." Her voice trembled. So did she.

He stopped in place. "You are right—I will not." He held up his hands in surrender. "Is there no persuading you from this course of action?"

She shook her head.

"Then go," he said. "Go quickly—do not tarry on your way." She turned and hastened toward the door while he was still speaking. "And promise me that you will somehow keep yourself safe."

She made no promise; she had already begun her flight.

Twenty-eight

She was sick of exploring, and desired but to be safe in her own room, with her own heart only privy to its folly.
                                                           —Northanger Abbey

arcy had not realized, during their first visit to the study, just how many documents its cabinet held. Now, after they had unrolled each one, the half dozen of greatest interest to him and Elizabeth lay spread on the desk.

Elizabeth stood nearest an architectural drawing of the ground floor, alternating her examination of it with surreptitious glances over her shoulder at the bear head on the wall.

"It is not going to come down and bite you," Darcy said.

"I know—I just cannot understand the appeal of having it in here—staring at one all the while," she said.

The sketch closest to Darcy depicted the castle ruins upon which the house had been built. "It appears that the original castle had two posterns—tunnels constructed to enable escape or sallies in the event of a siege," he said. "One led east, the other, west. However, there is no evidence of them on the architectural drawings of the modern Sanditon House."

"That does not mean they no longer exist," Elizabeth replied.

"Oh, I believe they still exist—or at least one did as late as a hundred years ago. But we still do not know where it enters the house or where it leads, let alone whether it remains in use today. In the course of time, either or both tunnels could have collapsed, or flooded, or been filled in, or had their entrances and exits built over."

"My guess is that Archibald's letter refers to the west tunnel, and that it exits somewhere near the grotto. That seems to have been his and Ivy's trysting place; he could go to meet her without being seen, or from there smuggle her into the house."

"Agreed. But who would know of it now? My impression is that the west side of the property sees little use. The hermitage has sat vacant since Mad Woodcock died, and the grotto abandoned since Archibald's death, if not before."

"I should think the groundskeeper would be aware of it."

"Perhaps—depending upon how well hidden the exit is. The grotto itself is so covered in overgrowth that I nearly missed *its* entrance. Even the groundskeeper might be unaware of a tunnel that has not been used since before he was born, with an exit that is *meant* to be hidden, on a part of the property that has fallen into disuse."

"Which would make it perfect for a kidnapper to enter and exit the house without being seen. However, where would he then take his victims, once he emerges from the tunnel with them? Especially in this weather? You and Mr. Hollis already checked for Lady Denham in the grotto."

"Yes . . ." He drew his brows together. "Come to think of it, Mr. Hollis tried to dissuade me from going inside. He claimed his lumbago troubled him and that he wanted to get back to the house before the storm broke. I wonder now whether he had another purpose for keeping me away. Regardless—from what I saw of the interior, I doubt that is where the missing ladies are being held."

"What of the hermitage?"

"It was Mr. Granville who visited that building during our search. He reported it empty and in very poor repair. If we want more details, we shall have to ask him."

She moved to a different side of the desk, where the architectural rendering of the cellars was spread, and examined it for the third time in fifteen minutes. "I keep studying this drawing as if the tunnel entrances will suddenly appear on it, if only I stare long enough." She sighed. "But they have not. I see only servants' passages that lead to the upper floors of the house."

Darcy consulted the drawing of the ground floor. "They appear to be rather disconnected—an inefficient arrangement. There are places where two or three rooms connect to each other, but not to the main servants' corridors, even if they are adjacent. The state apartment seems to have two of its rooms accessible to servants—but they are two different passages. What is the sense in that?"

"I suppose every house cannot be a Pemberley." Elizabeth looked at the first-floor rendering. "The master apartment has a similar arrangement, and I cannot see the sense in it, either. Perhaps the rooms or passages were constructed at different times? Mrs. Riley or Rebecca can tell us whether and how the servants' passages are used, if we really want to know." She paused. "Mrs. Riley might also be able to tell us something about the tunnels. She has been here long enough that she might have heard stories passed down through generations of servants."

Darcy consulted his watch. "This has taken longer than anticipated. It is time—past time—we returned to the portrait room. With luck, Sir Edward has come back by now with Sir Harry's watch, and if we do not find Miss Denham there, we need to alert the others to her disappearance."

"And that of Josiah Hollis?"

Darcy glanced at the renderings once more. Josiah Hollis had lived in this house some years as its tacit heir—long enough to have explored it thoroughly, inside and out. Josiah Hollis had tried to dissuade him from searching the grotto. Josiah Hollis had a grudge with the missing Lady Denham that spanned decades.

"I do not think Mr. Hollis has disappeared." He looked up from the drawings and met his wife's gaze. "In fact, I think Josiah Hollis might know more about these tunnels than anyone realizes."

As she fled to the portrait room, Charlotte did not need Sidney Parker's exhortation to hasten her steps. She wanted to put as much distance as possible, as quickly as possible, between herself and him. Their exchange had proceeded horribly, twisting sharply in directions she had never intended, like a runaway carriage violently pulled by horses whose driver has lost control.

She did not know what upset her more—the cause of their falling-out, or the quarrel itself. Her eyes grew warm as tears welled up. She continued down the corridor and around a corner, but found herself so distraught that she started feeling dizzy. It was not like her to allow emotions to affect her so. But then, she had been doing a lot of things tonight that exceeded the bounds of her usual behavior.

The dizziness became more pronounced—the fatigue of a sleepless night filled with emotional strain catching up with her. She stopped and placed one hand on the wall to support herself. Sidney's warning not to tarry echoed in her ears. Vexed as she was with him, she knew he was right about that. She would pause for only a minute—just long enough to regain her bearings.

A minute proved too long.

She sensed someone approaching behind her. Before she could turn around, before she could cry out, a hand covered her mouth. A strong arm encircled her in a firm hold.

And a familiar voice said, "My dear, remain silent, and all will be well—

"Trust me."

Twenty-nine

*"After a very short search, you will discover a division in the tap-
estry so artfully constructed as to defy the minutest inspection,
and on opening it, a door will immediately appear."*
                              —Henry Tilney, Northanger Abbey

*E*lizabeth and Darcy left the study and proceeded through the
library toward the door leading to the corridor. As they passed
the bookcases, however, Elizabeth noticed that the books which had
been lying out on their previous visit had been reshelved.

She stopped to take a closer look. "This is odd," she said.

"What is?"

"I am surprised to see these books rearranged since we were here
earlier in the evening. I should think every occupant of this house—
guest or servant—has been too engaged in more important matters
to trouble with their placement." She took a few steps back from the
bookcase. A thin gap ran its full height between it and the two cases
on either side. A glance at the others surrounding the room revealed
no such gap. "When we examined the drawings just now, did you
notice whether the library has a servants' passage behind it?"

"I did not note one."

"Nor did I." Had she, she might have been inclined to come out of
the study to take a look. As it was, she advanced to the reorganized
shelf and pulled off several of the volumes that had been lying loose
before, handing them to Darcy. Realizing what she was about, he set

them on a nearby table, along with their candle, and returned for more, removing them from the shelf himself.

The front row of books cleared, she reached for the row behind it—weightier volumes of more distinguished age and content. Behind a dignified edition of Shakespeare's plays, she discovered it: a lever. Grasping it firmly, she pulled.

The latch barely made a sound as it released . . . nor did the bookcase, as it swung back to reveal a passage.

"Well, now," Elizabeth said. "One wonders what else does not appear on those drawings."

Darcy retrieved their candle. "Let us find out."

The narrow corridor ran in two directions, one along the library's wall and toward the study, the other in the opposite direction, toward the bedroom wing. They took the former. The passage was rough—bare timbers and walls—but in good repair. They followed it until they reached a dead end. A wide wooden settle sat against the wall on one side, with a footstool before it and a small table next to it; elsewise, the space was empty.

"This is rather a let-down," Elizabeth said. "What is the purpose of a passage that simply ends without going anywhere? And who would have need of seating in here?"

"Indeed," Darcy said, studying the high-backed bench. Even the box seat was high; Elizabeth doubted her feet would fully touch the floor should she sit upon it. "This is hardly a space in which one would while away leisure hours."

He handed the candle to her and approached the bench. It was an old settle, with a hinged seat-top that opened for storage. He lifted the lid and she brought the candle near. Though the height of the seat made the space within unusually deep, it was empty.

"How very disappointing," she said. "We come upon a mysterious piece of furniture in the hidden passage of an old mansion, and all we find within are shadows."

"What were you hoping to find?" Darcy asked.

"Something—anything. I am not too particular. I might have been satisfied with a laundry list." As Darcy closed the lid, she passed the candle around the settle's sides. The only thing unusual about it was the seat's height. "Perhaps it was put here years ago simply to get it out of the way. It appears solidly built, but the surface of the seat is scuffed, and the bench height makes it impractical for use by anyone but gentlemen—tall gentlemen, at that. A lady would need the footstool just to mount the bench without looking like a child wiggling onto an adult-sized chair."

"So it is not tempting you to sit and laze a while?"

"Hardly. I think we are done here."

"Agreed." His eyes made one final floor-to-ceiling sweep of the space—and stopped on a section of the wall several feet above the top of the settle's back. She followed his gaze.

"Is that a hole in the wall?"

"I believe it is." Gripping the settle's back, he placed one booted foot on the seat and hoisted himself to stand upon it. The hole was now at his eye level. "Hand me the candle."

She did so. He held it up to the hole to look within, and released a low chuckle.

"What do you see?"

"Teeth."

"I do hope you mean somebody left behind a comb."

"Not quite." He extended his hand to help her up. "Come—see for yourself."

With his aid, she climbed onto the seat—a little more awkwardly than he had, ladies' gowns seldom contributing success to such action. Unfortunately, her effort resulted in disappointment; even on her toes, she was too short to be able to see inside the hole. Both agreed that any attempt by Darcy to lift her did not seem prudent—the seat was wide, but not *that* wide, and they did not want to risk either of them losing their balance.

"Here." Darcy handed her the candle and dismounted. He picked up the footstool and set it on the bench below the hole. She stepped onto it; the additional height proved just enough to enable her to look within the hole. The opening extended through the entire thickness of the wall, into the room that lay on the other side. That end was indeed ringed by sharp ivory points.

She looked at Darcy in confusion.

"The bear," he said. "In the study—you are looking through the bear's maw."

Her eyes widened and she turned to look again. "I cannot see anything beyond the teeth."

"That is because the room is dark. Were it lit, from this height you could probably see part of the room. More important, even if the view is extremely limited, you could hear what transpired."

"A spy hole." No wonder the bear had made her feel as if she were being watched. "Do you think someone observed us earlier—when the books on the shelf were disturbed?"

"Not only do I think it possible, I believe we and our fellow guests might have been spied upon in other rooms of this house throughout the evening. I suspect this is not the only such observation area in Sanditon House—in fact, spaces such as this probably account for the gaps between servants' corridors that we noted on the drawings. Some of them might even connect to the servants' passages via doors not obvious to those unaware of them, allowing someone to move from any room to another within the house without being seen— such as our kidnapper."

"Or Archibald and Ivy."

"Or the Hollis ghost . . ."

It took her a moment to catch his meaning, but when she did, she laughed.

"Who is not the ghost of previous Sanditon House masters at all," she said, "but whoever the present master happens to be, checking up on his staff to keep them on their toes. Should he make noise or do something else that inadvertently threatens to reveal his presence, it gets blamed on the ghost."

"That is my theory." Darcy reached for Elizabeth's hand and helped her down first from the stool, and then to the floor. "The passages, and fiction of the Hollis ghost, also provide the house's owner a way of keeping an eye on visitors he does not trust."

Archibald and Ivy again came to her mind. "Or of spying on his own family members. Archibald might have risked more than he knew by bringing Ivy into the house."

"If Archibald knew about the tunnels, he likely knew about these observatories. In fact, the tunnels might enter the house through these secret rooms, which would explain why they, too, are not represented on the drawings."

"I wonder whether his brother knew of the tunnels or the passages—he wrote that Oswald skulked around, trying to catch him in some transgression." Elizabeth mused a moment. "More pertinent to our present crisis, who knows about them now? Do you think Josiah Hollis is aware of them? He spent his youth being groomed as Archibald's heir."

"And he has spent his adulthood resenting Lady Denham for thwarting that plan. Knowledge of these passages would certainly provide him access to kidnap her—along with the other ladies. He could also use them to eavesdrop on the rest of us, staying abreast of our progress as we investigate."

"He has certainly made a point of absenting himself from us for significant periods of time tonight—including presently. I wonder whether the others have seen him since we left the portrait room."

"Let us go find out," Darcy said. "We have been too long away as it is. Let us also stop at Josiah Hollis's bedchamber once more en route, in case he has returned there."

They headed back to the library, where they closed the passage door and replaced the books on the shelf. "Are they in the same order?" Darcy asked.

"I believe so," she replied. "If not, we must simply hope the faulty arrangement goes unnoticed by anyone who might know the difference."

As they approached the wing containing most of the bedchambers, Elizabeth asked Darcy how he intended to coax Mr. Hollis into revealing the extent of his knowledge regarding the passages and tunnels. He was about to reply when they turned a corner and stopped suddenly.

Mr. Hollis lay prone on the floor—motionless.

Sidney Parker bent over him. Holding a candlestick.

Thirty

*"What one means one day, you know, one may not mean the next.
Circumstances change, opinions alter."*
— *Isabella Thorpe,* Northanger Abbey

t Elizabeth's sharp intake of breath, Sidney turned his head toward them.

"Mr. Darcy—Mrs. Darcy!" He rose. "I have been searching everywhere for you."

Darcy glanced from Sidney's face . . . to the candlestick . . . to Mr. Hollis . . . and back. Sidney gripped the heavy silver candlestick by its stem, its unlit stub barely rising above the nozzle. Mr. Hollis lay in a heap behind him. Darcy saw no blood, but with Sidney partially blocking his view of the body, he also could see no confirmation that Hollis breathed.

"What transpired here?"

"I wish I knew. I was trying to find Mr. Hollis—well, actually I was heading to the portrait room in hopes of finding Miss Heywood, but I was also on the watch for Mr. Hollis—when I came upon him like this."

Darcy studied Mr. Parker. Sidney's statements seemed to contradict each other, and his manner was nervous.

"Is he alive?"

"Yes—but unconscious. I think he imbibed too much wine. He

drank more than his share of it when he joined us in the portrait room after you left, and when last I saw him, he complained of feeling very sleepy. I have been trying to rouse him."

"With that candlestick?"

"What?" He looked at the candlestick in his hand as if it were a foreign object. "Oh!" He glanced at Hollis, then turned back to Darcy. "This does not look good, does it? I assure you—I have not used it as a weapon. Indeed, he does not appear to be injured—come see for yourself. I borrowed the candlestick from the portrait room to assist my search for Miss Heywood. Unfortunately, what remained of its taper soon sputtered out."

They approached Mr. Hollis's still form. Elizabeth knelt down to attend him while Darcy kept a close eye on Sidney.

"I thought you just said you were looking for Mr. Hollis?" Darcy said. "And before that, us."

"I did—I was—that is how it all began. Miss Heywood and I were trying to find you—"

Elizabeth suspended her ministrations to interrupt. "We last saw both of you in the portrait room. You left it together?"

"Yes."

"And now you are trying to find *her*? How did you become separated?"

He paused. "It . . . became necessary. When we parted ways, it was her intention to return to the portrait room to join you and Mr. Darcy." His expression became anxious. "Are you telling me that she never arrived?"

"We have not returned to the portrait room ourselves since we last saw you." Elizabeth's tone was subdued—a sign of her own growing dread. "Have none of the others seen her?"

"None of the others are there. Sir Edward returned with the wrong watch and has gone back to Denham Park for the proper one. And a servant arrived from Trafalgar House to report that Tom's son—the one with the cold—has taken a turn for the worse. Mary fears pneumonia and had hoped Diana could come to provide medical aid, but she must settle for Tom and Arthur. Miss Heywood and I were seeking you to inform you of their departure."

"Where are Mr. Granville and Miss Brereton?" Darcy asked.

"I do not know—they remained in the portrait room when Miss Heywood and I left, but were not there when I went back just now—there was only a note from Granville, saying that he and Miss Brereton had to leave the portrait room but that she was safe. I assume he was vague because he did not know who else might discover the note. At least, however, we need not fear for Miss Brereton's welfare. I wish I could say the same for Miss Heywood. Confound it all! I never should have let her leave my sight."

"No, you should not have." Elizabeth's tone was sharp, and in her criticism of Sidney, Darcy also detected a note of self-reproach. "Why did you?"

Sidney's gaze dropped to the candlestick still in his grasp. He shifted it from one hand to the other. "We . . . had a falling-out. Afterward, she wanted to be free of my company." He looked at Elizabeth once more. "I tried to persuade her to let me escort her back to the portrait room, but she refused so vehemently that I honored her wishes, though against my better judgment."

"May I ask what you quarreled over?" she said.

"It was a personal matter. I would rather not divulge the particulars. If Miss Heywood elects to discuss it with you, that is her choice, but I believe that my doing so would breach a confidence."

"Has it any bearing on our present crisis?" Darcy asked.

"No."

Darcy wondered what sort of "personal matter" could arise between two people who scarcely knew each other, that would result in Miss Heywood making such a rash and incautious decision. A few speculations passed through his mind, none of them favorable to Sidney Parker, but he let the subject drop for now.

"So you separated—and then what?"

"Miss Heywood headed back to the portrait room, while I tried to catch up with Mr. Hollis. We had witnessed him entering your apartment and stealing something from Archibald Hollis's clothing trunk—a miniature portrait, of whom I know not. He then took it to the long gallery and examined it beside a portrait of Archibald. For what purpose, I have no idea."

Darcy and Elizabeth exchanged glances. They knew whom the miniature depicted. Did Josiah Hollis know of—or suspect—the affair between Archibald and Ivy Woodcock? If he did, of what interest was it to him?

Darcy gestured toward Josiah's unconscious form. "Obviously, you managed to 'catch up' with him."

"Not immediately. First, I went to the portrait room, expecting to find you, Miss Heywood, Miss Brereton, Mr. Granville, and perhaps even Mr. Hollis or the returned Sir Edward. When I instead found the room vacant, I came up here hoping someone had returned to his or her bedchamber—and discovered Mr. Hollis, as you see him now, only a few minutes before you appeared."

Upon the last mention of his name, Mr. Hollis stirred and emitted a powerful snore. Darcy took it as a positive sign that he was drifting closer to consciousness.

Elizabeth shook him by the shoulder. "Mr. Hollis? Mr. Hollis, wake up."

"Yes, Mr. Hollis, do wake up," Darcy echoed, hoping his more forceful tone would penetrate the gentleman's inebriation. It seemed to help; Hollis stirred again, like a child who does not want to awaken. Darcy went to him and gave him a firm shake.

"I cannot believe Sir Edward was so careless as to bring the wrong watch, with so much depending on it," Elizabeth said. "How soon do you think we can anticipate his return?"

Sidney shifted uncomfortably. "We might not see him at all again tonight. But if we do, he will not have Sir Harry's watch in his possession."

"Why not?"

He hesitated. "Because I do."

He withdrew the watch he carried in his own fob pocket and gave it to Darcy for inspection. Elizabeth rose and came forward to examine it as well. Sure enough, it was the gold timepiece from Sir Harry's portrait, inscribed with the late baronet's name and date of ascension to the title.

Darcy, who had just begun to relax his guard with Sidney, regarded him warily as he handed the watch back to him. "How did you come to possess this?"

"I possess other information that I have been withholding—again, in confidence for someone else." He returned the watch to his pocket.

"However, for the safety of all the missing ladies, I believe myself obligated to divulge it now." He paused, appearing uncertain as to the reception his news was about to meet.

"I know who is responsible for Lady Denham's disappearance."

Thirty-one

"I have been a very liberal friend to Sir Edward. . . . For though I am only the Dowager my Dear, and he is the Heir, things do not stand between us in the way they commonly do between those two parties. Not a shilling do I receive from the Denham Estate. Sir Edward has no Payments to make me. . . . It is I that help him."
—Lady Denham, Sanditon

*E*lizabeth regarded Sidney in astonishment. "Who?"

"Lady Denham herself."

It was the answer she had least expected. What could he possibly mean by that statement—that some action on the dowager's part had provided the catalyst for her kidnapping? Darcy appeared equally surprised.

"I happened upon her when she was in London last Michaelmas," Sidney continued. "I had business in Gracechurch Street, and as I passed a pawnbroker's shop, she came out its door in such a state of agitation that she did not even recognize me. I stopped her and enquired whether she was in need of assistance. Glad for the sight of an old friend, she asked me to hail her a hackney-cab, admitting she was too distraught to walk on public streets. I offered to see her safely to her lodgings, and she gratefully accepted, sending her maid ahead by foot. Once inside the cab, however, Lady Denham said she did not want to return to her cousins' house immediately, and asked if we could go to a park and simply drive until she collected herself.

"In the course of our drive, she revealed that she had visited the pawnshop in hopes of reclaiming some articles she had taken there many years ago following Archibald Hollis's death, but had come to regret parting with. Though prepared for the likelihood that they had been sold, she was upset to discover that the pawnbroker himself was no longer at that address, and that a new broker now conducted business there. He had no information about the disposal of any of her items, but invited her to take a look at the finer goods he had on display—perhaps she could acquire suitable replacements? She declined, but as she turned to go, she spied an item in his case that she had not pawned, but immediately recognized: Sir Harry's watch.

"She asked the broker when he had acquired it, and from whom. He maintained his client's anonymity, but offered enough details— thinking to cultivate a sale—that Lady Denham knew without doubt that Sir Edward could not claim the watch had been stolen or had otherwise found its way to the pawnshop without his knowledge— the baronet had pawned the timepiece himself."

Elizabeth wondered why Sir Edward would do such a thing. A baronet presently building a cottage ornée on his estate could not be in such desperate circumstances that the income from a pawned watch would make a difference. But then, she wondered at many of the behaviors she had observed in him.

"You can imagine Lady Denham's outrage at Sir Edward's having sold for coin what ought to have been priceless in sentiment," Sidney continued. "She also took the sale as a slight against herself, for Sir Harry had not specifically bequeathed the watch to his nephew—it had been a gift she chose to give. After all she had done for him and Miss Denham, to be thus treated wounded both her pride and her heart. She questioned the affection he and Miss Denham had shown her through the years, and wondered whether it had been purely mercenary in motive. With no children of her own, she had intended to leave him her estate, but now reconsidered."

"If he valued a personal remembrance so lightly, what would he do with the whole fortune?" Elizabeth said.

"Precisely. Yet, who else was there to whom she could bequeath it? After decades of spurning her Brereton cousins' overtures of friendship out of the belief that they were financially inspired, she was discovering during her present visit that they were rather good people after all, but she still did not know any of them very well. And her

Hollis relations from her first marriage had given her such trouble in the past that she did not want to bequeath anything to them. 'I have half a mind to just leave my fortune to your brother to invest in Sanditon,' she said. 'He could name a building or two after me, and at least I would be remembered and appreciated by the strangers who come to visit.'

"'Now, Lady Denham,' I replied, 'there are people among your acquaintance who appreciate you—I, for one, and I have no need of your estate to motivate my friendship. You simply have to determine who your true friends are, and you will know what to do.'

"This set her thinking, and she calmed down, and by the time I escorted her to the door of her cousins' house, her spirits had improved. I left believing that I had done a good service by her, and thought no more of it.

"She, however, thought very much about it, for when I next saw her—at the hotel here in Sanditon, just before I met you with Tom—she told me she had devised a plan by which she could determine who among her friends and relations held genuine affection for her. She would host a dinner party, stage her own disappearance, then observe the guests' reactions to see who applied themselves toward efforts to find her, and who used her absence as an opportunity to achieve their own ends. When I pointed out that her true friends would be put to considerable distress over her welfare, she said their anxiety would be of short duration and meet with great reward. 'Besides,' she said to me, 'you of all people cannot criticize the plan—it was your suggestion in the first place.'

"I countered that I had suggested nothing so specific, but she was decided. That very morning, from a window in the long gallery, she had witnessed a clandestine meeting between Sir Edward and Miss Brereton that caused her to doubt even Miss Brereton's loyalty toward her, and she could not rest until she determined the young lady's allegiance along with everyone else's. Further, she insisted that I assist the scheme by observing from within the company and reporting to her at least once before she deemed it time to reveal herself. She also entrusted Sir Harry's watch to my care, with instructions to produce it when Sir Edward admitted he could not. It was her intention to appear at that time, to confront him and any others who had shown themselves to be less than sympathetic regarding her disappearance. Not wanting to provoke her displeasure, or cause her to doubt my own sympathy toward her, I reluctantly agreed."

"So you have known all along that Lady Denham was in no danger, and allowed this hoax to continue unimpeded." Darcy's tone revealed his disdain.

"Not quite—it has progressed in directions I did not anticipate."

"What of the other missing ladies?" Elizabeth asked. Beside her, Mr. Hollis rolled onto his side but remained asleep. "How do they fit into Lady Denham's plan?"

"Well, that is just it—they do not," Sidney replied. "There was never any mention of other people disappearing. When Susan vanished, I was as surprised as the rest of you, and thought it must be a coincidence—that she had indeed wandered down to the stillroom or some other place, and would reappear shortly. Either that, or perhaps Lady Denham had also tapped my sister to aid her design.

"When Diana disappeared, I became more concerned—she is not by nature one to quietly follow somebody else's plan without trying to take control of it herself. Nor would she countenance her brothers being put to distress over both herself and Susan missing. For that matter, even given Lady Denham's motive for the scheme, I questioned whether she would go so far as to generate that much anxiety within our family, when it was the Denhams, Hollises, and Breretons whose loyalty she wanted to test."

"Why did you not divulge all to me then?" Darcy asked.

"Because that is also when the note about Sir Harry's watch appeared—which was the signal for me to meet Lady Denham within the hour. I resolved to question her about Susan's and Diana's disappearances and, regardless of her answer, tell her that I was done with the scheme and that it was time to reveal herself."

"How did she respond?" Elizabeth asked.

"She did not respond at all—though I went to our designated meeting spot, she never appeared. I went back again after Miss Heywood and I parted ways, and still saw no sign of her having been there."

"So Lady Denham is indeed missing?" Elizabeth said. Mr. Hollis stirred again. He seemed to be responding to their voices—hers most particularly, as she was in closest proximity.

"Or she is somewhere in the house continuing to spy on us," Darcy replied. "As you and I saw for ourselves, there are places specifically designed for that purpose. She could be in any room of this house— perhaps even listening to us right now."

"What sort of places?" Sidney asked.

"Hidden observatories behind the walls of various rooms," Elizabeth explained. "We discovered one with a spy hole into the study and suspect there are many more, connected within the house by interior passages, and to points outside the house through old postern tunnels."

"I suspected the house might hold spy holes or something of that nature," Sidney said. "When I asked Lady Denham how she planned to conduct her observation, she was rather vague, so I figured she had some means she did not want to reveal. But of tunnels, I had no inkling they existed."

"We believe Mr. Hollis might be familiar with them." Though Darcy lowered his voice, Mr. Hollis stirred at the mention of his name.

"He did live in this house as its heir for a time." Sidney paused. "The presence of tunnels is disturbing news—it means that even if Lady Denham is still in the house, the other missing ladies could be anywhere."

"So you do not believe their absence is related to Lady Denham's plan?"

"Since Susan disappeared, I have been trying to think of what possible end the abductions could serve for Lady Denham, and have found none. I do not believe their absences are her doing, but rather, the work of another party. Further, if Lady Denham herself is indeed now truly missing, I believe the same individual is responsible for all their disappearances—especially now that you tell me of tunnels." He looked pointedly at Josiah Hollis and continued at a muted volume. "First Granville, then later Miss Heywood and I, followed Hollis as he moved through the house behaving suspiciously. If he is not the perpetrator himself, he is surely in collusion with the villain."

"I think it is time we forced him to wake and asked him some direct questions," Darcy said.

Doing so proved no easy matter. Mr. Hollis resisted coming to consciousness, and even when propped into an upright position, remained half asleep. His speech was slow, and he seemed to require much effort to find the words in his brain and operate his tongue to form them. He leaned his head against the wall behind him and opened his eyes but halfway, when he opened them at all.

"How much wine did he drink?" Darcy asked.

Sidney thought a moment. "Three, perhaps four glasses."

"That is not much, compared to what I have seen many gentlemen consume of an evening."

"True," Sidney said, "and he strikes me as a man who can hold his share of wine."

On the positive side, along with Hollis's person, his obstinacy was also sedated, rendering him less abrasive—compliant, even. His responses were simple and free of acrimony, if slow and slurred. He denied knowledge of the kidnappings, but did admit familiarity with the house's architectural secrets.

"Of course I know about the hidden corridors," he said, his s's stretching into hisses. "Discovered them myself when I was a boy, and used them to create mischief for the servants—until Uncle Archibald caught me at it. Didn't use them again until the night she returned."

"By 'she,' you refer to Lady Denham?" Darcy asked.

"No—the other one. But Lady Denham knew of the spy holes, too, and used them that night. As for the tunnels—" He released something like a chuckle, but in his somnolent state it came out more like a hiccup.

"Do you know where they lead?"

"One of them led to her becoming Lady Denham."

Darcy released an exasperated sigh and glanced to Elizabeth. "He is making no sense."

"Then it is up to us to make sense of it," Elizabeth replied. She looked at Mr. Hollis and addressed him as if she were attempting to extract information from Lily-Anne. "Mr. Hollis, what have the tunnels to do with Lady Denham's acquiring her title?"

"They are how she acquired Sir Harry." Mr. Hollis sat up a bit straighter and rubbed his temple. "One of the tunnels leads to Denham Park. She and the baronet wed so soon after her mourning ended, that I have always believed they must have been carrying on during it—perhaps even before Uncle Archibald died. The tunnel would have made it easy for her to go to him, or he to her, unseen."

"Denham Park?" Elizabeth said. "Does Sir Edward know of the tunnel?"

"Ask him. And if he tells you no, ask him how he managed to return here dry as dust from our search of the grounds, when all the rest of us got caught in the rain. Or did none of you notice that?"

Elizabeth, Darcy, and Sidney all looked at each other. "He also was dry when he returned with the false watch," Sidney recalled.

"I found a cobweb on him earlier in the evening," Elizabeth said.

"When was this?" Darcy asked.

"After Susan disappeared—when we thought she had merely wandered off. He claimed to have been searching for her in the attics."

Sidney frowned. "Why did he think my sister might have gone there?"

"He thought the Hollis ghost might have taken her. Or perhaps Ivy Woodcock."

Darcy released a sound of exasperation. "He and those ghosts! Every time a lady has disappeared tonight, he has tried to convince us that—"

He stopped. An unsettling thought occurred to all of them at once.

"That ghosts were responsible," Elizabeth finished. She mused a moment. "Was Sir Edward in someone else's company during any of the disappearances—someone who could vouch for his whereabouts?"

"I do not believe he was," said Sidney.

"Sir Edward—the kidnapper?" Darcy shook his head. "He is not that clever. And Miss Denham is among the missing women. Why would he abduct his own sister?"

"That little crosspatch is more likely to be an accessory to kidnapping than a victim of it," said Mr. Hollis. "Trying to pare down her competition for that poor Granville fellow she's been trying to reel in all night."

"Competition such as Lady Denham?" Darcy asked. "That is absurd."

"So is Sir Edward most of the time," said Sidney. "All I know is that five ladies are missing, including my sisters and Miss Heywood. And that I am tired of wandering around this house in the dark, looking for answers."

So was Darcy. Especially if the baronet could provide them.

"Mr. Hollis, where is that tunnel?"

Josiah Hollis remained too groggy to walk all the way to Denham Park; indeed, he had difficulty even reaching his bed.

"That is the last time I drink elderberry wine," he said as Darcy and Sidney assisted him into his chamber, where he could sleep off both the wine and its lingering influence. Elizabeth waited within earshot just outside the door. "I cannot recall its ever affecting me like this before," he mumbled.

The gentlemen helped Mr. Hollis remove his coat and boots. As he rolled into bed, he managed to stay awake just long enough to answer one last question from Darcy.

"If Sir Edward is indeed responsible for any or all of the ladies' disappearances, we cannot predict his state of mind upon our arrival, or of what else he might be capable," Darcy said. "Before we leave Sanditon House, can you direct us to the gun room?"

To Elizabeth, it seemed the tunnel led to the center of the earth, so extended a time did they follow it. She felt closed in and longed for fresh air. The lantern's glow struggled to illuminate the darkness ahead, but instead was swallowed by it.

She wished she knew what to anticipate when they reached Denham Park. Darcy and Sidney both thought it unlikely that Sir Edward would turn violent, but had taken the precaution of arming themselves with a pair of small military pistols they had found in the gun room. They carried them in the oversized pockets of the vintage frock coats they yet wore.

Just when she became convinced that the tunnel had no end, they came upon an unexpected fork. An opening on their left led to a stair; the main tunnel continued on as it had done.

"Apparently, Hollis did not see fit to warn us of this split," Sidney said.

Darcy brought the lantern closer to the stone wall to examine the opening. "He might not know about it." He shone the lantern farther into the opening. "This construction appears to me much more recent than that of the main tunnel."

"Which one do we take?" Sidney asked.

"The main one," Darcy replied. "Assuming it is the original tunnel, we know it leads to Denham Park."

He turned to head in that direction, but a faint sound caught Elizabeth's ear. "Wait just a moment," she said.

There it was—she heard it again. "I think I hear something. Let us go to the base of the stair."

They walked the twenty feet or so, then stood in silence, listening. It was a faint, sporadic sound, barely detectable.

"Voices," Darcy whispered.

They quietly climbed the stairs and came to a door. The voices behind it were stronger, but still too muffled to make out words. They sounded female. One of them, more forceful, rose above the others.

"That is Diana," Sidney murmured.

"Are you certain? Darcy asked. "The words are indistinguishable."

"I would know her tone anywhere."

Darcy studied the door. "It is less solid than I might expect. All the same, I hope we do not have to break it down. He tested the latch.

It gave.

Darcy pushed the door. It opened into an alcove, which they quietly entered. A larger room lay beyond, from which they could hear voices. Ladies' voices. All talking at once.

They stepped into it, then peered into the larger room beyond . . . wherein they discovered Susan, Diana, Miss Denham, and Sir Edward.

"Thank heavens you are here!" Sir Edward exclaimed, his expression full of desperation. "Please help me."

Thirty-two

Sir Edward's great object in life was to be seductive. With such per-
sonal advantages as he knew himself to possess, and such Talents
as he did also give himself credit for, he regarded it as his Duty. . . .
it was Clara alone on whom he had serious designs . . . She was
his rival in Lady D.'s favour . . . If she could not be won by affec-
tion, he must carry her off. He knew his Business.
                                                      —Sanditon

*P*ray, do not scold me—I do not think I can bear it just now,"
Sir Edward said. "I have been hearing enough of my folly from
my sister."

"It is no more than you deserve," Miss Denham responded. "Now
that the Darcys have arrived, may I go home?"

"You would abandon me just as more *guests* have joined us?"

Elizabeth scanned the parlor, taking in its old, mismatched furniture, bare wooden floor, unadorned walls, and heavy, closed draperies that gave the appearance of having been hastily hung. To her
dismay, she saw no sign of Miss Heywood.

Before she could enquire after her friend, Susan and Diana descended upon the new arrivals and drew them into the room as if
welcoming them to a party. Susan appeared very much as they had
last seen her, but Diana held a pungent compress to the top of her
head and approached in a less energetic manner than usual—which
is to say, that of a normal person. Both Parker sisters assailed them
with conversation at once.

"We have been waiting for you to arrive."

"Will Tom and Arthur be joining us, too?"

"I am so glad you are finally here!"

More practiced than Darcy and Elizabeth at maneuvering through the conversational barrage of his sisters, Sidney seized upon an opportune pause for air to interject.

"Where is 'here'? This does not look like any part of Denham Park that I have ever visited."

"We are in Sir Edward's new cottage ornée, of course!" exclaimed Susan. "It is not finished yet—we are the first to see it. Diana has been particularly helpful, offering Sir Edward and Miss Denham all sorts of advice as to its completion and fitting-up. Shall we ask them to show you through its rooms?"

Sidney glanced from Susan to Sir Edward, who remained several feet away still engaged with Miss Denham in a conversation he appeared to wish were not taking place. "How did you come to be here?"

"Have you forgotten? Sir Edward brought us here to keep us safe from Lady Denham's kidnapper. He said he told you and Tom that we had gone. Or perhaps it was Tom and Mr. Darcy."

"He did not utter a word about it to me." Darcy studied the baronet, taking his measure with a look that lasted long enough to attract Sir Edward's notice. "You say he persuaded you to come here for your own safety?"

"Not exactly," Susan said. "I do not recall the journey at all—I fainted before Sir Edward explained himself, or where we were going, or even who he was when he appeared in the dark, come to think of it. Regardless, I woke up here, and am grateful for his protection, even if unconventionally provided."

"Are you both well?" Elizabeth asked.

"As well as we ever are," Diana said. "Susan's sore gum is still giving her trouble, and she remains faint-headed from the leeches. I myself suffered a slight bump." She lowered the compress to reveal a dark, swollen bruise on top of her head.

"Good heavens!" Sidney exclaimed. "How did—"

"My own carelessness," she said. "But it is nothing to worry about. Doubtless, the injury looks worse than it is, and although I have likely sustained a concussion, it must be a mild one—as you can see, I am yet able to walk. The pain is tolerable—you know I am capable of bearing great agony with fortitude." She glanced at Sir Edward, who was following their conversation with an expression of increasing discomfort. "Now, our host, on the other hand—"

Diana leaned closer to her listeners, but did not lower her volume. "If you ask me, Sir Edward appears peaked. Do you not agree? I requested some herbs to prepare an infusion for him, but he has yet to provide them. I also lectured him at length about the need for better ventilation in that tunnel if he plans to continue using it regularly."

Sidney's gaze, which had been searching the room alternately with focusing on his sisters, now swept widely. "Has Sir Edward brought anyone else here? Miss Heywood, perhaps? I do not see her."

"Oh, yes!" Susan gestured toward a closed door opposite them. "She is in the next room, sleeping."

Relief suffused Elizabeth upon hearing this news. She would not have to confess to Charlotte's parents that she had somehow managed to lose their daughter. Sidney, too, visibly relaxed, though his expression quickly became anxious again. "Why is she by herself? Is she well?"

"Worn out, poor thing," said Diana. "She could scarcely keep her eyes open when Sir Edward brought her here. Miss Brereton, too—she is sleeping in one of the other rooms."

Miss Brereton, here as well! "I thought she was with Mr. Granville?"

"No, Mr. Granville asked Sir Edward to take care of her, and he was happy to oblige."

What had led to that request, Elizabeth could not imagine, but she was glad to now know Miss Brereton's whereabouts with certainty. They had found all the missing women except Lady Denham herself. There was still much to be discovered and uncovered, but Elizabeth dared to hope all would be resolved.

"Excuse me for a moment." Sidney started toward Charlotte's door with long strides. Elizabeth followed, wanting to ascertain with her own eyes that Charlotte was indeed safe and sound. They stopped when Diana outpaced them both and lifted a candle from the small table beside them.

"Miss Heywood complained of the headache when she woke earlier," Diana said. "I shall look in on her with you, in case she requires my aid."

"No—please stay with Susan and the others," Sidney replied, with a glance at Elizabeth that encompassed her in the request. "I will summon you if needed."

Recalling Sidney's admission that he and Charlotte had quarrelled, Elizabeth stepped back. Patching up matters between them might do more to relieve Charlotte's headache than any words Elizabeth could offer or medicinal remedy Diana could concoct.

Diana, however, stepped forward. "I was going to examine her again anyway—"

"You are needed more here," Sidney said. "If Sir Edward looks peaked, perhaps he is in need of nourishment. Have you yet shared with Miss Denham your recipe for toast-and-water? Nobody makes it like you do." He kissed her on the cheek, took the candle from her hand, and disappeared through the door.

A startled Diana stared after him, then turned around and strode to Miss Denham. "The recipe is very simple, actually—"

"I am sure our cook is quite capable of preparing it, and likely already has a recipe of her own." Miss Denham tilted her chin haughtily. "Besides, I do not think I have ever so much as entered the kitchen at Denham Park."

"Never?" Though Diana seemed a lady difficult to astonish, Miss Denham had accomplished it.

"I have servants for that."

"Well!" Undaunted, Diana straightened her shoulders. "How can you be sure they are preparing it—or anything else—properly, if you never learn at least enough to supervise? Come—this cottage has a kitchen, and it is time you became acquainted with invalid cookery."

"Mrs. Darcy, perhaps you could help me explain that mistresses of great houses such as Pemberley and Denham Park have no need to learn such things."

"Actually," Elizabeth said with secret delight, "I have an excellent recipe for gruel, writ out for me by the master himself of a great house in Surrey, that I will happily share with you once you have learned how to prepare toast-and-water."

Miss Denham released a sound of disgust and strutted from the room.

Willfully mistaking the younger woman's departure for an excursion to the kitchen, Diana hurried to catch up with her. "I suppose it is too much to hope that ingredients for eel broth are also at hand."

"Eel broth?" Susan exclaimed. "Wait for me!"

In the welcome silence that followed, Darcy closed the distance between himself and Sir Edward, whose countenance appeared still more peaked by the prospect of an imminent serving of toast-and-water being forced upon him. Elizabeth, too, drew close.

"Now that we are alone, let us waste no more time," Darcy said to the baronet. "What, exactly, is transpiring here?"

"Well, I—that is . . ." Sir Edward retreated a few steps, until the backs of his knees met a nearby chair. He almost fell into it, but caught his balance. "Um, you see—"

"Yes?" Elizabeth prompted.

He wandered behind the chair, running his hand along the top of its back—and testing Elizabeth's patience.

"Sir Edward?"

"Oh, hang it all! I suppose I must tell you everything, if you are to help me."

"We have not yet said we would help you," Darcy said. "But full disclosure would be a good start. How did all these ladies truly come to be here?"

Though no one else was in the room, Sir Edward came round the front of the chair again and lowered his voice. "I abducted them." He looked like a little boy admitting he had sneaked into the kitchen and stolen a biscuit. "But I did not mean to abduct all of them! Most of them were entirely accidental, you see."

"I do not see how somebody accidentally kidnaps a cottage full of women," Darcy replied. "So let us start at the beginning. Where is Lady Denham?"

"Lady Denham?" Sir Edward repeated the dowager's name as if he had never heard of her. "Why, I have not the faintest notion. If she was kidnapped, that was some other villain's doing. But her disappearance is the cause of all my misfortune since."

"You are the one who has committed the kidnapping." Elizabeth said. "How can you claim to be a victim of misfortune?"

"Her disappearance forced me to move forward with my plan to seduce Miss Brereton before I was fully prepared. As you can see"—he gestured toward the entry hall, only half papered, and the random assortment of furniture in the room where they stood—"the cottage is not quite ready to receive her."

Darcy's incredulity was evident. "Are we to understand that you planned to abduct Miss Brereton and bring her to a cottage not only on your own property, but within sight of the very house from which you stole her?"

"Not abduct—*seduce*. Given enough time, I intended to woo her into eloping with me willingly. Abduction was my contingency plan. As for the cottage, I was going to keep her here only until we could depart for a more romantic destination. I originally had a much grander scheme—taking her to Timbuktu, or at least somewhere on the Continent—but alas, the expense! My purse cannot afford it; that is the whole reason I must seduce an heiress to begin with, you see—to marry a woman of fortune. So, most regrettably, I had to settle for a seduction on the cheap."

"But Miss Brereton is not an heiress."

"Oh, but she might be!" he said. "Nobody knows the content of Lady Denham's will, and tonight's dinner discussion made me realize that I needed to hedge my stake by seducing Clara before my aunt's fate is known. If Lady Denham is dead, and her will names Clara as her heir, I will have secured my interest as her husband. If the will names me after all, I am no worse off for having a pretty new wife."

"And if Lady Denham is found alive?" Elizabeth asked. "Would she not be most seriously displeased at your having seduced Miss Brereton, or coerced her into marriage? The dowager could yet change her will."

"If she is alive, Clara has time to earn her pity, and I, her forgiveness."

"It has been five-and-thirty years since Archibald Hollis died, and she has not forgiven his family for their behavior regarding his will."

"Has she not? She invited Josiah Hollis to Sanditon House tonight for some reason. Everyone else present is a friend—she must be feeling more genial toward the Hollises than she has in the past."

Elizabeth, recalling the bitter expressions of resentment toward the Hollises that Lady Denham had voiced only the day before the dinner party, doubted that the widow had forgiven Josiah or any of his relations in so short a span. The fact that he slept in Sanditon House even now—with Lady Denham herself still missing—troubled her deeply. For better or worse, she had expected to find the dowager among the other missing women. At least Clara Brereton had escaped the full measure of Sir Edward's idiocy.

Or had she?

"Sir Edward," Elizabeth said sternly, "you have not physically forced yourself on Miss Brereton since bringing her here, have you?"

The baronet stared at her, his countenance utter shock. He stepped back in horror, forgetting about the chair directly behind him, and fell into it. "Good heavens! What kind of monster do you mistake me for? I would never violate a lady in that manner!"

"Then what is this talk of seduction?" Darcy towered over the baronet, who sprawled meekly in the chair. His voice was calm, deadly calm—and deadly cold. "Lady Denham's disappearance drove you to act sooner than planned, but by your own admission, in building this cottage you have been plotting to abduct Miss Brereton for some while, so that you could then 'seduce' her. What, precisely, did you intend to do once you were alone with her here, that would result in her consenting to elope when she had refused you before?"

"I meant to seduce her *heart*! I thought that if I could only get her away from Sanditon House and Lady Denham's influence for an extended period of time—more than a few stolen minutes here and there—I could win her love, and her hand in matrimony. But alas! I will never know whether I might have succeeded. Since bringing her here, I have been unable to court her—how could I, with so many other people milling about? The one conversation we did have, went badly—she expressed in no uncertain terms her displeasure with my scheme. So I have left my dear Clara entirely to herself, and according to the other ladies, the fair creature has slept nearly all the while."

Elizabeth was relieved that, however wrongheaded, entitled, and vain Sir Edward's intentions had been, they had not included ravishment. She was also glad to hear that Clara had not hesitated to assert herself with the baronet—and that he had been put to the rout.

"You still have not explained how the rest of the ladies came to be here," she said.

"Through a series of unfortunate errors," Sir Edward replied. "When I first realized I needed to elope with Clara as expediently as possible, I attempted to persuade her, but she rejected my efforts, as well as the marriage proposal I made after dinner. With no other recourse but to abduct her, I lay in wait for her to come to her chamber, then grabbed her from behind and whispered a warning to be silent. She complied by fainting, which made it easy for me to hoist her over my shoulder and carry her here through the tunnel. She awakened just as we reached the cottage. But when I set her down, I saw that—to my shock and dismay—I had entered the wrong bedchamber, and abducted not Miss Brereton, but Susan Parker."

"You could not tell the difference between Miss Brereton and Miss Parker?" Darcy asked.

"It was dark!" Sir Edward replied. "And I was nervous—I had never kidnapped a lady before!"

"Apparently, you have since gained considerable experience."

"Too much! I wish I had never begun. And poor Miss Parker—I do not know which one of us was more astonished to behold the other. What was I to do? Had she remained unconscious, I might have been able to return her without anyone's being the wiser, but now that she had seen me and this cottage, I could not very well bring her back to Sanditon House to tell the others what I had done! So I said I had rescued her from whoever—or whatever—had spirited away Lady Denham. (I thought this was rather clever, invented so spontaneously, and given her belief that Ivy Woodcock was to blame.) She agreed to stay here, where it was safe, but only if I would go back for Diana."

"I imagine Diana Parker was not as easily subdued?" Darcy said.

Sir Edward's eyes widened in painful recollection. "You have *no* idea!" He shuddered. "At first, I could not begin to imagine how to go about the business. Then I remembered the sleeping draught she had prepared for her sister, and devised a very clever (if I may say so myself) scheme to use Diana's own concoction to effect my design upon her. While everybody dispersed to search for Susan Parker, I stole into the sisters' bedchamber, hoping that in the curfuffle of discovering Susan's disappearance Diana had left it behind. Fortune smiled upon me! The phial was there, forgotten on the night table, and I immediately seized my prize.

"But as quickly as the goddess granted me luck, she imposed on me a trial to rival the labors of Hercules. Miss Heywood knocked upon the door, thinking she heard Miss Parker within! I quickly extinguished my candle and concealed myself behind one of the draperies just as she opened the door. Thank goodness the storm was in a state of fury at the time, for its noise drowned out any accidental sound I might make. I stayed in place many minutes after Miss Heywood left, until I was quite certain she was no longer in the corridor. Then I went in search of Diana Parker, planning to carry her away whilst all of you were still scattered about the house."

"But she was with her brother Arthur," Elizabeth said. "How did you intend to remove her from his escort?"

"I figured I would cross that bridge when I reached it, as they say. First, I had to find her in that vast house! I finally came upon her and Arthur in the morning room. Fortune blessed me again—she is a fickle goddess! The wind extinguished their candles, and Arthur left to relight them. Diana struggled to close the window, which was held open by the force of a strong gale. She was leaning nearly half out of the aperture to grasp the glass, when suddenly the wind shifted, and would have shut the window itself if she had not been in the way. The glass hit her head and knocked her senseless. With her thus unresisting, it was then an easy matter for me to carry her here."

"Were you not concerned that she had suffered great injury?" Darcy asked.

"Well . . . yes." His tone was unconvincing. "I did confirm that she was breathing. It would have been a terrible waste of time and exertion to transport her all this way, only to find her dead upon arrival. And imagine how much more trouble it would have been to carry her back and find an appropriate place to leave her! Really, one cannot fully appreciate the complex logistics of this kidnapping business until in the midst of it."

"Indeed." Darcy did not look at all appreciative. "With so many logistical challenges, how did Miss Heywood come to be here?"

"Miss Heywood was another unfortunate case of mistaken identity in the dark."

"And Miss Denham? Surely you did not mistake your own sister for Miss Brereton."

"Of course not! Do you take me for a simpleton? I brought her here to monitor the misses Parker whilst I returned for Clara."

"Whom you finally managed to abduct because there were no other single ladies left in the house?" Elizabeth said.

"Well, that helped—but in the end, my patience and perseverance were rewarded and Miss Brereton was practically delivered into my hands. When I did not have to use Susan Parker's sleeping draught to sedate Diana, I decided to administer it to Clara instead. So I added it to the wine in the portrait room—"

"You drugged the entire decanter?" Darcy asked.

"Well, *you* prevented me from merely adding a portion to her individual glass, so what choice had I but to pour in the full phial and hope she drank more later? It worked, however—when I returned to the portrait room after accidentally abducting Miss Heywood, I found only Mr. Granville and Miss Brereton within, and she so sleepy that she wanted nothing more than to go to her bedchamber. I chivalrously offered to escort her there and stand watch outside her door while she slumbered. She accepted, and I whisked her away. We made it no farther than the staircase before she lost consciousness altogether, and after all my failed previous attempts to carry her off, 'twas easily accomplished."

"Mr. Granville offered no resistance to your taking Miss Brereton off to her chamber alone?"

"Who is he to object? I am a longtime acquaintance of the lady, the nephew of her benefactress, and a baronet. He is some person unknown even to our hostess, who never met Miss Brereton before tonight."

Yes, Elizabeth thought, but Sidney said Mr. Granville had assumed responsibility for Miss Brereton's safety, a charge that, judging from his conduct earlier in the evening, she believed he had not only taken seriously, but performed willingly. What had caused him to consign her care to Sir Edward?

And then to disappear himself?

Thirty-three

Sooner than she could have supposed it possible in the beginning of her distress, her spirits became absolutely comfortable, and capable, as heretofore, of continual improvement by anything he said.
— Northanger Abbey

*M*iss Heywood?"

Charlotte fought to return to consciousness. She had fallen asleep regretting not having allowed Sidney to escort her to the Darcys, and now as punishment for her willfulness, the sound of his voice followed her into disjointed dreams. She could almost feel his hand upon her shoulder, trying to shake sense into her—as if the ache in her head were not admonishment enough.

"Miss Heywood, can you hear me?"

She could hear him, hear the urgency in his voice. *Yes, I know—I should have listened to you. Now leave and let me sleep.*

"Miss Heywood, do wake up . . . please . . . Charlotte?"

She forced open her eyes, blinking until her blurred vision cleared. Sidney Parker knelt beside her, his hand on her shoulder, his eyes assessing her intently. "Are you well?"

She was curled up on the seat of a chaise longue, her head resting on her arms, a light blanket covering her. She sat up—a little too quickly.

"My head hurts. I think it was the wine." She put a hand to her temple. "It must have been very strong—I did not drink much."

"I think any amount of that wine was too much," Sidney replied. "I suspect it was doctored."

"By Sir Edward?"

"It was he who brought you here, was it not?"

"Yes."

Sidney rose and helped her sit up a bit more, so that she could rest against the seat back, and tucked the blanket around her. When she was settled, he sat down on the edge of the seat, facing her. A single candle burned on a nearby table, its flame casting half his face in light, half in shadow. "Tell me how it happened."

"After I left you, I proceeded straight to the portrait room," she said, "but on the way I became dizzy and disoriented. I thought it was because I was distraught by our quarrel, or perhaps an effect of the wine. I stopped and steadied myself against a wall, intending to stay there only a minute or two, until the feeling passed. But then I sensed someone approach me from behind."

"My dear Miss Heywood!" Sidney's expression was equal parts concern and guilt. "Why did you not cry out? I would have come—surely, despite our quarrel, you knew I would have come?"

"I thought you were too far away to hear me."

"Someone else might have heard—Granville, Mr. Darcy—even a servant."

"I was faint-headed and not thinking clearly. I also lacked the strength to raise my voice to any significant volume. As it was, he seized me from behind and covered my mouth before I could collect myself enough to react. He called me his 'dear' and said I had nothing to fear, that I need only remain silent and all would be well."

A muscle in his jaw tensed. "I should never have let you leave my sight."

"I gave you no choice."

"I should have followed you, then."

"Had you stalked me, that would have frightened me more than Sir Edward did."

Remorse took hold of his countenance once again. In a softer tone of voice, he asked, "Were you very frightened?"

"When I first sensed him behind me, I was—I thought he was Josiah Hollis. But when he spoke, I recognized his voice and believed it was better to cooperate than to antagonize him by resisting. Ever since I met him, Sir Edward has impressed me as possessing . . . less-than-razor-sharp intellect. I believed that once we arrived at wherever he was taking me, I could devise a means of escape."

"Yet here you are."

"We did not go far before I fainted altogether."

"Despite having boasted to me earlier this evening that you are not generally given to swooning?"

Had their initial encounter in the gallery truly been only this evening? So much had transpired since, that to Charlotte it seemed at least a se'nnight ago. "You will recall that I reserved the right for some greater occasion. I should hope an abduction qualifies."

"It does, indeed. Though I would rather you had swooned in my arms than Sir Edward's." At her sudden look, he cleared his throat. "I would have known where you were, and that you were safe."

An awkward pause followed, and he became quite serious. "He . . . he did not hurt you, did he? Or attempt to force—"

She shook her head. "In fact, since bringing me here, he has paid me little attention at all."

"That is probably for the best. When you fainted, did you remain unconscious for long?"

"Just long enough for him to carry me here. When we entered the cottage, my arrival created a stir among the other ladies, and their commotion woke me. Your sisters were most solicitous, offering me what limited means of comfort were in their power, and assuring me that Sir Edward was really quite harmless. After a little while, Sir Edward retreated to another room, and they increased their ministrations on my behalf. While I appreciated their attention, it was . . ." She sought a word that would not sound ungrateful.

"Excessive?"

"You could say that."

The corners of his mouth lifted in a trace of a smile. "That means they like you."

"Flattering as that may be, I still felt very sleepy, and their well-meant care fatigued me further. Meanwhile, Miss Denham—who, despite Sir Edward's claim that he brought us all here for our own protection from Lady Denham's kidnapper, apparently was supposed to be acting as our warden—cast all of us condescending looks in sullen silence. So I came in here to sleep off the wine, or whatever it was that made me so groggy."

"Has your headache diminished since waking?"

"It has, though I am still tired."

"That is hardly surprising. It is nearly dawn, and this has been a long night even for those of us who did not spend part of it being abducted. Do you feel equal to standing?"

"I think so." She pushed the blanket aside.

He rose and offered his hand, which she accepted. After having spent half the night hand-in-hand with him, moving through the house in the dark, she found it almost natural to fit her hand inside his now—much more natural than quarreling with him.

His pull was stronger than she anticipated, and as she reached her feet, she overbalanced. He caught her in both arms and supported her, his hands cupping her elbows, his forearms beneath hers, until she recovered her equilibrium.

And then he continued to hold her.

Neither said a word. She dared not speak, for fear of everything coming out wrong again and reigniting their quarrel. He, too, seemed to be wanting to say something, but holding back. And so they stood there, their bodies far enough apart to be not quite in contact, close enough that she wished they were.

"Miss Heywood," he finally said, "I deeply regret kissing you."

His words drove away any residual trace of drowsiness. She stiffened. Mortification took hold and her face grew warm. She cast down her gaze to shield herself from his, and attempted to step away from him.

"No, I meant—" He tightened his hold. "I am making a mess of this apology! Diana was right when she said my mouth would get me into trouble—tonight it has, in a multitude of ways." His palms slid down her arms until his hands held hers in a firm, warm grip. "I meant that I regret the circumstances of the kiss, and the distress it caused you. More than anything, I regret that it made you distrust me enough to propel you into the reach of a villain—for a villain Sir Edward is, even if an incompetent one."

She raised her gaze to his again. "As for the kiss itself," he continued, pressing her hands more tightly, "I hope you will not consider it un- gentlemanly of me to say that I would not be averse to repeating it—someday—under different conditions—acceptable conditions for a lady whom I could never mistake for a housemaid, or mistake for anyone other than the gentle, generous, patient Miss Heywood who has suffered my company, not to mention my nonsense, with extraordinary forbearance all night."

Her breath caught in her chest. Part of her wished he would kiss her right now, propriety be dashed. (Most of her wished that, actu- ally.) But the part remaining—the dutiful Charlotte who would not disgrace her parents by engaging in too-familiar behavior with a gen- tleman to whom she was not even close to being affianced—asserted itself. She refrained from betraying any hint of her hope that "some- day" would arrive very soon.

His earnest expression turned to searching, as he tried to read her face. "Have mercy on me, Miss Heywood. Say something—anything— even if it is a command to take myself away and leave you in peace."

She realized, then, that she had neglected to speak at all, and had left him rather hanging in suspense. Squeezing his hands back, she said softly, "I might not be averse, either."

He smiled. So did she. And then he was indeed holding her close, long enough for them both to communicate through the embrace what neither was quite ready to voice aloud.

Thirty-four

The truth was that Sir Edward, whom Circumstances had confined very much to one spot, had read more sentimental Novels than agreed with him. . . . With a perversity of Judgement, which must be attributed to his not having by Nature a very strong head, the Graces, the Spirit, the Ingenuity, and the Perserverance of the Villain of the Story outweighed all his absurdities and all his Atrocities.
—Sanditon

*E*lizabeth nodded toward Sir Edward, who sat across the parlor in an ornate, high-backed oaken armchair amid a cacophony of female voices. "What should we do about him?"

"Sir Edward might be a fool, but he is a titled fool," Darcy replied. "And we have the ladies' reputations to consider. We must handle this delicately."

Elizabeth agreed. Though all present in the cottage ornée knew that no one's virtue had been compromised, if word of this night's events went beyond the confines of Sanditon House and Denham Park, gossips would not be kind. Yet even amongst themselves, Sir Edward's conduct could not be countenanced without his suffering consequences.

Sidney and Charlotte had emerged from the adjacent room, apparently in accord once more, and had joined the Darcys in conference. "Is it kidnapping if the captives do not want to leave?" Sidney asked. "Susan and Diana have remained willingly—or at least, not in fear of their safety. Even Miss Brereton does not consider Sir Edward a threat, only a nuisance."

"What about you, Charlotte?" Elizabeth asked. "As one of his abductees, what do you think?"

"Despite the fright he gave me at the time, I am not fearful of him now, and he has nobody left to kidnap."

"The irony," Darcy said, "is that, with Lady Denham now truly missing, in bringing all the other ladies here, Sir Edward might indeed have protected them from greater harm. Until we know what has happened to the dowager and who is responsible, they might be safer here than at Sanditon House. However, Sir Edward ought to sustain some sort of punishment."

Another glance at Sir Edward showed him shifting in his seat. Though the chair itself appeared so uncomfortable that Elizabeth could guess why it had been banished from the main house, the greater torture seemed to be the barrage of attention leveled at the baronet. Susan tried to cheer him, Diana tried to cure him, and Miss Denham steadily upbraided him. Miss Brereton, since wakening, had done her best to avoid him—an easy matter, as he, in turn, was so humiliated by the failure of his "seduction" scheme that he could not look her in the eye.

Elizabeth turned back to Darcy. "I think his punishment has already commenced. We can take additional measures later, after Lady Denham is found."

Sir Edward left his chair and came to them. "I just want everybody to go home and leave me in peace," he said. "How long is it until sunrise?"

"If you had Sir Harry's watch, you could tell us," Sidney said.

"Alas, when I returned to Denham Park for it the second time, I determined that, like Lady Denham, it has gone missing."

"I suppose that is a risk one takes when leaving items at a pawnshop."

Sir Edward's complexion became truly peaked. "You know about that?"

"I am not the only one," Sidney said. "It was Lady Denham who told me."

Beads of perspiration formed on the baronet's forehead, and he looked nauseated as he retreated to his oaken throne.

After consulting Sidney and Charlotte, it was decided that they would return to Sanditon House with Darcy and Elizabeth to continue the search for Lady Denham. Darcy hoped to find Josiah Hollis able to respond more coherently to interrogation, and to find Mr. Granville returned from wherever he had gone. The Parker sisters and Miss Denham would remain at the cottage ornée—or better still, remove under Sir Edward's escort through the tunnel to Denham House, where they could pass the time in greater comfort than in the partially finished and sparsely furnished cottage—until sunrise, when it was hoped that they could depart for Trafalgar House and tend to their nephew. The ladies were very much in favor of this suggestion; Sir Edward received it with resignation.

Elizabeth asked Miss Brereton which party she wished to be part of, and was unsurprised by her choice. "I would much rather go with you. I have tolerated enough of Sir Edward's imprudence and folly for one day, and I am too anxious on Lady Denham's behalf to sit idle."

Upon returning to Sanditon House, they looked for Mr. Granville in the portrait room, but did not find him. Elizabeth wished she knew what had prompted his removal in the first place; his prolonged absence made her uneasy.

"His continued absence makes me uneasy as well," Darcy said, "but we cannot continue to wander this house in the dark searching for people. We spent half the night looking in such a manner, and we cannot afford to lose more time. We are better off extracting additional information from Josiah Hollis and seeing where that leads us."

They found Josiah Hollis exactly where they had left him. He wakened more easily this time, and Darcy brought him to the portrait room so that the ladies might be present while he was questioned. Mr. Hollis glanced from Miss Heywood to Sidney with an inexplicable look of amusement, but said only, "Nice to see you both again."

"Nice to see you, too," Sidney replied evenly. "I would offer you more wine, but I am guessing you might decline."

Mr. Hollis winced. "I believe I have had enough for one night. I should have held out for port." He settled into a chair. "I was sleeping soundly. What is this gathering about?"

"Do you recall speaking with us earlier about the hidden corridors and spy holes within this house?" Darcy asked.

"Vaguely."

"You said you had used them to cause mischief as a child, but upon being caught, never used them again until the night 'she' returned. To whom did you refer?"

Hollis paused a long moment, as if deliberating whether to answer cooperatively or offer some smug remark.

"Ivy Woodcock."

"Ivy Woodcock!" Darcy's tone was sharp. "Do not tell me that you, too, insist on perpetuating the fantasy that the ghost of Ivy Woodcock haunts Sanditon?"

"I said nothing about a ghost," Hollis replied. "When I last saw her, Ivy Woodcock was very much alive."

"When was this?" Elizabeth asked.

"Forty years ago—about a month after my uncle married. She was old, as old as he."

"How do you know it was she?"

"Uncle Archibald and I were talking one evening as he walked to his apartment to retire for the night. When we reached his apartment, he invited me inside to continue our conversation. The new Mrs. Hollis was yet downstairs—my uncle, being so much older, maintained earlier habits than she, so there was no chance of our disturbing her in her adjacent rooms. We entered, and both of us were astonished to discover an elderly woman seated in his dressing room. A little girl—a wisp of a thing, perhaps six or seven—was with her.

"He stared at the woman for a full minute at least, and she just looked back at him, neither of them speaking a word. She had an odd expression—sad and happy at the same time. Finally, he whispered, 'Ivy?' She lifted her hand, which held a folded piece of paper, and extended it toward him, saying, 'I found your letter.'

"My uncle pulled his gaze away from her long enough to ask me to leave him. He said that we would finish our discussion on the morrow, and added that no one else need know about the visitor.

"Of course, that stoked my curiosity beyond anything. When I left the chamber, I went straight to a hidden room that looked into my uncle's apartment."

"Surely he was aware of the room?" Darcy said.

"In ordinary circumstances, he was perfectly aware of it. But that night, I do not think he was aware of anything but her."

Thirty-five

*H*e told her that he had never stopped hoping she was alive, and asked her where she had been all these years. She stepped out of their embrace and said, *"That is what I have come to tell you."*

The little girl became restless. Archibald found an old sketchbook and some pencils to occupy her, and Ivy seated her at the dressing table. He watched the child as she began to draw, then raised his gaze to Ivy. *"She looks very much like you did on the day we first met. Is she your grand-daughter?"*

"Ivy Rose is indeed my granddaughter," she replied. *"And yours."*

At this, Archibald was overcome. *"We . . . ?"* His voice broke; he could not even finish a sentence. Ivy took him by the hand and led him to the sofa.

She told him that after he left for Trinity Term at Oxford, she realized she was with child. Somehow his father, Victor Hollis, learned of it, and appeared at the hermitage one day while Ebenezer Woodcock was out. He offered her a bargain: She could leave Sanditon voluntarily, with enough money to find some other man to help her raise her child; Victor would arrange transportation to some remote part of northern England and create evidence in Sanditon that would imply she had died. Her father would be allowed to live out his years in the hermitage, but she would never communicate with Archibald, her father, or anyone else in Sanditon again.

If she refused Victor's offer, he would see to it that her bastard was never born—in an "accident" that left no question as to whether she had died—and her father would be driven out to spend his final days as a homeless wanderer.

Though it broke her heart, Ivy accepted the deal. "If I could never see you or my father again, at least I could bring your child into the world and raise him."

"'Him—'" he repeated. "The baby was a boy? We have a son?"

She smiled sadly. "We did. A beautiful boy who grew into a fine man and spent many years improving the family's fortune before meeting and marrying Ivy Rose's mother. He died two winters ago of pneumonia. Ivy Rose and her mother live with me now."

With the money Victor Hollis paid her, Ivy was able to pass herself off as a sailor's widow, and married a decent man who raised her son as his own. They had a comfortable, content life together, and Ivy grew to love him—though never in the way she had loved Archibald. When he died, she mourned him—then decided it was time she put her own past to rest. Figuring Victor was long dead and a threat to her no more, she journeyed to Sanditon not knowing whether Archibald himself yet lived. Upon her arrival she learned that he was very much alive—and had just wed someone else.

The news broke her heart a second time—if only she had come sooner. She would not begrudge him at last finding happiness; she had managed to snatch her share of it in the wake of Victor's manipulation. Despite having come all this way, she decided she would not attempt to meet him; she would not interfere with the path his life had taken.

However, she could not resist visiting the grotto once more—it would be where she made peace with her past, where she would finally have a chance to say good-bye to Archibald.

At twilight, she and Ivy Rose sneaked onto the grounds and made their way to the grotto. Discovering the flowing fountain with the statue of herself, which Archibald had installed upon inheriting the estate two decades after her disappearance, almost proved her undoing. Every memory they shared passed through her mind, and her resolve to avoid him wavered. When she found the letter he had left for her all those years ago, she was

*indeed undone. She could not leave—the grotto, the village, this earth—
without laying eyes on him one last time.*

*She found the tunnel entrance as she remembered, and entered the house
as he instructed. Once inside, she used the hidden corridors and spy holes
to determine which suite was his. And waited.*

*When she finished telling her story, they embraced again. Archibald con-
tinued to hold her, sharing what his own feelings had been at the time of their
separation and in the many years since—how he had returned to Oxford a
shadow of himself, and after completing his studies, returned home to a
house that felt even colder than it had before. How he had resisted his father's
urging him to marry and produce an heir, because he could not imagine
sharing his life and his home with anyone but her. How in his mature years,
as the master of Sanditon House, conscious of the weight of responsibility he
bore, he had reconsidered marriage, but could find no woman exactly like
her. It was not until he stopped trying to find Ivy in every woman he met, but
looked instead for someone nothing like her, that he found Philadelphia Brereton. Theirs was a companionate marriage, one that he entered to assuage
decades' worth of loneliness in his golden years.*

"You understand that I cannot be disloyal to her," Archibald said. "Though
I spent most of my life dreaming of a reunion with you, I have wed her, and
I cannot betray those vows."

"I know," she said. "If you could, I could not love you as I do."

*They talked and wept and even laughed, as the perfect accord they had
once known re-formed, until the hour grew late. Finally, both reluctantly
acknowledged that it was time for Ivy to leave. Ivy Rose had abandoned the
sketchbook and, after playing a while with and on the chamber horse, had
fallen asleep on its seat. Archibald stroked the child's fine, blond hair—the
shade his had been in his youth. The gesture inspired Ivy to take up a pen-
knife lying on the desk and cut off a single curl of Ivy Rose's hair. "So part
of her can be with you always," she said.*

*Archibald lifted the child, and she snuggled sleepily into his shoulder. He
held her in silence, his eyes closed as he absorbed the sensation of holding
his granddaughter in his arms. After several minutes, he opened his eyes
once more and looked at Ivy.*

"I want to give you some money."

She shook her head. "I did not come here looking for money."

"For Ivy Rose," he insisted. "For my grandchild. I could not provide for you and our son when you most needed me, but I can do something for her."

Again, she shook her head. "I took your father's money, and hated myself every day for it. I felt as if I had sold what was priceless between us for pennies and pounds—as if I had sold myself." Her voice wavered, and she wiped away tears. "He was so condescending as he handed it over—he made me feel mercenary and ashamed. I accepted it only to survive. Please, Archibald, do not let us part like this—quarreling over money."

Ivy Rose stirred, responding to the distress in her grandmother's voice. Archibald nodded in resignation: He would respect Ivy's wishes. When he spoke, his voice was fierce with emotion.

"I would give you anything—anything in the world within my power to give . . . but I will not give you money."

He asked for her address, which she provided; though they would not correspond, he wanted to know where she was in the world. He kissed her good-bye, and they embraced once more—a long embrace, for it had to last till the end of their days.

And then she was gone.

Thirty-six

Most grievously was she humbled. . . . She did not learn either to forget or defend the past; but she learned to hope that it would never transpire farther.

—Northanger Abbey

*T*hat is quite a secret you witnessed," Darcy said. "What did you do with it afterward?"

"Nothing," Josiah replied. "Even when my uncle allowed Lady Denham—excuse me, *Mrs. Hollis*—to oust me from the house and his will, I maintained his secret."

"In all the years you have harbored resentment toward Lady Denham, and given all the things that have been said on both sides, you never told her any of this—if only to injure her feelings or pride?"

"I did not have to. She already knew, because she witnessed it herself. As I came out of the observation room, I entered another that offers a different view of the apartment—and found her inside. I have no idea how long she had been standing there—how much she overheard—but she was weeping. We both started in surprise—two spies, suddenly face-to-face. I did not say a word—merely quit the room. I never alluded to what had passed in my uncle's apartment, nor our chance meeting afterward."

Elizabeth suspected that this surprise encounter was the reason Lady Denham resented Josiah Hollis so much. He not only knew that her husband loved another woman more than he would ever love her, but also had witnessed her grief and vulnerability at the moment she discovered that painful fact.

"In the trunk of Archibald's old clothing that many of us borrowed this evening," Darcy said, "there was a miniature portrait of a young woman. Do I assume correctly that it depicts Ivy Woodcock?"

"Yes."

"I understand there is also a miniature of Archibald from about the same time." He gestured toward the case in the corner. "Is it among those in that case?"

"No, that one depicts him at an older age. If there is one from his Oxford years, I have never seen it and do not know what has become of it."

"Ivy's miniature has disappeared from the trunk. Is there anything you would like to tell me about that?"

Josiah paused. "What makes you think I know something?"

"The trunk is in Archibald's former apartment, which you just admitted to knowing inside and out. What did you want with the miniature?"

Again, he hesitated, looking at them all, apparently deliberating whether to cooperate or stonewall.

What *had* Josiah wanted with it? Elizabeth wondered. Surely a likeness of Ivy Woodcock, while priceless to Archibald, held little sentimental value to Josiah. Sidney had said he observed Josiah holding it beside the gallery portrait of Archibald in his youth—which meant their affair had been on Josiah's mind earlier tonight, enough that he entered the apartment to steal her miniature. Did it have some bearing on Lady Denham's disappearance?

"Mr. Hollis," Elizabeth said gently, "not only is Lady Denham still missing, but now Mr. Granville is, as well. Whatever your feelings toward Lady Denham, can you not set them aside? If the miniature has anything to do with tonight's events, please tell us."

"Mr. Granville has disappeared?" Josiah asked. "When did this happen?"

"After you left the portrait room, Miss Heywood and I departed, as well," Sidney said. For some reason, this elicited a smirk from Josiah. "We sought Mr. and Mrs. Darcy, but did not find them. When I returned, Granville and Miss Brereton were gone. As you can see, we have since found Miss Brereton, but she does not know where Mr. Granville went."

Josiah regarded Sidney with a long, contemplative look. "How well do you know Mr. Granville?" he finally said.

"We have been friends for several years."

"Have you ever met his mother?"

"I cannot say that I have. Why do you ask?"

"Do you happen to know her Christian name?"

"I barely knew my own mother's Christian name—it is hardly something that comes up in conversation."

"Might it be Ivy Rose?"

Elizabeth gasped.

"From the moment Mr. Granville arrived, he looked familiar to me," Josiah said. "When you drew our attention at dinner to the similarity he bore to the portrait of Archibald in the dining room, I wondered whether he might be a distant Hollis connection, or perhaps a relation through Archibald's mother. But there was something else—or should I say some*one* else—familiar in him. With all the talk of Ivy Woodcock tonight, I finally realized who else Mr. Granville resembled: Ivy—and Ivy Rose, the little girl who accompanied Ivy here forty years ago . . . which would make Ivy Rose old enough now to be Mr. Granville's mother. I took the miniature to hold beside my uncle's portrait so that I could see both Archibald's and Ivy's features at once."

"And what did you determine?" Darcy asked.

"There is no doubt in my mind that Mr. Granville carries their blood."

Darcy turned to Sidney. "Do you think Lady Denham knew Mr. Granville's identity when she invited him to tonight's dinner? Or that Granville himself knows of their connection?"

"To my knowledge, they have never met, and she certainly gave no indication of familiarity with his name when she issued the invitation." He paused. "Though—now that I think about it, when I told Granville I had accepted the invitation on our mutual behalf, he asked a great many questions about Lady Denham. I ascribed them to natural curiosity about our hostess and the sort of evening he could anticipate, but in hindsight, an unusual number of his queries pertained to Archibald Hollis—more than one might expect regarding a hostess's long-deceased first husband. He also was interested in the fact that the marriage produced no issue, and curious about who might inherit the Hollis holdings upon Lady Denham's death."

"Regardless of Lady Denham's knowledge or ignorance of Mr. Granville's lineage," Darcy said, "it sounds to me as if Mr. Granville is well aware of any connection that might exist between himself and the Hollis family. The question is whether he has acted on that information tonight, and if so, how and to what end. We need to determine, as best we can, where in this house Mr. Granville has been since his arrival, and what he has been doing—or has had the opportunity to do."

"Do you think he is involved with Lady Denham's disappearance?" Sidney asked. "I cannot believe that of him."

"Whether we want to believe it or not, in the interest of Lady Denham's welfare we must consider the possibility," said Darcy.

Miss Brereton sank down on the sofa, where Mr. Granville had sat beside her earlier. "But he seems like such a nice gentleman. He was so attentive—offering his aid, bringing me wine. . . ."

"I don't know about you," Josiah said, "but if you ask me, the effects of that wine were no gift."

"Lady Denham's wine has never affected me as strongly as it did tonight," Miss Brereton said. "I actually fell asleep *while walking.*" She paused, an expression of distress overtaking her countenance. "Do you think the wine was adulterated?"

"Sir Edward admitted to having poured Susan Parker's sleeping draught into the carafe," Elizabeth said. "But we have no way of knowing whether Mr. Granville was aware it had been doctored."

"Maybe he was just trying to get her drunk so he could have his way with her," Josiah said. "Or have her out of the way."

"Mr. Hollis," Darcy said, "do curb your speech—consider the ladies' more delicate sensibilities."

Elizabeth assumed her husband referred to Charlotte's and Clara's sensibilities, for very little shocked hers anymore. In fact, the thought that Josiah had just voiced had also occurred to her—though phrased with less crass. Her mind now raced ahead, recalling numerous opportunities Mr. Granville had received or engineered, that a man with questionable motives could have exploited for his own benefit.

"Miss Brereton's quitting the portrait room with Sir Edward to go sleep in her chamber did free Mr. Granville to move about the house at will, with no one to question him," Elizabeth said. "He also roamed freely for a time when Susan first went missing—after you, Mr. Parker, parted ways with him. However, he spent much of that time trailing Mr. Hollis."

"What are you talking about?" Josiah said. "I was in my own chamber, sleeping, while you were all looking for Mr. Parker's sisters."

"Mr. Granville told us that he saw you coming from Lady Denham's apartment," Darcy said. "Afterward, Mrs. Darcy and I discovered that her papers had been ransacked. Do you know anything about that?"

"Only that if Mr. Granville claims he saw me near that apartment, he is either mistaken or lying. I have no need to pilfer any papers— I am under no illusions about her will containing anything relevant to me."

"You harbor no hope of inheriting Sanditon House?"

"That matter was settled long ago."

"If Mr. Granville is lying, then it is most likely he who rifled the papers," Elizabeth said.

"Unless it was Lady Denham herself," Sidney replied. "She did leave the ransom note during that same period."

"What?" Mr. Hollis exclaimed. "*Now* what are you talking about?" Miss Heywood and Miss Brereton also voiced surprise.

Sidney briefly explained that Lady Denham had been in the house during the early part of the evening, and why. "However," he added, "she truly went missing sometime before we all reconvened in here after the initial search for Susan."

"While Mr. Granville was wandering around the house incriminating me?" Josiah said. "Sounds to me like he was a busy fellow— first he kidnapped Lady Denham, then implicated me."

"He could not have kidnapped her then," Charlotte said. "He was still here when the ransom note was found, and later when Sir Edward returned with the false watch."

"Maybe he stashed her somewhere and came back," Josiah said. "This house contains no lack of hiding places."

"But Mr. Granville has never been here before tonight. Would he know of them?"

"If Mr. Granville is indeed Ivy Rose's son," Elizabeth said, "she might have told him of the tunnel that leads from the house to the grotto and hermitage."

"He examined the hermitage earlier this evening," Darcy said. "In fact, he volunteered to hike out there when we conducted our grounds search."

"And he returned dry, despite the rain." Sidney's expression was troubled; clearly this recollection, more so than the conjecture of the others, caused him to doubt his friend. He turned to Mr. Hollis.

"Show us the second tunnel."

Thirty-seven

"I do not pretend to determine what your thoughts and designs in time past may have been. All that is best known to yourself."
—Isabella Thorpe, Northanger Abbey

awn was just breaking as the six of them emerged from the tunnel into a small thicket between the grotto and the hermitage. The rain had finally ceased; dense fog now shrouded the landscape. Darcy was grateful that Josiah Hollis was among their party; otherwise, they might not have found the hermitage in the mist.

He was also grateful for the mist itself, however, for it cloaked their approach. Darcy and Sidney, yet armed with the concealed pistols they had taken to Denham Park, were able to creep right up to the hermitage. Sidney carried his weapon reluctantly, still hoping that they had allowed their conjecture to run wild regarding Percy Granville—that the friend who had in the first place received his invitation to this ill-fated dinner party by virtue of his connection to Sidney, had not betrayed Sidney's trust.

Darcy did not want to use his weapon either, but, able to predict neither what they would find inside the hermitage nor how events would unfold, they needed to be prepared for any eventuality. Elizabeth, Miss Heywood, Miss Brereton, and Josiah Hollis hung back several yards, where they would remain distant from any danger until informed that it was safe to approach. Darcy peered through one of the simple abode's two tiny windows. A single candle dimly illuminated the interior.

Mr. Granville was inside.

Fortunately, the unpredictable gentleman stood at the opposite end of the one-room dwelling, unaware of his observer. Darcy, however, had to remain cautious—the window held no glass; any sound he made could be heard.

Also inside was Lady Denham.

She lay on the remnants of an ancient straw mattress set atop a narrow bedstead made of rough-hewn branches. Not far away—nothing could be far in this humble space—two chairs flanked an equally rustic wooden table. The candlestick sat beside a paper on the table's surface.

Lady Denham appeared to be sleeping, but restlessly. She shifted often, no doubt uncomfortable on a mattress that was probably older and definitely more decrepit than she. Mr. Granville hovered near, alternately drawing close to see whether she woke, then retreating to pace off nervous energy. Debris littered the uneven stone floor—dead leaves, bits of broken pottery, thatch that had fallen in from the roof—and it rustled and crunched beneath his boots.

One of the chairs had been pulled out from the table. Mr. Granville sat down, facing the dowager, resting an elbow on the table beside him. But even then, he was not still. He repeatedly slipped his fingers into his waistcoat pocket until they at last simply stayed there, and he twitched his leg in steady rhythm as he watched Lady Denham sleep. The flame of the candle trembled.

Darcy stepped away from the window and motioned Sidney to follow him until they reached a safe enough distance to whisper.

"He is inside. So is Lady Denham."

Sidney deflated upon receiving confirmation of his worst imaginings. But he quickly recovered himself. "Has he harmed her?"

"It does not appear so. She is sleeping, and does not seem even to be bound or restrained in any way."

"Is he armed?"

"I saw no weapon. But he might have something in his waistcoat pocket."

"A pistol?"

"No, nothing so bulky." Their own pistols, though second-sized, created enough of a bulge in their coat pockets to be noticed by anyone who cared enough to look—but perfect concealment was not their object. Granville's waistcoat pocket was much smaller. "Something petite," Darcy said, "if anything at all."

"That is hopeful news, at least—perhaps we will not have to fight him. What is he doing?"

"Watching her. Pacing. Waiting."

Sidney nodded absently as his gaze followed the drifting mist to the small stone structure. He studied it for a time, then turned to Darcy.

"All right, then."

At the moment of Darcy and Sidney's abrupt entrance, Percy Granville was leaning over Lady Denham, his hands on her shoulders. He whirled round to face them.

"Parker! I—I was not expecting you." Mr. Granville's hands, which he had raised before him in an instinctive posture of defense upon being startled, dropped to his sides. He stepped back.

"I imagine not," Sidney replied. His stance was stiff, his manner cold and formal. "I myself did not expect to end the evening here."

"In truth, nor did I."

"In truth?" Sidney laughed, but it was a sound devoid of humor. "In *truth*? Do elaborate on what you mean by that—I am all curiosity."

Mr. Granville's gaze darted to Lady Denham. "I know this does not look good—"

"Well, now—*that,* at least, is the truth. No, this does not look good at all."

"I swear to you, Parker—and to you, Mr. Darcy—I mean Lady Denham no harm."

"Good G–d, Granville!" Sidney's voice was full of disgust, his expression one of disbelief and betrayal. "What are we doing here? What *are* you about?"

Movement from the bed drew Mr. Granville's attention back to Lady Denham, who had turned her head toward him. The dowager's eyelids fluttered. For a moment they partially opened, but then sleepily closed once more.

Granville raised his troubled gaze to meet Sidney's.

"I wish I knew." His own head shook in disbelief. "I never meant for events to go this far—everything has spun out of control."

"You were leaning over her just now, your hands upon her," Darcy said. "What was your intention?"

"I was trying to wake her. She has been sleeping a long while— I am growing concerned."

Sidney approached Lady Denham's reposing form, observing her closely. The rise and fall of her chest maintained no steady rhythm. Her eyelids were tightly squeezed shut. A muscle in her cheek twitched.

"I believe she is awake now."

Lady Denham's eyes flew open. She sat upright—no small feat on the sagging ropes that supported the deteriorated mattress—and scowled at her erstwhile conspirator.

"Sidney Parker, you are too observant by half."

Thirty-eight

"There is at times," said he, *"a little self-importance—but it is not offensive; and there are moments, there are points, when her Love of Money is carried greatly too far."*
——Thomas Parker, Sanditon

"How long have you been awake?" Sidney asked.

"Long enough." Lady Denham tried to move her legs over the side of the mattress, but there was no graceful way for the seventy-year-old dowager to extricate herself from the dilapidated bedstead without assistance. "Make yourself useful and help me out of this thing."

Darcy came forward to aid Sidney, and together the two gentlemen settled Lady Denham into one of the chairs. Mr. Granville stood back, trying to render himself as unobtrusive as possible.

To Darcy's eye, Lady Denham appeared unharmed. "Are you well?" Darcy asked her. "Has Mr. Granville injured you in any way?"

"I should say so! I have never in my life been so ill-used as I have by this pretender. This is an outrage! Presuming to speak to me about matters none of his business, and when I refused, drugging me and taking me from my own estate to—to . . ." She glanced around the dirty, cobweb-strewn room. "To this wretched hovel. Where are we? To what ends of the earth has he transported me?"

"Actually, this is *your* wretched hovel," Sidney said. "You have not left Sanditon Park—we are in the hermitage."

"Oh."

Darcy cleared his throat. "I meant physical injury, Lady Denham. The injury to your dignity we will address in a moment, but have you suffered any physical harm? You say Mr. Granville drugged you—"

"I gave her wine, with her own sleeping draught added," Mr. Granville said. "Nothing more."

"What sleeping draught? I never take medicine."

"The one Miss Diana Parker sent you."

"The same one she prepares for Susan?" Sidney asked.

"I believe so," Mr. Granville replied. "That is what she said this evening when she talked of it."

"How much did you give her?"

"The whole phial. I was hoping it would relax her and make her more receptive to hearing me out, but she fell asleep before I could even start the conversation."

Sidney's eyes widened. "Little wonder! To save preparation time, Diana fills the phial with multiple doses. It probably contained a week's worth."

Darcy inwardly shuddered at the thought of how lucky Mr. Granville was to have not inadvertently put Lady Denham to sleep forever. "How do you feel now, Lady Denham? Are you in need of a doctor?"

"A doctor? A doctor will only want to drug me more! Or stick leeches on me—and probably amputate a limb while he is about it, just for good measure. No! Do not even think about making my ordeal worse by bringing in a doctor! I am perfectly sound."

"If that is the case, several of your guests wait outside in great anxiety on your behalf, and they very much wish to see you to assure themselves of your welfare. Miss Brereton, in particular, has been terribly worried about you all night."

"Well, now, that is more like it! Yes, do bring Miss Clara to me. And the others."

"Mr. Granville, in light of Lady Denham's accusations, before we admit other ladies to this gathering you surely understand my need to ask whether you have any weapons on your person or in this room?"

"No—I give you my word."

"What about other items that could cause harm?"

"None."

"I assume you will not mind removing your coat so that Mr. Parker can check its pockets? And kindly show him whatever it is you are carrying in the pocket of your waistcoat."

Mr. Granville complied. The coat pockets were empty; the waistcoat yielded a small oval item that he placed in Sidney's hand. Sidney looked at it, met Granville's gaze, and returned it to him.

Sidney departed to collect Miss Brereton and the others, leaving Darcy with Lady Denham, Mr. Granville, and a silence so heavy that it outweighed all three of them. Ironically, both kidnapper and captive considered Sidney their truest ally and most sympathetic listener among all the guests, and were therefore reluctant to continue the interview with Darcy until Sidney returned.

Sidney's absence did not, however, prevent their commencing a squabble with each other.

"I wanted only to talk with you," Mr. Granville said. "A simple conversation, that is all. But you would not even let me begin."

"There is nothing you can possibly say that I want to hear."

"That does not absolve you of your moral obligation to listen."

"Moral obligation? Ha! You are a fine one to talk about morality, Mr. Granville. You—who repaid my hospitality by kidnapping me and bringing me to this—*place*."

Darcy thought Lady Denham was a fine one to talk about the obligations of hospitality, after the anxiety to which she had intentionally subjected her guests during the first half of the night. However, he kept that opinion to himself.

A moment later, Elizabeth and the others entered. Miss Brereton went straight to Lady Denham's side, her genuine expression of relief not lost upon the dowager.

"Miss Clara, you are a welcome sight. You will not believe the ordeal I have been through!"

Elizabeth was an even more welcome sight at Darcy's own side, where she joined him after paying her respects to Lady Denham and expressing her happiness in the dowager's being returned to her friends unharmed.

"What have I missed?" Elizabeth asked.

"Very little," Darcy replied. "But given the prologue, I think the principal drama is yet to come."

Both Miss Heywood and Miss Brereton kept their distance from Mr. Granville—a challenge in the snug space, which grew tighter with the addition of each person. Josiah Hollis was the last to enter. He scanned the dwelling from ceiling to floor, taking the full measure of its neglect: the cobwebs stretching across the corners, the squirrel's nest in the rafters, the bird droppings in the fireplace, the dry pine needles, leaves, and other detritus that had covered the floor before the eight of them had crowded inside, kicking up dust and displacing debris. It occurred to Darcy that Josiah was likely the only person present who had been inside the hermitage before last night, let alone seen it in good repair.

Josiah acknowledged the dowager with a nod. "Lady Denham."

"Mr. Hollis." Her tone was civil, no more, no less.

"I see you have redecorated since I was last here."

Lady Denham ignored Josiah's remark, instead turning to Sidney. "Now that everyone is assured of my well-being, can we return to Sanditon House? Most of the guests can go home now that the storm has passed, and the rest of us might as well be comfortable while we wait for the magistrate to come deal with Mr. Granville."

"The magistrate is in London, my dear lady; it might be days until we see him."

"Before we relocate," Darcy said, "perhaps Mr. Granville would like to explain what subject of conversation was so vital that he believed it justified kidnapping you." He pulled the other chair out from the table and, with a gesture, invited Mr. Granville to sit.

Mr. Granville remained standing. "Ivy Woodcock."

"Why do any of us need to talk about Ivy Woodcock?" Lady Denham waved her hand dismissively and shifted in her own chair. "Especially you?"

"She was my grandmother. My great-grandmother, actually. And Archibald Hollis was my great-grandfather."

"Impossible. Ivy Woodcock died almost a century ago, still a young girl."

Josiah Hollis crossed his arms over his chest and regarded her with an unwavering look of accusation. "You and I both know that is not true—your *ladyship.*"

The look Lady Denham shot Josiah in return was sharper than any words she could utter. "And you and I both know that nothing said here this morning can change choices made in the past. So why discuss any of this?" She turned her glare on Mr. Granville. "Especially with the ruffian who entered my house last night plotting to kidnap me."

"I never plotted to kidnap you, or to commit any other misdeeds against you," Mr. Granville said. "When I arrived at Sanditon House, my sole object was simply to make your acquaintance, to meet you in a context outside of our connection to Archibald Hollis, to judge for myself what sort of person you are so that I could determine the best tack to take when I returned the following day to request an audience with you."

"During which you intended to extort money from me, I suppose."

"No—merely to ask for answers to questions that have haunted my family for decades." He placed his hands on the table and leaned toward her. "When you did not appear at dinner and everyone speculated about your fate, I realized that the opportunity to learn anything directly from you might be lost to me forever, so I resolved to learn what I could in the course of my night at Sanditon House. That is why I volunteered to come out here, to the hermitage, when the gentlemen searched the grounds for you. I wanted to see where Ivy had lived, and use the tunnel she passed through to sneak into the house with Archibald."

He stood upright again. The cuffs of the eighteenth-century coat he still wore had ridden up, and he adjusted them as he continued. "That is also why I changed attire afterward, along with all the other gentlemen. Though the tunnel had kept my clothes fairly dry from the storm, they were soiled by my passage through it. But equally as important, I wanted to enter Archibald's apartment, to see his belongings and the rooms in which he lived, to see the things he valued." He picked up the paper from the table and handed it to Elizabeth. "You might have been looking for this."

Darcy spied over her shoulder. It was the sketchbook page that had disappeared from the chamber-horse drawer.

"My mother drew that as a child, during a conversation she over-heard between Archibald and Ivy. She told me she had hidden it in the springs of that contraption in Archibald's apartment, but I found it in the drawer."

"I now understand why she would have written 'Ivy,' 'Rose,' and 'Woodcock' on the page," Elizabeth said. "What is the significance of 'Tailor'?"

"It is my mother's maiden name—the one she bore when she created that drawing."

Lady Denham made a sound that could have been mistaken for a snort were she not a baronet's widow. "You expect us to believe you are who you claim to be based on a child's sketch you stole from my late husband's apartment?"

"Since the day I learned Sidney Parker grew up in Sanditon, I hoped one day to visit the village with him and somehow meet you. When he invited me to join him on this trip, I resolved to find a way to make your acquaintance—your dinner invitation was a lucky surprise. In the event that you did not believe my claim to be descended from Archibald Hollis, I also brought this." He reached into his waistcoat pocket, withdrew a miniature portrait of a young man, and held it up for her to see. "This is—"

"Archibald." Lady Denham said the name matter-of-factly, but her expression softened as she took the image into her own hand and regarded it. "I know my own husband, even if this likeness was painted more than twoscore years before we wed. Where did you obtain this?"

"He gave it to Ivy before he left for Oxford. It was one of the few possessions she took with her when his father drove her away."

Lady Denham handed back the tiny portrait. "Have you anything else to share, Mr. Granville?"

"Yes—not an object, but a fact. I also, I am ashamed to admit, entered your apartment in search of information. I confess this in the hope that by freely disclosing incidents of less honorable conduct, you will believe I speak the truth about the remainder."

"How did you penetrate the locked door?" Darcy asked.

"I did not—I accessed the apartment through the house's hidden passages. Archibald had shown Ivy the state apartment during one of her visits—and she spoke of it when reminiscing about her life in

Sanditon. Stories about its opulence and following the passages to find it were handed down in the family like fairy tales."

There was nothing magical or fairylike in Lady Denham's countenance and manner upon hearing Mr. Granville had violated her privacy. And that Ivy had visited those rooms decades before Lady Denham occupied them. "What did you take from there?"

"I looked through some papers in a letter case but heard someone approach in the corridor, so I had to quit the apartment rapidly."

"And then later implicated me for it," Josiah said.

"I am sorry for that," Mr. Granville replied. "I needed to deflect attention from myself. Thinking, as many did, that you were behind the disappearances of Lady Denham and the others, I figured one more transgression would easily be believed."

He turned back to Lady Denham. "I did take one item from the apartment—the sedative on the dressing table. Miss Susan Parker had gone missing by that time, and I thought it could spare Diana Parker the trouble of preparing a new one when Susan was discovered. I put it in my pocket and, in the course of other events, forgot about it until later."

"When you used it to kidnap me," Lady Denham said.

"That was never my plan. How could it have been, when everyone thought from the start that you had already been kidnapped?" Mr. Granville faced the others. "During the search for Susan, I returned to the portrait room before everyone else—and was astonished to discover Lady Denham within, leaving her own ransom note. She was as startled as I by the encounter, and I tried to use that to my advantage by initiating the conversation I had hoped to have about Archibald and Ivy. I poured her a glass of wine and, recalling the sedative I had in my pocket, added it, hoping it would make her more yielding about discussing the subject. Instead, it quickly rendered her unconscious.

"I panicked. I could not just leave her in the portrait room for everyone to find, and we were all due to reconvene very soon. There is a hidden observation chamber adjacent to the portrait room, so I deposited her in there, then took a circuitous route back to the portrait room so I would not be the first to have arrived. Though I outwardly maintained my composure with all of you—at least, I believe I did—

inside I was convinced that every noise I heard was Lady Denham waking up and trying to emerge from the observation room."

"I believe I heard such a noise, when we were gathered," Charlotte said. "I thought it was the sound of something falling."

"It was indeed—I later discovered that Lady Denham knocked an unlit candle to the floor in her sleep. I heard the sound myself while we were in the portrait room, and wished more than ever that all of you would depart. When you and Parker left Miss Brereton in my care"—he looked at Clara earnestly—"a charge that in any other circumstances I would have welcomed—I did not know how I would ever be able to disengage myself to deal with Lady Denham. So I poured you wine—untainted, I assure you—hoping you would become drowsy and retire. I hope, Miss Brereton, you can forgive me."

"Perhaps in time," Miss Brereton said. "But the wine was indeed adulterated with a sedative—by someone else."

His brows rose in surprise. "No wonder it affected you faster than I anticipated. Fortunately, Sir Edward returned, and I consigned you to his protection. With the room at last clear, I returned to Lady Denham. She still slept soundly. I could not simply leave her in place until she woke, or move her anywhere within the house—we might be overheard while having the conversation I yet hoped for. But where to take her?"

"So of all the places available to you, all the outbuildings and garden structures, you chose to bring me *here*?" Lady Denham said. "Why not the summerhouse, or the temple—someplace comfortable, or dignified, or at least . . ." She turned her hand to look at her fingertips, which she had absently allowed to rest on the table; they were smudged with dust and dirt. *"Clean?"*

"I brought you here because when you would not hear me out in the finest sitting room at Sanditon House—with its stately hearth and elegant furniture and portrait of your second husband bearing witness—I *wanted* you to see the hermitage. When I first stepped inside here, I was stunned by its primitive condition. This 'hovel,' as you called it, is where my great-grandmother lived while her lover enjoyed a life of ease at Sanditon House—the life that you inherited. Look around you—is this not picturesque? The epitome of simple, spiritual living? The perfect commune of man and nature—and all that other rubbish the well-off spout about hermitages while they entertain themselves by watching the hermits who live in them perform like bears in a circus."

"That all happened long before my time—before I was even born, let alone married to Archibald. It has nothing to do with me."

"While it did not then, it does now. I want to know whether Archibald Hollis ever made any provision for Ivy or her descendants—formally or informally. My mother says Ivy always spoke well of him—always described him as an honorable man—never blamed him for the cruelty she suffered when his father forced her to flee. Yet when she came back in her final years, told him she had borne him a child, and asked for his support, he refused to give her money."

"On what do you base that claim?" Josiah asked.

"My mother accompanied Ivy when she asked him. She was a child at the time, but remembers quite clearly waking up to hear Ivy pleading with Archibald that they not part quarreling about money, and his response that he would give her anything but."

"I witnessed that conversation, too," Josiah said, "and I was older than your mother. She misunderstood what she heard. It was Ivy who refused Archibald's offer of money, and my uncle conceded to her wishes."

"Just like that?" Mr. Granville said. "He never made another attempt?"

"I did not say that."

Josiah crossed his arms over his chest and looked at Lady Denham. She made a great business of smoothing her skirts as she avoided his gaze. Eventually, he said, "Are you going to tell him, or shall I?"

That captured her attention. Lady Denham stared at Josiah a long time, but he did not back down.

"I shall tell him," she finally said. "But not here."

Thirty-nine

"Do not let us quarrel about the past."
—*Elizabeth Bennet,* Pride and Prejudice

*T*he scene in the portrait room back at Sanditon House was
much the same as it had been the night before, with the noticeable addition of Lady Denham. All five Parker siblings were in atten-
dance, the health of Thomas Parker's son having improved following
an early-morning house call by his aunt Diana while Sidney and the
others were confronting Percy Granville. Both Denham siblings were
also present, the Sir having received a summons from her ladyship,
and the Miss still hoping to engage Mr. Granville's interest before he
left the village. Josiah Hollis, Miss Brereton, Charlotte, Elizabeth, and
Darcy completed the party, and the guests had grouped themselves
in twos and threes about the room. All of the gentlemen, to their
unanimous relief, were wearing their own clothing once more.

Josiah glowered at Sir Harry Denham, who observed the proceedings from his usual vantage point above the fireplace. "It galls me beyond anything to see that portrait occupy a place of honor, while my
uncle Archibald's is banished upstairs," he said to Darcy. "It is disre-
spectful. None but a Hollis, or someone of Hollis descent"—he looked
at Mr. Granville, beside him—"should preside over this room."

In the corner opposite, Lady Denham regarded the image of her second husband with an expression of pride and wistfulness. "That portrait is one of the few objects I took with me from Denham Park when I moved back here after Sir Harry's death," she said to Elizabeth. "All the rest, as part of the late baronet's estate, went to Sir Edward. There are some who disapprove of my having moved Archibald's portrait to the gallery of his ancestors, and hanging this one in here. But I was married to Sir Harry longer, and with him I did not live in Ivy Woodcock's shadow. Everywhere in this house I am surrounded by memories of Archibald; I wanted one memory of Sir Harry here with me."

She looked across the room to where Sir Edward stood with Miss Denham. "Unfortunately, my nephew is not quite the man his uncle was. I am still astonished and appalled by his recent behavior. Plotting to abduct Miss Clara! A young lady under my protection! His conduct is an outrage against us both. Clara tells me he had been trying to woo her for some time. I witnessed one of his attempts—the morning you came to call, I saw the two of them just on the other side of the paling in Denham Park. I thought she had met him for a prearranged tryst, but she told me just now that he surprised her there and made an unwelcome effort to persuade her to elope to Scotland. The audacity! And then for him to enact his ill-conceived abduction scheme and draw the Parker sisters and Miss Heywood into it as well—have you ever heard of such idiocy?"

Elizabeth replied that she had not. "You told all of us that you will administer Sir Edward's punishment," she said. "Have you yet determined what it will be?"

"More than our magistrate would bother to do," Lady Denham replied. "Because Sir Edward is a baronet, the magistrate will look the other way so as not to injure the Denham name. Indeed—I, too, will ensure the name is preserved—along with Miss Clara's reputation and that of Sanditon as a whole. We cannot let word of these abductions get abroad, or that will be the end of Sanditon's prospects as a genteel watering-place for families of good character."

"You also must ensure that Sir Edward never takes it into his head to abduct Clara or anyone else in the future."

"I have a plan for that. After giving him a dressing-down he will never forget and exacting a promise to never repeat his actions, I am sending him and Miss Denham on an extended trip to a place very far from here, in hopes that they both find rich spouses."

"A tour of the Continent?"

"No—the West Indies. I hear there are plenty of heiresses and wealthy plantation owners there. By the time Sir Edward returns with a bride, perhaps Miss Clara will be settled in an establishment of her own."

Overhearing his name, Sir Edward wandered into their conversation. After he had voiced repeated enquiries as to the dowager's health and offered expressions of relief at her having weathered both the storm and her kidnapping without ill effect, Lady Denham looked pointedly at Sir Harry's portrait.

"Sir Edward, I understand that in my absence you had difficulty producing Sir Harry's watch."

"I—" The baronet seemed about to offer either a desperate excuse or an inflated apology, but stopped himself and answered, simply, "Yes."

"That is because I have it." Lady Denham withdrew the watch from the folds of her skirts and allowed it to swing from its chain. "You and I both know where I discovered it."

Having just regained his color hours before, Sir Edward appeared a bit peaked again. "Yes . . . yes, we do, and—"

"Let us withdraw to discuss the matter. And several others."

Sir Edward returned from the tête-à-tête humiliated and humbled. From each of his abductees, he begged pardon in express terms, supplemented by enough poetic quotations and polysyllabic words beyond his understanding to render his apology as unintelligible as it was heartfelt. Miss Brereton received particular assurances of no further attempts at courtship, which she graciously accepted.

As the baronet slunk away, Lady Denham's gaze followed him, then next fell upon Mr. Granville. "I think I am going to forgive him," she declared. "Not immediately, but in time."

"Sir Edward, or Mr. Granville?" Elizabeth asked.

"Both, I suppose. Sir Edward is my nephew, and despite his folly I can never stay angry with him for long. Mr. Granville is Mr. Hollis's great-grandson, and I have been haunted by the ghost of Ivy Woodcock for far *too* long. Mr. Hollis would not have wanted that—for me, or for Mr. Granville."

They crossed the room to where Percy stood with Darcy and Josiah. "Mr. Granville," Lady Denham said, "it is time for that private conversation you have been seeking."

Josiah's gaze followed the pair as they left the portrait room and turned down the corridor. He appeared pensive, but not at all curious.

"You know what Lady Denham is going to tell him, do you not?" Elizabeth asked.

Josiah turned to her and Darcy. "Yes. I have read Archibald's will. Back when he died and his widow gained control of everything, we—his Hollis relations—asked to see it. As his erstwhile heir, I served as the family representative."

"Did Archibald leave anything to Ivy Rose?" Elizabeth asked.

"Archibald left everything to Ivy Rose."

At first, Elizabeth thought she could not possibly have heard Josiah correctly.

"Everything?" Darcy appeared equally incredulous. "Then how has Lady Denham retained control of the estate?"

"Lady Denham was given a life interest in the property. For the remainder of her years, the income is hers. Upon Lady Denham's death, the entire estate, minus a few modest bequests, goes to Ivy Rose or her issue."

"I imagine you and the rest of the Hollises are not pleased about Ivy Rose inheriting the estate," Elizabeth said.

"The rest of the Hollises do not know the terms of Lady Denham's occupancy; they, like the rest of the village, believe Lady Denham owns the estate outright—and I ask that you keep your knowledge to yourselves. While Uncle Archibald was not ashamed of his union with Ivy—he would have married her, had his father allowed it—he did not want to embarrass his widow by exposing her to gossip about Ivy Rose's relationship to him."

"He sounds like a good man," Elizabeth said.

"He was. He did right by me, even after his new wife ousted me from Sanditon House. He paid for my education, looked after me from a distance in a godfatherly sort of way, and left me a bequest that

I will receive upon Lady Denham's passing, on the condition that I never expose her secret—which I never have until last night, when I thought her life depended on it. And even then, only after I tried to piece together myself what was transpiring.

"As for my own opinion regarding the ultimate disposal of the estate, I have no quarrel with Ivy Rose inheriting it. A man's property should go to his children. What has stuck in my craw all these years is that Lady Denham has a comfortable fortune of her own, and therefore no real need for Sanditon House—particularly during the years when Sir Harry was alive. While she resided at Denham Park, Sanditon House sat without any family in residence. Ivy Rose and her husband could have been living here—Percy Granville could have grown up here. Lady Denham has always had it within her power to give the house to those who have a moral claim to it even if their legal claim is dormant until her death. Instead, she lives practically by herself in a house so large that she does not use half of it."

A little while later, Percy Granville and Lady Denham reentered the portrait room. Though they did not seem especially friendly, there appeared to be peace between them. They parted in the doorway, Mr. Granville with a respectful bow.

Lady Denham next summoned Josiah Hollis. As Josiah took his leave of them and walked toward the dowager, Darcy's gaze followed him.

"Last night I thought Josiah Hollis a bitter, self-seeking rat," Darcy said. "Today he seems a decent, honorable human being. Did we misjudge him initially, or has he transformed overnight?"

"Both, I think," Elizabeth replied. "For decades, he has been carrying the secrets of Archibald and Ivy's liaison, Victor Hollis's treachery, and the disposition of Archibald's estate—and secrets have a way of rotting one from the inside." As she watched Josiah leave the room with Lady Denham, she noted no sign of lumbago or any other misery. In fact, his steps seemed lighter. "Now that he has finally released those secrets—even if only to us—he must feel a great sense of relief."

The discussion between Lady Denham and Josiah Hollis was of a different character than her conferences with the others. Apologies did not come easily to her ladyship, nor the self-awareness required to recognize when one has given injury. But she had hosted the dinner party in the first place out of a need to get her house in order—both literally and figuratively—and had invited him to get a sense of who she was dealing with, now that they both had aged, to ensure that events of the distant past would not cause surprises in the future. She had discovered that the past was not so distant after all, and that its repercussions could and would be felt despite her efforts to contain them.

By the time their conference ended, they had reached a state of truce.

Mr. Granville approached the sofa where Sidney was in conversation with Charlotte and Miss Brereton. Charlotte detected hesitation in his step, as if he were unsure of the reception he would meet from his friend.

Sidney greeted him cordially, if a bit more stiffly than was his usual style with Mr. Granville. "You look none the worse for your meeting. Is all now straight between you and Lady Denham?"

"I believe so. In exchange for my silence about my relationship to Archibald Hollis for the remainder of her lifetime, Lady Denham will not seek legal redress for my having stolen her away to the hermitage."

"That sounds like a fair arrangement," Sidney said. Gesturing toward an empty chair beside the sofa he shared with Charlotte, he invited Mr. Granville to sit with them.

"More than fair." Mr. Granville gratefully accepted the seat, and the implicit olive branch proffered along with it. "It took three generations of prudent marriages and hard work for my family to accrue fortune enough to educate and raise me as a gentleman. Were I to stand trial for kidnapping, our fledgling claim to gentility would be destroyed, and I will have undone in one night what took several lifetimes to build." He shook his head, his countenance filled with incredulity, as if he spoke of someone else rather than himself. "It was a rash act, a transgression I regretted even while I was committing it, and I still do not quite understand myself how events reached that point. I can, however, say with certainty that such a thing will never happen again. I apologized to Lady Denham, but I also apologize to you all. I served you a poor return on your friendship and trust."

"Lady Denham was also guilty of deception last night," Sidney said, "and I was party to it. So we are none of us innocent." He looked at Charlotte and Miss Brereton. "These two ladies excepted, of course." He met Charlotte's gaze, and his countenance began to take on its usual liveliness. "Unless, Miss Heywood, you are about to astonish us with a confession?"

"Not this morning." If Charlotte had a confession to make, it was that the same night that brought so much anxiety to them all, had also occasioned feelings of a very different nature, which she was just beginning to comprehend, and which required more time to explore— preferably in the company of Sidney. So, as in the end no real harm was done, she could not unequivocally say that she wished the whole evening had never happened, for even her own, absurd, abduction had led to something good.

"I am glad to hear it, for I believe we have all enjoyed enough surprises for one day." Sidney held her gaze a moment longer, and Charlotte was just wishing Mr. Granville and Miss Brereton would be possessed by a sudden impulse to leap up and take a stroll about the room when he turned back to his friend. "So, Granville, had Lady Denham anything else to say?"

"I am also permitted—commanded, more accurately—to call at Sanditon House regularly. She has assigned me a project: the renovation of the hermitage into a proper cottage. She claims the end purpose is to lease it out to visiting families, but I believe the process of overseeing it is a test of my merit." He seemed about to reveal more, but apparently decided to hold his own counsel for now on the remainder.

"A test you will easily pass, I wager. What do you think, Miss Brereton? Can Granville redeem himself in Lady Denham's eyes? In yours?"

Mr. Granville waited in hopeful anticipation as Miss Brereton assessed him.

"I think so," she said at last. And offered a smile.

Forty

My readers . . . will see in the tell-tale compression of the pages
before them, that we are all hastening together to perfect felicity.
—Northanger Abbey

*L*ady Denham thwarted the expectations of all her would-be
heirs by living to the age of ninety. When she did pass away,
she left the majority of her personal estate to Clara, who by then had
long since put aside the name Brereton—in exchange for the name
Granville. A courtship that began during Percy's visits to oversee the
hermitage renovations, and that continued after the project was complete, flourished under Lady Denham's approbation. The new couple
made their residence at Sanditon House, and by the time Percy came
into his inheritance, a bequest that permanently established their
family there seemed so natural that nobody thought to wonder why
the former estate of Archibald Hollis passed to him.

Her ladyship's sole bequest to Sir Edward comprised the return
of Sir Harry's portrait to Denham Park and Sir Harry's watch to the
present baronet—with stern instructions to value the timepiece
more than he had upon first receipt. As luck would have it, Sir Edward did not need a monetary remembrance from Lady Denham to
ensure the continued welfare of the baronetcy, for while in the West
Indies he indeed found a young heiress whose parents Sir Edward

seduced with his title. Providentially for all concerned, she brought to the marriage not only enough money, but also enough sense, for them both.

The dowager's provision for Miss Denham was more generous, and settled upon her while Lady Denham yet lived. The exact amount of the gift is immaterial, for no matter what its size, in the eyes of its recipient it was less than she deserved, and in the eyes of potential suitors it was insufficient recompense for spending a lifetime as her husband. However, when supplemented with funds from Sir Edward's new wife after a year spent living in the same house as Miss Denham, Esther's dowry proved enough to entice a junior diplomat who spent much of his time abroad.

Susan, Diana, and Arthur Parker returned to their home in Hampshire, where Arthur eventually met and married a gentle, patient young woman who was not only an excellent cook but understood the dangers of Damp and the comfort to be had in a good fire—in the right season. In mitigating his sisters' influence, she brought out what was best in him, and he became a less indolent, more active gentleman. Upon their brother's marriage, Susan and Diana left the house to the newlyweds and permanently moved back to Sanditon, where they lived in a state of blissful infirmity and frantic activity until they died of old age.

Finally free of the burden of carrying others' secrets, Josiah Hollis became a less acerbic man. He made peace not only with Lady Denham, but with the past, and in doing so realized a happier future than the one to which he had resigned himself. Like his uncle before him, he married a younger woman late in life. She appreciated what was good in him, forgave his faults, and bore him an heir who carried on the Hollis name.

As for Sanditon itself, the resort never achieved the size and renown of Eastbourne or Brighton, and therefore attracted no French visitors at all, which suited Lady Denham quite well. It did, however, become such a well-reputed bathing-place among genteel families that its popularity justified the building of Waterloo Crescent and all but shut down the competing town of Brinshore, which delighted Thomas Parker. And once its reputation was established, the village went on to enjoy many years of prosperity, which pleased its third major investor, Colonel Fitzwilliam.

Although Mr. Granville departed Sanditon the day following the Great Misadventure, Sidney Parker remained, and accepted Thomas and Mary Parker's repeated invitation to remove from the hotel to Trafalgar House. That he extended his visit to Sanditon longer than originally planned, and did not name his departure date until Miss Heywood had determined hers, was a coincidence not lost upon any who knew him.

Though guests in the same house, the two were well supervised; indeed, there is no safer place for a young lady than the company of a captivated gentleman . . . who has an adoring niece and three nephews under the age of seven, who follow their uncle everywhere. Little Mary even accompanied them on the daylight walks Sidney had promised Charlotte, ambling between them or skipping ahead as they strolled along the Terrace or down to the shore.

They did occasionally find opportunities to engage in private conversations, and their attachment increased with each one, until suddenly it was the day of Charlotte's departure. Encountering each other in the morning room while Charlotte waited for the Darcys to collect her, they unexpectedly found themselves quite alone.

"Mr. Parker," she said in surprise as he entered. Setting aside the needlework that had been mindlessly occupying her, she rose and started toward him, but stopped after only a few steps.

"Miss Heywood." His gaze swept the room at knee height, seeking small chaperones in hiding. When no giggles issued from behind the furniture, he came forward until they stood but two feet apart. Each felt there was still so much to be said that neither knew where or how to begin. They regarded each other in silence for a moment, then laughed at the unnecessary awkwardness between them.

"I was hoping for an opportunity to wish you a private good-bye," he said. "Are you ready to leave Sanditon? Has four weeks in the company of Parkers proved long enough?"

"I am ready to be with my family again," she replied. "But I will miss the friends I have made here." She would most especially miss Sidney, and wondered when and how she might next see him. "And you—are you traveling directly home when you leave here, or will your journey take you elsewhere first?"

"There is one stop I plan to make." His light tone belied the seriousness of his expression. "I hear there is a village named Willingden not too far distant, which might be worth visiting."

"Indeed?" Her heartbeat accelerated, as it did whenever he was very near, but she endeavored to maintain her composure. "There are two Willingdens in Sussex. Take care you do not confuse them—especially if you are seeking the one with a surgeon."

"Actually, I want the one *without* a surgeon, for I hear that should I happen to sprain my ankle while passing through, there is a family who might extend me hospitality for a fortnight or so while I recover." He moved another step toward her.

"That seems a rather hazardous way of securing an invitation."

"Perhaps it is," he conceded. "But I want very much to become acquainted with them."

She very much wanted her parents to become acquainted with him—and to like him as much as she did. "Have you any connection to the family?"

"I know one member. It is a new friendship, but one I believe of mutual regard." His gaze held such warmth that she could feel it. "And that I dare hope will endure indefinitely."

"Well, that sounds promising. Perhaps, then, you should simply present yourself."

He took her hands in his, and closed the final step. "Would I be welcome if I did?"

"To at least that member. And by the time you arrive, she might have said a word or two on your behalf to ensure a favorable reception from the rest."

"Then I shall proceed there with all acceptable haste upon quitting Sanditon tomorrow."

The authoress leaves it to the reader to decide whether Sidney Parker then kissed Charlotte Heywood, and whether the young lady was at all averse. And if he did kiss her, whether the kiss confirmed

Sidney's hopeful perception that in the final moments of their unexpected embrace behind the drapery panel, she had begun to kiss him
back. And whether this second kiss might have lasted just a tiny bit
longer than either of them intended going into it.

And upon parting, which of them marked more impatiently the
time between Charlotte's arrival home and the hour at which Sidney
could reasonably appear.

Epilogue

"It is settled between us already that we are to be the happiest couple in the world."

—*Elizabeth Bennet,* Pride and Prejudice

*E*lizabeth took pleasure in watching the attachment between Sidney Parker and Charlotte Heywood blossom. It brought back memories of her own courtship with Darcy. Though the circumstances had been very different, the early-days feelings of joy and discovery were not.

For this reason, she and Darcy deferred their impulse to end their Sanditon adventure prematurely. Though both felt they had experienced quite enough of the village, Elizabeth wanted to allow Charlotte more time with Sidney before they took her home. The fact that Lady Catherine awaited them at Brierwood had nothing to do with their staying the full fortnight they had originally planned. (Well, perhaps it did. But only a little.)

On their last day in the village, Lady Denham invited Elizabeth and Darcy to tea, which was served with an apology for all the trouble her staged disappearance had cost them. As they took their leave, the dowager invited them to stroll through Sanditon Park as much as they wished before leaving the grounds. Elizabeth asked Darcy to show her the grotto.

They walked out to it. Elizabeth drew aside a section of the over-grown ivy hanging before the entrance and stepped within. Darcy followed.

Despite—or perhaps because of—its untamed state, the atmosphere inside felt peaceful. Though it was dim, enough late afternoon sunlight penetrated the ivy to illuminate the fountain statue. Elizabeth quietly regarded the form of Ivy Woodcock captured in the hope and promise of youth.

From behind, Darcy put his arms around her.

"You said they never stood a chance." Elizabeth leaned against him, feeling his solid strength at her back. "And in their youth, perhaps they did not. But I wonder, had Archibald not just married Philadelphia Brereton when Ivy returned, whether they might have spent their final years together?"

"No one will ever know." Darcy turned her in his arms so that he could see her face as he held her close. "But I do know that I look forward to spending mine with you—and an eternity thereafter."

———

Sometimes, on warm summer nights, the breeze blowing through Sanditon Park parts the cascading ivy at the grotto's entrance just enough to form an opening in the verdant curtain.

If one listens carefully, above the distant crash of waves might be heard a sound resembling laughter.

And if the moon is full, and at precisely the proper angle in the sky, one might almost see two misty figures appear, join hands, and enter.

Author's Note

How much unexhausted talent perished with her, how largely she might yet have contributed to the entertainment of her readers, if her life had been prolonged, cannot be known; but it is certain that the mine at which she had so long laboured was not worked out, and that she was still diligently employed in collecting fresh materials from it.

—James Edward Austen-Leigh, nephew of Jane Austen
A Memoir of Jane Austen, 1871

Dear Readers,

When I finished writing the sixth Mr. & Mrs. Darcy Mystery, *The Deception at Lyme (Or, the Perils of Persuasion)*, readers immediately began asking me, "Now that you have written one mystery for each of Jane Austen's novels, where will the Darcys go next?"

While I considered several possibilities, one stood out as feeling the most natural—for the characters, the series, and my own development as a writer.

We would go where Austen herself went.

After she finished writing *Persuasion*, her last completed novel, Austen began a new untitled book set in the fictional seaside village of Sanditon. From dates written in her own hand on the first and last pages of the manuscript, it appears that she worked on the novel from 27 January through 18 March 1817 before setting it aside. Her health failing, she never returned to the story and died at age forty-one in July of that year, leaving behind eleven and a half chapters (approximately 24,800 words) of a first draft.

Author's Note

Although unfinished, the draft—which eventually came to be known by the title *Sanditon*—is as rich as Austen's other works. In those few chapters she sets her stage, populates it with memorable characters, and infuses the whole with humor reminiscent of her earlier writings. Then, just as Sidney Parker arrives in town and heroine Charlotte Heywood calls upon Lady Denham at Sanditon House for the first time, the fragment ends. The story Austen planned for Charlotte, the Parker siblings, the Denhams, and Sanditon's other residents will forever remain a mystery.

As you might have guessed by now, I love a good mystery. And the Darcys have become experienced at solving them.

The Suspicion at Sanditon is not the tale Austen would have told, had she lived long enough to complete her novel. That lost tale is one that only she could tell. But like all the previous Mr. & Mrs. Darcy Mysteries, the story between these covers is woven from threads Austen left behind. As a fragment, *Sanditon* abounds with loose threads: a setting currently undergoing transformation, relationships and situations rife with possible plotlines, dynamic characters left in a state of suspended animation. I wanted to give those characters a story, one that, with Austen's indirect guidance, I could tell.

Although I had read *Sanditon* before (the first complete transcription of the fragment was published in 1925 by R. W. Chapman, and others have been published since), this time I immersed myself in Austen's handwritten manuscript. I read the draft in her own hand so that I could study it from the perspective of a novelist—a fellow practitioner of the craft—rather than through the filter of other transcribers, many of whom had approached it from a more scholarly perspective. I wanted to see every crossed-out sentence, every added phrase, every punctuation change—to see her writing in process, and learn all I could from the experience. (For a first draft, it is strikingly clean— truly genius in action.) Creating my own transcription, word by word, comma by comma—working with her words on such an intimate level—was like an apprenticeship with a master.

When I had done, I began writing my own story, and you hold in your hands the result. I hope you have enjoyed the Darcys' Sanditon adventure. If it has inspired you to seek out Austen's fragment to meet her characters firsthand, you can obtain *Sanditon* (often as part

of a collection with other Austen novels or minor works) from your favorite bookseller or library. (To view Austen's handwritten manuscript,
see the note below.) If my story has inspired further interest in the
Mr. & Mrs. Darcy Mysteries, I invite you to visit me at my website,
www.carriebebris.com, to learn more about the series, forthcoming
books, and author events, or to sign up for my electronic newsletter.
While there, consider dropping me a note—I always enjoy hearing
from readers! I thank all of you who have already shared with me
your thoughts about the series. Your words mean a great deal to
me, and I remain—

Your most obliged and
humble servant,
Carrie Bebris

Notes on the text

All quotations from *Sanditon* are from my own transcription of Austen's
1817 handwritten manuscript, accessed in electronic facsimile through
Jane Austen's Fiction Manuscripts: A Digital Edition, edited by Kathryn
Sutherland (2010), available at www.janeausten.ac.uk. In most cases,
I preserved Austen's spellings, capitalizations, punctuation, and em-
phases. I have written out superscripts, abbreviations, and numerals;
ampersands are changed to "and." The long "s" form of the lowercase
letter "s"—printed as ʃ—is changed to a short (i.e., ordinary) "s."

Sources of Sir Edward's literary quotations

15 *Assoiled from all encumbrance of our time:* William Wordsworth,
"Occasioned by the Battle of Waterloo—February 1816."

32 *The best-laid schemes of mice and men often go awry (The best-laid
schemes o' mice an 'men/Gang aft agley):* Robert Burns, "To a Mouse,"
1785.

66 *on this gay, dewy morning:* Robert Burns, "Lovely Young Jessie,"
1793.

66 *fair imperial flow'r:* William Cowper, "The Lily and the Rose,"
1782.

91 *If this be dying . . . there is nothing at all shocking in it. My body hardly
sensible of pain, my mind at ease, my intellects clear and perfect as ever.*
Samuel Richardson, *Clarissa,* 1751.

99 *not to see the lady of this castle . . . who disappeared so strangely:* Ann Radcliffe, *The Mysteries of Udolpho,* 1794.

155 *She walks in beauty, like the night/Of cloudless climes and starry skies;/ And all that's best of dark and bright:* George Gordon, Lord Byron, "She Walks in Beauty," 1815.